BROKEN REFLECTIONS

BROKEN REFLECTIONS

RON SHAW

First Edition: November 2024

ISBN 979-8-9891240-4-6 (Paperback)
ISBN 979-8-9891240-5-3 (Hardcover)
ISBN 979-8-9891240-6-0 (Ebook)
ISBN 979-8-9891240-7-7 (Audiobook)
LCCN 2024911100

10 9 8 7 6 5 4 3 2 1

Editor: Leilani Dewindt
Cover Design & Interior Layout: Danna Mathias Steele

Published by Evocative Impressions, LLC

Evocative Impressions, LLC
P.O. Box 6
Sandown, NH 03873
evocativeimpressions.com

CONTENT WARNING

Broken Reflections contains themes and content that some readers may find distressing. Please be advised of the following potential triggers:

Violence
Descriptions of physical violence and injuries.
Supernatural battles and confrontations involving harm.

Psychological Distress
Exploration of mental health issues, including identity crises and existential angst.
Depictions of psychological torment and emotional suffering.

Death and the Afterlife
Themes of death, dying, and the afterlife.
Descriptions of Purgatory and supernatural realms.

Substance Abuse
References to drug overdose and substance abuse.

Dark and Eerie Atmosphere
Settings and scenarios that may induce fear or anxiety, including dark and surreal landscapes.

Manipulation and Betrayal
Themes of manipulation by supernatural forces.
Instances of betrayal and treachery among characters.

Existential and Philosophical Themes
Deep exploration of existential questions and the nature of reality, which may be unsettling to some readers.

Supernatural Elements
Interactions with ghosts, spirits, and other supernatural beings.

Please read with care and take breaks if you feel overwhelmed. Your mental and emotional well-being is important.

By the breath of the void,
in the court of the nameless king,
Through the labyrinth of the cosmos,
the ancient song we sing.
By the darkened sun,
the secrets of time shall yield,
With the echoes of the past,
the unseen dimensions revealed.

- *Necronomicon*, attributed to Abdul Alhazred.

PART 1

ECHOES OF IDENTITY

PROLOGUE: JOHN

The bitter taste of ipecac and vomit clinging to my tongue served as an unwelcome reminder of how my night had been going. It was a night of sex and more than a healthy dose of drugs. The last damn Vicodin I took had pushed me over—or could it be it was the half bottle of Grey Goose that did it?

When the paramedics got me into the ambulance they gave me the choice of chugging down the ipecac or having my stomach pumped once we got to the hospital. What the hell, I thought, it was nothing more than another substance to toss into the cocktail I had already mixed in my stomach.

Once the vomiting started, it wouldn't stop. I swear I was puking out everything I had eaten since the third grade. All the retching was making it hard to breathe, and eventually I passed out.

I was becoming aware of my surroundings again and noticed this was not the emergency room. This was far too nice to be any hospital I had ever seen. Scanning the room I saw a man, his height dwarfing any man I'd ever encountered. He wore a cloak, blacker than the darkest of nights.

This had to be the after effects of the drugs. Yet, they should have been out of my system by now. This stranger appeared out of thin air. One moment I was looking at the dark bathroom across from me–a dull glow of indigo light came twinkling through. Then he rolled in like the morning fog from the light. With each blink of my eyes, the glowing became brighter and the stranger larger.

Closing my eyes tight, shaking my head, I thought, *this has to be an aftereffect.* They mustn't have gotten all of the drugs out of my system. Why else would I be seeing a man such as this walking through my mirror? Why else would there be this peculiar indigo light filling the room? I scrunched my eyes tighter, so tight I could feel the cut above my right eye beginning to rip open again.

"Mr. Tyler," said a voice I had never heard before, "you mustn't clench your face so hard. I couldn't imagine you standing in front of your board looking like a constipated fool. Could you?" The stranger's laughter echoed through the room. Laughter at my expense, no less.

I wasn't accustomed to people speaking to me this way. I relaxed my face and opened my eyes. "Who the fuck do you think you are speaking to me like that?" It was clear this man had no idea who I was.

"That is of no importance to you at this moment, Mr. Tyler. What is important is that you listen, and with great attention, to what I'm about to tell you."

As the stranger leaned in, I could feel the warmth sucked out of the air and then a suffocating squeezing of my lungs. From his lips came a chilling whisper. Each word striking me like a sledgehammer to the gut. It was an unearthing of secrets long ago buried. Secrets I had paid a king's ransom to ensure no living person would know. Yet this stranger knew them all— and knew them in detail. How could he know such things?

He didn't stop there. The stranger continued repeating the many misgivings and bad deeds from my life. One by one, they echoed through my ears. Each one breaking deeper into the depths of my mind and soul. I could feel my very existence shattering around me. I could no longer control the guilt and emotions I was feeling. At that moment my eyes betrayed me. With the force of a river bursting through a dam, the tears began falling. I hadn't cried like this since I was a child.

"Stop, now, please," I whispered to the stranger. "Please… please… please… Stop it all!"

The stranger was stepping back as I looked up through tear-filled eyes into his. Those eyes, I will never forget them. Glowing a deep indigo color sucking the feeling of life right out of me.

"Mr. Tyler, your life is of no value to me. How or why your attempted overdose failed is beyond even my understanding. For a man who has been so successful at accomplishing things in life, it's rather a joke to see you fail at something as simple as this. Tsk, tsk, Mr. Tyler."

As the stranger moved closer once again, I could see a belt in his hand. It was the two-thousand-dollar Italian leather belt I had been wearing when they admitted me. "I have a more important purpose for you… For us. To both reach our potential, Mr. Tyler—you'll need to die."

"I… I… don't… want… to… die." The words came out of my mouth with each hyperventilating breath.

"What you want is of little concern to me. You're a poison to this world, and now we shall have an opportunity to extract that poison from it."

He created a loop with the belt and slid it down over my head, then further down until it rested around my neck. I wanted to stand up and run, but I couldn't manage to make any part of my body move. As if by some unseen force I found my body paralyzed. Desperate pleas to my limbs for movement were met with no response. If I couldn't move, how was I to get up and fight off this stranger?

He whipped the end of the belt forward. It felt as though a boa had begun its deadly squeeze around my neck. Tighter and tighter, the choking feeling wouldn't stop.

The pressure in my head was getting worse. I could hear the blood coursing through it with each beat of my heart. My eyes were starting to bulge out from their sockets. No more air. My hyperventilating ceased, along with any other breaths.

The stranger pulled tighter on the belt yet again. I was dragged to the foot rail of the hospital bed where he tied the belt into a knot from its highest point. For good measure, he got me up onto my knees, leaning me forward away from the bed. This, bringing me deeper into the stranglehold of the belt, ensured I had no chance for a final breath.

"I'm afraid I can't stay with you until your moment of sweet demise, Mr. Tyler. No worries though. The end will come soon enough for you. Now, I must be off as there are other pressing matters that require my attention. Tick tock, tick tock, the hands of time wait for no one, Mr. Tyler."

I felt his cold hand touch my head. As I closed my eyes, there came a moment or two where I could feel pins and needles running a course through my body. Here it was, a final surge of life. My lungs burned as they craved any bit of precious oxygen, but there was none.

A wave of darkness rushed over me, even the voids of space had more light than the shadows which ingested me. Pain, fear, any sense of being—it all washed away.

From nothingness, a new light came to my attention. It started as nothing larger than a pin drop far off in the distant darkness. With each second that ticked by, the light would double in size. Before I could comprehend what was happening, the light washed over me.

It was a rather disorientating feeling. With the light came the screams and cries of a million voices. I couldn't understand what they were saying, which gave me no relief. As quickly as the light had come, it was gone, and I found myself standing in the hospital room again.

A chilling sight met my gaze as I looked back to the bed. It was my own lifeless body. Like a child's disregarded ragdoll, I lay propped up with only the belt, firm around my neck, to hold me in place. The gasp that escaped my mouth carried and echoed through the room. The shock of this sight sent me stumbling backward, falling onto the cold tiles of the bathroom floor.

How could this be, I wondered? Steadying myself, I rose from the floor and took a step towards the bed, towards my body. I was a few steps away when the door burst open, and the nurse for the evening rushed in.

"Get Dr. Adler now," she yelled to the orderly peering through the doorway.

I watched as this tiny nurse maneuvered my body, getting the belt free of my neck. As she did, the lifeless sack of skin that had been mine fell to the floor with a hard thud. Watching this unfold, from the corner of my eye something captured my attention. It was that indigo light again. Now it was coming from behind me.

I turned to the mirror but couldn't see myself. Rather, I saw what appeared to be a never-ending hallway filled with the indigo light. The hallway was growing larger, and the light brighter the longer I stared into it. Appearing as if it were some strange optical illusion, it continued to grow.

Turning back once more, I looked at the nurse trying to resuscitate me. Her minuscule hands pressed deeper and deeper into my chest with each thrust. Glancing back into the endless hallway, I noticed something else. Off in the distance of this chilling light was the silhouette of a person moving towards me.

As it always had, my own curiosity got the better of me. Stepping into the light, I almost immediately felt a loss of self that I had always known. It was as though my very being was now nothing more than a timeless void.

The sounds of the hospital room were fading into a far-off murmur behind me. I pressed on further into the light and approached the silhouette.

As the figure got closer, I noticed this was not the stranger I had seen before. Rather it was another man who might be only a few years younger than myself.

The man moved closer, and I opened my mouth to say hello, but no sound came out. He appeared to be speaking back to me as well, but there was nothing other than the hollow silence of this endless void.

When he and I passed one another, our eyes met for the briefest of moments. In that short space of time came a flash of light so bright that I found myself blinded for a moment. My vision soon returned, and with that, I found ahead of me I could see an end to the hallway.

There, beyond the doorway, stood the dark stranger again. His face held a sly grin as he slammed the door shut without word or warning, taking what light there had been away with him. Silence, to a maddening degree, was all that remained.

Back into a void of nothingness. Without a clue of what else to do, I felt myself try to walk, or at least I thought I was. Where to? That, I was unsure of. It was then, from out in the distant darkness, a voice came: "Hello, John. My name is Elizabeth..."

CHAPTER 1: CLAY

THE MONOTONOUS TICKING OF THE CLOCK MARKED the seventh hour on the fifteenth day since I'd clawed my way back into the world of the living. Each second had been a sharp reminder of my escape from Purgatory, each minute dragged on in this sterile room at the Appalachian House.

I sat in a plush green chair, staring out over the Blue Ridge Mountains when Emilia, John's wife, stormed through the door. "I swear with the amount we are paying this place, you think I could get a straight answer!" Her voice faded into the background, merging with the trumpet-like sounds of the adults in a Charlie Brown special.

"John, are you even listening to me?" Her voice boomed back into my awareness.

I blinked, trying to regain focus. She wasn't talking to John, but to me, trapped in his body. "I'm listening," I muttered in a voice still foreign to my ears.

She sighed, exasperated. "Don't you even want to know how our children are doing?"

Children. John's children, not mine. My fist clenched, feeling the soft fabric beneath my fingers. "Sure," I said, doing my best to feign some interest. "Tell me about them."

Her eyes searched mine, looking for something—anything—familiar. "They miss you, you know. They're confused and don't understand why you haven't come home."

I bit back the sharp retort that sat on the tip of my tongue. How could I explain that while she saw the man she thought was her husband, inside was a person who had just escaped the cold reality of Purgatory? I hadn't had time to process it myself. Since I'd been back, I'd been captive in a psychedelic haze of drugs. In the moments I wasn't sedated, my mind was in a constant state of replaying my final moments in Purgatory.

"I'm trying, Emilia," I said, my voice hoarse and dry from the medications. "I'm trying to understand what's going on myself."

She shook her head, tears welling up. "You've always been distant with me, John. But the way you've been these last two weeks is even colder and more distant than usual."

In that moment of vulnerability, I saw Ava's face instead of Emilia's, her eyes filled with the same pain. The guilt gnawed at me. "I'm sorry," I whispered, looking back to the mountains. "My mind is a clusterfuck of thoughts; I can't seem to find clarity in anything." I stood and placed my arm around her shoulders, offering what comfort I could. "I've been so absorbed in my own shitstorm that I've neglected your feelings. I promise to be more present, to listen better, when you come."

My actions must have come as a shock to her. She lifted her head so suddenly that it slammed into my face. I felt my teeth and lips ache from the impact. "I'm sorry, John," she said, rubbing the back of her head. "Did you seriously just try and comfort me? You must be more mentally disturbed than the doctors think."

This confused me. "Isn't that what one person should do for another when they're upset?" I asked.

A perplexed look came over her face. "Yes, it is. But John, in the thirteen years we've been together, you've tried to comfort me, what, a total of two times? Once you were as high as a fucking kite, and the other time was after my mother passed away."

There was that awkward silence that comes after such a revealing insight. Whose skin was it I'd jumped into? John Tyler was a man, at least according to his wife, for whom empathy was a foreign visitor. It was in the midst of that thought it occurred to me that I'd been no better in my own life. There'd been so many opportunities where I should've given more of my attention to Ava, but hadn't.

After that morning, Emilia became warmer with me. I asked more pointed questions to determine who John Tyler was and the life he'd lived. It seemed to make Emilia feel better to talk about these things. But the more I came to know, the more I learned to despise him. In John, I had found a person who could give my dick of an uncle, Joe, a run for his money. I could say many nasty things about Joe, but at least he cared for his wife and spawn-of-Satan children. I wasn't getting the sense that John felt the same about his own family; I got the impression the only person John Tyler cared for was himself.

As Emilia left, I turned back to the window, the Blue Ridge Mountains stretching out before me. The morning mist rose over them, a reminder of the world I'd left behind. I wanted to go back, to find some semblance of peace, but I knew that wasn't possible. Not now.

On cue, Dr. Adler, my attending psychologist, walked through the door. He glanced at the replaced mirror in the bathroom and then back at me. "How are we feeling this morning, John?"

He believed he would be able to cure me of my "debilitating mental disease." At least that's what he'd told me and Emilia.

I heard him one afternoon outside my door, talking to a few of the nurses. "That's John Tyler in there. *The* John Tyler. You know, the tech millionaire! Can you imagine if I'm the one who helps get him better? I'm sure the family will be more than happy to pay me a generous reward." Later, I overheard him telling a psychiatrist: "If I can't fix the bastard, I can still profit from him. I mean, who wouldn't pay to keep this shit out of the tabloids?"

I clenched my jaw. "Just fine and dandy, doc."

He scribbled something onto his clipboard. "Any further... episodes?"

Dr. Adler was a real piece of work. So far in our sessions, he managed to do two things: annoy me and awaken the constant anger I held inside.

I shook my head. "No more little green men, no bleeding walls. Just me, Jim Morrison, and Jerry Garcia over here enjoying the psychedelics you keep delivering to my ass."

The psychedelic effects had been amusing to me, but the aftereffects of the sedatives were anything but pleasant. They made every piece of food taste like I was eating a dry rice cake. And the worst of it was the constipation. I forgot how uncomfortable it could be to be so full of shit.

Adler's eyes narrowed; the man hated my sarcasm, and I knew it. "Good. I'll take that as progress. Remember, John, we're here to help you. The more you cooperate, the sooner you'll be better."

"Well, once you stop sticking needles of fun juice in my ass, I might start to feel better."

"John, you know we're only doing what's needed to keep you safe and from further harming yourself. Your wife still seems quite concerned." He looked back at the bathroom mirror again.

After he left, I took notice of the mirror. The same mirror I had once shattered, now whole again, glowing the indigo color I had learned to fear and despise. My mind, still in a fragile state, found it hard to accept seeing this damn light again. There had been no sign of Az since I made my leap through the void of his gateway. Yet, here it was, glowing that oh-too-familiar color.

"Clay… Where are you?" The voice came from all around, filling the vacant spaces of the sterile room. "Clay… Please come back to me. I need you." There was no doubt that was Ava's voice. Was that her calling to me from Purgatory, or had they slipped me yet another new medication?

Stepping into the bathroom, I saw a glow filling the mirror. I reached out to touch it, and the glow instantly vanished. All that remained was a reflection that I've yet to get used to staring back at me.

In some ways, the shape and features of John's face were more than similar to my own. The difference, when looking at my face, was that one could see the lines forming from living a hard life. Examining John's face, you could see he had paid a lot of money ensuring his skin and body were well taken care of.

I ran my hand up and down the mirror. Turned the bathroom light off and on. Opened and closed the door a few times. I even tried saying Az's name three times in the dark. Neither the indigo light nor Ava's voice would return to me.

To say I was frustrated was an understatement at that moment. Telling myself it was because the doctor pushed on my emotions and it had worn me thin was the only thing that kept me together. It could be; after all, it hadn't even been an indigo light that I had seen. I assumed this was some sort of Purgatory PTSD that I was experiencing. I was feeling exhausted, and as much as I was trying to avoid my dreams, I was in the living world again. Not sleeping would have consequences for me.

No sooner had I closed my eyes than the dreams began again. There I was, shoving Ava back, making my crazed dash past Az, leaping into the darkness of the gateway. Yet, this time, in the dream, I noticed something I hadn't seen or paid attention to in my crossing. Out in the distance of the darkness, there was… Elizabeth. This was the same woman who Grayson had been friends with and the same one who Az had used to deceive me. There she was in the darkness—smiling at me.

Had she been there when I crossed over? Was she there watching as John Tyler and I passed by each other in the dark void? I guess the better question would be: Was that her or another trick Az was playing on me? I knew from Grayson's tale that she had also crossed through the gateway. It could be that she had gotten stuck there. It was too hard to tell what's real anymore or what was a projection from Az. For all I knew, this was nothing more than fabrications from my unconscious mind.

These dreams continued on a daily basis. Each time I closed my eyes, it was the same. Except now, I was aware of Elizabeth when I saw her. Every damn dream, there she was, smiling at me. What I wouldn't give to be able to talk with Grayson or Ava about any of this. If I told Dr. Adler or one of the staff at Appalachian House, I would be inviting them to provide me with more medication. If I told John's wife, Emilia, I would only frighten her, and again, the odds were that I would end up with more medication. I traded an existence captured in Purgatory for that of a world where everyone believed I was crazy. Every deed has a toll that comes due, and this must have been my penance for having broken free of the chains of Purgatory.

Thinking back to my sessions with Dr. Adler, it could be that this was my anger leading me into further poor decisions. When alone at night, I began going to the bathroom mirror and talking to Ava. I still wasn't sure that it was her I heard there. It gave me some relief, though, to believe there was a chance she was hearing me.

"Ava, I'm so sorry I left you. I swear I didn't see any other way at the time. It seems that no matter the cost, my anger keeps winning and I'm making the dumbest fucking choices because of it. I will find a way back to you, Ava. I will find a way to make this all better. I will find a way to not let anger rule my world. I love you, Ava. I will see you again soon."

They couldn't keep me in this place forever, could they? I needed to figure out what it was that they all wanted from me. Dr. Adler was easy, feeding his ego or his pocket. For Emilia, I would need to learn more about her life with John. I also needed to convince her that I was sane, and that I wasn't going to make another attempt on my life. I had to wonder, might she be the key to my freedom?

CHAPTER 2: ARIANNA

BLINK... BLINK... BLINK. I'D BEEN STARING AT THE SAME incessant blinking cursor on my laptop for the past two hours. I had my notes. I had my memories of our conversations. I had all that I needed to continue writing out Clay's story—as I promised him. But there was this unfamiliar weight settling in on my chest. It continued to grow more intense each time the cursor blinked at me. I felt like someone was placing stones on my heart. Each hour that ticked by, they added another stone, making me feel the true weight of these emotions. It was a mixture of sorrow and something darker, something more volatile. It kept me from moving forward.

It had been nearing two weeks since I had last seen Clay; his absence had wound the high-tension strings of my emotions. Following his leaving for Crossroads, the strings stretched even tighter each day. My heart filled with feelings of emptiness and an ever-growing sadness. Feelings like this were anything but new for me; they were ones I had done a fair job of repressing for many years. I found myself asking: What is the true cause of these feelings? Where would the rabbit lead me if I followed him into Wonderland? Was I even sure I wanted to dig that deep below the surface?

I couldn't deny there was a spark Clay brought back to me that had been missing from my life. The more I thought about it, the spark was less about Clay and more about having a meaningful purpose each day. Not that I had been unhappy before that. It was that before, I felt more like a sideshow freak with a gift for talking to the dead. I was an amusement to the people who called me or scheduled meetings with me. When Jamie called me, her case was the first that sounded like the real thing, and it was. My connection to Clay had blossomed so fast, it was as though we had always known each other. It was in that time with, and now the loss of Clay, that has brought me back to ten years earlier when I lost my Eddie.

The mention of Eddie was like a scab on my heart and soul that kept getting picked at. It didn't matter how old the wound was, so long as you keep picking at the scab it never has the chance to heal. His name alone would leave me sitting at the edge of my seat fidgety and unstable. Clay, being the observant person that he was, could see the shift in my mood when he broached the subject. Remaining respectful of my boundaries, he never probed further than what I was willing to discuss.

I found a remarkable amount of similarities in Clay and Eddie's personalities. From the sarcastic sense of humor, to the still-like calmness I felt in their presence. It is no wonder that spending time with Clay brought up such vivid memories of my time with Eddie. It wasn't just reminiscences; it was an immersion into the emotions tied to those memories—feelings of safety, the comfort of familiarity, and a lingering sense of love that echoed through our interactions. These were emotions I had long suppressed since Eddie's departure. Now the days spent with Clay had unraveled the tightly sealed compartments where I had stored those sentiments, allowing them to flood back into my consciousness, raw and unfiltered.

The cursor was still blinking and I had been thinking for far too long. It wasn't as if I had other things to do or places to be. I hadn't had regular work in the last three years. I made most of my money from helping those who claimed to have hauntings; though only one-in-five actually did. For now though, I didn't need to work again for a while. The money that Clay had paid me would more than cover my meager expenses. I felt I at least owed it to him to complete the catalog of his memories.

As I immersed myself in Clay's memories, my dedication to documenting every detail became a form of solace—a way to honor my promise to him and perhaps uncover the truth behind his vanishing act. Reading back through my notes, it's funny that all this information was written in my own hand, but it felt like I was meeting Clay again for the first time. I wasn't only typing his story to my computer, it was being etched into my heart.

Aside from chronicling his life I had made another promise to Clay. If I didn't hear from him again, I would start looking for him. After two weeks and no word from him, I was becoming more concerned with what fate had befallen him. Had he made it back to the living world like he planned to? Did his fiancé betray him, or had they reconciled their differences and she had made it out of Purgatory with him? The worst of these thoughts were those of if he hadn't escaped. What if instead Azrael had done what he was threatening to do? Would I find Clay, with his memories erased, wandering around Purgatory without a clue? As my thoughts threatened to consume me, a sharp knock at the door shattered the silence, jolting me back to the present. The sudden intrusion startled me, but it was the look of distress on Deanna's face that sent a shiver down my spine.

Before I could say come in Deanna marched in. The look on her face was one of pure distress. "Damnit, girl, you should've told me what that boy was up to!"

No question about it, Deanna was pissed. I now knew that something had happened with Clay, but how much of it would Deanna share? "What are you talking about?" I asked.

"Don't play coy with me, Arianna. You knew damn well what he was going to try, and you didn't tell me! Whatever that boy has done, it's causing a ripple effect not only in Purgatory but across all realms, both of the living and the dead."

Her eyes narrowed, mirroring the stern expression my biological mother used to give me. Memories flooded back of that same gaze preceding a reprimand, whether deserved or not. Deanna's familiar look spoke volumes, conveying a silent disapproval and signaling trouble ahead. I knew from her piercing gaze that things were far from good, stirring a sense of unease within me.

"Arianna," she said. "I need you to tell me everything that you know about what Clay's plans were. Don't skip or leave out any damn bit of information this time."

It took some time for me to get Deanna calmed down enough to understand what she was talking about. In the twelve years I had known her, I'd never seen her so worked up by something. Under normal circumstances she was very particular about her appearance; today she was a disheveled mess. Her snow white hair looked like she had stuck her finger in a light socket and her blouse was half tucked in and half untucked in the back of her skirt. What choice did I have but to come clean with her on it all? I also wanted to know what had happened to Clay. He had to have made it somewhere if this much hell had broken loose.

"Yes, Deanna, I knew he was going to try and return to the world of the living, but I didn't help him with that. All I did was spend time capturing the memories that he had remaining in the event he were to end up like Hamilton. Clay only wanted a way, should Azrael erase his memories, to have a path back to them. I saw no harm in doing that."

"Still, Arianna, you should've told me what he was planning. Whatever it is he did or tried to do has opened up a rift between the realms of the living and dead. I don't know the extent of what damage might have occurred yet, but I can assure you that whatever it is there have been changes in Purgatory. Hamilton came to me two days ago and told me a silent chaos has broken out. It would seem that none are coming or going from Purgatory anymore. And he was going on and on about a change to the light. Believe me, Arianna, this isn't good for any of us."

"Deanna, I don't even know if Clay was successful."

"Are you not listening to me? The realms of the dead do not change on a whim like the weather my dear. Whatever that boy did he was successful at one thing: leaving a trail of chaos behind him."

"The last I spoke to Clay was before he went over to that bar, Crossroads, on Halsted, to meet with his fiancé. She had been working with Azrael, and he was trying to learn more about how she had ended up here. Even more so, why she was working with him. It had me worried that he was walking into a trap. It was bad enough that Azrael showed up here..."

Deanna gave me a sharp look. "You mean, you saw him? You saw Azrael?"

"Yes, I did, and let me tell you, from the look and feel I got from him, he isn't someone that I want to see again any time soon. As for Clay, I haven't heard from him or seen him since the night he left. He said if he got back to the land of the living and remembered, he would be in touch with me. Since I haven't heard from him, I've been keeping an eye out at places he said he went to in Purgatory, but still, no sign of him."

Deanna sat in a prolonged silence, staring off at the antique floor mirror in the corner of my living area. She took a sharp breath as though something had sucked all the air out of her lungs. Her expression changed from the one of anger and concern she had come in with to one of curiosity.

She finished her tea, stood from the table and walked over to the mirror. I followed behind to see what it was that had caught her attention. When I was not more than a step behind her, she turned and walked back to me.

"I knew my time was coming, but lady love, I didn't think it was going to be like this…"

"What are you talking about, Deanna?" I asked.

She kept talking as she walked away, though she continued to glance back at the mirror. "He will come again, he knows where you are and your connection to that boy. Damn it, Arianna, I told you to be careful. I wasn't ready for this yet."

I heard what Deanna had said but I couldn't understand why Azrael would be coming after Deanna or myself. Whatever Clay had done was between him and Azrael. This had nothing to do with either of us. It made no sense to me.

Before I could ask Deanna any more questions, she had gathered her things and was heading for the door. "I will be back, sweet girl. I must go find Hamilton and have him get a few things ready. I'd recommend that you make sure all your living affairs are in order. I'll do what I can to protect you, but I'm just an old lady readying to stand against Death."

Deanna closed the door and I walked back to my pillow corner and sat down. I considered for a moment what living affairs I had. There were none. The only things I had were the memories of Eddie and a promise to Clay. I still had hope that I'd hear from him or find him before things could get worse. He might have known how to stop whatever was coming from Azrael. I needed to find him, wherever he might be.

CHAPTER 3: CLAY

"JOHN, WHY DON'T WE GO BACK TO THE NIGHT OF YOUR overdose again. I'm feeling that if we can get back to right before those events, we'll begin to have a better picture of your state of mind."

"Dr. Adler, to be honest with you, I don't remember shit about the events of that night. The first thing I can recall with any clarity is yourself and Nurse Mildred standing above me talking. Even those memories become foggier by the day. I'm sorry to say that if we need to begin before then I'm not going to be of much help in my therapy."

I wasn't lying to him. I had no clue what John Tyler had been up to before I woke up in his life. These were the normal conversations Dr. Adler and I were having each day. Most days he would become this incessant pest pushing harder and harder. When he wasn't asking about John's past he was digging into the events that happened when I arrived at Appalachian House. What did I remember? Why did I find it necessary to shatter the mirror when I saw my reflection?

I tolerated this because, what choice did I have? I had no immediate pathway to escape. Dr. Adler in the meantime had become convinced that I, as John, was experiencing a form of PTSD. "This," he would say, "I have no doubt is stemming from your overdose and attempt on your life." Part of me wondered what had been so wrong with John's life that led him down the road to his own death.

After all I had done to get back to the world of the living, why had this man been so eager to leave it? His wife and children were still here. He seemed to not want for anything, ever. Did he think he was going somewhere better? It had me wondering if the living could see what a fucked up place Purgatory was, would they be so eager to take their own lives?

As for John, I could have walked a thousand miles in his shoes, but that gave me zero fucking clues of what was in his head that night. The only part of me that crossed over was my consciousness. I may have looked and sounded like John, but there was no remanence of his memories or personality in here. It was only me that remained on the inside.

I was doing my best to stay as pleasant as possible during these trivial sessions, but Dr. Adler would have them drag on for hours. I'd never been good at sitting still for a long period of time. Add having to talk about what I was thinking and feeling—I had to question if I hadn't come to the world of the living but rather to my own personal hell. Even when it would appear we had reached the end of a topic, the dear doc would come around and take another whack at it. I was beginning to feel like an emotional punching bag.

By the third week of these sessions I had taken more than I could stand. My responses to the doctor's questions were more that of a petulant child than a grown man. In the later hours of these sessions I'd taken to mocking the doctor. The longer the session lasted, the worse my responses to him became. The only thing that was on my mind right now was Ava. I still hadn't found a way to get out of here and out of here is where she was. This was a hospital, but to me it felt like another damn prison and right now, Dr. Adler was the warden.

I had been pushing every button that Dr. Adler had exposed and his patience with me had come to a swift end. "Damn it, John! You're the most stubborn patient I've ever had." Rising from his chair and pushing it back against the wall, he left the office in a huff. What the hell am I supposed to do now, I wondered? Do I sit here and wait to see if the doctor comes back? What is the official protocol for a rehab hospital?

It was a few minutes of sitting in silence before Dr. Adler returned with another gentleman. "John, I'd like for you to meet Dr. Dawood. He's currently working as a guest here at Appalachian House while his local office is being built. He has a world renowned practice and is taking our profession to new heights. I've asked him to sit in and observe the rest of our session. It is my hope, since we've made so little progress, that he might provide some insight to a better mode of treatment for you. Do you have any objections to that?"

"Whatever works for you doc." I wanted my response to be as indifferent as possible. There was something right away about this new doctor that had stuck me with a growing sense of curiosity.

I was expecting, since he now had a colleague in the room, that Dr. Adler might take a new approach. Didn't happen. Apparently the doctor liked to keep throwing the same shit at a stained wall. With the same questions coming at me again, I'd lost any focus on what was being asked of me. My attention was still very much focused on Dr. Dawood, who had taken a seat in the corner to the left and rear of me.

Dr. Dawood was a tall man with a tawny complexion. It was his attire that I found most unusual, at least for this setting. Much of the staff at Appalachian House took to dressing in a rather casual fashion. Which surprised me. The people that could afford this hospital were those of means. I figured they would have been more comfortable with suits around, but Emilia had told me a different story. Here was Dr. Dawood, dressed much more like I would have expected a person in his profession to dress.

He wore a light gray three-piece suit, carried a mahogany cane hooked on his right arm, and a gray bowler hat with blue trim in his right hand. Looking over at Dr. Adler who was wearing a pair of faded jeans and a USC hoodie, it was easy to differentiate the styles. Beyond the clothing there was something peculiar about Dr. Dawood that I couldn't yet put my finger on.

"Damn it!" shouted Dr. Adler, bringing me back from my fixation. "John, can you please try and focus on what we're discussing here. Where is it that you keep drifting off to? I would love to know." He turned his attention to Dr. Dawood, who was still sitting silently in the back corner. "You see, this is the behavior I was telling you about."

"Dr. Adler, would you mind if we consult in the hallway for a moment?" asked Dr. Dawood.

"Yes, but of course, Dr. Dawood."

The two men exited and I could see by all the hand flapping Dr. Adler was doing that they were having an animated discussion. It was only Dr. Dawood who returned after that conversation. It seemed that he had dismissed Dr. Adler. I wondered how the good doctor's ego was feeling now.

"Mr. Tyler, I'm going to be taking over your sessions for a time. I'll follow up with Dr. Adler, of course, on your progress, but from here on out you'll be my patient."

My first reaction to this news was a hearty laugh. "And what makes you think you're going to be able to do any more for me than Dr. Dipshit was able to?"

"For now, let's say that I have a better familiarity with cases such as yours. If you give me a chance you may find that we have more common ground for our discussions." He didn't wait for me to confirm or agree to his taking over, though he carried on as if I had. "For starters, why don't you tell me more about yourself, Clayton Mitchell. That is what you like to be called, is it not?"

"Clay will do fine, thanks."

This was a surprising approach for the doctor to be taking. Dr. Dawood wanted to keep talking about my life, as in my real life, not the life of John Tyler that the others had been trying to learn more about. "You see doc, you asking those questions… I'm hesitant to answer. How am I to know that you aren't like the rest of the doctors around here? It seems any time I've spoken about anything other than being John Tyler it doesn't end well for me. In fact, most of the time it ends with another needle jabbing into my ass and me on a six-hour trip down happy fucking highway."

"I understand your apprehension, Clay. I'm, however, not the other doctors. I can assure you that unless you become violent or outright delusional, there will be no need for more sedatives to be administered to you."

Over the course of several sessions I chose to let my guard down bit-by-bit and started sharing the story of how I, Clayton Mitchell, ended up in the body of one John Tyler. I couldn't help but to feel patronized by Dr. Dawood at first. I was sure that he was asking these questions for nothing more than his own entertainment. With more sessions, though, I could see that when he asked questions he would listen to what I had to say with such an intent ear. His follow up questions always seemed to come from a point of genuine interest rather than just moving through the clinical motions.

The more comfortable I became, the more I shared with Dr. Dawood. There was one piece of information that I left out of the story. At no time did I ever mention Az directly to the doctor. I instead referred to him as "a troubled entity."

I still wasn't convinced that Dr. Dawood wasn't Az crossed over into the world of the living. I remembered Deanna telling me that Az had the ability to walk amongst the living. Why not pose as a therapist and drive the nails deeper into my wrists? It might've come off as paranoid behavior, but fuck it! Go through what I went through in Purgatory and tell me you wouldn't be feeling a touch on the paranoid side. It didn't matter anyways. My suspicions of Dr. Dawood were soon validated.

It was at the beginning of a session, a week or so into our meetings, that Dr. Dawood started off with, "Clayton, please tell me more about this Azrael character you last spoke of."

Like I said, I never said his name to the good doctor or to anyone since I had returned to the land of the living. My anger was boiling up. That son-of-a-bitch Az had followed me through. I felt myself ready to attack him right then and there. There was another voice in my head, though, one with better reasoning. It said, "Let this play out a little longer, Clay. You have no idea what might happen to you if that is Az. You have to remember you are in the land of the living again. Play your cards right, and you may just find your ticket back to Ava."

If this was Az, I decided I was going to make him break character. I began to give Dr. Dawood my account of Az and I did all that I could to make him sound far more heinous than he was. I only hoped that if this was Az, his pride-filled ego would force him to reveal himself to correct what I was saying. It never happened though. Dr. Dawood sat there nodding his head as I rambled on with my stories. Either Az had gotten better with his self-control or Dr. Dawood was in fact who he claimed to be.

As this session was coming to an end, I noticed something that any other day may not have stood out to me. There wasn't a single reflective surface in this room that I could find. During all our sessions, the windows were always draped, no mirrors, no glass anywhere—with one exception. In the corner of Dr. Dawood's office there was an antique grandfather clock. At the back of the clock behind the pendulum was a narrow mirror that spanned the height of the clock.

As Dr. Dawood moved from the chair he had been seated in over to his desk to grab a pen, he passed in front of the clock. I thought my eyes were playing tricks on me—there was no reflection of the good doctor in it. Yet, clear as day I could see my own, well, John Tyler's.

Dr. Dawood turned and caught sight of what I was staring at. "Well, it seems you have figured me out, Mr. Mitchell."

Snapping my head back to Dr. Dawood, I saw that he was looking at me with a very familiar pair of icy blue eyes. In a panicked response, knowing one false move could mean the end of my existence in all realms, I pushed Dr. Dawood's desk towards him. Boxed against his bookshelves, I took the opportunity to charge back to the office door. Fuck… it was locked! *Of course it's locked, you asshole,* I scolded myself, *this is a damn recovery hospital.*

I turned to reassess my options and saw where Dr. Dawood was… too fucking close, that's where he was. The doctor was now only inches away from me, his eyes shimmering an icy blue death. I watched as his hand reached forward and touched me on the shoulder. I scrunched my eyes shut, not knowing what might come next.

Where there had been anxiety and alarm, there was now a sense of peace and calmness. I hadn't turned to dust; that was a good start. But I could still feel Dr. Dawood's hand upon my shoulder, and I could still hear the monotonous ticking of the clock.

"My… my Clayton. I can see that Azrael has done quite the number on you. You're close to being as broken as they come. But my friend, you're not so far gone that we cannot repair you."

I eased my eyes open, looking back into Dr. Dawood's. "You've nothing to fear from me, Clayton. I'm not here to harm you. Quite the opposite, actually."

"That's exactly something that Az would say. Too many deceptions. Too many tricks!"

"Let me assure you, Clayton, I'm not Azrael. I am, however, of a similar origin as him and share a similar role in our universe."

"And I am supposed to just eat this up and believe everything you say now? Take you on your word alone? That's how this is all going to work, is it? Do you take me as some fool? I've been beyond this world. I know the deceptions."

"Very well, Clayton, if this is how it must be," Dr. Dawood says.

Before my eyes, Dr. Dawood transformed from the well-put together therapist I had been getting to know to a much taller version of himself, covered in what I could only guess to be some sort of hieroglyphic tattoos. He was now dressed in a tunic of pale color and adorned with shining gold stones. It looked like something I would have imagined they wore in the age of antiquities in Egypt.

Dr. Dawood raised his right hand; upon it was a tattoo. This one I recognized; it was the eye of Ra and it was glowing the same blue color of his eyes.

"Clayton, Death takes many forms. Azrael is only one of those forms and I'm yet another. Not all deaths are the same or as understandable as those of you in the living world think them to be. The form you now see before you is the form I've chosen for the purposes of the job I must do. As was the form you saw of Azrael, the one he had chosen. Even these are not our truest of forms. Nor is the form you see of Mr. Tyler, the form you saw of yourself or that of others around you. These forms are skins you wear for a time but in the end shall always shed."

Dr. Dawood stepped back from me, walking to the desk. As he did he returned to the human form I'd come to know. "I see in your eyes, Clayton, that you no doubt recognized some of the markings on me. To simplify this for you, I've been called Anubis, The Weigher of Righteousness, by some. I am a guardian to existences beyond those you are familiar with."

"Sorry doc, still having a hard time believing you're not Az. I've seen him take many forms and have heard him say many things. All lies. Your transformation and story do nothing to help me believe what you say."

Dr. Dawood bent, picking up the papers that had flown from his desk when I pushed it. "I understand this may be hard for you to accept right now. I'm willing to work with you on that trust. I am afraid, however, that our time to do that is going to be limited."

Walking over to the antique grandfather clock, Dr. Dawood opened the door and began winding its silver hands. "You see, Clay, when you crossed the gateway back into this existence, you caused a great disturbance. One that I'm not sure you are ready to understand. You now inhabit a body that does not belong to you, and you're now in a realm to which you no longer belong."

I kept my back to the door watching Dr. Dawood as he checked his watch to the clock, then closed the door, turning back to me.

"And what exactly is it that you need from me, Dr. Dawood, or whoever the fuck you are?"

"What I need from you Clayton… what all the realms of living and dead need from you, is to help us find Azrael before he can do any further damage."

CHAPTER 4: AVA

I stood with my fingers trembling above the doorknob, I questioned if I should turn it. The sickening feeling returned in a swirl of sour waves. My head spun like a jacked up merry-go-round. For two days I had repeated this process over and over. Standing at the door, the knob in my hand, ready to leave the coffin like confines of the apartment above Crossroads. Each time it led back to the stiff sickening feeling that ran through me.

The days before still lingered fresh in my mind like a nightmare refusing to fade with the sun. I saw it all playing out: Clay shoving me to the floor, sprinting past Az to dive through the whirlpool of indigo light that was Az's gateway to the realms beyond Purgatory. It's those last few seconds that have continued to haunt me.

Az's rotted third arm reached out, touching the bottom of Clay's foot. There was a flash of blinding light and a boom so loud and powerful that it shook the world down to its very core. When the light faded, both Clay and the gateway were gone.

Az escorted me up to the apartment. I could see by the rapid darting of his eyes and the downturned hook of his lips that something hadn't gone as expected. I wanted to fight him. I wanted to run—run and never look back. I was so tired though. It felt as if I had taken a handful of allergy pills and chewed them down like candy. When Clay left, something changed.

Whatever happened changed the course of this realm. I caught a glimpse out the window on our way up the stairs when I noticed the sky. It had gone from the familiar indigo color of a perpetual twilight to that of blue so dark it looked more like a never ending midnight.

Like all the other times I had tried, I let go of the doorknob and sat back on the bed, defeated. It only took a few moments before the sickening feeling went away, but the thoughts and the memories, they lingered. I still had no real idea what had become of Clay or why he had to go and cross through the gateway. If he had made it back to the world of the living, what would that mean for me? Was I doomed to become one of Az's mindless nitwits? Or if Clay had made it, would he find a way to bring me back as well?

I forgave him for leaving me, though I still didn't understand why he had to go. Az threatened him, but we still had the door behind us. We could've run off together. Together, that was all I wanted. But something had changed in Clay since his death. Much of his personality was still the same, but there was that underlying anger I hadn't seen in him during our lives together. I'm not saying he was a saint, but there was something much darker in his anger when it came to Az. It was blinding him and causing him to make decisions like a child throwing a temper tantrum.

The other question that swam through my head was: Where the hell was Az? He had what he wanted now—me, without Clay. Yet there hadn't been a sight or word of him. This is where I delved into a back and forth conversation with my inner self, trying to rationalize my behavior.

"Why are you still sitting here, Ava?" half of me asked.

"Because Az could come back at any minute, and I don't want to suffer a painful demise," the other retorted.

"Do you think just because you sit here he's going to make it any easier on you? You sitting here only makes it easier for him to find and do what he wishes with you."

"Yes, but where can I go? Clay and Az were the only two that I had in this place. One is gone and one is an insane sociopath with supernatural powers."

"Ava, get off your ass and go back to the door. Turn the knob and leave this place before it's too late. You can do this. Now go!"

I got up, ran to the door, touched the knob—to the same result again. Frozen in the fear of an unknown future. Anxiety flooded my body in tsunami-like waves. I crashed to the floor, the tears running down my face. It was then that I heard something drumming up from the floor below me.

It came in soft percussive waves at first and then grew stronger. Thump thump. Thump thump. The rhythm repeated. Then my cries became one with the sound of a slide guitar echoing out a deep and mournful blues run. The music was a sweet symphony to my ears. I knew this song, and for a moment I found myself lost in its story. When it ended I found a new life, a new energy inside myself.

Rising up from the floor, I grabbed the knob, and this time, I turned it. The sweet sound of music flooded and filled the gray space of the room, bringing with it light and a new hope. Letting the music lead me step-by-step down the stairs, I found myself one step closer to freedom. Each sweet song the band played brought a new reason for hope back to my heart.

Unconsciously, I started humming as the melody found my soul. Then a realization came to me: I had not sung a single song in many years now. The last time I could recall singing was when I had spent time with my parents. I knew in my heart there were still so many songs in me, but each time I would try to sing my throat would go dry and I would choke up.

I didn't leave the bar but sat there until the band wrapped and the bar closed for the night. I then went back up to the apartment and went to sleep. Each night, however, I came back down and each night I could feel a little more strength. A little more like myself again. In the darkest hours I still yearned for Clay to be back with me. It may be that we were worlds apart now, and finding each other again still felt near improbable.

It was this vicious game that the universe was playing on us. Let us get close enough and then yank us away back into new turmoil. These thoughts made me cry out to him, though I doubted he could hear me.

It was his last words to me that now held meaning. He wanted me to find some woman who had been helping him. How the hell was I going to find someone in a city of millions of people, living and dead? It was like trying to find Waldo in a sea of red and white stripes. All I had to go off of was a name: Arianna.

It had been nearing two weeks now and still there had been no sign of Az. Leaving the cramped apartment of Crossroads became less daunting with each passing day. Expanding my comfort zone down to the bar and taking in the music that was bringing the fighter out in me again. I needed to get further than this though. If I was going to find this Arianna woman, I needed to get beyond the doorway of Crossroads.

Despite my longing desires, doubts gnawed at me. Would finding her truly make a difference? After what I had seen happen to Clay with my own eyes, how could I even think it was possible for him to exist, let alone me find him. Still for his sake and for my love of him, I had to try. I was also not blind to the fact that the longer I was away from him it became much more probable that my memories would soon fade. It took a dream to finally get me to cross the threshold and back out into the city.

The dream was of Clay, at least I thought it was him. We were in a place that was a darkness like one that only can exist in a dream. I could hear Clay's voice speaking out to me. "Light is all there is in the end, Ava. All we have is light."

"I don't understand what you're saying, Clay. Where are you, where are we now?" I pleaded, confusion evident in my voice.

"Our only way beyond the darkness is to let in our real light."

His words, like riddles, danced beyond the grasp of my fingers. "Please," I implored, "help me understand." But he remained silent.

I could only assume it was him, though all I saw was a beautiful blue and gold light shimmering in front of me. The colors had me captivated, but when I reached out to touch the light there was a heat so intense I immediately recoiled back and at the same time snapped awake from the dream. All that remained in my head that morning was a mission to find Clay.

On my first venture outside of Crossroads, the anxiety made my stomach feel as though it had been trapped on one of those pirate ship rides. The ones that swing you back and forth, higher and higher. I stayed close to the bar in the event that I did run into Az. It would be much easier, I thought, to make up some excuse to feed him. After a few hours of wandering nearby there was no sign of him. As I began my way further out into the Chicago neighborhoods it struck me for the first time, since all this happened, how dark this new color was that replaced the familiar indigo. That wasn't the only thing I noticed.

Since Clay had made his jump through the gateway I had not seen the Indigo Alarm going off. That was the name I gave to the small fluctuations in the indigo light when Az would pass through the gateway with new Purgatory arrivals. Aside from the new hue, there had been no changes. This realm was lingering in a state of constant darkness.

It made the differentiation between night and day near impossible by sight alone. The best chance a person could have was to observe the living and see what they were doing while out on the street. Were they dressed in business clothes for the day or partying it up in the night? This also had a change on how those with me in Purgatory were behaving.

When Az had been present things were calm, well, as calm as a place like this could be. There was an increase in the activity of the non-living. It wasn't a good increase though. There was a sense of alarm for those that had been here for some time. I tried to engage them in conversation but that effort remained as fruitless as it had ever been. They may have been more active but their brains were still the mush that Az had converted them into. I left them aside and focused my energy back on the task of finding Arianna.

Thinking back to the conversations I had with Clay and the few days I spent following him, I knew my best chance to locate Arianna would be to head over to the Lake Shore Drive and Belmont Harbor area. I had never seen which building Clay had gone into; I only knew that he always headed back in that direction.

A short walk later and I found myself staring out into Lake Michigan from Belmont Harbor. My mind aloof, a familiar voice greeted me. "Beth… Is that you, Beth?"

It was the old homeless man who had been so kind to me when I first got here and again when I got back from my parents. Without the little bit of knowledge he shared, I'm not sure I would have ever found my way around.

It occurred to me that I had never shared my real name with him. On top of that, I again couldn't remember his name. Feeling a little guilty on both counts, I knew what I wanted to do. "I'm so sorry. I know we've met a few times before but I can't remember your name."

A big toothy grin came across his face. "That's okay, Beth. Happens all the time that I can't remember no damn names myself. Grayson is the name."

"It's nice to meet you again, Grayson. I do have something I need to confess to you. You see, when I first met you I had just gotten here. I had no idea who or what to believe. So I was rather surprised when you started talking to me and, well, I wasn't fully honest about who I am."

Grayson took a step back and started sizing me up. "That you behind there, Azrael? If so, you best just come on out and face me in your true skin."

"Nnn… no… no… no. I promise you I am not Azrael. I meant that my name is not Beth. It's Ava."

He took another step back, looking me up and down again. "Now I see what all that fuss musta been about. I take it you are *the* Ava."

"What's that supposed to mean?"

"Ava, let's go find us a place to sit down and talk. I'm thinking we've got a friend in common, and I want to know what has happened to my boy."

CHAPTER 5: CLAY

DR. DAWOOD NEEDING MY HELP TO FIND AZ? IT FELT like a punchline to a cosmic fucking joke. Wasn't he the one with the supernatural mojo? The angel of death or whatever? Why couldn't he locate Az himself? It's not like I could pop back into Purgatory at will and give him directions. But there was one reason I even entertained the idea—finding Ava. I had a hunch Az wouldn't be far from her.

I couldn't hold back my frustration. "Dr. Dawood, or whoever the fuck you are, why should I help you find Az?" My skepticism bled into my words. "Sure, I want to find Ava, but if there's a way to avoid Az, you can be damn sure I'll take it. And don't tell me you can't teleport into Purgatory. You claimed to be like him, or was that another lie?"

"Clayton, it's not that easy. As I've told you, I'm like Azrael so much as I help to usher those from this living world, as you call it, into the next. Each death is different, and where you end up depends on a multitude of different things."

I cut him off. I wasn't in the mood to hear the same spiel that Az had already delivered to me. "Look, I've got it, doc. Az told me all about the place of good, the place of bad, and of course his favorite—the place of indecision."

Dr. Dawood's lips curled into a thin grin. "You make it sound like there are three distinct locations, Clayton." His amusement was palpable. "But I'm afraid Azrael might have misled you. When I say each death is different, I mean precisely that. There's no one-size-fits-all destination. We'll delve deeper into this later. For now..."

My frustration boiled over. "If everyone goes to a different place, how do you explain all those people I saw in Purgatory? What about me and Ava—we were there together. Same place, same time. How does that fit into your theory?"

Dr. Dawood's tone shifted, more serious now. "We'll discuss this further later. For now, consider whether you'll help me or not. Know this though, Clayton, the body you're in... it's not yours. Whether you help me or not, you won't be staying in it for long. I suggest you return to your room. We'll reconvene tomorrow at nine."

I left the office feeling bewildered, as if I hadn't learned anything at all. Why the hell did things like this keep happening? Why did it always need to be more complicated? Returning to my room I grabbed the chair, pulled it in front of the window, and stared back out to the mountains. What risk was I taking by agreeing to help Dr. Dawood? The thought lingered as I gazed at the mountains, their silent grandeur contrasting with the chaos within me. And why did these entities, whatever they were, always seem to rely on people like me and Ava to carry out their bidding?

This all felt as though I was falling into another one of the traps Az had set for me. The only thing that kept me thinking that Dr. Dawood was not Az was the moment when he had touched me. I hadn't fallen dead, but rather I was overcome with a feeling of calmness and serenity that I'd never known before. Az had touched me at least twice; neither time could I remember it being a pleasant experience.

The more I pondered, the more I wondered what it would take for me to trust Dr. Dawood. His comment about it not mattering what my choice was, I wouldn't remain in this body, still sat heavy with me as well. What was it he meant by that? Is someone going to kill me if I choose to not play along with this game? In the end, none of these questions mattered. What did matter was finding my way back to Ava. I wasn't sure how I was going to get there, but getting back to Chicago, back to Crossroads, had to be the start of it.

Arianna had also been on my mind. I had made a promise to contact her once I got back to the living world, but Appalachian House restricted my phone access. If I could get a message out to her she may be able to help me get away from this place. Not to mention she and her friends had connections to the afterlife. They could be my eyes into a world I could no longer peer into on my own.

So there it was: I needed to play along with whatever games might be happening here. I wasn't ready to give unconditional trust to Dr. Dawood yet, but I would play along for now and help the doctor. As far as I could see, it might be my only logical way of reclaiming my freedom from the Appalachian House.

I drifted into sleep, dreaming not of nightmares but of the most beautiful and vibrant hues of blue and gold. They surrounded me, danced through me, carried me away on waves of tranquility. The dream then bled into the first time I met Ava at UIC. That sparkle in her emerald eyes. She was so close in the dream I could taste her kiss when I woke the next morning. That dream of Ava, it was a memory lost in the vacuum of Purgatory. It was back now, but how?

I recounted my dreams to Dr. Dawood during our morning session. "How did my memories come back out of thin air? I thought those were gone for good."

"Clay, that means you are awakening. If you let more of that anger of yours go, you will see more of this existence for what it is. If we are to get you back to Ava and find Azrael there must be more of this to move us forward."

CHAPTER 6: AVA

I WAS STILL SHAKING MY HEAD IN DISBELIEF AFTER AN hour of speaking with Grayson. "You two were never further than a mile apart. To think I'd met you two times before I ever come across that boy. He'd been searching high and low for you for some time when I first met him. Only thing on his mind was to find you and finding a way out of this place. I warned that boy time and time again about playing with fire, but he wouldn't listen to a thing ol' Grayson had to say."

"I caught up to him and realized that too. But Grayson, why would you share the location of the gateway with him? You knew how dangerous it was and how dangerous Az can be. Look around us, Grayson; all this is because Clay crossed through that damn gateway."

"Ava, if it wasn't me, he was gonna find that damn thing on his own. But what got to me was when that no-good son-of-a-bitch–excuse my language, miss, but that's what Azrael is–started posing as Elizabeth. Something had to be done. So..."

"So you sent Clay into the lion's den wearing armor made of porterhouse steaks. Grayson, you knew as well as I did Clay would never have been a match for the likes of Az."

"No ma'am. And I don't think you much believe what you said either. Be mad at me all you like, but you know there's something special about Clay. It's just that boy's anger... he tries to control it... but the wrong damn way. He holds on to that like a baby holds on to its bottle. All that anger makes his temper quick and he makes bad choices."

"That still doesn't excuse you sending him there. How did you even know the gateway was there, or that it existed for that matter? Az told me that no one else here knew about it."

"Does it surprise you that he would lie to you? Maybe I sent him there 'cause it," he pointed around at our darkened world, "all this... it needed to happen. Sometimes a person gets a feeling they gotta do something and well, that's what I done. Don't mean I don't feel bad if something ill come to Clay, but..."

"Well, something bad did happen to him. I told you, Az touched his foot with his third arm. Then... boom... Clay and the gateway were both gone."

"It may be he's not gone for good. It may be he's made it beyond the gateway. Miss Ava, let me tell you a little more 'bout how I come to know about that gateway and more of the story of my dear friend Elizabeth."

Elizabeth's tale was an interesting one; it was also one that I had recognized from Az. When he had first shown the gateway to me I had asked him if anyone from here had ever gone through it. He said there had been one and now I knew who she was. I still wasn't sure why Grayson thought it was wise to share that information with Clay. He saw what happened to his friend Elizabeth and claimed he had not wanted the same for Clay. Yet, he told him where to find the damn thing. By the end of the story I had chosen to accept it all for what it was: a bad dream I've yet to awake from.

"Grayson, I still need to see if I can find Clay. I know there may be little hope in it now, but I still have to try. One of the last things he said to me was to find a woman named Arianna. It wasn't a name or person I remembered from our lives. I suspect she was someone that he had interacted with once he was in Purgatory. Do you know who or where she is?"

A sullen look came to Grayson's face, "I'm afraid I don't know much about her. I know she was from the living world and she could see and speak with the dead. Clay didn't share much more than that with me in regards to her. I know he'd been staying not too far off of Lake Shore but where exactly that is... well, that's beyond me. Might be, however, if she could talk to folks like us there could be some others in the area she'd spoken with. If you like I can help you search around. I know a thing or two of where to find folks like us."

A friendly face and company was more than welcome right now. I hadn't shared it with Grayson, but deep down I was still fearing that Az would be coming to find me soon. I hoped that having him around would give me the courage to keep going. We set out on our search for the mysterious Arianna.

As Grayson and I canvassed the lake shore trail, questioning others like us about Arianna, most recoiled at the mention of the living world. "Grayson," I interjected, pulling him aside, "let's try a different approach to get them talking. You have to remember that Az was pretty damn strict about not talking to the living. With you asking them that they may be under the impression you're working for him." He took a moment to consider it, nodding his head.

"Yes. I can see where that might set these airheads off." Despite our efforts, many of them were already too far gone to provide us a solid response. When the lakeside area search began to feel fruitless, Grayson led us back to other areas that he'd known Clay to be frequenting in his time here. That eventually brought us to a place called the Green Mill Tavern on the upper end of Broadway.

The Green Mill is a popular jazz night club, but what had made it more famous was that it was once owned by Jack "Machine Gun" McGurn, a member of Al Capone's Chicago outfit. They even have a seat marking where Capone had once sat. I looked around as we entered, thinking I might see the long deceased gangster, but I can assure you now… he's not here. There were a few other non-living folks like us, though most were unwilling to give us the time of day.

"Grayson, there is no one here that is going to talk to us. I'm beginning to think that we're not likely to find any person in this existence that will be willing to share with us if they know a person on the other side that can talk with us."

As Grayson pondered my suggestion, a voice with a British accent interrupted our conversation, emanating from a booth behind me. "I would dare to say miss, you are asking the wrong people then."

Turning around to the booth behind me, there was an older man with salt and pepper hair, a narrow and pointy face, and wearing more tweed than any person should ever wear at one time. I pulled out the chair and sat down across from him. "Okay, well, now I'm asking you. Do you know any living people that can talk to the dead."

"Don't be foolish my dear. I don't know anyone who talks to the dead."

I was getting pissed. Why had this asshole stopped me if he was only going to waste my time? "Okay buddy, thanks for nothing."

"Miss… I'm sorry, what is your name?"

"Not that it matters, but it's Ava."

"Miss Ava, I meant only that they do not talk to us. That would be a sign that they were losing their mental faculties. I do, however, know a living person that can talk with us. But before I tell you any more, I must know why you would be looking for such a person."

CHAPTER 7: ARIANNA

 within me, like currents converging in a cosmic river. I felt a tingling sensation spreading across my skin, as if I were being touched by unseen hands. Waves of emotion washed over me, dread and uncertainty, like the universe itself was ripping into the threads of my soul.

Lost in the recesses of my emotions, thoughts drifted back to another time, to another loss that shaped the contours of my soul. I found myself attempting to balance them all. A balancing act that made me feel as though I were on a tightrope hundreds of feet in the air; no safety net below to break the eventual fall. What Deanna shared with me did nothing whatsoever to quell the flood of emotions I'd already been battling against. It was the thoughts and memories of Clay that had opened the dam of this raging river. Now memories of Eddie were taking me from the shallows to the whitewater of the rapids in this river of emotions.

It had been a cold and blustery day in the winter of 2006. Eddie and I were still so young then as we entered our final year of college. It was a winter that had been particularly relentless.

Storm after storm buried the city under a sea of white. Finally a window of several days came with no new storms and the roads and trails were clear and dry. Eddie wasn't particularly good about staying inside for long periods of time. He'd been getting restless to get out and go for a run. Late on the evening of February 12th, he found his moment.

It was almost nine-thirty at night, and I pleaded with Eddie not to go. "Please, Eddie," I begged, "it's already so late. Can't you wait until morning?"

He flashed me his warm smile. "I won't be gone long. I just need to shake off some of this built-up energy. Take a long bath, and I'll be back by the time you're done." With a kiss on my forehead, he zipped up his jacket and stepped out the apartment door.

I finished my bath, no Eddie. I read half a book, still no Eddie. As it got near midnight I called the Chicago police to report him missing. "Sorry, ma'am. Until it's been twenty-four hours there is nothing we can do. If he hasn't come back by tomorrow please call us again. In the meantime, try calling him again and maybe some of his close friends. Could be he stopped somewhere and lost track of time."

They found his body a week later on the shore of Montrose Beach. How Eddie had ended up in the lake in mid-February—no one was really sure. However, it was more common than one would think for a person to fall into the frigid waters of Lake Michigan in the depths of winter. Some, in time, washed up on the shore; others ended up pulled deep into the lake's murky blue chasm.

Reflecting on Eddie's tragic end only heightened the emotional turmoil I was experiencing. His loss left a void in my life that I struggled to fill. I fell into a dark depressive state and it would in time lead me to a moment of desperation. A week after Eddie's death I stood on the shore of Lake Michigan staring into the same dark waters I'd lost Eddie to. Sometimes loss is so painful it blurs the eyes to any other means of recovery. And now, now here I am again. Another loss digging through scabs of the past; the emotional blood flowing again. While Clay was not mine and we'd never been in love like Eddie and I had, I still felt a love for him—and he was gone. As Eddie's tragic end faded from memory, I returned to the present, yet the eerie sensation of being watched persisted, unsettling me once more.

The afternoon blurred to night as Clay's words and memories appeared on my laptop screen. The Book of Clay, as I was calling it, was getting closer to final. Taking a moment to stretch, I glanced over to the windows on my right and caught a pair of the bluest, icy cold eyes staring at me. From the reflection of the window I'd have sworn whomever these eyes belonged to was standing right behind me. I swung around to see nothing but the emptiness of my apartment.

It wasn't the first time I had sensed a presence in my apartment. I often saw spirits or the non living plainly, like living people, but some moved like morning fog. Someone was here with me; I could feel them lurking about.

Whatever or whoever this was, they were not leaving me with a pleasant feeling. I got up from my seat, went to the kitchen, and grabbed some white sage. Smoke drifted from the sage as I walked around the apartment, trying to clear the uneasy feeling. When I could no longer feel the uncomfortable presence, I closed my laptop and headed to bed.

Eddie stayed close to my mind that night—my dreams haunted by his presence. I saw him trapped in a place where there are no forms, only the faintest of light. There were others trapped with him in this place. I couldn't see them or where we were. I only felt their energies devouring my own.

Eddie's energy being the strongest, I felt my way over to him. I got close enough that I could feel his breath on my skin. Reaching forward to embrace him yet, there was nothing there to grasp. Dark laughter filled the void, followed by a soft whisper in my ear: "We'll meet soon, Miss Stone."

I pushed back to see the eyes that had been peering upon me earlier. Blue lights glowing in a sea of darkness. It was all that I could see. I tried to run, but found myself falling instead. I kept falling and falling until I felt my body slam into cold water. I was sinking below and no matter how hard I kicked to get back to the surface the weight of the water pulled me deeper. As my air was running out, that was when I snapped awake in my bed. My body was covered in beads of perspiration, sheets soaked as though the water from my dream had awakened with me.

I got out of bed and began burning more sage. I poured myself a glass of wine—I didn't care that it was five in the morning. I needed something to settle my broken nerves. I sat in the cushioned corner of my apartment, sipping the wine until I again drifted back to sleep.

It was noon when I woke again, a wine glass half-full still in my grasp. I needed to talk to Deanna. Whatever had come into my apartment, into my dreams, was unlike anything I'd ever felt. She would know more about this and its connection to what had happened with Clay. I tried throughout the day and into the evening to call and text Deanna—she never responded. She always responded. Was this the work of Azrael? Had he already found a way to Deanna?

CHAPTER 8: AVA

Some people enjoy conversation, while others tend to talk excessively. Forty-five minutes had crawled by, marked by Grayson's tapping foot and my restless fidgeting, as Hamilton's incessant chatter showed no signs of simmering. His diarrhea of the mouth reminded me of a scene from *The Goonies*, where Chunk, captured by the Fratellis, spills every detail of his life without reaching the point. That's precisely how I was feeling. I was wishing for a metaphorical blender to move things along.

"You see, before I found myself in this ghastly existence I'd been a Paranormal Researcher of sorts. I can't tell you how relieved I was when I came to find out that there was indeed "another side" beyond the veil of the living. But my lord, did it have to be… well, this?"

"Yes, I'm sure that came as quite the shock," I said. "What about this person you say you know that can talk to us?"

"Yes. Yes. Let me tell you, many people in this world claim to be mediums and speak to those in our world. So, my dear woman, what you learn once you have given your final curtain call is," he looked around like a child before saying something inappropriate, "how bloody full of shit they all are."

And he was off on another four more tangents before I could bring him back to learn there had been only one of the many he'd known that could in fact talk to us.

"It sounds like you had quite the life," Grayson said, trying to be courteous.

"I couldn't tell you in all honesty. I made the mistake of not taking Azrael's warnings about speaking with the living as valid and then poof… memories gone."

I clenched my fists, growing increasingly irritated by the possibility that Hamilton was fabricating stories just for the sake of conversation. "How were you able to share all that with us?' I questioned, my tone edged with skepticism.

"Oh, yes. Well this lady, the one I told you about, she was able to share much of my life with me. You see before I ended up in Purgatory, she and I'd been friends in the living world. She shared much of what had been erased with me."

"Can you take us to meet her? I promise I have only a few questions about a person I'm trying to find."

"I may be able to. But first I need to pay her a visit and make the request to her. What type of person would I be if I just brought you along without giving her due notice? I'd be a real wanker, that's what I'd be. Tell you what, meet me down the end of Navy Pier two days from now. There is a statue there…"

"Yes, I know the place," Grayson said.

"Good, good. I will meet you there and so long as she says she will see you we can be on our way."

As we exited the Green Mill, Hamilton veered off, leaving Grayson and me to make our way south on Broadway. "Grayson," I interjected, pondering aloud, "it must be her, right? Arianna, the woman who can speak with the dead. How many individuals in this vast city possess such a rare gift?” Grayson furrowed his brow, his eyes darting in thought for a moment. “According to our friend there might have been a lot who claim it, but fewer that can actually do it. Still, it has to be a small enough community of them that even if this woman isn’t Arianna, it might be that she knows her.”

“God, I hope so. Grayson?”

“Yes?”

“Is it selfish that part of me is still worried about losing my memories and not just finding Clay?”

“I wouldn’t say it’s selfish, Ava. Even when we have the best of intentions there is that part of us that will fight like the dickens to save itself. Losing your memories is losing part of yourself. So I’d say what you’re feeling sounds ‘bout right to me.”

It was easy to see why Clay had gotten along well with Grayson. He had that sage-like wisdom at times that you would not expect to come from him.

“If you don’t mind me asking, what are you going to do with yourself for the next two days?” It was a great question he’d asked and I had given it no thought until that moment.

“I suppose I’m going to head back to Crossroads.”

Grayson’s eyes widened in alarm and confusion as he processed my decision. “Why on God’s green earth would you want to go back there? You should be staying as far away from Azrael as you are able to.”

“I know I should, but until we find this Arianna woman and more especially, until we find Clay, I need to keep Az’s suspicions down. Besides, where else am I going to go? Crossroads is the last place I have left that was a part of my life. A small part, but a part no less.”

“I don’t see it as being wise. No telling what could happen if Azrael gets a hold of you. Then there would be no finding this woman or Clay. There is this cemetery not too far down the way. There are a few caretaker huts and gatehouses that you might be able to stay in. Something about the cemetery, Azrael will not enter its grounds."

I leaned in and gave Grayson a grateful hug. "Thank you for your concern, Grayson. I'll see you in a few days down at the pier. You have my word on that. For now I'm going back to Crossroads. You keep yourself safe and I'll see you in two days."

He headed back towards Wrigley Field as I continued south on Halstead to Crossroads. All that he was saying was true. I knew there was a danger involved with going back to a place where Az had been so present, but something told me it was where I needed to be.

CHAPTER 9: CLAY

"HERE'S THE DEAL DOC, I'M GOING TO HELP YOU WITH one condition; you've got to assure me that no harm will come to Ava. I've already done too much stupid shit that's put her in danger. I don't feel much like adding something else to that list."

Dr. Dawood must have been expecting this as there was no pause before his response. "Clayton, I've no way to give you assurances on things that are out of my control. Azrael's realm is beyond my reach, which is why I'm asking for your help. I will do everything I can to help guide you so that there's as little chance as possible for others to become involved. But you will get no one hundred percent assurances from me on anything."

"Okay doc. I'll help. It doesn't seem like I have many other options available at the moment." He was holding the cards and again I was stuck waiting to see what hand I was dealt.

"Thank you, Clayton. The first thing we need to do is get you away from the Appalachian House." He was right about that. I'd already spent far too long in this hospital—time I could've been using getting back to Chicago. Time I could've been using to get Ava free from Purgatory and here with me in the living world.

"Thank you for stating the obvious. Tell me something that I hadn't already figured out. Like, how exactly do you plan on doing that? So far, I've been able to see this hospital has almost as much security as a prison. Not to mention you're a guest doctor here. I don't suspect they're going to let you just walk out the door with me. Then there's the issue of the fact that John's wife is here every damn day. If she's not confronting me, trying to see if any of John is left in here, she's bitching out Dr. Adler and the staff about the treatment that I'm provided."

Dr. Dawood was silent for a moment as he considered this reducing my confidence that he would be able to keep Ava or myself from danger should something happen. "Clayton, you see, she might in actuality be the key to getting you out of here."

"You think Emilia is the key to getting me out of here? I had been thinking that at first too doc, but she'd much rather keep me in this kennel than set me back into the world. I've tried making things better with her. I'm just not sure it's doing anything."

I watched as Dr. Dawood glanced down at the papers in his hand, his brow furrowing in concentration. "You should learn to trust your intuition. You're here voluntarily, Clayton. John entrusted his medical decisions to his wife when he entered the program." He paused, meeting my gaze with a meaningful look. "You'll need her cooperation if we're going to get you out of here."

"I suspect that it was unwilling or unknowingly doc. From what I remember my first night here was also John's first night here. Something tells me that before I woke up in his body he still hadn't recovered from whatever he'd binged on. Can't we find a way to declare that power of attorney invalid? That John was not of his right mind when it was done? Anything other than trying to deal with that woman. Doc, she is impossible."

"No Clayton. She's the one you must convince. John will have no legal grounds, there are legal documents that precede this incident that would support the current situation."

"Great. Winning her over will be as easy as putting frosting on a hot cake. I don't know how I'm going to convince her to let me out of here. She knows I'm not her husband but there is a part of her that keeps looking for him here. She may not like him very much, but she is sure as hell invested in him coming back for some reason. If what you suspect is right and I don't have a lot of time in this body, is it even possible to return John to it?"

"Unfortunately, no, Clayton. You've seen the trouble caused by your own crossing back into this world. It was never meant to happen. Bringing John back would only further exacerbate the issue. I would recommend that you ease Mrs. Tyler into the idea that her husband is gone and will not be returning to her. She needs to understand there is more at stake here and her husband's sacrifice will prevent something more catastrophic from happening."

"No offense doc, but that kind of talk might have gone over well in the age of pharaohs, but these days, it's not going to work so well."

"Well then, Clayton, it's up to you to figure it out. Make sure it happens as quickly as you can. We need to have you out of this hospital in the next week."

My fingers drummed against the armrest of the chair, my foot tapping out an unsteady rhythm on the linoleum floor. "A week?" I scoffed, my voice tinged with disbelief. "Feels like I've been running against the clock since I woke up in this damn hospital."

"That can be the way of things sometimes. For now, there is one other thing I need you to work on."

"What's that doc?"

"You need to get control over your anger and learn how to release it in a more effective way."

"What do you mean my anger?" I felt my fists clenching involuntarily, the tension spreading to my jaw as frustration surged within me. "I'm fine," I muttered through gritted teeth, forcing a strained smile that failed to reach my eyes.

"Clayton, you need to look deeper. The anger is there and if you hold on and keep festering in it, I fear what we have to do will not end up well for you or any of us."

More puzzles to solve. How would I win over Emilia? And all this about anger—I couldn't understand it. Sure I've gotten angry before. What the hell would you do if you had the Angel of Death running up your ass? What would you do if you and your fiancé had been taken before your time? Tell me one person that wouldn't have some residual anger after that. Dealing with that would have to come later. Right now my focus needed to be on Emilia.

I needed to let her know that her husband was not coming back and on top of that, I had to convince her to let me walk free. It would seem the fun never ends for Clayton Mitchell.

CHAPTER 10: AVA

BACK AT CROSSROADS, I STILL HAD NO SIGHT OF AZ. AS I settled in beside the gateway, anxiety gnawed at my insides. Each passing moment without Az's return intensified the tempest within me. Doubts crept in, whispering sinister possibilities threatening to overwhelm my resolve. Was Az's prolonged absence a sign of abandonment, or was he weaving a darker scheme beyond my comprehension? Uncertainty loomed over me, obscuring my thoughts and clouding my judgment. Despite Grayson's warnings echoing in my mind, an inexplicable compulsion tied me to this desolate post, a prisoner of my own conflicted heart.

No matter how long I sat and waited, the gateway had not opened. In those long hours after midnight while I sat and watched there was something Az had once said that came back to me. He had told me the day he first showed the gateway to me that there were others, that this was not the only one. He never said more than that on the subject, so it remained a mystery to me what they looked like or where their location was.

Left with nothing other than my own thoughts, the questions came drudging in. Was it possible that he'd abandoned this gateway, moving on to a new one? Would this gateway even work again after what had happened with Clay? The longer I waited the more questions came. What had become of Az? Was he gone? If so, what was happening in the world of the living? Were people no longer dying tragic deaths? Or worse, were the dead stuck in the living world with no way to cross over?

There were still several days before I would meet back up with Grayson and the gentleman calling himself Hamilton. If I sat waiting like this until then, I was sure I would find myself on the brink of madness. I've no idea what I should do with myself other than wait and watch. My body and mind at last grew weary and exhausted. With nothing better to do I returned to the apartment above the bar and fell into a deep sleep filled with dreams.

In my dream, I wandered through shifting shadows and vague shapes, where reality twisted like a serpent coiled around a vine. There, I found a woman bathed in an eerie glow, her face hidden in shadow. She lay pinned beneath a towering mirror, its surface reflecting fractured images of me as I approached. The nearer I got, a sense of unease washed over me. Her cries pierced the silence, reverberating through the void, each word I could scarcely comprehend. I rushed to her to see if I could help and move the mirror from her body. I came to a sudden and abrupt stop a few feet away from the woman. There was a dark chasm between us, and I couldn't find a way to cross it. The woman was still crying out. Her cries were faint at first, but soon they began to come through clearer. "Clay! Clay, where are you? Please, I need your help!"

I awoke short of breath, my fingernails digging into my palms. That woman—I'd never seen her before, in life or death. Why was she calling for Clay? I needed to shake this dream before it consumed me. I had to keep my head clear right now. After the unsettling dream, I was left feeling uneasy. I headed downstairs to the bar from the apartment above. The dimly lit space felt familiar, with the scent of stale beer lingering in the air. As I entered, I noticed a woman sitting by the stage. She was someone like me—dead. She made her way to the stage, then greeted me, breaking the silence between us.

"Hello dear," said the woman. "I suspect that you must have been the one he'd been making such a fuss about." She sat back and crossed her legs. "I wasn't planning on coming to this place, but it seems that my destiny wasn't my own to choose. We have some things to discuss, young lady, so why don't you sit down. My name is Deanna, and we have a mutual concern."

CHAPTER 11: ARIANNA

I KEPT GLANCING AT MY PHONE, HOPING FOR A MESSAGE from Deanna, but it stayed totally silent. My stomach started feeling all twisty and weird, like a bad vibe that just wouldn't go away. I decided it was time to pay a visit to my old friend. I set out to Deanna's, a small three story building on West Belden in the neighborhood of DePaul University. As I entered her neighborhood it brought back the memories of when I first met Deanna.

I'd been a student at DePaul, and Deanna, at the time, was a professor of psychology and nearing retirement. It was my final year and I had her as my professor for an advanced psychology class—psychology of the paranormal. It wasn't until after Eddie's passing that we came to know each other more intimately.

It was Deanna who'd recognized the withdrawn behavior that I was demonstrating. Following one of the classes she pulled me aside. "Miss Stone, I've observed some changes in your demeanor lately. The news about your boyfriend, Eddie, must have been incredibly difficult for you to process. Grief can be a formidable challenge, particularly when faced alone.

If you ever feel the need to discuss your feelings or seek support, please know that my door is always open to you."

I'd been quick to dismiss Deanna's concerns. Deep down, however, I already had my plan in place. My mind and body wanted only to be back with Eddie. Soon I would join him in the icy depths of Lake Michigan.

I made my attempt in the first week of March. It was early morning, the winds were blowing strong across the lake, creating large waves to crash on the concrete shoreline. I sat down on the edge and slid my feet into the frigid waters. I didn't have time for much after that. One wave was all it took to push, then pull me over the edge into the ice bath of the lake.

Out of pure instinct I found myself panicking at first, but the cold soon took over my body and my will to fight subsided. I can still remember how fast I'd lost consciousness. It came with great relief. There was no fear in me in those moments. I'd fallen into a peaceful serene darkness. Then, from the darkness, I saw a rainbow of colors floating around me. As I fell deeper into this place I began calling out for Eddie—there was no reply—from him. Rather, there came a small child-like man who looked at me with mild amusement as he took my hand.

"My dear," he said, "the world still has a need for you. This will not be your time and it isn't the way to find your lover again."

"But I don't want to go back," I pleaded. "I'm tired and I can't fight it any longer. There is no love left in the world without Eddie. There is nothing remaining there for me."

"You have a greater purpose and in time it will become known to you. For now I must bring you back."

I could feel this child-man pulling me back through the waters to the surface. "No," I began shouting. It did me no good. Before I could stop it, the rainbow colors faded into the distance and I found myself lying on a hospital bed. My skin, blue and freezing. A tube was shoved down my throat and wires connected to beeping machines.

I later learned that when I pushed off into the water there was a man who'd been running nearby on the lake shore path. He saw me go in and without thinking jumped in after me. Lucky for both of us, he was a strong swimmer and had comfort with cold water.

Because of the man's heroics the story made the local news. Rather than say what I'd been doing, I told those who asked that I'd carelessly gotten too close to the edge and had fallen in. Deanna had seen the news coverage, but in her wisdom knew better what I had done.

The next week when I returned to classes Deanna again grabbed me at the end of class, bringing me along to her office. I'd been so broken at that juncture when Deanna dug in I spilled much of my life story to her. I would confess what I had been doing that morning at the lake and also shared what I'd experienced in those moments under the water. I was expecting more of a surprised look from Deanna, but it hadn't shaken her at all.

Instead, Deanna invited me to keep coming back so that we could continue our conversations. It was in these hours hanging about Deanna's office that I first came to meet her friend and colleague Hamilton. When Deanna introduced us she explained to me that he worked in the world of paranormal investigations and she wanted me to share my experience with him. It was only a few weeks later that I would have more than my own experience to share with them both.

Coming back to reality I found myself standing at the entrance of Deanna's building. I rang her buzzer several times with no response, so I did what any city dweller would do—pressed them all. I finally got a response from one of the residents.

"Yeah, she's not here. They took her out by ambulance about two days ago. Can't say I've heard or seen anything else since then other than that damn cat of hers. The paramedics left her door wide open and that cat got out and was crying all damn night. Finally I got up and put it back in her apartment with some food and fresh water. Not a soul has been up to look in on the poor thing. You family or something?"

"Not family, no. They all passed away years ago. I'm her close friend and colleague. Would you mind buzzing me in so I can check on her cat?"

"I don't think I should be letting a stranger into the building, miss. This ain't none of my business. I already called the super to come take care of the cat and use his keys to lock that door up. He should be here in another twenty minutes or so. If you want to get in I'd suggest waiting around till then. If he decides to let you in, that's up to him. None of my business what he does."

He wasn't much help with getting into the building but I now knew why I hadn't heard from Deanna. As I settled onto the concrete steps, the warmth of the day embraced me, but a different chill crept over me, the kind that comes from uncertainty and waiting. Wrapped in anticipation, I hugged my arms around myself, feeling the weight of each passing moment as I waited for the building's super to arrive. Time seemed to stretch endlessly, the minutes dragging like heavy chains. Lost in the rhythm of waiting, my thoughts drifted back to a haunting encounter from the past...

It was a month or two after I'd taken my ice bath in the lake. I was sitting in my living room working on a term paper when I looked up and saw a young girl sitting in the chair across the room from me. I looked to my door thinking in my haste I must've left it open when I came back from campus. It had to have been one of the neighbor's kids that wandered in. But the door was still closed.

"Umm… hello. How did you get in here?"

"My parents used to live here and so did I."

"Are you lost and this was the only place you remembered?"

"I'm not lost! I've been here longer than you have. I was here the day you moved in with Eddie. I liked him. I'm sad he's not here anymore. You were much happier when Eddie was here."

"Yes, I was. If you've lived in this building that long, how come I've never seen you before. Which apartment do you live in?"

"Well, this one of course. I've lived here for a long time."

"I've never seen you before. Where did you come from? You should tell me so we can go find your parents."

"You won't find them, they died like me. But, I don't know where they went after we died. I ended up here in our apartment and have been here since. I haven't talked to anyone in a long time. There was this one man who came when I first got home. He scared me. I hid for a while after he left."

I got up and moved closer to the little girl. I went to take her hand but as I grabbed for it, I ended up with a handful of the chair. The girl let out a giggle. As I realized what had happened I took a step back. The girl laughed more now and began swinging her feet as she sat in the chair.

"I like you Arianna, you're funny."

"You… you're dead. But how… how can I see you? If you've been here for a long time, how come I've not seen you before?"

The little girl shrugged at me and went back to swinging her legs before getting up to stare out the window. "Someday mommy and daddy will come back to get me. Won't they Arianna?"

I didn't know what to tell her. I spent time after that getting to know her and was able to locate information on her family. They had lived in my apartment back in the early eighties. The little girl's name was Sandra. She and her parents had died in a freak car accident on Lake Shore Drive.

At my next meeting with Deanna I shared this experience with the little girl. Deanna smiled at me. "Well, know that you are in good company."

"Yes, my dear, you are," Hamilton said as he rounded the corner. "We were waiting to see if the gift had fallen on to you after your… erm… experience."

"I have had the same gift as you since I was a very young girl. It will take you time to get used to seeing and speaking with them, but that is what we are here for," Deanna said.

It had been shocking to learn this about Deanna. I looked over to Hamilton, "And you have this… gift as well?"

"No, my dear. I've not been that fortunate. I am what you might call an individual who has an interest in learning more about the afterlife."

There were many days I thought it was more of a curse than a gift in those early years. As time went on I learned to appreciate how I could help and give closure to those on both sides of the divide.

"Can I help you, miss?" I'd been so lost in my own thoughts I hadn't seen the man approach me. This must be the building's super.

"Yes. I'm a close friend of Deanna St. James. I came to check on her and one of your residents said that she'd been taken away by ambulance. I'm looking to get in and make sure Arcane, her cat, is doing okay. I would be really appreciative if you would allow me in."

"Not something I'd normally do, but to tell you the truth I'm not much of a cat person. Tell ya what, If you'd be willing to take that cat I will be happy to let you in."

"Why would I need to take the cat?" I asked. "He should just need to be fed and given some fresh water."

"Oh… no one has told you. I'm sorry miss but Mrs. St. James died on her way to the hospital. I'm only here to lock up her apartment until her next of kin can come take care of her belongings."

The words crashed into me like a sudden gust of wind, leaving me breathless and unsteady. Darkness encroached at the corners of my vision, and the earth seemed to sway beneath my feet. My heart raced, echoing the inner chaos, as the world blurred and spun in the wake of Deanna's sudden departure. Overwhelmed by grief and disbelief, I reached out to grip the railing, seeking stability, but found none. Then, as if my body could no longer bear the weight of the news, I felt my legs give out and my body go tumbling down, succumbing to the overwhelming tide of emotion. I curled into a ball at the foot of the stairs and began hyperventilating. This couldn't be real, it just couldn't.

"Miss, are you alright… miss?"

The world faded out around me. This was all too much. A tingling sensation ran through my body and everything turned to black. In the darkness I found icy blue eyes staring at me yet again. "Won't be long now, Arianna. I'll be coming for you very soon. You can be sure of that."

CHAPTER 12: CLAY

I WAS PACING THE CHECKED FLOOR OF MY ROOM WONdering how to have this conversation with Emilia. She would come back, as she had everyday that I'd been here. By now she'd surmised that I wasn't her husband. Yes, I looked like him and to her ears I sounded like him, but that was as far as the similarities would go.

Emilia had given me the impression that she didn't want John back. The enigma that she was, for one reason or another she also seemed scared to lose him. Until now I hadn't taken much time to ask her many questions about herself or their life together. I'd improved at answering her questions and engaging in conversation but not inquiring about anything below the surface. The time we'd spent together at first focused on her trying to convince me that I was John. Dr. Adler had put it to her that I was having a psychic meltdown and she needed to keep talking to me as John to help me break through that. Once my actions convinced her otherwise, conversations leaned more to who I, Clayton Mitchell, was, and how I'd come to be in possession of her husband's body. "There are a lot of people, including myself, who'd love to know that right now," I told her.

When Emilia arrived for her daily visit I was still pacing the room. Out beyond the windows I could see the sun burning off the morning clouds over the Blue Ridge Mountains. I'd forgotten how beautiful that could be.

Emilia came up behind me, placing her delicate hand on my shoulder. Turning to her, for the first time I caught a glimpse of her smile. It was bright and as welcome as the first warm days of spring. I could only hope that it would stay that way after our conversation.

"Mind if we grab a seat and chat?" I asked.

"I'd rather not sit right now. I've been in the car for the last hour driving here. I need to move around a bit. Are you okay to walk and talk?" she replied.

I wasn't allowed far beyond this room and the session rooms I would meet the doc in. Because of who John Tyler was and the fact that Emilia could be very persistent, Dr. Adler allowed us to walk out to the hospital garden area.

It was nice to get a breath of fresh air. One not reeking of the stale disinfectant that wafted through the Appalachian House. Emilia and I walked around the building, still not saying much to one another, until we came to the garden. There I found a bench that sat under an old willow tree. I knew Emilia didn't want to sit, but I'd already been pacing all morning.

At first Emilia continued walking to the tree. When she turned back to me I went with a direct request. I didn't have it in me to try anything more clever at the moment. "Emilia, what will it take for you to sign off to allow me to leave this place? I know I'm here so long as you decide that to be true. So tell me what it will take."

Looking down at the ground she dragged the tip of her toe in a small circle in the dirt below her. "Where is it you're wanting to go? Back to work? Back to the clubs? Back to the unfaithfulness?"

I sighed. "I thought we'd gotten past this. I'm not John, Emilia. As much as I may look and sound like him—it's not him in here. I've no recollection of what he did before I came into his body or what his personality was like. I need to know what you want or what you need to release me. There are things bigger than either of us, things that I can't explain because I don't fully understand them yet. All this stemming from the fact that I've somehow ended up in your husband's body. What will it take, Emilia?"

She was twirling her hair around her finger. It reminded me so much of Ava. God I missed her right now. I needed to figure this out and get back to her.

"If I let you free will you get John back to me?" she asked. "I mean if you leave, are you leaving his body too?"

"To be honest, I don't know. I know that I have to get back to where this started and from there I've no clue what the hell I'm supposed to do or what'll happen. I'm not going to be dishonest with you and promise you're getting John back. That isn't for me to say. What I can promise you is that if I see him, I can tell him how much you love and miss him."

Emilia had covered up her face and for a moment I thought she was crying, then as she lifted her head back up, I could see she was laughing.

"You really think that's how I feel about him? You want to know what life with John Tyler has been like for the last twenty years? You want to know the hellish torment myself and my children have been through because of him? Oh sure, in the public it seems like he's the fucking Pope. I'll tell you behind closed doors, he's the antichrist. A no good cheating bastard. He never cared about me or the children. You want to know what that son-of-a-bitch did not more than a few weeks ago? He took his children and I out of his will. It was no surprise for him to remove me; I knew he was planning to run off with that skank he'd been parading around half the country. Taking me out was fine, but his own children? What kind of man does that?"

She stopped to catch her breath for a moment. I looked over and could see that laughing turned to tears this time. I stood up next to her and placed an arm over her shoulder. "I'm sorry he was such a bastard to you, Emilia. But I'm not him. Holding me here will do nothing to repair the damage he's done."

She wiped the tears on her jacket sleeve leaving a long mascara stain. "No, there's nothing you can do to repair the past, but you can fix the future."

"I'm not following. Can you break it down for me?"

"You want out of here, right? Do whatever big thing it is that you have to do. You need me to sign off to make that happen, right? Well, I'll tell you what, you want that and I have something that I want. I want John's will corrected."

"I don't see how I'm going to be able to help with that."

"You look like him. You sound like him. We'll need to see if your signature looks like his, but what else do we need? I can bring you to the lawyer's office with a list of changes that you want made. We place all John's assets in mine and the children's names. You do that for me, and I'll sign the damn release papers."

"I… I suppose we can try it, Emilia. Won't he just change it back if I am somehow able to get him back in here?"

"You said it yourself, there's no guarantee that he even gets back. I have to at least try and get this squared away for the children. Would you deny a mother that?"

"I'm not trying to deny you or your kids anything. I'm just trying to understand what it is you're wanting to do. It's none of my business what happens with your husband's money or anything for that matter."

"You may need to start being concerned with that. You may not be him, but to the rest of the world you are him. If you think it is going to be so easy for you to walk out that door here and not be noticed, you are fucking delusional. John is known everywhere and no doubt by now someone in this place has leaked the fact that you… John is here. Like it or not we're going to need each other to get what we both want. Now, are you in or not?"

What else could I do but say yes to her? She had a handful of aces and I was playing with a pair of threes. "Yes, Emilia, I'm in. How long will it take to get a meeting with the lawyers?"

"I'll handle that, John… I mean, Clay, right? Gotta get used to calling you that. I should know your name if we're going to be working together."

"It is, but probably better if you keep calling me John. I need to get used to responding to that if this is going to work."

Emilia walked me back to my room and said she would continue coming to visit every day while she got all the details worked out with the lawyers. After she left I headed to Dr. Dawood's office to pay him a visit. I only hoped he had more news he could report back on how the fuck I was supposed to find Az again. Little did I know, all the answers would be waiting for me, hidden in plain sight, beckoning from the shadows of my reflection.

CHAPTER 13: ARIANNA

It had taken all my willpower to get home after finding out about Deanna's death. I knew deep down that the time would be coming soon when Deanna would no longer be around. I'd not expected it to be so sudden like this. She may have been on in her years, but she was still in good health for her age. It had been not more than a few days since she'd stopped over to confront me about Clay, and now, now she was gone.

It still wasn't clear to me what Deanna had died from. After I got back to my feet from passing out, Deanna's super was of little help. "Miss, I ain't got all day. Look, it ain't my business, but the old lady kicked the bucket on her way to the hospital. If you need more details, you're better off talking to the cops. Now, if you're still up for it, I can let you in to fetch her cat. Otherwise, I'll be calling animal services in a minute."

My head was still feeling light, but I couldn't pass up the chance to get into Deanna's apartment. It was my best chance at seeing if there were any indications of what might have happened. I also wanted to make sure Arcane would have a good place to go at the end of the day.

The super only allowed me into Deanna's apartment long enough to collect Arcane, his food, and a few other related cat items. I tried to look for hints at what happened as I moved about the apartment but the super kept pushing, "Miss, I ain't got all fucking day. You want to get that cat or what? I got stuff to do."

Nothing looked out of place. Deanna was very particular about the cleanliness and arrangement of items in her apartment. It was something she'd become sensitive about over the years. She would always say, "After all these years of the non-living visiting me I've grown tired of those that like to surprise me. You learn with time my dear that they cannot resist moving things about when they get bored."

As I walked back to the door, I noticed a large crack in the mirror above the faux fireplace. Additionally, I observed that the mantle clock stood frozen at 2:33 a.m. In all the years I'd been coming to visit Deanna, I'd never seen that crack in the mirror, and she made it a point to wind the clock to the right time every evening. To anyone else these things may have looked inconsequential, but I knew at that moment that whatever happened to Deanna was not a natural death.

With Arcane's carrier in hand, I hesitated by the cracked mirror. Something compelled me to reach out and touch the fracture. As soon as my fingers brushed the cold surface, a vision overtook me.

The room around me faded, replaced by an eerie, indigo-lit space. I saw Deanna standing in her living room, looking frightened but defiant. The air around her seemed to ripple, and then he appeared—Azrael, dressed impeccably in a dark suit with an indigo waistcoat. His eyes were icy blue, glowing with a malevolent light.

"Deanna, your time has come," he said, his voice dripping with condescension. "You should have known better than to meddle in my affairs."

Deanna stood her ground. "You can't take me before my time. I still have work to do."

Azrael laughed, a dark, chilling sound that seemed to echo endlessly. "Time is a luxury you no longer have. Consider this a lesson in humility."

He raised a hand, and the air around Deanna shimmered. She clutched at her chest, gasping for breath, and then she collapsed. The vision shifted, showing Azrael standing over her lifeless body, a satisfied smirk on his face.

I wanted to scream, to lash out, but I was just a spectator in this nightmare. The scene faded, and I heard that dark laugh again, echoing as the vision dissipated.

"Miss, I ain't got all fucking day. You want to get that cat or what?" The super's voice jolted me back to reality. I was still in Deanna's apartment, my hand on the cracked mirror, the vision lingering in my mind.

"Yeah, I... I'm coming," I muttered, shaken to my core. I gathered Arcane and his essentials, but my mind was racing. Deanna had been murdered, and I had seen it happen. Azrael had struck again, and now I was more determined than ever to stop him.

When I got home I did the best I could to get Arcane settled in. Having a moment to sit down I took advantage of it. I hadn't forgotten what happened and what I'd seen when I blacked out. Pushing it aside for the time I was at Deanna's was the only thing that kept me from falling into a pool of despair at that moment. With all that behind me, all my mind could see were those cold blue eyes and all I could hear was that wretched voice echoing between my ears.

I had no doubt of who's behind this, but I was starting to wonder if he's the one who got to Deanna. Could she be trying to reach out to me from beyond? If she is, she might have reached Hamilton. He's my best shot at uncovering more about this mess. Right now, a big glass of wine and a long shower to clear my head sounded perfect.

Standing in the shower I let the water rush over me. It was the one thing that felt real at the moment. Losing Clay and Deanna in the same month was too much for me. A crash of something in the bathroom brought me back from my thoughts. "Arcane… What're you doing out there?" That poor cat, a new apartment, he'd likely tried climbing something that wasn't nailed down.

Wiping the shampoo out of my eyes, I opened the shower curtain. No Arcane. The mirrored door of the medicine cabinet swung open, facing me in the shower. I should've seen my own reflection in it. I didn't. Instead, I stood looking down a dark and narrow hallway. An indigo light glowed from the furthest end. How was this even possible?

I rubbed my eyes again, and as I reopened them, I could see the indigo light had gotten brighter and closer. From behind the light a door opened and I could see a figure walking out. It was getting closer to the back of the mirror. Before he got to the very edge I knew who he was. I'd seen him when he came to talk to Clay. Those icy eyes I'd been seeing—I had no doubt now—were his.

I jumped out of the shower, slammed the mirror door shut before leaving the bathroom. I heard the glass shatter behind me. I saw Arcane in the hallway, scooped him up and ran to my bedroom. *Shit… shit… no damn door.* Why the hell did I take the door down and put these beads up?

I got to the far side of my bed holding the cat against me. He was not pleased as my hair and naked body were still soaking wet from the shower. Arcane showed his displeasure with a scratch to my face, causing me to let him go.

"My my, we should stop meeting like this Miss Stone."

He walked towards me. I wanted to run, I wanted to scream, but I couldn't. His eyes grew larger the closer he neared. The flesh rotting away from bone. He reeked of death and was on top of me before I could move. Could these be my last minutes as a mortal? Clenching my eyes I prepared myself for what was to come. I stood there wet and naked, shaking to my core. A heinous laugh came. "Miss Stone, I've no intention of killing you—at least not at the moment. It might do you well to open your eyes and get yourself more comfortable. You and I have things to discuss."

"What, so you can kill me at the end?"

"We shall see if your death becomes necessary. You'd be wise to do as I say for now if you do have any desire to remain in that mortal flesh of yours. I know you've tried to leave it before. Always happy to lend a hand with that Miss Stone. Now, I need you to tell me everything that happened and what it was that you told our friend Mr. Mitchell."

CHAPTER 14: CLAY

WHEN I ARRIVED BACK AT DR. DAWOOD'S OFFICE I FOUND the door locked. I knocked several times, each time a little louder. Looking through the small wire mesh window I couldn't see anyone in the office. The absence of Dr. Dawood outside of our sessions struck me as odd. Deciding to return later, I left his office, pondering over the implications of his transient presence.

I headed back in the direction of my room, as there weren't many places I had access to at the Appalachian House. It was either to the cafeteria, to the therapy offices, the single common lounge area, or back to your room. Emilia wasn't here right now so it was unlikely I would get back out into the garden. Of the choices I had, none were the least bit appealing at the moment.

Not too far past the lounge I noticed one of the emergency doors was ajar. Looking around I saw no other staff nearby. "Hello," I said, pushing the door open a little further. Expecting to find that a staff member had snuck out for a cigarette or a few drags from their vape, I pushed it open even further. The door swung wide open, and I took a step closer to the outside. Leaning out, the weight of my body pushed the door the rest of the way open. Looking to the left, I saw nothing. I looked to the right, but not a soul was there either.

I didn't feel much like getting reprimanded for trying to escape and lose what wandering privileges I had earned. That was one thing I could say for the Appalachian House, it didn't matter if you were Jeff Bezos or John Tyler; they made it their mission that everyone followed the rules or faced consequences.

I was pulling the door closed when I noticed it. There in the grass at the side of the building was a gold medallion about the size of a quarter. As I picked it up I could see that it had an eye on it. It wasn't just any eye, but the same eye that I saw tattooed on Dr. Dawood's hand.

I was wondering if this was his and if so, what was it doing outside the half opened door? Had something happened to Dr. Dawood? I mean, why not? It would be just my luck that once it looks like things might be moving in the right direction, the one person helping ends up gone. Not like that's happened to be me before or anything.

I picked up the medallion and placed it in my pocket. I took one last look around before pulling the emergency exit door shut. On a whim of curiosity I turned and headed back to Dr. Dawood's office. Still no sign of him nor an answer at the door.

Back in the cafeteria a few minutes later I got myself some food. Since I'd been back everything continued to taste like overcooked cardboard. It was strange, I might have been alive again, but there were times it was as though the senses I had didn't work the way they should. Was it because John lacked these senses or was it because, as Dr. Dawood had said, I didn't belong in this body?

Leaving the cafeteria I felt a sudden onset of tiredness come over me. As there was no set schedule for us here I headed back to my room to rest.

When I got back to my room the door was wide open. I swore I'd closed it before I left. Had Emilia come back to my room rather than leaving after our walk? Or, was this just the day that I would be finding open doors all around me?

I stepped into the room with a heightened sense of caution. No Emilia. No staff. No one—period. Taking stock of the room, I noticed not a single thing was out of place. I walked back, closed the door and took a piss. As I was washing my hands I couldn't help but look at the face in the mirror, staring into the eyes of a stranger. From all that Emilia had shared with me this morning all would point to this being a rather unpleasant stranger to reside in.

Looking back up after I turned off the faucet, it was no longer John's reflection I stared into. Now, I looked into a dark place. An expanding darkness. I closed my eyes for a moment; as I opened them again the darkness was gone and John had reappeared.

I was too tired to ponder this shit any longer today. Lying on the bed, I felt a cool sensation forming in my right pants pocket. Reaching down I pulled out the gold medallion I'd found earlier. It was freezing cold to the touch and there were strange vibrations pulsed through it. Gripping the medallion in my closed fist, I soon drifted off to sleep.

We never know when dreams happen or how long they will last. For some they seem to last for hours or days. Yet, it may be the span of only a few minutes in your waking reality. Dreams give one a feeling of being disconnected from the self. That was what I was feeling in that moment, a disconnect from the living world. A connection only to the realm of dreams.

I found myself back in Chicago sitting on the shore of Lake Michigan. It was the concrete steps where Ava and I had gone on our second attempt at a first date. It wasn't her beside me. In this dream it was Arianna I found there. "Clay, I need you to hear me right now," she said in a whispered tone. Her presence and words had caught me by surprise. I hadn't noticed the large wave before it came crashing down on us.

It pulled us into the lake, Arianna was carried away from me by the water's pull. No matter how hard I tried I couldn't swim closer to her. Another wave came slamming my body against the concrete shore. I could feel myself sinking, the cold dark waters all around me. I pushed with everything I had trying to get back to the surface. The harder I tried to go up, the faster it pulled me down. I felt a hand grab hold of my ankle. My first instinct was to kick and fight. I looked down and through the dark waters could see a familiar tattoo on the hand that was pulling me. It was the eye. The eye on the medallion. The eye tattoo on Dr. Dawood's hand. I surrendered my fight and let the hand pull me down.

Down became up, up became down. I surfaced from the depths of the water to find this was no longer Chicago. It was someplace different, some place foreign to me. I was in a river and a hand was pulling me toward the river bank.

"I was beginning to think you'd fight me the whole way down."

I cleared my eyes and saw Dr. Dawood sitting beside me on the river bank. He was again out of his business clothes and dressed as though he'd ransacked an ancient Egyptian history museum.

Coughing out the water I'd swallowed I managed to choke out, "A little warning might've helped with that. What the fuck did you expect me do to? I felt like I was drowning and I'd just watched Arianna get swept away. I was busy trying to save myself and her."

His eyes widened and jaw went slack. "What do you mean you saw Arianna? You should have been the only one. There should have been no other person with you."

"Well, doc, she was. I don't know what to tell you."

"Clayton, our time is shorter than I'd suspected. We can't have these conversations in the living world any longer. Things can be heard there and there are still many things in all these realms that I can't explain to you. But here, here we are safe—for a time at least. I can share more with you and hope that in this space I can free you from the poisons that bind you."

"Where exactly is it that we are, doc? Last thing I remember I was taking a nap at Appalachian House."

Dr. Dawood looked at me shaking his head. "The body you possess is still back at the Appalachian House sound asleep. It is your essence or soul that is here with me now. As for where we are, it's a place that's outside of the bounds of the space and time that you know. What I have to explain is about to get much more complicated Clayton. Why don't we take a walk as we talk."

Reaching out a hand, he pulled me to my feet. Looking around I saw that whatever or whenever this place was, we were in the midst of a dark night. "So you brought me to ancient Egypt, doc?"

"No, that isn't where we are. It is only made to look that way. Each of us, the Guardians of the Eternal Light, have places created to aid those passing from one form unto the next. This one, that you are experiencing now, is mine. You experience it as ancient Egypt because those were the people that presented me with my name, Anubis. Before them I still did what I've done since the beginning of my memory. With their gift of a name, I created this place as my gift to them."

Before us stood a grand temple, its towering sandstone pillars adorned with intricate carvings that seemed to dance in the flickering light of oil-burning urns. Entering the temple I could see hieroglyphics on the walls. Each presenting a vibrant glow in a cool blue as Dr. Dawood passed by.

We passed through three sets of doors until we reached the center of the temple. In that chamber I found a single stone table and two chairs. Approaching the table I could see that the top was a large mirror encased in gold. The round-eyed medallions adorned the corners. When I first glanced into the mirror I didn't see John as I'd been expecting. I saw myself, in my own body again. Black clouds then pushed in from the edges until they had completely filled the mirror.

"Why did I see myself and not John in that mirror?"

Dr. Dawood settled into his chair, his robes billowing around him as he gestured for me to take a seat opposite him. "You see what you recognize as yourself Clayton. You're not John so it's natural that you'd not see him. However, what you saw in there is not you either. The body that you knew isn't the first you've known. Nor will it be the last. It is but the one you can best remember at this time."

The sound of shattering glass jolted me awake, propelling me from the bed in a flurry of tangled sheets. Heart pounding, I scanned the room, searching for the source of the disturbance. I jumped from the bed looking around to investigate further. It was in the bathroom, it had to be. Running into the bathroom I found the mirror cracked from edge to edge.

I needed to get to Dr. Dawood and tell him about this dream. I also had to tell someone about this broken mirror. If they thought I broke that damn thing again. it would be another round of sedatives. That was the last pile of shit I wanted to step in right now.

PART 2

LABYRINTHS

CHAPTER 15: AVA

"SO YOU'VE MET CLAY? AND YOU KNOW WHO THIS Arianna person is?" I asked.

"Yes, my dear, on both accounts," Deanna replied.

"Great. That means we can go to her and find out what she knows. Clay told me she was the one I needed to find. Though I'll need to go find that gentleman that was going to help us. He told us, Grayson, the friend I told you about, that he knew a woman in the living world."

"This man, where did you meet him?" Deanna asked with curiosity.

"Ah… We found him over at the Green Mill in Uptown."

She let out a soft sigh. "I'm sorry to disappoint you, Ava. I'm the woman that Hamilton was going to take you to see."

I couldn't hide the confusion from my face after that. "I'm sorry, he said he was bringing us to see someone that was alive. From where I'm sitting, you are anything but a living person."

"Yes, now. Up until yesterday, I was alive. That is until Azrael came along to end it for me."

"That couldn't be possible. I was here the whole time. The gateway," I said as I pointed to the emergency door behind her, "it's right over there. It never opened."

"Well, here I am. I'd say it was very much possible." She eyed me with a veiled suspicion. "How is it that you seem to know so much about this gateway and the comings and goings of Azrael?"

My eyes betrayed me before my words ever could. "I was… um… working with him for a time."

Deanna slid back from the table. "And what type of work was it that you were doing with him?"

"No. No. No. It wasn't like that," I protested. "I was helping those that had come here. I was helping them get acclimated. Get comfortable. Helping them understand the rules Az said existed in this place. The rules we all have to adhere to. I swear I didn't do anything bad to a single person. As far as I knew, until Clay told me otherwise, Az wasn't that bad of a per… well, whatever the hell he is. All that changed when he told me about how I'd been his choice. Told me that he took both Clay and I before we should've been here. It was all so much. It happened so fast I…" I sat down on the stage placing my face in my hands. Had I done something wrong? How many people had suffered or been hurt because of what I was doing for Az?

A frail and tiny arm slid over my shoulder and then embraced me in a hug. "I can't tell you it's all going to be okay, Ava. But I can tell you that I see no bad in you. If something bad happened to any of those people touched by Azrael, it was not on account of you. Now, if you don't mind I'm interested in hearing more of what Azrael said when he last spoke with yourself and Clay. Before I ended up here with you, we noticed something strange happening between the realms of living and dead. I only knew it had something to do with Clay.

My dear friend Hamilton, whom you've met, was trying to find out more for me."

She paused for a moment, letting out a deep sigh. "Oh… I will need to go find my dear Hamilton. He still has no idea of what's happened."

"I'm supposed to be meeting him and my friend Grayson tomorrow." Offering her a tentative smile, I suggested, "If you like, you can stay here with me until then. I'm happy to answer any questions you may have. Then, we can go meet him together." I hesitated, feeling a pang of guilt for asking her to stay, but the thought of her company was strangely comforting. "I know it may be a lot to ask, but... I'm sorry. It gets so lonely sometimes."

"That sounds like a splendid idea. Let's go sit and chat more about this predicament we've found ourselves in."

Over several hours, I learned about Deanna's unique life— her tenure as a professor at DePaul University, and the many years she moonlighted as a medium. "To think I spent almost the entirety of my life speaking with the non-living and now here I am." She gave a slight laugh, though it was hard to distinguish if it was because she found the situation humorous or if it was all she could do not to cry.

She told me of her meeting with Clay not long ago. He'd been asking questions about Az and Arianna had contacted her for help. "My question to you, Ava, is," she said, "what exactly happened? When I last spoke with Arianna she'd mentioned something about a gateway. Do you know what she was talking about?"

I pointed behind me to the steel emergency exit. "It would appear right here behind us. From what I understand, it serves as a passage for Az to travel between the realms of the living and different realms of the dead. Az would exit through it and when he'd return he'd have a new person with him. He told me that no person could cross through it alone." I paused for a moment, thinking again about how I'd not seen the gateway open, and yet, here was Deanna, a new person in Purgatory. It put my amygdala on high alert. I'd seen Az take the shape of a woman to fool Clay. He'd taken the appearance of a little girl to fool me. I couldn't help but wonder, was he doing it yet again?

"Deanna, if you don't mind, I have some questions for you before we continue discussing the gateway or Az. Can you tell me what you remember and how you came to be here? I've met a lot of newcomers, but I must say, none have seemed as well-adjusted and functional as quickly as you."

Deanna tilted her head and looked down her bird-like nose at me for a moment. Letting out a sigh of frustration, she said, "I see. You take me to be Azrael. Well, I'm glad to see you appear to be a touch more aware of your surroundings than your fiancé was." As her frustration simmered, her posture stiffened, and she continued, "Very well. If you need to hear my final moments before we talk more, I do hope when I'm done with this you might have a little more trust in me, Ava."

A pang of guilt struck me for not believing her sooner. "I hope you'll understand my mistrust, Deanna. It's what happens when you've been here as long as I have."

"Yes. Yes. Now do you want to hear or not?" She was giving me the stern look that only an educator knows how to deliver. I gave her a nod, and she shared a brief version of her last moments in the living world with me.

"I was visited by Azrael, who told me my time was up. There was an argument, and during my attempt to confront him, I was struck down by a clock. I fell into darkness and woke up here. It's clear he had plans that required me to be here, in Purgatory."

The details she shared filled in some gaps but also left many questions unanswered. "It does sound like Az, at least the way he spoke to you. He can be a condescending prick most of the time. What I'm still a bit confused about is how he got you here without using the gateway. There was a point when he mentioned other gateways, but never went into much detail beyond that."

"If Azrael is indeed who we think he is, it's possible he possesses the ability to create a gateway at will, regardless of location. At the moment, however, I'm not concerned with finding his gateway. In fact, I'd like nothing more than to get further away from it."

Deanna stood up and walked to Crossroads' front door. As she placed her hand on the knob she looked back at me. "I know you may still not trust me, Ava. Staying here, however, only allows for us to be sitting prey for Azrael. I need to go back to my apartment and see what's become of my sweet Arcane and see what other memories might strike. You're welcome to come if you like."

I felt a moment of hesitation. The comfort of staying at Crossroads was tempting, but the urgency in Deanna's voice and the need to understand more about what was happening pushed me to decide quickly. "You're right, Deanna. Let's go to your apartment. Maybe we'll find something that can help us."

I followed Deanna out of Crossroads without hesitation. On the way to her apartment I couldn't help but search each window, each alleyway, each dark corner—Az was waiting for me out there somewhere.

CHAPTER 16: CLAY

I GOT TO DR. DAWOOD'S OFFICE WANTING TO TELL HIM about the conversation we'd shared in my dream and about the broken mirror. I couldn't allow curiosity to let me forget about that. Looking in from outside the office door... everything from my previous visits was gone. The desk, the books, the chair I had sat in. The only thing remaining in the office was the grandfather clock. Its methodic *tick-tock tick-tock tick-tock* reverberating across the empty office.

Turning the doorknob I found the room unlocked. As I entered the office I was looking for any signs of what might've happened. There was no way I'd slept that long. How had all the furniture been cleared away in that time?

"Mr. Tyler?" the voice came from behind me. "Mr. Tyler, what are you doing in here? All unoccupied rooms are out-of-bounds for patients."

Dr. Adler was standing behind me with that same damn quizzical look he always has when he sees me. I'd love to smack that look right off of him. "I was down here looking for Dr. Dawood. All his stuff was here this morning and now it's gone.

I stepped in for a moment for a look around. Do you happen to know where Dr. Dawood has gone?"

The look on Dr. Adler became even more sour, something I didn't think was possible. "Mr. Tyler, there's no Dr. Dawood at this institution. Could you perhaps be confusing him with someone else?"

"You're the one that had him take over my case! You introduced him to me, Dr. Adler. How can there not be a Dr. Dawood here?" My voice grew tense. I couldn't afford to let them think I was losing it again.

Dr. Adler approached me with baby steps before placing his hand on my shoulder. "Mr. Tyler, I think you may still be having side effects from the sedatives. Come, let's get you back to your room. We can sit and talk more about this Dr. Dawood there."

I walked with him back to the room, where he closed the door behind us. "Can you tell me more about this Dr. Dawood, Mr. Tyler?"

"He was the doctor you brought in to see me after you lost your shit with me in the last session we had together. I'm not sure what you're trying to pull off here. Is this one of your quack ways to make mc think I'm going insane when I'm not? Where is Emilia? She will tell you she's seen him and we've spoken of him."

"Mr. Tyler, I can call your wife or we can discuss this when she comes back tomorrow morning. I'm going to look and see if there was another doctor meeting with you. Would you mind..." As he was getting up he looked into the bathroom seeing the broken mirror. "Mr. Tyler, care to explain what happened here? Were you trying to harm yourself again?"

"What? No. That's part of what I was going to find Dr. Dawood about. I was lying here taking a nap when I'd been woken by the sounds of the glass breaking. I have no idea what caused it, but I was going to report that to him."

"I see," said Dr. Adler. I could hear the disbelief in that shaky voice of his. "Well, I'll have maintenance come up and get that repaired. Can you promise me that if I leave here you're not going to try and harm yourself?"

"Yes. I have no desire to hurt myself. I'm as curious as you when it comes to Dr. Dawood. I promise I will not harm myself. I'm going to sit on my bed and wait for you to come back."

It was about an hour before Dr. Adler returned. Not too long after he left, a maintenance person came to replace the mirror in my bathroom. I didn't move beyond the room or the bed for the entirety of that time.

When Dr. Adler returned he was wheeling a small black table with a laptop on top of it. He didn't close the door this time and I noticed a nurse and a few orderlies posting themselves outside my door. What in the holy hell was going on now?

"Mr. Tyler—I want to show you something. I'm going to ask you to remain seated on the bed for now."

"Yeah, sure doc. Show me what you've got."

He came over, opening the laptop. "I went to our security team and had them pull the video of the office where I found you. These are clips of that office from over the past week. Please watch them carefully."

When he pressed play I saw the empty office of Dr. Dawood, looking like it had when I'd been there a short time ago. Dr. Adler sped up the video and I saw myself enter the office. Okay, I wasn't getting it. Why was he showing me a video of me entering the office today? Then I noticed the timestamp in the corner of the video—it was from a week ago.

I watched myself go to the middle of the room and sit on the floor. The video was grainy but I was able to see that I was talking to someone, but there was no Dr. Dawood in the video. I kept watching—there are more and more videos like this.

I saw the altercation that I had with Dr. Dawood when I suspected him of being Az playing out on the video. I was fighting back against no one. The desk I had pushed was not there. The only thing that had ever been in that office was the grandfather clock.

As the video stopped I shook my head, realizing the gravity of the situation. "Is this some kind of fucked up joke? Did you have someone edit that video and superimpose me into an empty room? I know I saw furniture and there was a Dr. Dawood there." My mind raced with the implications—if they thought I was hallucinating, they'd drug me for sure.

"Mr. Tyler, please try to remain calm. I realize that seeing this may cause you some stress. This could be a temporary effect of everything that you've been through."

Walking back across the room—Dr. Adler kept his distance from me. I stepped to the door and kicked it shut. I knew Dr. Adler was probably shitting himself at that moment knowing he was locked in here with me. It would be a few minutes before the nurse with her pudgy fingers would get the right key to open the door.

I dashed back across the room, grabbing Dr. Adler by the collar of his jacket. "You listen to me, doc. I've had it with everyone trying to fuck me over in this place. So I'm gonna make myself very clear with what I say next. You're gonna leave this room and you're gonna call Emilia. You will tell her to get back here as soon as she can. And… when those dipshits in the hall unlock the door and come in here you're going to tell them everything is a-okay. Are we clear, doc?"

"Mr. Tyler, please try to control yourself..."

"Fuck that shit, doc. The time for control has come and gone. I'm going to level with you. You know who I am and how far my reach extends. I promise you if you drug me one more goddamn time and fail to do as I've asked I will make the necessary calls to shut this fucking place down for good. Understand me now, doc?"

I wasn't sure where this sudden boost of confidence had come from but man what a feeling it was. Dr. Adler nodded his head in compliance just as the nurse pushed the door open. I could see the syringe in her chubby fingers as she eyed the doctor. "Nurse, that won't be necessary right now. Mr. Tyler is going to be compliant and sit on his bed until we exit."

I straightened out Dr. Adler's collar, "That's right, doc. Remember what I said and don't try pulling any clever shit on me." I turned away from him, sitting back on the bed. I could feel the medallion creating a cold spot on my leg again. I could only take it as a sign that it was time to take a nap again while Dr. Adler got in touch with Emilia. What else was there to do but dream?

CHAPTER 17: ARIANNA

AZRAEL ALLOWED ME TO GET DRESSED BEFORE DIRECT-ing me to go out into the living room. I could feel nothing but a sick revulsion as this thing looked upon me. I'd seen him once before, but only for a moment and at a distance. This time, he was far too close to me. Although he appeared human, the putrid odor of death grew stronger as he approached. The closer he stepped it felt as though the air was being sucked from my lungs and my skin began to chill.

I sat on the floor against the westward facing window, grabbing a pillow to serve as a barrier and in hopes of getting some warmth back to myself. We sat there for a time, and he didn't speak. He was pacing back and forth across my apartment with utterances under his breath. I didn't dare speak and risk angering him. I knew I needed to be as smart as possible or else I would find myself dead.

Now that he was here I'd become more certain that what I'd seen at Deanna's was his work and now he'd come for me. I still had no idea what had happened to Clay after he left. He, this thing, had been there, what more did he hope to learn from me and by killing sweet Deanna?

Turning his attention to me, he walked across the room, tilting his head with curiosity. "Miss Stone," he said calmly, ""would you care to share with me what it was that you told Mr. Mitchell?"

"I… I don't understand. Told him about what? There were many things that Clay and I spoke about in our time together. Your question is too vague to answer fully or truthfully."

"You'd do well not to play stupid with me. You know damn well what it was that he was going to do!" His eyes intensified, glowing a deep indigo as he drew nearer.

"I knew nothing more about the gateway than what he told me about it. Before I spoke with him I'd never heard of such a thing. All I knew is that he wanted out of where you had him and he thought the gateway was his way out. Now you answer a question: What did you do to Deanna? I know it was you so don't play coy with me."

Laughing to himself, he said, "Well, she was in my way of getting to you of course. She was nothing more than a means to an end. I promise you she meant nothing to me."

Anger was rising like the fires of hell within me only sur-mounted by the guilt I was feeling knowing my helping Clay was the cause of Deanna's death. No. No, it wasn't! I had to stop telling myself that. It was this vile thing that had brought her to her end. I wouldn't feel guilty because of the evil in him. I wouldn't let him project those feelings onto me.

"I'll ask you once more, Miss Stone, what was it that you spoke about with Mr. Mitchell?"

"We spoke of life and death. We spoke of his life and his death. We spoke of the afterlife you brought upon him. We spoke of your deceitful treachery used to control the people in your realm."

"I would hardly call them people. They lose that status when they crossover."

"Would you like to hear the rest of what I have to say or not?"

"I'll hear what I want to hear and when I want to hear it. You say this is all that you've talked about. Do you even have the slightest idea of what a mess that idiot has caused? He's ruined everything that I'd been working on for several millennia. All because he couldn't forget the living world, forget his precious Ava!"

The silent raging and pacing began again. No longer looking at me, he studied the floor as he marched in small circles in my living room.

"No, he couldn't just take things for what they were. She was one of the last damn ones I needed. Hell, if he'd played along he would've quickly moved on! And now… now I have to go and clean up this mess across many different realms. When he crossed back over he defied the rules of the universe. That gateway was destroyed because of him. Now I must resort back to an older means of moving about."

"The mirror," I said in a hushed tone as I thought out loud.

"What?" his concentration was broken. "Yes, genius, the mirror."

"But why did you have to take Deanna? Why is it that you've come for me? It would seem that your trouble is with Clay, not us."

"You all played a part in this. Don't you see, each of you had contact with him. Each of you guided him to the point where he could desecrate my domain. Defile my plans. Now, you all must come! I can think of no other way to correct what's happened."

His attention was again drawn away from me as he slipped back into a rambling rage. "It should've just been Ava. She was one of the last ones to complete it all."

He wasn't paying attention to me, and I wanted to get near the kitchen, closer to the door. Unsure if one could outrun death, I had to make a move. Staying here would only lead to my demise—I wasn't ready for that.

I'd made it behind the kitchen island and could still hear his rants. So far so good. Scooting to the edge of the island, my door was now visible. A single dash forward and I could reach it, but shit… it's locked. That meant I'd have to take a few seconds to do that once I reached it. A few seconds was too much. I kept crawling, moving slowly so as to not gain his attention. Looking back over my shoulder, I watched the path Azrael was taking. Each time he walked further down the hallway, farther away from the door. I had to time this just right.

Time slowed, each of his steps echoing in my head. He reached the end of the hall, the farthest point from me and the door that he would reach. Pushing myself from the floor I sprinted ten feet to the door. I grabbed the lock, turning it. Click, click. Shit that was too loud. I had the door open, but made the mistake of looking back over my shoulder. Azrael… he wasn't there.

Still needing to get out to find another place to be, I turned back to the door. I swung the door open fully and was met with what could only be described as a nightmarish creature. Something that you never speak of, even if you remember it. His flesh was rotted down to the bone. No eyes, only glowing orbs of deep indigo. Draped in cloaks black as pitch. He came towards me. Stepping back as fast as I could, I tried to run, but he was too fast. I was tripping over my own feet. I tumbled backward, my head slamming into the corner of the kitchen island. Sharp pains fired through my body. The last thing I felt was the second impact as my body and then head smacked onto the hard floor.

CHAPTER 18: CLAY

I THOUGHT MY DREAMS WOULD GET ME BACK TO DR. Dawood. I should've known better; nothing ever goes the way I expect it to. The dream began the same as the last. I found myself back in Chicago sitting alone along the shore of Lake Michigan. A few moments later, Arianna was back beside me. This time, however, I entered into a state of lucid dreaming much quicker. Aware of what this was, I remembered the wave that had come before. As it splashed up over us, I wrapped my arms as tight as I could around her.

Submerged, the water was swaddling and pulling us down lower and lower into the darkness of the lake. Arianna was panicking and trying to push away from me. Looking into her eyes I shook my head no. I needed to help her stay calm and ride this out. Her eyes grew wider and she was now gulping water, trying to get air. I'm not sure if it was the sight of seeing her do this, but I pulled her in closer and kissed her. Had I been hoping this would stop her panic or was it something else? I wasn't sure, but I found myself with the sour feeling of guilt blossoming in my stomach. This was only a dream though, right?

As the kiss broke, the world turned on its axis. Up became down and down became up. We were back in the river I'd come to before. The place I found Dr. Dawood, albeit this time there was no Dr. Dawood. I used the last of my energy to drag Arianna up the river bank before collapsing into the cool mud to catch my breath.

"Clay? Is that really you? But how... How can this be? I must be dreaming?"

Moving the drenched hair out of my face I looked over to her. "This is a dream. How else could we be in the same place?"

"I was just in my apartment, Clay. He was there with me, then I don't know what happened but I somehow ended up with you. We were sitting on the shore and that wave washed over us. Clay, I don't think I'm dreaming. How could I be?"

"He? Who is the 'he' that was with you?" I knew what she was about to say, but I didn't want to believe it was true.

"Clay, it was Azrael. He came to my apartment. I can't remember every detail but he was there and I was trying to get away from him. It's so foggy right now. I'm so tired all of a sudden Clay. I need to sleep. Can you stay with me while I rest?"

"Yes, but not here. Come with me, it's a short walk we have to make and we'll have a safer place for you to rest." I put her arm around my neck and mine around her waist as we made our way to the temple. I was hoping Dr. Dawood would still be there. We needed to talk about what in the hell was happening while Arianna rested.

There was no way she was here. People don't share dreams. This was my dream. This was nothing more than a strange fabrication buried deep in my subconscious. It was manifesting into a dream. I've been listening to Dr. Adler too much.

Passing through the third door into the center chamber I noticed changes since I was here last. The table and chairs were no longer in the center of the room. Instead, there was a cot to one side of the room and in the center there was a round pool with steam rising from its waters.

I guided Arianna over to the cot and laid her down. "Close your eyes and rest. I'll be here with you."

She grabbed my hand, squeezing it tight. "I'm so happy to have found you again." Her grip went slack as she eased into a fetal position and drifted off to sleep. Once I was sure she was asleep I went looking around the chamber. I could find no indication that Dr. Dawood or anyone else for that matter was here with us. I went to make a closer examination of this new pool that had appeared.

The water, crystal clear with reflections dancing on its surface, had a refreshing eucalyptus smell to it. There were stairs all around leading down into the center of the pool. Getting down on my hands and knees I edged closer to it. As my eyes came over the water I could see a reflection—it was me. But it wasn't just me. There was something behind me. I went to turn but was too slow. Whatever had been behind me shoved me forward and I went head first into the water.

The dreams felt so real that I'd begun to lose a sense of what was a dream and what was reality. I could still taste Arianna's lips on my own. The ice water soaking through my clothes—was this the dream, or was Arianna the dream? It was Emilia's voice cutting through the haze that brought me back to what I knew was reality.

"What the hell did you do, Joh… Clay?" Her words pierced through the confusion, a sharp reminder of the world beyond my dreams. "I got a call from a more than pissed off Dr. Adler saying that you demanded I get back here. You know that I have kids at home. You know that I'm all that they have, so why the games?" She may have not been Ava, but the look in her eyes burnt a hole in me the same way.

"I'm sorry for the dramatics, Emilia. I really am. I had no other choice. I needed to get you back here. They were about to try and sedate me again. I can't afford for that to happen and I can't afford to stay here any longer. I need you to authorize my release today."

"Damn you, we had an agreement. You stay here until after all the work with the lawyers is done. Why should I let you out any sooner? So you can run off and break our deal? I don't think so!"

"Emilia, for fuck's sake, I'll come with you and sign the damn papers, but I can't stay here. They showed me videos today of my sessions with Dr. Dawood and they are using them to claim I'm unstable. I can't let them keep doing this to me!"

"Who the hell is Dr. Dawood? You've been seeing Dr. Adler since you got here."

I paused, realizing that mentioning Dr. Dawood was a mistake. "Forget about that. The point is, they're trying to keep me here by any means. I need you to trust me and get me out today."

"Okay… I really don't think it would be a good idea for you to come into my home with the children in your current state of excitement. This is just not…"

"Don't you fucking dare, Emilia! You leave me in this place now and you'll never, and I mean never, get those will changes made. You seem to forget that I've already been dead and know some of what goes on beyond here. I have no problem getting myself back there again. It only hurts for a moment."

She stepped back, realizing what I was saying now. Though I know she didn't have a lot of love for her husband, she did have a need or desire for his money. She turned and walked over to the window watching as the sun set over the mountains.

"Fine. I'll release you, but we can't go back to the house. I don't want to give the children any false hopes that their father has recovered and is coming back. I need to make a few phone calls and have someone take the kids for the night. Then I need to call the lawyers and have them get the paperwork ready for early tomorrow morning."

She walked out into the hall to make her calls and I assumed to find out what the sign out process is as well. After weeks in this place and the time I spent dead, I was finally going to get back out into the world. I knew I needed to get back to Chicago and I needed to find Arianna. It was the only way I could prove to myself that what I'd experienced was just a dream. Arianna was my last hope of finding my way back to Ava. And time was running short.

CHAPTER 19: AVA

THE WALK BACK TO DEANNA'S APARTMENT TOOK A GOOD half an hour, with my concern growing that it might take even longer. Cautious at first, due to her age when she crossed over, Deanna soon shed her hesitance upon realizing the absence of her former aches and pains, forcing me to match her new-found brisk pace.

Upon reaching the door, she hesitated before turning to me with a puzzled expression. "I... I don't have my keys," she confessed.

"Oh," I replied with a reassuring smile, "you needn't worry about keys anymore. The doors open for us as needed."

Reaching forward I turned the knob to let us in. As I stepped inside and looked up I felt my stomach drop when I saw another person standing over near the window. I'd almost backed over Deanna who had pushed past me, going right up to the gentleman I'd seen. By the time she reached him I realized it was the same man Grayson and I had met at the Green Mill.

"Hamilton," Deanna said. "I'm so glad to see you. We have much work to do, old friend." He turned, looking over at her. I saw the realization on his face as he observed the indigo hue covering her.

"Deanna… I… I'm…"

"Yes. Yes. Yes. I'm dead. Let's get past all that right now. I'll tell you what happened shortly, but we have more important things to discuss."

Deanna gave Hamilton a hug and then walked around him into her apartment. "Arcane," she called out. "Arcane where are you, mommy's home." She called out more, looking for her cat in all his favorite napping spots, but the cat wasn't in the apartment. When Deanna entered the kitchen she'd noticed his food was also missing.

Deanna joined Hamilton and me in the living room. "Arianna must have come and taken him. She's the only one who would have known where his food was. She's also the only one that could have taken that cat without getting scratched half to death. We'll need to go to her shortly."

Sitting down on the edge of the reclining chair, I saw the rapid change in her expressions. Eyes widening. Her mouth fell slightly agape. "This is where I was right before it was all over." I followed her gaze over to the mantel above the faux fireplace to see the mirror cracked from corner to corner. Deanna got up and walked over. "This clock is out of place. It's what he hit me with." Her attempt to grab the clock and move it had failed. It was then that the reality of our interactions with the living world became a reality to her.

"It takes a little to get used to," I said. "In time you'll find with a touch of will power and concentration you can touch things in the living world—for a short time anyways." I was trying to sound reassuring for her, but there is nothing you can do to ease this part of a person's transition. The more they come to realize their disconnection from all that they knew, yet, still being able to see it all, hear it all… it breaks them down.

Hamilton recognized this as well and came over to Deanna. "I'm glad to see you, my friend, but oh how I wish it was in a different light. You, out of all, Deanna, do not belong in this godforsaken place." Turning to me, he said, "And to my new friend: How is it that you came across Deanna?"

"She found me," I replied. "Well, I suppose it was more so she was looking for the gateway and we found each other there. But, what now? I still don't understand what's happening. I watched Clay jump through the gateway. Az touched the bottom of his foot. There was a large boom that shook hell on earth. Now we have fifty shades of indigo outside, making this place even more depressing than it was before. If that's even possible. Can either of you explain what in the hell is going on here?"

Deanna, still looking at the crack in the mirror, said, "This story started many years ago. Long before Clay or yourself became involved. Even long before Hamilton became involved. I've always had this connection with the worlds beyond. It was through my Aunt Elizabeth that I'd become comfortable speaking with the dead. I never knew her in life as she died several years before I was born. What I'd known of her came from family photographs and stories my mother and grandmother would share. She was a singer, you know. A mighty good one at that. My mother often shared stories about her and her travels around the country performing. Little did my mother know, Aunt Elizabeth was also sharing her own stories with me.

"I often observed Aunt Elizabeth lingering about at family gatherings, though she remained silent. At the age of seven or eight, I never thought to mention this observation to anyone. There was always this beautiful smile on her face that warmed me to the soul. There was this one Christmas when I was eleven and mother and I'd gotten into a rather intense argument.

Over what… I could no longer remember. I did what any eleven year old might do and stormed off to my bedroom, slamming the door behind me.

"I didn't hear the door open but as I looked up with my tear soaked eyes I saw Aunt Elizabeth standing at the foot of my bed. Just standing there looking at me. I wiped my eyes and looked back at her. It was then she realized I'd always been looking at her and not through her. It was also the first time I'd heard her speak.

"She told me that while she understood I was upset, it wasn't nice the way I'd spoken to mother. She instructed me to march back downstairs and make my apology. As you can imagine, I was in a state of shock hearing her speak. I'd gotten used to seeing dead people here and there, but none had ever spoken to me until she did. I rushed back downstairs to apologize to mother and told her that Aunt Elizabeth told me that I should. Mother just shook her head, taking it as some childish nonsense, and then carried on with her conversation with the other adults."

Deanna became silent and lost again in her story. I wondered when and where her mind was now. I watched as she ran her fingers over the cracks in the mirror. When she came back to us to continue her story I moved closer to her to see what it was that she'd found so fascinating about these cracks. I put my own hand up to the cracks. I could feel them. I suspected that may have been what was captivating her. Taking another moment tracing the cracks, she went back to her story.

"Following that day, Aunt Elizabeth and I engaged in numerous conversations delving into various topics, including the realms beyond the living. Her guidance expanded my understanding, even touching upon subjects my mother deemed taboo. Despite her openness, certain boundaries remained in our discussions. I'd asked her many times about how she died and what she remembered of it. What the world where she was looked like. These questions were always met with a changing of the subject. She'd feed me a short response of, 'in your own time and in your own way you'll find what this side looks like. I'll not take all the secrets of the world from you.' Though I didn't know why, I could always see a sense of anxiety and fear in Aunt Elizabeth when we spoke.

"She stayed with me over the years as I grew. She was my support when my own parents traveled beyond. I'd asked her why I couldn't see them and she told me that like books, there are different endings for each person. Theirs had taken them to a place where they were no longer visible to us. As I got into my midlife our visits became less frequent. Then, one day, back in the late 1980s, she disappeared. I've never seen her again.

"I had others that I talked with in her world by then. They could only tell me that something there had changed. There was a thunderous roar that rolled through and then the sky changed to what I can only guess now is this shade of indigo we see."

"Actually," I said, "the indigo hue intensified after Clay entered the gateway, transitioning from a lighter shade to its current state."

Deanna pondered on it for a moment. "Perhaps their fates were intertwined all along. I've gone on a tangent. I'm sorry. Where was I? Oh yes. Before Aunt Elizabeth's disappearance, I began observing a man in her vicinity, always at a close distance. I'd tell her and she said not to pay any attention to him. He was nothing I needed to worry about. I'd forgotten about that man until I saw him standing in my living room before he so kindly took me with him to this place."

"So you're saying that Az was stalking your aunt before she disappeared? I find that easy enough to believe. It seems everyone he takes an interest in ends up disappearing. Thinking about it now, Az did mention once when I asked him if anyone had crossed through the gateway. He said there was a woman who had tried but he'd prevented it, and it caused the indigo light. Maybe it was your aunt he was speaking of, Deanna?"

"Yes, maybe it was. Hamilton, have you seen Arianna at all?"

"No. Haven't seen her since our last visit with her and the boy."

"I think it's time then that we get over there. I have this feeling we're going to find more than just her there."

"But without the gateway..." I started to say.

"He's using the mirrors, Ava. I don't know many places that lack mirrors, so he can go when and where he likes. We can discuss more on the way, but we must go—*now*."

CHAPTER 20: ARIANNA

"CLAY," I CALLED OUT, BUT SILENCE GREETED ME. HE promised to stay with me. Where had he gone? How had I ended up here? I recalled running towards the door in my apartment and then falling backward. Then... there was Clay and a rushing wave... and now, this strange temple.

Opening my eyes I realized I was still in that temple. I wasn't sure how long I'd been out for. I could make a guess that if I was still in this place that it may not be a dream. It was a struggle for me to move from the cot and get my feet back on the ground.

The light in the temple was nothing more than a glow like the moments before the sun breaks over the horizon. It allowed me to make out nothing more than my immediate surroundings. In the center of the chamber was a table with two chairs. I could've sworn that when Clay and I first came in here there'd been a pool of sorts there.

Artwork I recognized as hieroglyphics decorated the pale sandstone walls. I recognized some of the symbols as they came up often in my line of work as a medium. I saw many symbols of the canine-headed Egyptian god Anubis along with the Eye of Horus. I couldn't believe how authentic they looked. The ground was a similar light sandstone color of the walls, though there it was, in parts, covered with grains of sand. Where in the hell had I ended up?

"Hello, Miss Stone. If you like you can take a seat. You've been through a lot and you will need to take it slow for now."

As I glanced towards the chamber's entrance, I saw a tall man covered in hieroglyphic tattoos. His eyes glowed a cold blue, and with each step, scents of lavender, peppermint, and cedar filled the air.

He came over to the table and took a seat. I approached him with a good deal of caution. It was his eyes that made me weary. They were the same blue I'd seen with Azrael. "Who exactly is it that you are and where am I?" Grabbing one of the chairs, I positioned myself as far away from him as I was able.

"Who, or what I am, is a matter of whom you ask. I've gone by many names. As you might see by the artwork that adorns this chamber, there's a familiar name you may know me by—Anubis. As to where you are, Miss Stone, it is a place of my own design. A place where I can come when I need to… how is it said in your time? Oh yes, be off the radar."

"How was it that I got here?"

"Do you not remember coming with Mr. Mitchell? How it was he got you here, I'm still trying to understand myself. This isn't a place for those of whom are living, but rather, a place for their essences once they have shed the mortal skin. The only reason Mr. Mitchell is able to get here is because he's not in his own mortal skin. His essence can, let's say, jump around. Something others in your living world lack the ability to do."

"Wait, that means he made it? He got through the gateway and returned to the living… and…" My brain was piecing the puzzle together, "and that was him. That was really him that

I saw when dreaming about the wave that brought us here?" The thought that I'd actually felt Clay, knowing he was in the living world, meant that he might be coming to Chicago soon.

"How do I wake back up and get back? If Clay is able to come and go, doesn't that mean when I wake up I should be back home in Chicago?"

"Unfortunately, Miss Stone, I can't provide you with an answer yet. Your presence here is quite unusual. At this moment, all I can say is that your essence has been temporarily displaced. Do you happen to recall the moments before you came across Mr. Mitchell in your... dream?"

I had to sit and think about that. It hadn't been so long ago, yet, for one reason or another, the last day was a blur. The harder I tried to remember it, the more I was unable to. It was as though the day never existed and my first memories began when I was sitting with Clay. There was also that kiss. Clay had kissed me when we were under the water. But why? Had that happened for real?

"I... I can't remember. I can remember my past and what happened when I met with Clay, but where the memories of the moments before have gone, I..."

Adjusting himself in the chair he reached his open hand across the table. I'm not sure what compelled me to do so, but without thinking, without hesitation, I reached my hand towards his. "If you'll humor me, Miss Stone, please take my hand for a moment. I assure you, I mean you no harm."

Placing my hand into his, an artic chill coursed through me. So cold—I could feel my hand begin to numb. Then, there was the most beautiful warmth. A warmth you feel in the spring. A warmth the sun creates as it falls down upon you creating this sense of aliveness and joy. How was this possible from a single touch? I closed my eyes. The sensation was so strong I needed to dull my other senses to give my full appreciation to this.

"Miss Stone, I must tell you, whatever has happened, your mortal life is hanging in the balance. You're not dead but you're on the precipice. That may have been how Mr. Mitchell was able to bring you here. For now, you'll stay here. We'll keep you safe."

When he let go of my hand my senses returned to normal, the world feeling much duller than it had been not moments ago. It was then that the realization that something had happened to me and I was nearing death became frightening. I needed to try remembering what happened.

With eyes wide open my hand was still stretched out, palm up, in front of me. He said, "I understand your confusion and lack of memory. It's very common for those when they first arrive in a place such as this."

"You still haven't told me where this is. Is this like the waiting room to heaven or hell or something? I can do without word riddles and vagueness right now, if you don't mind."

"Yes. In simple terms, you're in what you would call the afterlife. Though, you've not left the mortal world, yet. It's like a lucid dream from which you may never return. This particular place is one that I hold dearly."

Glancing around the chamber, I asked, "So, you lived during the time of the Pharaohs? Your name being Anubis and all, along with this setup," I gestured to the artwork, "I can't imagine this existing in any other time or place."

"Life and Death, as you know them, are not the same as I know them, Miss Stone. I've always been alive, as have you and everyone else you know. This was a time when the people knew better of me. Worked beside me to do what I must do. I know this may sound something of a word game to you, but you're not in place to understand nor appreciate what I can and will one day share with you. For now, it would be best if you allow yourself more rest. Your mortal skin is out there and we must find a way to determine what has and is happening to it. The more energy you use here, the higher the likelihood remains that you shall stay here. Do you understand, Miss Stone?"

"Yes. I think so. This is still feeling so much like a dream to me."

"And dream you will."

Lying back down on the cot, I rested my head looking back at Anubis. "Will I see Clay again?"

"You may. If he's brought you here, he can return. He may not realize what has happened. Nor does he understand he has the power to come and go as he wishes. It would seem both you and I are in need of a conversation with him. For now, you're my guest. Please rest, Miss Stone, you're safe here."

I closed my eyes with a hope that when they opened again I would find myself back in my apartment. Drifting into a warm darkness, I couldn't stop thinking this was still nothing more than a dream. Things as strange as this only happen in the movies, not in real life. Then again, what did I know? If anything, life as a medium had taught me how little it is that we humans understand. When given the chance our brains will do the best to explain the unexplainable to us. For now, though, I let those thoughts stop. For now, I would let myself sleep.

CHAPTER 21: AVA

WHEN DEANNA, HAMILTON, AND I LEFT HER APARTMENT we headed east back towards the lake. I'd stopped believing things happened by chance not long after I arrived here. It came as no surprise to me when I spotted Grayson across Halsted when we crossed it at Addison. Calling him over I re-introduced him to Hamilton then introduced him to Deanna. His eyes moved over to Deanna and a look of befuddlement came to his face.

"My apologies miss," he said to her. "It's just, you look like an older version of this friend I once had. So peculiar."

Deanna smiled and shook his hand. As we walked the rest of the way to Arianna's apartment I took the time to catch Grayson up on all that had taken place. How Deanna had come to an untimely death at the hands of Az, but more importantly, that she'd come in contact with Clay when she was still in the living world. I was about to tell him the story about her Aunt Elizabeth when we arrived at Arianna's apartment. The topic of conversation changed rather fast when we entered the building.

As we went inside, the sight that greeted us was chilling. Shards of glass lay scattered across the floor, gleaming in the dim light like fragments of a shattered mirror. The steel mailboxes looked as though someone had taken a torch to them, coating them with a dark film.

Grayson's voice trembled with apprehension as he voiced his concerns, his words punctuated by an edge of fear. "I don't like one goddamn thing about this," he muttered, his gaze darting around the dilapidated surroundings. "We'd be best to turn around and get the hell outta this building."

"Do as you like," replied Deanna. "If Arianna is here, I intend to check on her and get her out of here."

"I'm go… go… going with Deanna," Hamilton stuttered out. I was certain had he been able to, he would have pissed himself as he said it.

I stood looking from Grayson to Deanna and Hamilton. "Sorry, Grayson. I've come too far to turn back. If Arianna is my key to finding Clay, I've got no choice but to go forward."

Grayson dropped his shoulders and shook his head. "You and that damn man of yours ain't so different. The both of you leading me down paths that keep putting me in the shittiest of places! Man oh man. I'm not liking this one damn bit." Stepping back through the door, he followed the rest of us up the stairs.

Grayson and I had fallen several steps behind as Deanna and Hamilton marched up the stairs. It came as a surprise when we reached the landing to see them both standing in front of a door staring at it.

"Are we gonna just stand here in the hall looking at the door or is someone going to open it?" I asked.

"It's locked!" Deanna said, looking back at me. "Both Hamilton and I have tried. It will not open."

I pushed my way forward and turned the knob. Indeed, the door was locked. In the years I'd been here I'd never found a door that wouldn't open. There was no place that we couldn't get into if we needed to. Why or how was this door locked to us? It defied the rules as I understood them.

"Locked doors are locked for a reason. People are either trying to keep something in, or keep something out. My guess is that in this case they are trying to keep us out. I don't have much of an argument against that," Grayson said.

"Grayson, you don't have to stay with us," I said, feeling annoyed with his persistence on us leaving.

"No ma'am. I have to. I don't like it, but I can't let nothing happen to you. Clay wouldn't ever forgive me if I did."

Turning back to the door I knocked three times. I turned the knob again and the damn thing opened. I looked back and the others were staring at me. "I don't know," I said. "I figured what the fuck. If you can't open a door, knock and see if someone answers." If I only knew what was on the other side I might not have been so annoyed with Grayson.

We walked in not more than a few steps before we were again frozen in our tracks. This time it came due to the woman lying on the floor with a pool of coagulated blood around her head. Her hair was part blonde and part black—the black coming from the dried blood clinging to it.

As Deanna brushed past me, a surge of urgency pulsed through her. Kneeling beside Arianna, her fingers trembled as she reached out to touch her friend's battered form. The sight of Arianna's blood-soaked head pierced through Deanna's heart, igniting a storm of emotions within her. "Oh Arianna," she murmured, her voice thick with emotion. "I tried to warn you, but you stubborn girl, you wouldn't listen." With a heavy sigh, she leaned in closer, her breath catching at the sight of Arianna's shallow breaths. "She's still clinging to life," Deanna whispered, her voice barely above a hush, as if afraid to disturb the fragile thread that bound Arianna to this world.

"That won't last much longer," came a voice booming down the hall.

From one of the doors at the far end of the hall, out stepped Az. Grayson and Hamilton turned back to the door, but it slammed shut before they could cross the threshold.

"Don't be in such a rush to leave gentlemen. Let's all sit down and get reacquainted with one another. Shall we?"

"I'm not leaving Arianna there," Deanna shouted at him.

"Miss Stone? No need to worry about her. I promise you, she'll not be running away any time soon. Now, I suggest you all take a seat. I'm feeling a rather foul mood growing and it's best we not let you folks have to experience that right now."

CHAPTER 22: CLAY

IT WAS AN HOUR RIDE FROM THE APPALACHIAN HOUSE to Richmond, Virginia. Emilia had chosen a hotel there that we'd be staying at for the night. The hotel in Richmond wasn't the upscale spot you'd imagine for a tech mogul and his spouse. That's precisely why Emilia picked it.

I learned on the drive to Richmond that she'd learned after the first few years of John's emergence into the public eye that the smaller mom and pop places were more likely to leave you be and keep to their own business. Staying at bigger hotels she'd found there was always someone who knew someone. The staff at those hotels were always willing to give tips to the media about which big name was currently staying there.

For this trip she wanted to keep everything as quiet as possible. Since John or I'd been at the Appalachian House, she'd been heading up the operations at InterFaze, John's company. She'd convinced the other executives and board members that John had gone on a retreat to recenter himself and plan for the rest of the coming year.

The other executives seemed relieved by this, but a single leak from the press that John was back in Richmond would turn that into a fiery ball of shit. Emilia had been cleaning up John's messes for many years and didn't have it in her right now to try and clean up another.

The hotel had a single room left, and it had only a single queen bed. Emilia and I looked at one another as we entered the room. "I'll take the floor," I said. Emilia found this amusing.

Laughing at me, she said, "We're both adults. Like it or not you're in the body of my husband; a man at one point in my life I'd felt something like love for. We can share a bed for one night and it'll not be the end of the world. After all, we're only going to be sleeping."

"You may be comfortable with it, but I'm not. I have a fiancé that I very much love and this doesn't feel right to me."

She walked to the small closet, looking around for a moment. When she turned back she had two more pillows and a blanket. Throwing them down in the middle of the bed, she said, "Will this make you feel a little better? We can have a barrier between us. Sounds like most of what my marriage to John has been like. Always something or someone between us."

Tears welled in Emilia's eyes, her fingers combing through her hair in agitation. I didn't want to make this more of an emotional deal than it needed to be so I gave in. I told her that I'd sleep on the bed with her so long as the pillows remained between us. I was no longer in the mood to talk about this so I went over to the bed and lay down.

"I'm going to take a shower… This has been a long day," Emilia said as she went into the bathroom. She left the door cracked open just enough so that the steam from the hot shower could be seen escaping. I reached over to the nightstand; it was sticky with an unknown residue that made me shudder to think what it may have been. I snatched the remote and flipped on the

TV for background noise. Finding an infomercial, I let it play, hoping to drown out the chaos in my mind.

I didn't think I would find sleep. To my surprise, once my head hit my pillow, it was only a matter of moments before I drifted off. I'd been hoping that I would return to the dream I had with Dr. Dawood or even the one with Arianna. They'd felt so real. I was sure if I could talk to either of them again I might have a better clue of what was going on. As of right now, I still had no idea what I was going to do after the will papers were signed tomorrow morning.

I drifted into a dreamless sleep, only to awaken with Emilia's head nestled against my chest the next morning. So much for respecting the pillow boundary. I looked over to the digital clock radio on the nightstand beside me. It was only five in the morning. I wasn't sure what time Emilia had fallen asleep or what time she normally woke. I also wasn't sure how long I could lay here with her resting on my chest. It wasn't that she was an unattractive woman, far from. She just wasn't Ava. The only other woman I'd lain in bed with was Arianna and at that point I was dead. There was no contact that could be made between us. Emilia's touch felt foreign against my skin, a stark reminder of the unfamiliarity of our current situation. Lost in contemplation, I began counting stains on the ceiling until Emilia's movement brought me back.

Sensing an opportunity, I tried to subtly shift away from her, but my efforts were futile. Instead of me being able to move away from her, she'd wrapped an arm around my waist, pulling me in tighter. I lay there, stiff and still. *Please, let this woman wake up soon,* I pleaded.

It was another hour like this. I lay there counting stains on the hotel ceiling. When she woke I think her position caught her by as much shock as it had me. Emilia rolled quickly to the other side of the bed. "I'm so sorry, Clay. It's been so long since I had John in the same bed as me. I meant nothing by it."

Shaking it off I went to get myself ready to meet with the lawyers. Emilia had brought one of John's suits with her. Apparently, I landed in the body of a man who wears thousand dollar suits as his casual daywear. She was kind enough to bring along a razor. "There's no way," she said, "anyone in the office is going to believe there's not something wrong if you show up looking like Grizzly Adams."

After we finished getting ready, Emilia drove us downtown to John's lawyer's office. "Just follow my lead and try not to say too much. Oliver is John's lawyer and his favorite buddy to go out whoring with. If there's someone that knows John better than I do, it's Oliver."

When we entered Oliver's office he seemed more than surprised to see me, but even more surprised to see Emilia standing beside me. "John, so good to see you. Emilia." He gave her a curt nod before turning back to me. "To what do I owe the pleasure today? John, I thought I heard you were on a safari or something."

"We're here to make changes to John's will and some adjustments to the business ownership. You'll have to forgive John. He's come back with a touch of laryngitis and hasn't been able to speak so well the last few days."

I don't know where she pulled that gem from, but good play Emilia. The less I had to say the better it was for both of us. I reached out my hand to Oliver and gave him a firm handshake. That was accompanied by a look letting him know I wasn't in the mood for bullshit today.

"Okay… Emilia. What types of adjustments are we making today? I can take notes and have one of my paralegals get it typed up for us in a day or two."

"Oh, thank you, Oliver. There's no need for that though." She reached down into her bag and pulled out a stack of legal documents, slapping them onto Oliver's desk. "We had some time and you weren't available. I had my attorney draw these up for us. All we need from you today Ollie is to observe John's signature and sign as a witness. We don't want any questions about the authenticity of the documents."

"Emilia, you know I'm not going to just sign off on this without reading it first. What kind of service would I be doing John if I didn't dig through this with a fine-toothed comb? Do you really take me for a foo..."

"That will be quite enough, Oliver." I made the voice as scratchy as I could. It was all I could do to sit there and listen to this asshole for a second longer. He was making me think too much of dear Uncle Joe. "I know damn well what's in those papers, Oliver. I'm in full support of the changes, which you can read later if you like. You're my lawyer and my friend. But make no mistake, today you're my lawyer to whom I pay a considerable amount of money. And today, you're going to do as Emilia has asked you and bear witness to my signature. Any further questions, Oliver?"

"N... No, John," he stuttered, nearly falling out of his chair. I'm not sure what he and John had previously discussed, but I was willing to bet this was a big change from that.

"Good," I said. "Now have someone get me some goddamn water. My throat is fucking killing me."

Oliver got up from his desk nearly tripping over himself as he headed out of his office door.

Turning to Emilia, I noticed her stunned expression, her eyes wide with disbelief. She began to speak, but I waved off her words, preferring silence for the moment.

Once Oliver returned with my water I took a few sips and then pointed to the conference room across the hall. "There's a lot of paperwork, let's move in there so we have some room to spread out."

In all, it took just under an hour of signing document after document. First I would sign, then Emilia would sign, then Oliver would sign. When we were done signing, Emilia and I sat and waited while Oliver had his intern make copies. As we were leaving I told Oliver I'd be in touch soon. The contents of the documents remained a mystery to me. Whatever it was, it brought one hell of a smile to Emilia's face.

As we walked back to the car, and clear out of view of Oliver's office, Emilia jumped up, wrapped her arms around me, and placed another kiss on my cheek. "Thank you, so much. You don't know how much what you did is going to help out my children… and me."

"I don't mind helping you, but you'll still have to contend with John if he makes it back. I still have no idea what is going to happen and what the fuck it is that I have to do. He may never come back or he may come back with vengeance."

"Either way, it doesn't matter. What you, we, signed back there, it has a clause that says it can't be amended for another twenty years. Even if he wanted to change it, he couldn't without a long legal battle. All he can do is abide by the clause which leaves everything to me until the children reach the age of twenty-five. After that, it's all theirs and I can wash my hands of it."

I gave her a smile. John must have never known how smart of a woman he married. Emilia drove to the hotel and when we went in she brought two bags with her. "We're going to need to make a few changes to your appearance before you leave here. John has a very recognizable look to him. Something tells me that right now neither one of us wants to deal with unnecessary John sightings." She pulled out a pair of hair clippers and black hair dye. "You can kiss that hair goodbye, and the dye is for those eyebrows. Sit down and let's get this over with."

Two hours later I was as bald as the day I was born and had a new pair of ebony eyebrows. She dressed me in an old hooded sweatshirt, dark denim jeans, and a pair of worn-in Adidas that felt like heaven on my feet. We were at the Amtrak station in Richmond and I was getting ready to board a train north to Washington, D.C.; from there I was off to Chicago.

Emilia had paid for a sleeper car from D.C. to Chicago. This would allow me as much privacy as I needed and would also keep me out of too much public exposure.

She gave me a final kiss on the cheek before I left to board. "Thank you again for everything. I hope that it all works out for you. Oh… and if you see my son-of-a-bitch husband, kick him in the balls for me." I gave her a nod, tipped my head down and boarded the train.

As the train began to depart, I made my way to a seat for the short journey to D.C. Despite my exhaustion, I remained vigilant, knowing I wouldn't be able to rest until I reached the safety of the sleeper car.

CHAPTER 23: ARIANNA

I SAT ON A BENCH AT NAVY PIER, MY EYES FLUTTERING open to a dreary sky painted with dark, purplish hues. A wind was blowing in off the lake rustling papers and other loose debris about. Looking around, I noticed other people, their clothing seemingly from another time, adding an eerie atmosphere to the scene. They seemed oblivious to my presence, lost in their own world, perhaps from a century or more before my time.

As I gazed at the dilapidated building nearby, its weathered exterior spoke of a forgotten past. Despite the warnings echoing in my mind, an irresistible pull drew me towards it, my curiosity battling with a growing sense of apprehension. Every step forward felt like a leap into the unknown, but I couldn't resist exploring further.

Approaching the crumbling edifice, an indigo light emanated from within, casting a mysterious glow that beckoned me closer. Pushing open the creaking door, I stepped into the dimly lit interior, every horror movie I'd ever watched warning me against such reckless curiosity. Yet, curiosity kills the cat, they say, and today, I am the proverbial cat.

Inside, the air was heavy with the scent of dust and decay, and the floor lay strewn with remnants of a vanished age. A thick layer of dust covered everything, undisturbed for decades. My footsteps echoed in the silence as I made my way deeper into the abandoned structure, drawn by the promise of discovery.

Beyond the door sat a counter where they would've collected tickets or payments from visitors when this place was open. From beyond the turnstiles I saw a light glowing behind a giant red and white striped curtain.

"Hello?" I said as I stepped beyond the counter and pushed my way through the turnstile. There was no response, so I tried again. Still nothing. I walked further in and saw that the curtain was actually a drape covering something. I reached up and took a hold of the fabric. It made an echoless swoosh as I pulled it down. Along with the drape, all the dust that had accumulated on it came free as well. For a few moments I was lost in a gray snowfall.

As the dust cleared I saw—myself. A whole lot of me. There were so many mirrors and they were all facing me. Some showed a direct reflection of me while others distorted either my height or width. In the middle of this wall of mirrors was an open doorway with a small chain latched across it.

I looked around, still not seeing anyone else. The closer I got to the doorway I could see the indigo light coming brighter from the inside of the house of mirrors.

Leaning in I saw more mirrors and the indigo light reflecting off a few of them. I wanted to know where this light was coming from. I slipped under the chain and stepped in.

When I was younger, I remember going to fairs and navigating my way through other amusements like this. The trick I'd learned was to keep your hands in front of you and use your feet and the floor as your guide. Your eyes would only deceive you if you relied too much on them. The further I wandered into this labyrinth of mirrors it became clear this was no ordinary mirror maze.

I did my best to keep my eyes down and follow my feet—I found my eyes drawn upward to the light causing me to veer in a direction to get closer to it. I'd been working my way through the maze for what felt like a half hour or more. Yet, I'd gotten no closer to the light. It continued to reflect at the same size since the time I'd entered.

My better judgment kicked in and I decided it was time to turn around and get out of here. I turned to retrace my steps through the dusty floor but as I spun around I found only a mirror behind me. How could that be? I'd just walked through here. Maybe I'd turned too far when I spun? I turned again. Another mirror and the tracks of movement in the dust in a small circle around where I stood. It was as though I'd spent hours walking in circles on a four-by-four section of the floor.

I looked up and turned my body around, first clockwise, then counter-clockwise. All to see reflections of myself. There was no way forward, no way back. My heart pounded in my chest, my breaths coming in short, panicked gasps as I realized the gravity of my situation. Lost amidst the labyrinth of mirrors, I struggled to suppress rising waves of fear and doubt, each reflection a distorted echo of my own terror.

Closing my eyes I took a deep breath, trying to not let the panic overtake me. When I opened my eyes I was no longer looking at myself in the mirrors. Each mirror showed reflections of other people.

They were blurry at first, but as they began to become clearer, I saw faces I recognized. It was Deanna, and then I turned and saw Hamilton. There was another woman who I didn't know but recognized her as Clay's fiancé from the picture I'd seen. There was also another older gentleman that I didn't recognize.

I made one last turn and there behind me, in the mirror, was Azrael. I stepped back towards the mirror I'd seen Deanna in. Azrael was getting larger in his mirror. I wanted to get away. I turned back to find Deanna was no longer there. None of the mirrors were the others that I'd seen—they were all Azrael. The indigo light I'd seen, now shining from his eyes.

The mirrors began closing in on me. Each step I took echoing in my head. THUD… THUD… THUD.

Either time was slowing or my movements were. I was bringing my hands up to my face but they couldn't move at their normal speed. I looked around again and the mirrors were only a few feet away from me now. Azrael, still growing larger and more viscous looking. Only three inches away. I was feeling claustrophobic and couldn't take it any longer. I screamed, screamed so loud.

My screams echoed through the maze as Azrael's menacing reflection loomed larger with each passing moment. I heard a large crack, and then another. Looking again I could see all the mirrors beginning to spiderweb. Desperation clawed at my chest as I searched for an escape, my mind consumed by a primal instinct to survive at any cost. There was a loud whoosh like that of a strong wind. Then came the sounds of shattering glass. Each mirror breaking apart, the glass floating in place. Then, without warning, all the pieces began blowing in every direction. Behind the mirrors, there was nothing but darkness.

The pieces of glass moved so fast that I'd not realized they'd cut me. Looking down I could see my body was drenched in red. It ran from my arms, my chest, my legs, my face. I felt nausea coming over me as I fell down to the dusty floor. I couldn't breath, couldn't move. Falling into a dark void, the last of my breaths came out, screaming, "Help me!" Then there was nothing but a cold darkness, no feelings remained.

CHAPTER 24: AVA

WE ALL SAT HUDDLED IN A CORNER OF ARIANNA'S APART-
ment, except for Deanna. She'd defied Az's commands and stayed
with Arianna where she'd fallen. Az paced across the room, not
saying much to us, and we didn't say much to one another. The
only voice we could hear was that of Deanna repeating, "Poor
sweet, stupid girl," over and over as she stroked Arianna's hair.

Sitting there was driving me crazy. Even more so was
watching him pace. What was the point of this? For us to sit
and watch him walk in circles while some poor woman died?
I needed something to fill this void. Looking around the little
corner area we were crammed into, I saw an open laptop. On
the screen I saw a title page: *The Book of Clay*.

What on earth was this woman writing about Clay? What
did she know about him? He, at most, had only been with her
for a short time before Mount Shitstorm had erupted. I wanted to read it, but I knew that would disrupt the nauseating
silence and likely set Az off. Before I'd gotten the chance to
think any further on this, the silence came to an abrupt end.

I hadn't been the only one who was getting frustrated at our
sit and wait situation. Looking over to Grayson I saw his hands

twitching. There was this look in his eyes as he glared at Az; if looks could kill and we weren't already dead, Az would've been.

It happened so fast. One moment Grayson was sitting there and the next he was up on his feet in pursuit of Az. "Damn you to hell Azrael!" he shouted. The sudden pause in Az's pace showed he was as surprised as the rest of us.

"First, I watch you take Elizabeth from me. Then you go and pretend to be her to confuse that boy. Then you do God knows what to him. You took that sweet lady over there and brought her to this damn place. And now… now… you motherfucker… you go and leave this poor woman bleeding on the floor. All so you can keep pacing and muttering bullshit to yourself? For what man? I've had enough of this shit and this fucked up existence you keep us all in. So either you open that damn mouth of yours and start explaining some shit or I swear to all that is holy I'm gonna reach in and rip that damn third arm of yours off! And for good measure I am going to beat you with that motherfucking thing!"

Grayson never had a chance. By the time he was a foot away, Az's eyes had grown into indigo orbs and his third arm was already out from under his waist coat. He grabbed hold of Grayson, still keeping the third arm at bay, and swung him towards a mirror that was standing in the corner of the room. The mirror began glowing the same color that the gateway used to. And like that, Az shoved Grayson through the mirror. He was gone.

That one act set everything else into motion. Az walked back from the mirror, his third arm leading the way. Hamilton was not as lucky as Grayson. When the third arm made contact with Hamilton's throat, he turned to a pile of ash and fell to the floor. Seeing Az's eyes now on Deanna, I moved as fast as I could to get in front of her. "Az! Stop this right now. You have to expect when you beat people down there's gonna be a point when they've had enough. What are you even doing here? You took my life early. You took Clay's life early. For what? Now you're going to, what… make everyone disappear from existence?"

"Everything you've ever known is an illusion, Miss Sanderson. Everything you've ever been or ever thought you've been is all one big illusion. This world, the world you lived in—none of that was for you. You think you had a life of free will where you could come and go as you please. You can have your double chai latte and whatever the fuck it is you do. But no, none of that is real life. What's real is the fact that for all my existence I've had to usher you foolish things back and forth. For what? You never seem to understand your purpose. I could only take so much of this nonsense. A few thousand years ago I found a way to keep the cycle from happening again and again. In time, I knew it would free me from the chains that have bound me. You were to be a piece of that, and I would've shown you the way to your own freedom, to your own peace. But no. You couldn't even do the simplest part of letting those dear sweet memories of a false life be washed away. Now, it's your own ignorance that will do you in."

Az came closer. I did what I could to shield Deanna and Arianna from him. Though I knew it wouldn't do much good. Az was far more powerful than I was and if he chose to, he could swat me out of the way like a bug. The only chance I had was to keep distracting him with words. Words that might calm him from this tirade he was on.

"Az, I'll go with you. I'll let my memories fade, but please, let these two go."

"It's too late for that Miss Sanderson. You had your chance to be part of this and you squandered that trying to save your poor precious Clay. Now is the time for action. The season of death has come."

He pushed me back. Looking up as I landed on the floor I saw his third arm was out again. It appeared that he was now going to do to Deanna what he'd done to Hamilton. Instead, he pushed her out of his way and went for Arianna.

He got down on his knees and grabbed her throat. Both Deanna and I had the same idea, though it was a poor one. We charged at Az, but even together, he flicked us away like we were nothing more than fleas. I went flying across the room, and Deanna crumpled to the floor like an old ragdoll, unconscious. He turned back and resumed choking Arianna.

I saw her body begin lurching and shaking on the floor. She was fighting. Something in her was trying to keep her alive. Az's touch alone should've killed her—it was as though something or someone was protecting her.

An unintelligible uttering came from her mouth, but her voice soon grew stronger through Az's suffocating grip. "Help me! Help me! Somebody help me!" I couldn't respond. The last time Az had thrown me had left me numb and unable to move. Looking at Deanna I saw she was still unconscious. As quick as they'd started, Arianna's shouts subsided.

The whole room, or the world for that matter, fell silent. Her body moved no more. Proud of his accomplishment, a grin came over Az's face. He was getting to his feet. "Well, that issue has been dealt wi..."

From Arianna's lifeless body, an ear-deafening scream spread across the room. It was a scream unlike any I've ever heard before. It was so loud and painful; I brought my hands up to my ears to try and muffle it out. I could see it was having the same effect on Az as well.

He put his hands to his ears and fell back to his knees. The screeching continued for a moment longer. It lasted long enough that the mirror in the corner of the room shattered into a thousand pieces. Only then did Arianna go silent again.

I heard her take a final raspy breath. What I saw before me was no longer Arianna. It was nothing more than a suit made of flesh and bone.

It took a moment more before Az recovered from the screaming. As he looked from Arianna to the mirror and back again it was clear he was confused about what had happened. Getting back to his feet, he walked back and kicked Arianna's corpse. No movement. He pulled his pocket watch out and looked around the apartment. "This is impossible. She should… she should be here by now."

Moving quicker now, he went over to the mirror. He began pushing pieces of the glass around with his foot as he stood shaking his head. Something struck him, and he ran out into the hallway. I took this opportunity to move over to Deanna and check on her.

She rolled to her side and had a view of Arianna. The tears in the old woman's eyes said more than words could've. "I know," I said, "I'm so sorry."

I rested my hand on her shoulder, and she placed hers on top of mine. "She's not here—that's a good sign. She's been saved from any more of this torment."

Az stormed back into the room like he was taking the beaches of Normandy. There was something different about him. A look. One I'd never seen him wear before—fear.

"Both of you, get to your feet now! We're leaving this place."

"What makes you think we're going to go with you?" I asked.

His response was to come grab both of us by the arm and pull us from the apartment. Fight, as we may try, it proved useless against his grip. Forced to follow, we came back to a place I knew too well. We arrived at Crossroads.

Az slammed the door open, throwing Deanna and me down at the back of the bar. He turned and went upstairs to the apartment. I knew this was a place of safety for Az. What I didn't know is what would come next for Deanna and me.

A cheap over the door mirror is what Az had in his hands as he came back down the stairs. It looked like something I had years ago in my college dorm room. He placed it in front of the emergency exit where his former gateway had been. As if it knew where it was, it began to glow that familiar indigo. Az's third arm came out as he turned back to us. I knew then what our fate would be.

CHAPTER 25: CLAY

THE TRAIN RIDE FROM RICHMOND TO D.C. HAD BEEN quiet and so far not a single person had recognized John Tyler in disguise. I'd made the transfer over to the Chicago bound train which would take me through Pittsburgh, then Cleveland before taking me home.

Now that I was in the privacy of a sleeper car I could let my guard down a little. The sleeper car had private rooms with two benches that faced one another and could fold out into a bed. It also had a private bathroom. The only reason one would need to leave its comfort is for food. For that, you'd have to head to the dining car. I wasn't hungry at the moment. All I wanted to do was get a few hours of sleep. I didn't know what was ahead of me in Chicago, but I could guess it wouldn't be a pleasant homecoming. This was likely the last moments of peace I would have for the foreseeable future.

I watched the burnt out factories and countryside pass by outside my window. It reminded me of a song my father used to sing by Arlo Guthrie, "Hobo's Lullaby." I began singing it softly to myself as I rested my head against the window. Soon this lonely hobo was back to the world of dreams.

This sleep brought dreams, but no rest for me; at least not the mental kind I was in desperate need of. I found myself again back on the shore of Lake Michigan. This time, though, there was no Ava or Arianna. This time there was only myself and the emptiness of the lake. The wave came again, as it had the times before. Swept again into the depths of the freezing cold lake I'd become so accustomed to, now I no longer fought against it. I let the water wrap its cold hands around me and pull me into its depths.

When I surfaced from the river I took a deep breath as I pulled myself onto the muddy riverbank. As I got to my feet to push forward to the temple all I could think was that there had to be a better way of getting to this place.

Approaching the temple entrances I looked up noticing something I'd not seen on my last two visits. The urns were now burning with indigo flames. I could've sworn that before the flames were your typical orange or reddish. No time to worry about that now; in I went.

Through the long corridors and several doorways, I made my way to the chamber at the center of the temple. The pool I'd been pushed into was no longer visible. Rather, the table from my first visit was back in its place. Also back was Dr. Dawood, patiently waiting at the table.

The table was set with a large carafe and two earthenware cups. Looking at me then to the grandfather clock in the corner of the room, he said, "I was wondering if you'd find your way back here, Clayton. I'm glad to see you. But… I must bring you some unfortunate news."

Looking behind Dr. Dawood I saw Arianna still stretched out on the cot where I'd left her. "Is she okay?" I asked. "I didn't know what to do. She ended up here with me the last time I was pulled through. I'm still trying to figure out if this is nothing more than a dream or if there is a connection here to reality. This is a dream… isn't it, doc?"

"No. This isn't a dream. Yes, you're able to come to this place while the body of John Tyler sleeps. This place is as real as any place you've ever been before. Miss Stone, that you see over there, she too is as real as the person you met in Chicago. There have been some unfortunate happenings, Clayton." Motioning to the chair across from him, he added, "Please, take a seat."

Taking the chair I moved it so that I could see both Arianna and the doctor. "When you found Miss Stone she was in a state between her human existence and her existence in this world. Something happened when you brought her here. The temple has offered her some protection, but only in this realm. Out there where her flesh and blood were, she remained at risk. I found her here and have watched her since. About an hour ago she transitioned to existing only in this realm."

"Meaning what doc? That she's dead in the living world?"

"I'm afraid that is the case, Clayton. She temporarily disappeared from my view. Only a few moments at the most. Then she reappeared and I could see that all her essence came with her. I've no doubt that Azrael has had a hand in this. I can feel his panic, and he is moving faster towards whatever his end goal has been."

As the reality of Arianna's death sank in, a suffocating tightness settled over me, crushing my chest with the weight of her loss. With trembling hands, I reached out, grasping for something—anything—to anchor me in this swirling sea of grief. "I'm going to fucking kill him! I don't know how, but I'm going to do it."

Dr. Dawood scolded me. "You must control your anger. It will serve neither you nor Miss Stone any good."

"Control my anger?" I was seeing red. "Control my fucking anger? This son-of-a-bitch takes Ava, takes me, now he takes Arianna and I'm supposed to not be angry about it? I told you doc, I'm going to find him and I am going to kill him. I'll not let him do this to anyone else. Poor Arianna, her only involvement was writing down my memories in case Az were to wipe them out. She had nothing to do with anything else I did or planned. And now… now she's dead and who knows what else he might do to her. You tell me not to be angry… you might as well tell the wind not to blow!"

The light in the temple began flickering, an indigo light forming in the mirror at the back of the grandfather clock. "Clayton," yelled Dr. Dawood, "get a hold of your emotions. You're going to lead Azrael right to us. We're in no place to face him yet. Please! I ask you again, calm your emotions. Once you are calm we will talk about this more. I have things that we must discuss. Things you must learn. You'll have your chance at Azrael; this I promise you. Please, though, if you're to give yourself a fighting chance against him, you must calm your emotions."

Taking a few deep breaths I walked over to Arianna. As I knelt down beside her, I took her hand in mine. "For you and Ava." I let my anger subside for the moment. As I did, the indigo light in the grandfather clock receded as well.

"Thank you, Clayton. Take a few more moments and when you're ready we'll discuss many things. Starting with why I had to leave the Appalachian House the way that I did."

I walked around the room for another minute or two taking in all that was happening as I did. Could this be nothing more than another dream? After all, the last time this had happened I still woke back up in the world of the living. This was my subconscious getting the better of me again. The only choice I could see was to run down this dream and see where it led me.

"Okay, let's get this moving doc. I have no idea how long I'll stay in this dream and I'm sure there's more I need to take away from it."

"Clayton, I don't know if I can be any clearer about this. This is no dream. You will come to appreciate that soon enough."

Dr. Dawood gestured towards a door at the back of the chamber. As I walked through the doorway I could see it was a hallway of sorts. The ground was heading downward at a slight slope. I could only see around thirty to forty yards ahead where it came to a corner. The walls, much like the rest of the temple, were decorated in Egyptian hieroglyphics and paintings. I didn't understand any of it and the pace of Dr. Dawood on my heels told me that now was not the time to be asking him about it.

When we reached the end of the hallway, it turned the corner and stretched into another hallway. This one was shorter and had a set of stairs leading even further below ground level. "Where exactly are we headed doc?"

"For what I must show you we must have as much silence as possible. We're almost there, it's just down these stairs and one more hallway after that."

When we got close to the end of the last hallway I saw a pair of golden doors. The handles were adorned with the Eye of Horus and Eye of Ra on respective sides.

Dr. Dawood pulled the great doors open. Inside was the round pool of steaming water I'd fallen into. How had it gotten here if it was in the main temple before? I saw no lifts or holes in the floor where it could have been raised or lowered.

As we entered I didn't see any source of light inside. There was only the luminous glow glimmering in from the hallway.

"What exactly is it that we're doing down here and how much safer is this than upstairs? This still feels very much like a dream to me."

Dr. Dawood seated himself on the edge of the pool and motioned for me to enter and sit next to him. I walked over and as I got closer to the pool I could feel that it was in fact not heat making the water steam. It was freezing cold and the steam was a reaction to the desert air. This couldn't have been the pool I was shoved into before. That water had been warm like a freshly drawn bath.

"Clayton, there are many things you will come to understand in a very short time. As I mentioned to you upstairs, you'll need to be able to control your anger. There's a metamorphosis that you must undergo. How you respond with your anger is going to determine a great deal of what is to come. Not just for you, but for all of us."

He reached his hand down into the icy waters of the pool and without warning splashed a handful of it up into my eyes.

"Hey, what the fuck doc? Was that really necessary?"

"Your anger Clayton. Control it. Stop letting it control you. What you must go through is going to cause much more anger than a splash of water in the face. Now focus for me. Focus on all the things that make you angry. Find all that you remember from childhood to this moment."

He slid closer to me and placed his hands on my shoulder. "Close your eyes and concentrate on those memories. Feel how you felt in those moments when you'd been wronged in life and in death."

I was hesitant to close my eyes, but I did as I was instructed. No sooner had my eyes shut than I heard the great golden doors slam shut. The noise alone, never mind my curiosity, drove my eyes to open again.

The room was dark except for the indigo flow from the cold pool waters. "Clayton," Dr. Dawood said, still seated beside me, "you can trust me. I'm here to help you, not harm you." I closed my eyes again. "Now focus on what I've told you."

It was rather vague to have to think about everything that had ever made me angry in my life. There are always the big things that you remember and hold with you. For me, that was my parents being killed before their time. Ava, killed before her time. My own untimely death, and now the same for Arianna.

I could feel the anger from those memories. It was like a swelling wedge in my stomach. Then came more. My anger at the way Uncle Joe had treated my father, treated everyone in the family. The way he'd acted at my parents' funeral. The fact that he tried to take what money I had after I died. That was it; the floodgates flung open. All my anger came roiling to the surface.

Dr. Dawood must have seen it. He placed a reassuring hand on my shoulder. "Do you feel it all now?" he asked. "Do you have all those memories?"

"Yes. I think so."

"Good. Now you need to let them go. Every last one of them."

"And how exactly am I supposed to do that, doc?"

"Forgiveness, Clayton. Forgive all the misgivings you've felt in your life. Forgive those you've placed the blame on. Most of all, forgive yourself for the blame you've laid upon your own back." Dr. Dawood took my hand and placed it in the cold water. "Forgive Clay. Let the waters wash your anger away."

I began to forgive everything and everyone that I could remember. Each time I forgave something or someone I could feel the weight on my back getting lighter. At last, there was myself to forgive. I grew hesitant again. Could I forgive myself for the life I lived? Yes. I had to. This was the only way I could help Ava and Arianna.

Taking a deep breath, I dug into the depths of my feelings and forgave myself, letting go of the last of my anger, but it wasn't easy. The memories of my mistakes, my failures, the times I let people down—they clawed at me, refusing to let go. The shame, the guilt, they were like chains wrapped tightly around my soul.

Images of Ava flashed before me. The times I wasn't there for her. The moments I let my anger get the best of me, hurting those I loved. I felt the sting of those moments, the sharp pain of regret. How could I forgive myself for those?

I felt a tear slip down my cheek and into the water. "I'm sorry," I whispered, my voice cracking. "I'm so sorry, Ava. For everything."

The water seemed to respond, the indigo light pulsing gently. It was as if it was urging me on, pushing me to confront these emotions. I took another deep breath, diving deeper into my memories, into the darkest parts of myself.

"I forgive myself," I said, my voice growing stronger with each word. "I forgive myself for my mistakes, for my anger, for my failures. I forgive myself for not being perfect. For not always being there. I forgive myself for being human."

The words felt like a release, a letting go of the weight I'd been carrying for so long. The chains of shame and guilt began to dissolve, the anger dissipated into the cold waters.

The weight was gone. The room, silent.

Opening my eyes I still saw the indigo light of the water visible. I looked for Dr. Dawood but he was no longer sitting next to me. I rose to my feet and turned. "Dr. Dawood, where did you go? I've let my anger go. What do I need to do now?"

When I spun back around there was Dr. Dawood, both of his hands pushing towards me. He grabbed on to me and pulled me towards the pool. "Now, Clayton, you must die again."

We fell through the water, and I woke back on the train heading to Chicago. I wasn't alone in my room, Dr. Dawood was standing in front of me. In his hand was a curved blade with a golden pommel. I knew what he was about to do but my hands couldn't move fast enough. The blade slipped into my chest, causing a sharp burning pain. It was ripping through skin and muscle right down into my beating heart. Before my heart stopped I looked up at Dr. Dawood, saying my last words as John Tyler: "*Why?*"

CHAPTER 26: AVA

AZ GRABBED DEANNA WITH ONE HAND AND ME WITH the other. The third arm was there dangling between us. Lucky for both of us, it had yet to touch us. "You want your precious Clayton so much? Now you're going to get a chance to see what's become of him." He pulled us through the gateway.

For a moment, my eyes were blind from the bright indigo light. Deanna was trying to fight Az, but it was a fight she wasn't winning. When I was able to open my eyes again I thought I'd gone blind. My eyes were open, yet there was nothing but pitch blackness.

Looking to the left, I saw nothing. Then to the right and down, still nothing. It wasn't until I glanced up that I could see the faint indigo glow coming from Az's eyes. As my own eyes began to adjust I could faintly make out Deanna still in the grips of Az's other hand.

Though I couldn't see motion or things moving by, I did have a sense we were moving and there was other movement in the darkness. Where was it that he was taking us? He'd said Clay was gone once he came through the gateway. How was it he was going to take me to him? Did that mean he was going to turn me to dust as he had Hamilton?

We traveled on in the darkness for a time. Then out in the distance I saw what looked like hundreds of stars, but they weren't stars. They were the eyes of hundreds of people.

I couldn't stand having Az drag me around like this. I pulled back against his hold on me and made my best attempt at breaking free. "Go ahead little sheep," he growled. "Run off now and you'll be lost and alone for all time. Even though you see the others beyond here, you don't know the way."

"Where are we, Az? Who are those people?"

"Miss Sanderson, you'll find soon enough that you know many of them. Having helped train all these people to forget. It was you who saw to it that I was able to deliver them here. And now, you'll join them in their fate."

He threw Deanna and me down on what felt like the ground, though I could not be sure of the surface in this darkness. It was cold like concrete against my skin, but there were also vibrations coming from it that I'd never experienced from the ground before. A hand reached down and pulled at my arm. Out of self preservation I pulled back in fear.

"It's all right Miss Ava. I'm not gonna let this fool hurt you."

"Mr. Devo. You surprise me again. You shouldn't have survived, let alone found my… collection. Oh well, you can join them as well."

Grayson moved in front of me and began pushing me further back into the crowd of lost souls. He paid no further attention to Az. Looking back over my shoulder, I could no longer see the glow of Az's eyes in the darkness. It hit me that I'd not come alone with Az. "Wait!" I shouted. "Deanna's here with me, we can't leave her."

"It's okay dear. I'm right here with you. I can't see who in this awful darkness, but some kind soul has my arm and is leading me along behind you."

Turning back to Grayson, I asked, "Where the hell are we?"

"Your guess is as good as mine. When he tossed me through the mirror I landed hard. I sat there in the darkness for a while. I was confused as to where I was, but once I got my senses back I picked a direction and started walking. It felt like I'd been walking for days when I started to see lights off in the distance. I'm sure you know now that they weren't lights, they were these folks' eyes. Well, anyways, I got to them and they started walking away from me. I followed, not wanting to be left in the darkness. The rest of it, well you're going to have to see that for yourself Miss Ava."

"I would love to see anything." I wanted to see that this was Grayson. His voice sounded the same, but there was something in the way he spoke now. Something had changed. The only way I would know it was him for sure was to see him in some form of light. My thoughts were interrupted when another hand grabbed on to me. It felt more delicate, more feminine of a grip. "Hello, Ava."

"I recognize your voice, but I don't know who you are. I'm sorry I can't see you."

"It may help you if I start yelling and telling you to get the fuck out of my apartment, lady." She gave a light laugh.

"Oh my god! Krissy? Is that really you? But no. You… you made it through to the place of light. Az said that you'd been freed from your guilt and you'd moved on there."

"He moved me alright. Along with many others. It was no place of light, Ava. He left us alone in this darkness to wander. But, it isn't as dark as he thinks."

I heard a loud *BANG BANG BANG,* as if someone were striking the knocker of a very large door. A small crease of light came first and then began to grow until it was the width of a person. It started at the ground and the light continued up into an infinite space. Though I tried, I couldn't see where the light ended.

One by one I watched a line of people form and begin to enter into the light. I stood back watching until it was Grayson and I remaining. "It's okay, Miss Ava. You can come back out if you go in. It's not any final place for us to stay. I had a quick look before we heard you coming and we came back out just fine."

He placed his arm across my back and guided me forward. Stepping through we went from this immense darkness into a world full of light and… sunshine?

It took a moment for my eyes to adjust. I hadn't seen real sunshine in many years. Turning back I expected to see a massive door, yet it was nothing more than a crack in a large rock, maybe nine to ten feet in height. I could've stopped and examined it closer, but there was sunshine.

Everything here had been washed clean of that dirty indigo light that stained the realm we'd been in. As we walked further away from the rocks I could see we were in a valley. There was a stream we passed that had the clearest and coolest water I'd ever seen or felt. Scattered trees jutted up along the hilltops and stream and just beyond them I could see a white stone structure rising up from the earth.

It looked small at first, but that was because I'd only been seeing the top of the building. As we rose to the top of the valley I saw across from us a twin valley. There at the base was a beautiful Greek or Roman temple made in the finest white marble. The nearer we got the larger it became.

I was looking around at the people we'd come through with. I saw faces I recognized aside from Krissy. And I confirmed the voice I heard was Grayson, but still, I couldn't help seeing that something had changed in him. It did make me sad to see all these people and know that it was partly my fault they'd ended up back in that darkness.

The temple had many people there. Most sitting about and talking. When they first saw Deanna, Grayson, and me approaching, they became instantly quiet. *Oh god, what are we walking into now? Have we gone from strange to stranger?*

There were hushed whispers as their eyes set on Grayson. Then at last we reached the temple entrance where a young lady stood sentry. She took Grayson's hand. "She will be most glad to see you here," she said. The girl then moved on to Deanna, taking her hand. "She will be glad to see you, but most sad that it was here you've landed." The girl said nothing to me, she only turned and waved for us to follow her. The three of us were looking back and forth to one another, not having the slightest inclination of what this girl was speaking about.

After being escorted through several doors and chambers of the temple we came to its center. It was a chamber no larger than forty feet by forty feet and in the center stood a round, crystal clear pool. "Please wait here," the girl instructed us as she scurried out another doorway.

"Where do you think we are? Did we all end up in the light place or is this another one of Az's mindfucks?" I asked.

"There's something different about this place, that's for sure. I think..." Grayson was suddenly speechless in response to this woman who entered from the door the girl had exited. "I... I..." Grayson fell to his knees and the woman came over and embraced him.

"Okay. Okay. Get to your feet Grayson." The woman looked over to Deanna. "My sweet niece. I'd hoped to never see you here. But, I'm glad to see you lived to an older age. I suspect if you are here that means Azrael got to you and something has happened."

Deanna wiped the tears from her eyes. "Aunt Elizabeth… so this is where you've been all these years. I was right to suspect it'd been Azrael you'd been chasing. Oh Auntie."

"Aunt?" Grayson said with the same amount of confusion I was feeling. His eyes were darting back and forth from Deanna to Elizabeth. "I knew she looked familiar. Well, I'll be a… She's your niece. I'm sorry Elizabeth. I should've done more to protect all of them from this, from him."

"It's okay Grayson. We're all here now. I had expected to see someone coming not long ago. I knew when the world shook as it did that someone else had crossed through Az's gateway. I half expected to see you, but instead, we got him." Elizabeth pointed to a man sitting facing away from the pool.

My heart dropped to my feet. Could it really be him? After all this time he'd landed here. I ran over, placing my hand on his shoulder. "Clay?" He turned around and I found myself mistaken. This wasn't Clay.

"Who?" he asked in the harshest of tones. "Lady, who the hell are you and please get your damn hand off of me!" I stumbled back into Elizabeth.

"Not who you thought, I see. He's not the friendliest person. What I need to know now is, who is it that you thought he was?" Elizabeth looked around at all of us. "And I need to know what the hell has happened out there."

CHAPTER 27: ARIANNA

I WAS NOTHING. I WAS EVERYTHING. LOST IN A PLACE absent of space and time, a sense of disconnection washed over me like a tidal wave. Memories of my life didn't flash before my eyes; rather, they engulfed me all at once. Every hope, every fear, every ounce of love and pain, all there in a single moment, followed by empty darkness. I felt myself floating in the nothingness, a mere whisper in the void.

Above me, tall and narrow mirrors began to fall one by one, forming a barrier around me. My brain screamed for movement, but I couldn't distinguish one body part from another. The mirrors continued to fall, closing in around me.

Looking into the mirrors I didn't see myself, only other mirrors. The gaps between the mirrors tightened. I could hear each one as it connected with the one beside it. Click… Click… Click. The mirrors were locking into place.

As the mirrors connected, enclosing me tightly, I felt like a caterpillar trapped inside a glass cocoon. There was a faint clicking sound that was growing louder, like the stress of fracturing glass under too much weight.

What started as small cracks had now expanded, spider webbing through the mirrors, until the glass shattered all around me. I jumped up, gasping for breath. I searched my surroundings, questioning whether it had all been a dream. As the haze lifted, I found myself back in the temple where Clay had left me, the cot still beneath me. Clay hadn't returned, and Anubis was nowhere to be found.

I walked over to the table in the middle of the room and took a seat, trying to make sense of what in the hell I'd experienced. First, the room where I saw Deanna, Hamilton, Clay's fiancé, and the other man. Then, Azrael—his presence still haunted me. The sensation of glass tearing through me felt agonizingly real, yet my skin bore no wounds. It had to be a twisted dream.

"Hello again Miss Stone." I heard the voice booming from behind me. It was Anubis, and he was wiping his hands as he walked back through one of the darkened doorways. He tilted his head, looking me over. "This is most unfortunate. I'd thought it was the case and now I've no doubt it is."

"What... what's unfortunate?" I asked, my voice trembling with uncertainty.

"I'm sorry, Miss Stone, but it seems your time in the world you knew has come to an end. You've transitioned fully to this realm. Your essence has departed from the body it once inhabited."

"Ironic, isn't it? After spending years communicating with and encountering the deceased, now I find myself among their ranks. But, where are the others? Where's Deanna? Eddie? Clay? It's as if they've vanished."

"Clay did come back, Arianna, but I'm afraid you've just missed him. He had to go on… a journey. One I hope to see him return from before too long."

"Where's everyone else that I knew? Shouldn't I be greeted by all or at least some of my loved ones that I've lost over the years? It looks to me that you are the only person in my afterlife."

"Miss Stone, there's no afterlife as you may have imagined. Life is continuous, like chapters in a book. Your experiences here are but a single chapter in a much larger story. It may take time, but you'll recall the different chapters that have shaped your journey. I assure you, I'll provide more details soon. My hope is to share this with the both of you."

"With us both?"

"Yes. I have my hopes that Clayton will return to us in a matter of time. When I share this history, this story, I would like it to be with both of you. It makes it much easier when one can support the other through the change.

"For now, you're free to roam the temple and beyond. As I've told you before, this is a safe place. It takes some time to get used to the transition, but the exhaustion will wear off. Rest when you're able to. I've other things I must see to. I'll return before long, Miss Stone, and we can talk more."

Anubis nodded before departing through the doorway, leaving me with a whirlwind of unanswered questions and the profound exhaustion of transition to the afterlife. As I stood alone in the temple's solemn silence, I couldn't shake the feeling of uncertainty gnawing at my core. Yet, amidst the shadows, a glimmer of hope flickered—the hope of reuniting with Clay and uncovering the secrets awaiting us in this enigmatic realm.

CHAPTER 28: AVA

AFTER ELIZABETH CAUGHT UP WITH GRAYSON AND Deanna, she pulled me into a small chamber within the temple. Inside, a statue of a Greek or Roman goddess stood solemnly, its identity blending amidst the shared characteristics of both ancient civilizations.

For what felt like an eternity, I stood in silence before Elizabeth's voice pierced the air, breaking the stillness of the chamber. "Her name is Persephone," Elizabeth said. "She's the Greek goddess of the underworld. This temple we are in belongs to her." The door to the chamber creaked shut, sealing us within its confines.

Looking around the chamber, I said, "My apologies if I've forgotten to say hello to her. I must have missed her when I walked in."

"Grayson's right, you're a zesty one. You may come to meet Persephone if we're able to stay here long enough. I think by now you have an idea of who I am."

"I might. I suspect you're *the* Elizabeth. The one who escaped Az and was the first to cross through the gateway alone. Though, some things aren't adding up for me; or at least not to the accounts that Az and Grayson provided me. Let's see, if I recall Az's version you were erased from all existence. If we go by Grayson's version you should be missing the lower half of your body."

She laughed. "Is that what Azrael told you? He erased me from existence? My, he has gotten quite the imagination since I've last seen him. As for what Grayson told you, it wasn't a lie. Something did happen when Azrael's third hand touched me. Once I landed in this place, however, it was undone and I was whole again. Now, enough about me. I've heard a tale that you were working with that beast. Is that correct? What would have ever led you to believe he could be trusted?"

"We all aren't you, Elizabeth. I was doing the best that I could to survive the circumstances in front of me. Our stories are a little different."

"It may be they are. It may also be that some circumstances aren't so different, Ava. We were both ripped from our lives well before our time was up. It may be that I was also scared and naive when I first entered purgatory and did what I must in order to survive. You're not the first one that he's tricked, Ava."

Was she implying that she'd worked for Az? I couldn't hide the look of confusion from my face. None of this added up to what Grayson had shared with me. "So how is it then that you didn't know about the gateway until later on in your years in Purgatory? How is it even possible that you got away from doing work with Az? He'd left me with no choice to continue on, that is until he disappeared after Clay was gone."

"Grayson knows what I shared with him and that is only part of the story. In regards to the gateway, Azrael never confided in me the way he did with you. Maybe he learned from what happened with me and decided that he needed to show you more trust. Or, it could be he knew by showing you and telling his version of my tale that it would keep you scared enough not to try and access it. I can't really speak to how he thinks. If I knew that none of us would be here.

"If you don't mind, I'd like to get back to understanding what has happened recently. Outside, the man you saw, you seemed to recognize him for a moment. Yet, when he turned I could see the look of disappointment that washed over you. I take it he wasn't whom you expected. He arrived the same day that we felt the world shake, which means he is in some way connected to your story. I, along with many others here, have tried speaking with him, but that man is so unpleasant. He either grunts or gets up and walks away whenever anyone tries to talk to him."

"I don't know that man. I thought it was my fiancé. Clay had ended up in this existence and had not long after fallen onto Az's shit list. Az, at one point, even portrayed himself as you in a ruse to gain Clay's trust." Elizabeth's lips formed into a sour pout. "Clay became aware about the gateway from Az's need to brag about it and later learning your story from Grayson. He became obsessed with getting himself and me back to the world of the living. That's when we found each other. We didn't have a lot of time together as I'd been working with Az and knew about the deception. It all came to a boil when I was telling Clay he needed to lay low. I'd been trying to learn more about what Az was doing. Clay wouldn't back off and Az cornered us. That's when I learned both Clay and I had been taken by Az before our time. He took me because he said he needed me to help with the work of aiding the new arrivals. He said it was what I was meant to do. He took Clay, because I refused to let go of my memories and Clay was a key to helping me keep those. Az thought if he could rid me of Clay, the memories would soon follow. I would be his."

"I see. That's quite the story. What, may I ask, happened that caused the world to shake the way it did?"

"During the confrontation Az came after Clay. He told him he was going to rid him from existence one way or another. Clay dove through the gateway. Though as he was crossing I saw Az touch the bottom of his foot with his third arm. I suspected that Az, in that moment, had done what he intended to—erased Clay from all existence. That was the same moment the world shook and the sky became dark as night."

"I wonder then who it is that our guest might be. By all accounts, it should've been your Clay that came to us. Somehow, this discouraging man has come to us instead. What I do know of our guest is that his name is John Tyler. I don't know how he arrived here but I found him wandering in the darkness not long after the disturbance. Beyond that, I don't know much more."

"How do you even know his name if he hasn't spoken to anyone?"

"There are some things that I've learned in my many years here that I don't wish to share. It was a gift, I guess you could say, that I didn't ask for; it was given to me by Azrael. I'd rather not think about it any more if it's all the same."

Elizabeth was visibly shaken by whatever it was she was remembering. I thought it best not to push much more on the issue. I was feeling lucky that whatever Az had done to her, he'd not done the same to me.

Elizabeth motioned for me to follow her back outside. "It is time that both you and I have a nice long chat with Mr. Tyler. We need to know what he knows or what he remembers."

"Do you think he'll even talk to us?" I asked. "He seemed so cold when I approached him earlier."

"My dear, we're not going to leave him the opportunity to refuse us."

CHAPTER 29: CLAY

I SHOULD'VE BEEN PISSED. DR. DAWOOD HAD JUST shoved a knife through my chest. For one reason or another I felt no anger over the situation. I understood that it had to happen. I wasn't sure why it had to happen, I only knew it did.

Death the second time was still a rather painful experience, but after the pain of this death subsided there came a new experience. The first time I died there was a never ending exhaustion and the experience of waking up in Purgatory. This time I'd faded into the darkness again, but there were no flashbacks of the death or the life I'd known. It could've been because I'd only known it for such a short time.

In this death, after a short visit to the darkness I found myself again sitting on a Chicago bound train. There at my feet I saw my dead body. Well, in reality it was the dead body of John Tyler that I'd borrowed for a time. There should be a sense of guilt about his death, but after all I'd learned from Emilia it seemed a proper ending for this shitbag.

She and the kids would have the support they needed and could live lives without wanting for anything. I could only hope that the money they were about to come into wouldn't ruin who they were as people. Having more creatures like John or my Uncle Joe in the world was never a good thing.

I sat for a few moments examining John's body. The knife that Dr. Dawood had used to stab me was gone. Good luck to the cops trying to find the murder weapon in this case. For a moment I wondered if all unsolved murders were in fact caused by supernatural events like this. Looking back at John, most of the blood that spilled was now coagulating, though the wound still had a small rivulet of blood flowing. The majority pooled up on the floor and ran towards the door and the train car's hallway. I suspected it wouldn't be long before one of the porters saw the goo seeping from under the door and came in to investigate.

I was still feeling no anger. Whatever Dr. Dawood had done before he decided to knife me was working. In fact, it wasn't just a lack of anger I was experiencing. All my typical nervousness and anxiety were absent. I was feeling only what I could explain as extreme contentment. I dare say it was bordering on a feeling of euphoria. It's kind of like that feeling after you've had a good "ahhhh" type of sigh.

The train was outside of Pittsburgh when one of the porters finally entered the room. There was a lot of confusion and shouting amongst the three porters as they did their best to figure out this situation. Most of their concern was how to keep the other passengers from seeing what had happened and preventing mass alarm on the train.

When the train came to a halt in Pittsburgh the conductor had contacted the local police to investigate. I sat watching and listening to them hypothesize about what had happened to this man. When they identified the body as John Tyler, a whole new level of chaos was introduced. They knew that this was going to draw the media in like flies to shit. Everything they did from here on out would be placed under a magnifying glass.

It didn't take long for me to grow bored watching and sitting on the train. In my first death I'd never left the confines of Chicago. I still had to get back there, but this was a chance for me to explore more of the world beyond the living.

Stepping off of the train I looked to the sky and noticed that unlike what I'd seen in Chicago, there was no indigo color to the sky here. It looked… normal. The sun was shining and the sky was a beautiful blue. It was a nice day so I decided to go for a walk.

The rest of the afternoon I walked and as the sun came down I found myself on the outskirts of a small farm. In a way, it reminded me of Great Aunt Tilda's place back in Sparta. It was getting late, and I thought it would make a nice place to get sleep before continuing on my journey west.

Approaching the barn I found the door open wide enough for me to squeeze myself through. It was dark inside but I could hear the distant neighing of two horses down the far end. I found a ladder not more than ten steps from the door, and as I had hoped, the top loft was covered with loose straw and fresh bales of hay. A perfect bed for the night.

Settling myself in for the night I was still basking in this delightful feeling of contentment. I closed my eyes and drifted off. I should've learned my lesson by now; sleep is never normal and full of rest when I need it to be. I went from my dream back to the temple, though I no longer got there through the lake. This time I woke next to the same pool that Dr. Dawood had shoved me through.

Wandering back through the hallways approaching the center of the temple, I could hear two voices talking. I stayed back from the door for a moment listening to the conversation. It was Dr. Dawood and a woman's voice I could hear. It was Arianna; she'd woken up.

Turning the corner of the doorway, before I could say a word, Dr. Dawood spoke up, "We're glad to see you back, Clayton. Come sit, we have much to talk about."

CHAPTER 30: JOHN

I'D BEEN STUCK IN THIS FUCKING HIPPY COMMUNE FOR what felt like ages. I knew it wasn't that long, but with all their happy-go-lucky bullshit, it sure as hell felt like it. I should've stayed in the darkness when that woman started calling out to me.

Anytime a person knows your name and you don't know theirs, it's always a reason to be wary. After having someone strangle you and then passing through some mystical fucking mirror I thought, what the fuck? How bad could it have gotten from there? A whole lot worse…

She led me through the darkness to this Roman bathhouse or whatever it is. When we got here she put me in this room with a small pool and proceeded to ask a ton of questions about some man named Azrael. I said to her, "I have no fucking clue who you're talking about lady. You just found me wandering around in… in whatever the fuck that was. Do I look like I've been out chatting it up with your friend?" That didn't dissuade her.

Day and night she and the others kept coming back with more questions about this gateway, this guy Azrael, and some shit about Purgatory. I made it a rule in my life to never repeat myself. Either people are smart enough to listen the first time or they can fuck off. I'd had enough of this Elizabeth woman and her little friends coming to ask questions that I had no answers to. It wasn't my problem they couldn't accept it. After three days of that I stopped talking with them all together.

After a few days of the silent treatment, they stopped coming. Once they let me out of the room, I wasted no time in trying to escape the Heaven's Gate clan. I walked for hours in what I thought was a straight line, only to end up back at the goddamn temple. The whole situation was absurd; it felt like I was walking in circles, with the temple appearing no matter which direction I went. The freaks on the farm seemed to find it amusing.

A group called the searchers roamed the area, venturing into the darkness to find others left behind. I tried to shadow them, hoping to learn their secret exit route. But no matter how hard I tried, the guards always stopped me from getting too close, thwarting my attempts to uncover their escape route.

I decided that a better approach would be for me to lay low for a time and hope they would soon forget about me. While I waited for things to calm down I spent the days sitting at the edge of the temple staring off to the horizon. Then this morning there was a commotion and all the searchers got into a huff and ran off. When they got back to the temple they had three new people with them.

I figured they were more of the lost who ended up here. However, it appears that one of them thought she recognized me. She came up behind me calling me Clay. I had no clue who the hell Clay was or who this ginger bitch was and told her as much.

The head cult leader, Elizabeth, seemed to take notice of the ginger bitch recognizing me and ushered her away. Looks like she might get the same type of welcoming I'd received. With all the attention on the newcomers I thought this might be my chance to go. I was getting up when I saw Elizabeth and this other woman approaching me. *Great, now I'm gonna have two of them up my ass.* I was beginning to feel like I was back home with my wife, Emilia.

Funny, I hadn't thought about Emilia since I'd been here. I wondered how she was celebrating my death. Oh wouldn't that bitch be in for a surprise when she found out all my money had been left to Jasmine.

It had been a sex and drug infused weekend in Vegas. None of the cheapshit either. I'm talking about a quarter kilo of the finest Colombian blow. We were having ourselves one hell of a party when the idea came to me.

Emilia bored me from the moment the honeymoon was over. But, I wanted to avoid too much media attention around my other… tastes. Keeping a reliable wife around helped with those optics. That was ten fucking years ago.

I started fucking Jasmine about four years ago and she became everything to me that Emilia wasn't. She helped me keep the excitement in my life that I so needed. She pushed me to the end and could keep me dangling by the short hairs. I thrived off of that shit.

I'd finally found my balls again and gotten to the point I was ready to leave Emilia, but damn what would the media say? I'd already purchased a ring for Jasmine, but she said she wouldn't take it until she had something more concrete. She wanted to see divorce papers.

It would take time, but I had another way to prove I was serious. I called my lawyer, Oliver St. Cyr; he was one of the only people that knew all the shit I'd gotten myself involved with. I told him to get the divorce papers together but not to file them yet. The second thing I told him was to remove Emilia and the kids from my will and to replace them with Jasmine as my sole beneficiary. He asked me if I'd lost my fucking mind at which point I reminded him that I was paying him to do a fucking job and not question my decisions. An hour later I had an updated version of my will faxed to me in Vegas.

I showed it to Jasmine, and she extended her hand. I slipped the ring onto her finger. We partied and fucked the rest of the night away. I hadn't realized how hard I'd partied that weekend until I got home.

I was still zooming from the last few lines I snuffed down on my private jet on the way back to Richmond. When I got home Emilia knew where I'd been, and she was on a fucking rampage. I wasn't in the mood for her shit and the drugs had gotten me in a foul mood.

She yelled at me, telling me how worthless I was. To prove to her how worthless I was I went into the bathroom, grabbed a handful of pills from our medicine cabinet and swallowed them down with a bottle of vodka.

I'm not sure what the fuck I was thinking. I like my life and had no reason to want it over—too much blow, what can I say. The next thing I knew I was zooming down the highway with a paramedic trying to get me to chug a bottle of ipecac. After that I was falling in and out of consciousness. Then I woke up to some tall fucker strangling me with my belt and that crazy mirror shit. What a fucking ride this had been.

My thoughts were abruptly interrupted by the sound of footsteps. With a curse, I snapped out of my daze, realizing I hadn't heard Elizabeth and ginger bitch approaching behind me. Whirling around to face them, I growled, "What the fuck do the two of you want? I'm not really in the mood for your redundant questions again."

CHAPTER 31: AVA

IT WAS ABOUT THE WELCOME I'D EXPECTED FROM HIM. Looking closer at him now I'm not sure how I confused him for Clay. It had to have been the way he was sitting and the way his hair looked. Beyond that John Tyler and Clay were nothing alike.

John has a classical square jaw, dark hair, and good looks that most women would swoon over. If that didn't get them I'm sure those hazel eyes could perform some hypnotic magic on their own. *Jesus, get a hold of yourself Ava.* This wasn't the type of man I was ever attracted to in my life and more importantly, I had Clay.

"Mr. Tyler, you have such a poetic way with your words. Though we would love to hear more of your prose, we've come to find out more about how you ended up out in the darkness. I now know you didn't get here the way I'd originally thought, thanks to Miss Sanders..."

"Can you please just call me Ava? I really can't stand this Miss stuff. Az did the same damn thing. Let's skip the fucking formalities and get to the point."

Elizabeth pulled back with a shocked look on her face as if I had offended her. *For the love of all that is holy, we're dead and she is getting her panties in a wad about my language!* I looked over to John who was sitting there grinning like a child enjoying a show of mischief.

"Now see, that's what I'm talking about! Finally, someone with a spark in this damn place. I'll chat with her and see if she's got anything interesting to say. You left me locked in a room and watched with amusement as I tried to figure a way out of this shithole. I've no time to talk with the likes of you."

John motioned for me to come sit beside him as he shooed Elizabeth away. She was hesitant, looking worriedly between the two of us. "Shoo ya old bird," he yelled at her again.

"Ava, I'll talk with you again later. Mr. Tyler, be nice to her or we'll make sure you get back out into that darkness like you so want."

John and I watched as Elizabeth walked back into the temple. When she entered he turned back to me. "So, Ava, is it?"

"Yes, and you're John. Now that we have that out of the way, can we have a real conversation here?"

"I said I'd talk to you. What makes you think I'm just gonna spill my guts to you? You haven't earned that yet."

I started getting back to my feet. "Okay jackass, I can see you're going to waste my time. I have other things to worry about so have a nice..."

"Whoa. Whoa. Whoa there. Settle down. We can talk, but I'm not doing all the talking. Let's play a game of quid pro quo. I answer one for you, you answer one for me."

I sat back down beside him. "I swear, John, if you start wasting my fucking time I'm done and I'll tell Elizabeth to toss your ass back out there. Now, can you tell me who you are?"

"John Tyler; I thought we had that established already."

"A little more than a name might be helpful. Who were you when you were alive?"

His ego was devastated with that question. "You mean you've never heard of me before? John Tyler, the tech genius? The man who made Appalachia the new Silicon Valley of the east?"

"Oh, so you were the John Tyler who…" I started laughing having added the *were* in there to remind him of his fate. "No, I have no fucking clue who you were."

John put his hands up where his heart should be. "A knife right here, Ava. That's all you need to know at the moment. I'm big in the tech and business world."

"You were," I reminded again.

"I beg your pardon?"

"I said, you were big in the tech and business world. In case you haven't noticed, you're no longer alive."

"So you all keep saying. It could be that I'm in a coma and all of you are nothing more than figments of my imagination. Now it's your turn. How do you know our lovely host Elizabeth?"

"I don't know her. Today's the first time I've met her. She is an acquaintance of one of my travel companions and the aunt of the other. I've only heard stories about her."

"So you don't know her and yet you trust her?"

"I've no reason to doubt my companions that she's a good person. Now, the next question for you. What's the last thing you remember before ending up here?"

"I was in the darkness, the same as you, I suspect."

"No. Before the darkness. Do you remember how you died and what happened around your death? Did you see anyone? Talk to anyone before you went into the darkness?"

"Who's Clay?"

"You haven't answered my question yet."

"I did. You need to be more specific with your questions if you want specific answers. Now, who is Clay?"

"Clay is my fiancé." He sat looking at me like there was more to come. "More specific questions, right," I said, giving my shoulders a shrug.

"Touché. Before I kicked the bucket, I was high as a kite. What I recollect, I can't tell if it's real or just a drug-induced hallucination. Why'd you think I was Clay?"

"It was the way you were sitting and the way your hair looked from behind. I… I thought it was him."

"I did see someone before I died. Again, I don't know if this was real or the drugs. He was a tall man who carried a pocket watch. He knew many things about me but didn't have the courtesy to share anything about himself."

"And right after you died, did you see anyone?"

"Nuh-uh, my turn. So, this Clay, is he stuck in the dark too?"

"I… I don't know. There was something that happened and I'm not sure where he's gone. That's why I was so hopeful that you were him."

"Yes. Just before I got into the darkness I saw a man that looked a little like myself. We were trying to speak to one another but I couldn't hear a fucking thing. It was like we were both mute or something."

"Did you see where he went? Was he with you in the darkness?"

"You're really suckin' at this game, Ava. My turn now." John leaned into my ear, whispering, "Are you as turned on as I am? I bet we could sneak off and have some fun."

I'm most certain he didn't see my right hook as it made contact with his jaw. "And we're done here you fucker."

"Oh, come on," he pleaded, "a little fun could do us both some good."

He kept laughing as I stormed off back to the temple. He was a fucking pig, but he'd dropped some useful info, or at least I hoped it was useful. I needed to find Elizabeth. If Clay'd been lost in the dark this long, who knew what had happened to him.

CHAPTER 32: CLAY

ARIANNA JUMPED UP, RUNNING TO ME. AS HER ARMS wrapped around me, an unfamiliar mix of relief and unease flooded my senses. It was strange, almost foreign, to feel her warmth against me. Questions churned in my mind, doubts clawing at the edges of my consciousness. Did she truly understand the gravity of our situation? Did I?

"I didn't expect him to come after you, let alone bring you here. I would've..."

"Clay, what's done is done. I knew when he got Deanna it wouldn't be long before he came for me."

"He got Deanna too? Man, I created such a mess..."

She put her hand up to my chest. "Stop. This isn't about feeling bad for yourself right now. We," she said, pointing over to Dr. Dawood, "have been talking and there's much to be done. He said you'd be coming back and there are things you and I must learn together. Are you willing to learn with me, Clay? Or are you going to storm off on another personal crusade? Just so you know, the correct answer is 'I'm with you, Arianna.'"

I wasn't sure how much I trusted Dr. Dawood at the moment considering he'd recently shivved me on a Chicago bound train. I needed to have a conversation with him first. I still wasn't mad—my anger was nothing but a fleeting memory. The conversation was needed for a few of my questions to be answered.

"Can I have a few minutes alone with Dr. Dawood?"

Arianna was looking at me as though I was crazy. "Who's Dr. Dawood?" Looking back at the table, she realized, "Oh, you mean Anubis. Is that what he told you his name is?"

"He told me who he claims to be. Dr. Dawood is the name I first knew him by so I am a little more used to that right now. Please, allow me a few moments with him and we can sit down and talk about what might happen next."

"Okay, have at it." She walked back over to the cot and sat down.

Looking towards the table I could see Dr. Dawood patiently waiting for me. The way he was looking at me it was clear he was waiting to see what type of reaction I'd have towards him.

"Did you have to stab me through the heart, doc? I understand the necessity of my death to fix this, but the unexpected knife was a bit much."

He nodded, understanding that I wasn't the sour and angry Clay that had returned to him. "I admit," he said, "it was a little dramatic. It was however what was needed. For you not to return to Azrael it had to be sharp, sudden, and it had to be me to do it so I could claim you. Had anything else happened to you it would've been right back to Azrael and I cannot let that happen. I have two of you here now and with your help we can put an end to this once and for all."

"Wait, so I would've ended up back there? Isn't that what we wanted to happen?"

"Eventually, yes. But not yet. You need more time. Releasing your anger and dying again are only the first steps in a longer journey that must be taken. Your anger may come back again, Clayton. You must remember that until we've come through what lies ahead you must keep that in check."

"I understand doc. As of right now, I feel no anger, only a need for resolution and making sure no more unneeded deaths come from Azrael."

"Death indeed. It's best that we should include Arianna back into the conversation now. This is something that you both need to go through together. Is there anything else you need to ask before we proceed?"

"I may have more questions later, but let's move forward for now. It's late, and I'm tired as hell."

"Very well. Arianna," he called across the room, "will you please come join Clayton and me? It's time for us to begin."

As Arianna approached the table the light of the temple dimmed and Dr. Dawood was no longer Dr. Dawood. Where he had been now was the most beautiful light I'd ever seen, floating above the table.

CHAPTER 33: AVA

"AND WHAT WAS OUR FRIEND ABLE TO TELL YOU?" Elizabeth asked.

"Other than the fact that he's a misogynistic asshole? We can say it's very likely that Az is the one who killed John. I'm not sure of the reason yet. It also sounds like while he was coming into the darkness he came across Clay. John said he wasn't able to speak with him; something about them not being able to talk or hear one another. Do you think that means that Clay is still lost out in the darkness?"

"That's very unlikely. Despite the vastness out there, we would have encountered him by now if he were still lost. Whatever happened to Clay, he's beyond Azrael's reach and the darkness."

"Do you really think it's possible that he made it back to the world of the living?"

"I thought I could do it myself once, but here I am trapped by the darkness and this place given to us by Persephone. Speaking of which, she would like to speak with you."

As Elizabeth said that it had me rethinking my decision to trust her. The expression on my face gave away what I was thinking to her. "Yes, Ava, she's real and wants to talk to you. Do you really doubt the reality of such a person after having met Azrael and knowing what he is? Did you not think others like him existed? There are still many things you don't understand."

"And where exactly am I supposed to find her?"

"The pool in the other chamber."

"So what, am I going to be talking to some kind of magical reflection or something?" Elizabeth grabbed my arm, her nails digging into my skin. It was the first time I'd felt physical pain since my death.

"Hey, watch it!" I shouted at her.

"No, you watch it. I tolerated that bratty attitude of yours out there with John only because I thought it would play well. Anything to encourage him to talk more with you. I'll not tolerate it any longer. You'll need to learn, Ava, that while you may have an intelligent mind and a compassionate heart, how you treat those not in need of your help is just as important as how you treat those that do."

She kept a hold of my arm and dragged me through the doorway to the chamber that had the round pool. It rose up from the ground with beautiful blue and green stonework around the edges. When I got closer I could see a bright orange flame made of the same stonework at the bottom of the pool.

Elizabeth let go of my arm and I started rubbing the area where her nails had gotten into me. What the hell was this bitch's deal? She might be the queen bee around here, but she might try to deliver her messages with a little more tact.

"So here's the pool, what happens…" I turned and caught the back of Elizabeth as she exited the room. No sooner had her foot crossed the threshold of the doorway when a door I'd not seen slammed shut, closing me inside.

"What happens now?" a sweet soothing voice asked from behind me.

Turning, I saw a radiant orange light filling the room. I raised my hand to shield my eyes from its luminance.

"It's okay, Ava. You can look now."

It took a moment for the spots to clear my eyes from the bright light. As they did, I saw a woman standing before me close to my own height. Dark hair curled over her shoulders with tight ringlets resting on her cheeks. She wore a white robe and on it a broach holding the same flame design as the bottom of the pool.

"Step forward," she commanded, "I'm not going to hurt you."

With hesitation and caution, I approached her. "How did you… you were just a ball of light and then you're here…"

"We're all light my dear. What you see now is the way I present myself so those on your level can see me. It's the same for all of us, even you."

I did my best to contain my laughter. "Sorry, last I checked I didn't consist of a bright light. I am… well, was flesh and bone, now I'm not sure what I am. Though I can still feel my flesh and bone."

She flashed a pleasant smile to me; seeming amused by my naivety. "You may call me Persephone."

"Yes, Elizabeth told me your name."

"What is a name my dear? Nothing more than a label to identify. I've had many names, as have you."

"Not so sure about that. As far as I know I've always been called Ava."

"Ava was only the name your parents in this life gave you. It's not the only name you've ever had; nor will it be the last you have. Ava, come sit with me by my pool. We have so much we must discuss."

"Shouldn't we get Elizabeth and the others?"

"No. They're not needed. What must be said and what must be done is for you alone. The others aren't ready to forget yet."

I pushed away from her scrambling back to my feet. "That sounds a lot like something Az would say. He was always so keen on making sure we'd all forget."

With a flash, Persephone disappeared. I turned to the exit to get the others and there she was behind me. She put her hands out towards me. I closed my eyes tight; if this was Az I didn't want to know what was coming next.

Then, a sensation of fire coursed through my body. It was uncomfortable at first, but as it spread, I felt… alive. More alive than ever before. Opening my eyes I saw Persephone aglow in front of me.

"I told you, you've nothing to fear. I'm not Azrael. Forgetting is part of what needs to happen, but not the way he has you forget. He has you forget to control you. We, I, ask you to forget so that you may remember."

CHAPTER 34: ARIANNA

"WHAT EXACTLY DO YOU MEAN WE HAVE TO FORGET TO remember?" I asked.

"Before you entered the existence you just ended you surrendered your memories from the others you've had. You surrendered the knowledge of where we, yourself, Clay, and I, have all come from. The only way that you'll get that knowledge back is to willfully forget the life you came from. You must sacrifice the smaller for the larger."

"I'm not liking the sound of this, Dr. Dawood," Clay said, rising from the table and starting to pace. "You do remember I told you about Azrael and all he kept wanting out of Ava, myself, the others in Purgatory, was to forget. To shed our memories. He said that's how we rid ourselves of guilt and move on to the place of light or the place of darkness. How is this any different?"

"You must be willing to make a sacrifice, Clayton. It's a leap of faith and you must put your trust in someone. Both of you can either believe that I'm here to help you or that I'm in cahoots with Azrael."

Clay looked at me, shaking his head. He didn't want to go through with this. I knew how much he'd gone through to preserve and protect his memories. I didn't see him giving them up even if he trusted this man.

"Anubis, or Dr. Dawood, whichever you prefer. Can you explain why it's crucial for us to do this now? Shouldn't it be done at our own pace?" I asked.

"Under normal circumstances, yes. It would be done at one's own time and choosing. These, however, are not normal circumstances. To do this is still at your own will; I'm only asking you to consider doing it sooner."

"You keep mentioning something's gone horribly wrong, but you haven't given us any concrete information," Clay said to Dr. Dawood, his frustration mirroring mine as we questioned the validity of the doctor's explanations.

"Without you remembering all of who you are, it will be too hard to explain, let alone for either of you to understand. The best I can give you at the moment is that Azrael has been collecting lives for a long time."

"Isn't that what all of you do? Collect the lives of the living?" I asked.

"This is why I need you to remember," a frustrated Dr. Dawood restated. "Dear Arianna, there's no living and dead. Every existence is life, it's different levels of living that you experience." He came over and placed his arm on my shoulder. "We don't collect lives, we guide those who need to be moved from one form of living to the next. What Azrael is doing is keeping those he takes and storing them so they cannot pass to their next form. He's hiding them away. We're still not sure what it is he's trying to do with them, but he's captured enough now that there's an imbalance felt throughout existence. Clayton's stunt of jumping back into another existence made it apparent that Azrael is getting out of control. The risk of someone returning has the possibility of upending all existences that we know."

"And somehow Clay and I are supposed to be able to stop this? Look at us both! He took both of our lives already."

"He took your existence of flesh and bones, this is true," Dr. Dawood responded. "But he didn't take your lives in their truest sense. You are still very much alive in the realm beyond mortal death. Here 'alive' means having consciousness, having purpose, and having the ability to act, even without a mortal body. It will not be just yourself and Clayton; there is another who must also drink of the Waters of Lethe and be born anew."

"The Waters of what? Listen doc," Clay said, "I don't have time to dick around with word games right now. I still need to find out what's happened to Ava. If he still has her every second that ticks by puts her in further danger.

Dr. Dawood explained, meeting my gaze, "Yes, you'll learn more about Eddie. But this is the only way I can assist you," he added, emphasizing the necessity of the sacrifice.

The mention of Eddie was a punch in the gut to me as much as the mention of Ava was for Clay. I looked to Clay to gauge his reaction. A shoulder shrug was what I got from him. I was done with not knowing and this feeling of dependence on others. If there was more to know and if Dr. Dawood was telling us the truth, then so be it. I would drink the Waters of whatever and get on with it.

"Fine," I said. "Give me the water. I'm in no mood to stand around and debate this any longer. If this is what I must do to learn more and to get beyond this—so be it."

"And for you, Clayton?"

Clay turned, walking away from both Dr. Dawood and me. He kept walking through the doorway he'd come from earlier. Dr. Dawood grabbed my arm and guided me to follow Clay. Traveling down a series of hallways we ended up in a room with a round pool in the center. Clay was kneeling down next to it with a hand splashing in the pool's water.

"These are the Waters of Lethe." Dr. Dawood's voice echoed throughout the small chamber. "From these ancient waters the memories of the living world you've each known will be extinguished. In return, your memories from all your existences can be restored to you. You'll also return to your true forms. The experience is not fun, but I promise the pain of it lasts only a moment."

Dr. Dawood handed me an emerald encrusted chalice and directed me over to Clay. I handed the chalice to Clay, and he dipped it down into the pool.

"For everything that you've been shall soon return. Drink long and deep of the waters. Allow them to cleanse the past."

Clay's hand trembled as he reached for mine, his fingers interlocking with mine in a tight grip. With a deep breath, he brought the cup to his lips, his knuckles turning white against the emerald chalice. He sipped down all the water then reached down and refilled the cup for me. As I brought the cup to my lips I could feel the water, cool and refreshing at first. But as it hit my throat I felt as though I was choking on fire. My eyes began watering. I went to cry out in pain but my voice was no longer there. My tears felt like they were burning my flesh away.

In a panic, I looked over to Clay, and he was having the same reaction to the water. He was clawing at his throat and trying his best to cough. "You mustn't panic. The pain will pass," Dr. Dawood said to us.

I watched as Clay's skin began melting off of him. It started from his head. It was like watching a human candle melt down. First his flesh, then his muscle, then his organs. All melting down to piles on the floor. When there was nothing but bone left, he was still grabbing at his throat, yet, now it was his spine.

There was a hot white flash of light and then the bones and all that had melted turned to nothing more than a great big pile of ash. That's when I noticed my own skin beginning to melt.

Agony seared through me, each drop of water scorching my throat like liquid fire. Once it hit my eyes, I could no longer see, only feel the pain as each bit of me turned into nothing. Then another flash. The last thing I heard was Dr. Dawood's voice calling out, "Soon you shall return and we will talk of many things. May your travel be safe."

CHAPTER 35: CLAY

I DIDN'T HAVE TIME TO STOP IT ONCE THE CHANGE started. I'd still been hesitant about drinking the water, but I could see that this was what Arianna wanted to do. Like it or not our fates were locked together.

The fire burned inside of me and before I could warn Arianna, I felt myself disintegrate. It was a feeling as though for a third time I had died. There came that sense of disconnectedness that I'd experienced each time—though there was something more now. It was as though I was watching a movie or maybe I was in the movie. I didn't know at that moment because I couldn't recognize myself.

I was in a great vast darkness at first. Then an explosion of light expanded and began to create and touch everything as it ripped into billions of pieces. It was a beautiful sight to watch. I realized in my admiration that this was the formation of a universe and it was all being created from the light.

I watched from a distance as each star, each planet, each being were all created by the light. It was as if some unknown architect was weaving individual strands of light together to make these new and wondrous things. Then I saw the earth.

My curiosity took me closer to this world and I could see beasts upon the land and in the sea. They evolved and changed into new versions of themselves as time rolled forward. I began noticing as each beast of the earth died a light would return out into the darkness for a time before returning to the earth or other distant worlds.

Humans came along not too long after the beasts. I watched as they built and tore down cities that consumed the small planet. As their time aged, so did their curiosity of what the light had made. Unlike the beasts they had stronger mental capacities and began naming all that the light had created, including themselves. However, their light seemed to become trapped on the planet.

Because of their deeper intellect and formation of emotions they were refusing to leave those with whom they developed bonds with. There came a calling that many of us heard from the heart of the purest light. It said to us that some are needed to remain as greater lights and it would be their job to make sure the human lights found their way back to the purest light again.

I found myself connected with three other lights nearby, separate from the watchers guiding humans. We traversed the expanse, marveling at its wonders. Gradually, we began to disappear and reappear, taking human forms on Earth to share our knowledge. However, one light failed to return, triggering alarm as our collective brightness dimmed.

The watchers joined together as they suspected it may have been one of their own who was trapping the light in a place out of their reach. There weren't many places the light didn't touch, but whatever was making our light duller, had found such a place. We were all sent down at that point to help find why other lights were disappearing. The problem was our capacity while on earth to understand was diminished. Both on the way in and out we are required to drink the Waters of Lethe. On the way down to forget our light birth and past experiences and on the way back to collectively remember it all.

For me, that was fifty visits ago. During my last visit, I embraced the identity of Clayton Mitchell. It marked the beginning of a path fraught with challenges and revelations. That was the visit where I found my end by the hands of a watcher named Azrael. Now, I must return in all my forms, most importantly in my truest form of a radiant blue and white light.

The air was dry and I could feel the chalice back in my hand again. The hot Waters of Lethe were still a sting upon my lips. Opening my eyes, as myself again, was always refreshing.

Looking to my right I could see her yellow light still coming back to us.

"I see you've made the journey safely."

"Yes, doc, I have."

I stood up and walked over to Dr. Dawood, taking his hand. "It seems such a long time since we've seen each other, yet, it has been no more than a few moments. Please continue to call me Clay. I've grown fond of this identity and think we will be needing it."

"Yes, I would agree, we will. How much do you remember?"

"It is still coming in waves. As of now I remember being born from the heart of the light and the missing lights," I said. "How long before she comes back to us?"

"It shouldn't be much longer now. You're both going to need to rest and rebuild your strength. I will get her off to rest as soon as she's back. As you have been, you are still my guest. Please rest and we shall talk again soon."

As I prepared to leave the chamber, a thought struck me, causing me to pause. "Wait, Doc. I thought drinking the Waters of Lethe was supposed to make us forget our last lives completely. Why do I still remember everything about being Clay?"

Dr. Dawood sighed, a look of regret crossing his face. "I owe you an apology, Clay. I didn't explain everything about the Waters of Lethe. The truth is, the waters can have different effects depending on your willingness to sacrifice the memories of your last life. If the sacrifice is made with a full heart and true intent, your most recent memories can remain intact, while allowing you to access deeper truths. However, without that willingness, the waters could have adverse effects—erasing memories in a more destructive way, leaving gaps that could confuse and disorient you."

I absorbed his words, feeling a sense of relief mixed with confusion. "So, it's about intention?"

"Precisely," Dr. Dawood confirmed, though his eyes shifted slightly, as if measuring his next words. "Azrael erases memories by force to control, but when you willingly release them, it is to unlock greater understanding. It's a conscious choice, not a loss." He paused for a moment, as if considering whether to say more.

I nodded, the explanation settling in, but a seed of doubt had been planted. Was he telling us everything? I pushed the doubt aside for now, focusing on the task at hand. "And what about how we look? I know we're all light, like you and Azrael, but we still look like ourselves from our last lives."

"That's a choice, too," Dr. Dawood explained. "Many choose to retain the appearance of their most recent life because it provides familiarity and comfort. It's a way of holding onto an identity they understand, especially in a realm that's constantly shifting."

"So, we can appear any way we want, but we choose what feels right," I said as the understanding began to settle in.

"Exactly. This realm is about freedom of choice, in both form and memory."

I went back to the center of the temple and lay down on the cot. I still didn't know what was ahead, but I knew this was the beginning of something much bigger than any of us could comprehend.

As my weary eyes began to close, I sensed Dr. Dawood's presence drawing near, his footsteps echoing in the temple's hallowed halls. Beside me, Arianna's gentle form found solace, her warmth a beacon in the darkness. In that fleeting moment, amidst the quiet hum of our intertwined lights, I understood the weight of our shared destiny. Together, we would navigate the unknown, bound by the threads of fate.

CHAPTER 36: AVA

When Persephone told me about drinking the Waters of Lethe, she seemed not surprised at all by my response of, "Okay, give me a damn cup."

"You don't know yourself," she said, "but, I do. The flame in you still burns brighter and fiercer than so many others. Always one of my favorite lights to return."

I had drunk from the waters. It was a strange yet familiar process that I knew I'd done before. I remembered my other three lights and the times we had traveled together. I found it funny that Clay and I had found each other again on this journey. Time and time again, that seemed to happen. Though all our lights were very different, there were four of us who always came back to each other.

As I reminisced, it hit me: the indigo light, the color of Az's light. It glowed because he'd somehow touched all of us in the reality we'd been in. Yet, it still didn't explain the change to the light once Clay had crossed through the gateway. There was still so much more to figure out.

I slept for what felt like several months after I'd been transformed back to my real self. In reality, it was only a day and a half. When I woke I found Grayson and Deanna sitting in the room with me. Looking at them, I realized it was the first time I saw them as the light they were. I wondered if this was how Az had always seen us.

Deanna's light was a brilliant amethyst color, and Grayson's—his—was the most brilliant of those among us. All around him was a glorious glow of gold and silver. I wished the two of them could see this, knowing in time they would— as long as we remained free from Az.

When I walked over to them Grayson sprung from his chair and gave me a bear hug. "Ava, are you okay? Elizabeth said you'd gone to see some Persephone woman and we weren't allowed to see you. Then when we finally did see you again you were out cold. Please tell me that they didn't hurt you or anything like that."

I couldn't help but notice the continued change in how Grayson spoke. I smiled at him; it was easy to understand now the light that he was. A true and loving person, always the one to sacrifice to make sure others were taken care of. There was something else about him. Something I should've known but still hadn't remembered. I leaned in and gave him a kiss on the forehead. "Thank you, Grayson. Yes, I'm quite well. Much better than I've been in a long time. We'll have more to talk about, but first, I need to speak with Elizabeth again. Can you tell me where she's gone?"

Grayson looked down at the ground, then back to me. "Well, see… since she was the one who had led you to that woman… She and I had a bit of an argument. I told her she had no business leaving you without one of us by your side. Anyways, she went back into that hallway and hasn't been out in the last twelve hours or so. I'm not sure if it leads out of this place or what. I was going to find her myself shortly if she hadn't come back."

"Thank you, Grayson. That won't be necessary. I think I know where she's gone. I'll be back soon and all of us will have work to do."

I followed the hallway back to the chamber with the pool and, sure enough, found Elizabeth sitting by the water's edge with the bright light of Persephone glowing from within. "So now you remember?" Elizabeth asked as I approached.

"I do remember most, yes. Some of it is still coming to me but I suspect in the next few days it will return to me."

I looked down into the pool and the light of Persephone quickly faded. "Guess she didn't want to talk to me any more at the moment. "

"She spoke out to you? Out of all the years I've been here I've only seen her, and she has given motions. I sort of knew what she needed me to know and did it."

"Yes, she spoke to me. Tell me, Elizabeth, has she ever told you about drinking the waters of the pool?"

Elizabeth waved her fingertips through the water. "Not to worry, Ava. I'm very well aware of the Water of Lethe and what they do. I'm also very much aware of what we all are. I don't need to drink the water to know that."

"Then why haven't you drunk the waters to return to yourself?"

"We all have a role that we must play in what's happening and what's yet to happen. Until I know that all those captured by Azrael have been set free, I will not allow myself to return to the light. I must stay here and guide them through the darkness."

"I see. Can he get into this place?"

"The short answer is yes. We are in a place that the light touches. He may not know it yet, but as with all of us, if the light can touch it, we can be there."

"And Persephone, she, as his equal, isn't able to do anything about this?"

"That, I don't understand myself. I've asked the same question many times. No, is the only response she ever gave me."

I put my hand out to help Elizabeth up. "Come with me. We need to talk with the others. I will not remain captive in Az's or anyone else's world. We'll find a way out of this for everyone."

PART 3

SPLINTERED REALITIES

CHAPTER 37: ARIANNA

THINGS SEEMED CLEARER FOR CLAY; FOR ME THE WORLD was still a foggy mix of realities. I was grasping the basics of it, but some part of me was resisting this change. It was an overwhelming wash of emotions, and I needed time to process this. I left Clay and Dr. Dawood and returned to the pool chamber.

As I sat looking through the water I could see at the bottom of the pool what looked to be a tiny emerald amulet. As I reached my hand into the water to pick it up I could see through my skin a shimmering yellow light. This is what I really am—nothing more than light.

With the amulet in hand I spent a moment studying it. Nothing so special about it on first inspection, the only thing I could see was my own reflection. If I could even call it that any longer.

As footsteps echoed down the hallway, a wave of frustration and a deep need for solitude washed over me. Each step reminded me of the urgency to confront Azrael, whose enigmatic plans posed a threat to more than my own realm. My weariness stemmed not only from the cosmic stakes but from the way

Clay and Dr. Dawood treated me like a princess in distress. I needed this moment alone not only to collect my thoughts but also to prepare myself for the upcoming confrontation, which promised to reshape far more than my own fate.

Glancing back into the pool there was indigo light glowing from the center. It hadn't been there a moment ago. There was only one person, or thing, I know that comes with that color—Azrael.

Clay and Dr. Dawood entered the room as I was standing up. I went to tell them about the light in the pool when I felt a cold wet hand wrap around my ankle. It pulled me so hard and so fast I didn't have a chance to move away from it. By the time Clay and Dr. Dawood got into the room I was knee deep in the water. I clung to the stone edge of the pool for dear life. The hand pulled harder and harder. Clay ran to me, grabbing on to my arms, trying to pull me back. "Azrael's got me!" I shouted.

Dr. Dawood's inaction puzzled me as Clay struggled to pull me from the water's grasp. His eyes, filled with conflict, met mine. "I can't help you," he murmured, his voice almost lost in the chaos. His deliberate choice to remain on the sidelines deepened my confusion and heightened my suspicions of his true motives.

Further and further I sank under the water until at last my head was below the crest. The last thing I saw through the water was a blurred image of Clay's hands reaching for me. Sucked down into the shadows, another world of darkness awaited me.

I could no longer feel hands on me, but I could see that I'd become encapsulated in an indigo light. Each second in Azrael's light was a suffocating eternity. His light was dulling my own. After a series of several flashes I was back at Navy Pier again. Back to the house of mirrors from my dream.

I could feel his cold putrid hand squeezing my arm. "They thought they could take what's mine. They thought I would just lie down and accept their foolishness. I promise you, they have no idea what I'm capable of," Azrael growled.

He guided me through the main entrance into the house of mirrors, but would not step beyond the entrance hall. I could see the tarps I remembered pulling down had been placed back over the outer mirrors. Only the dark entrance to the maze remained visible.

Azrael's voice cut through the darkness as he taunted, "I sent you here before, Miss Stone. That was but a prelude. Now that you've revealed your true form, you face even harsher realities. Their foolishness has only sped up my plans. Anubis might be playing checkers, but I'm playing chess—and this game spans across realms." This revelation made the stakes clear: Azrael was playing a cosmic game, using us as pawns to achieve an unknown end.

"Why are you doing this, Azrael? What do you want with me? And why imprison us—what have we ever done to you?"

He hissed back at me, "Like I've said before, you're just pawns in a much larger game. Your light, and the others', will serve a greater purpose when the time comes." He pulled my arms behind me and led me to the entrance. "Enjoy your stay, Miss Stone."

As I was shoved through, I turned to try and fight my way back out, but the door slammed shut. Looking back I could see that the maze had changed. The first room I found myself in was a series of tall floor mirrors encased in dark wooden frames. They looked very much like the one in my apartment.

I stood by the door contemplating what I should do. I'd been here before, and the maze went on and on. I reached for the door I'd come through before moving away from it. I made that mistake last time when I left and then could not get back to it. I couldn't even feel where the door had been. No doorknobs or seams of the door could be felt. Banging on the door would be pointless. What? Was Azrael going to answer it and reconsider? Highly unlikely.

There was only one hope for me: to wander forward into the mirror maze. I could only pray that Clay and Dr. Dawood would be smart enough to find me before the hour got too late.

CHAPTER 38: JOHN

There had been some sort of commotion over at the temple when a large envoy marched off. I knew they were heading back out into the darkness. I did notice however that Elizabeth wasn't with them. I found this unusual as she was more often than not the one to lead them out.

Keeping a safe distance, I followed them as they marched down through the valley, only coming to a stop when they reached a large pile of rocks. I watched as they walked behind the rocks, one-by-one, and never returned from the other side of the pile or anywhere further down the valley. This had to be it! It had to be where they were crossing in and out of the darkness.

I could see they'd left four guards to watch. Making a move right now would be pointless. Instead, I walked several hundred yards back from the rocks and planted myself at the base of a giant willow tree. They couldn't stay gone forever. From what I'd observed of their previous expeditions, those who left were only gone for a few hours at most. I would wait here until they returned and then once they, and the guards, were gone, I'd search the rocks and make my exit.

There was a sense of excitement growing in me that I might be free from these people. I'd grown beyond tired of being their captive. About the only thing that had gotten a rise out of me was that ginger bitch, Ava. It was funny how much she reminded me of Emilia when I first saw her.

I was still puzzled why she'd so suddenly become as important as she had to Elizabeth. I knew something had happened to the ginger bitch. Not long after she'd gone into the temple Elizabeth had come back and grabbed the old goat and homeless man and ushered them into the temple. I wondered if the feisty little redhead had found her own way out. No, it couldn't have been that. I searched every inch of that chamber when they held me there. There was one way in and one way out. There was more to know about this, but if I was being honest, I hoped I wasn't here to learn about it.

A few hours had passed when I saw the search party reemerge from the rock pile. I kept my eyes on them on their march back to the temple. Once they had crossed over the top of the valley I wandered down to the rock pile and began to investigate. My only thoughts now were on getting the hell out of here.

My initial inspection of the rock pile turned up nothing unusual—just a jumble of stones. But the urgency of escape pressed on my mind; there had to be more to these rocks. I circled them again, my hands brushing over the cold, hard surfaces, searching for any sign of a seam or hidden opening. I was so fucking close to getting away from here, yet I had no clue how these rocks turned into a door. It wouldn't be long until someone noticed I wasn't sitting in my usual spot and they would come back looking for me. There was still a sense of determination to get free, but I wasn't going to be stupid. I could come back and search another day, but not if they caught me first.

As I made one last round of the rock pile, something I'd overlooked caught my eye—footprints in the dirt, not just mine but others, converging at a single point. It was the largest of the rocks and I was sure that I'd checked it on my previous passes. Stepping back up to it I could see no lever or knob to open it. I began pushing anywhere I could get my hands to, but still nothing.

Exhausted, I slumped against the base of the largest rock, my frustration boiling over. "Open up, you goddamn rock!" As I leaned back, my head thudded against the rock, finding an unexpected hollow. Surprised, I pressed against it, and with a grinding noise, the massive stone shifted, revealing a dark passage.

I sprung to my feet, turning to see that beyond the rocks I was staring into the darkness. Taking one look back in the direction of the temple I saw no one coming for me. I stepped forward into the darkness as the large stone slid back into place, stealing the last bit of light from my vision.

For a few moments, I hesitated, my eyes straining against the pitch-black darkness that the opened passage revealed. *How the hell do those freaks come in here and move about?* I'd never seen them with flashlights or anything like that. It was so damn dark in here. No matter how long I waited, my eyes couldn't adjust to it.

I wasn't sure what the ground consisted of. It was a hard surface that felt very much like a stone or concrete slab under my feet. With as much caution as I could take, I put one foot in front of the other, moving further into the darkness. Each step was calculated to ensure I wouldn't trip. I walked in this manner for at least a half an hour before I grew tired with the slow pace. I had to move faster before the tinfoil hat crew came after me. Thus far I hadn't come across a single obstruction. This ground was as smooth and flat as a new pane of glass.

I quickened my pace when I saw a glowing orb off in the distance. I wasn't certain if my mind was playing tricks on me or if this thing was for real. *Only one way to find out, John,* I thought.

Another hour of walking and the damn thing was still there but not getting any closer. More determined than ever to find out what this was I pushed on. It wasn't until the second hour of my walk that I could see the orb of light growing larger.

The closer I got it, I began to see that it wasn't an orb. The light had only appeared that way from afar. It was instead a series of rectangular shapes. They look a lot like… they're… windows? But windows to what? Was there another place like where I'd come from that these windows looked into?

Another hour had come and gone. Had my curiosity not gotten the best of me I would've given up this trek hours ago. When I finally reached the windows, the size of them was un-real. Each one had to be standing somewhere around fifty feet in height and twenty feet across. The light I'd followed wasn't coming from them, but through them. I walked up to the first of the windows and could see it opened up into a room or hallway with hundreds of mirrors wrapped around it. The light was not coming from a specific place; it sort of wrapped around or coated everything.

I kept moving along the windows. They had to lead me somewhere, right? When I pressed against the glass of the win-dows I felt a subzero cold take over my body. It was as if I'd jumped into a frozen pond in the depths of winter. Pulling my hand back the cold sensation subsided.

There was something familiar about this light. I'd seen this before, but where? I was trying to recall when something mov-ing on the other side of the window caught my eye. Looking closer I saw a woman. She entered where the first of the win-dows began.

"Hey! Lady! Right here," I called out to her. Nothing. I tried a few more times to get her attention but either she was deaf or the windows were sound proof. I began banging on the glass of each window that she passed. Each time my skin made contact with the glass the chill of death returned to me. It didn't stop me, and each time I banged harder.

"Take it easy you damn imbecile!" came a voice out of the darkness. "It doesn't matter how loud you yell or bang, she's not going to hear you. If you really like Mr. Tyler, I'm more than happy to place you in there with her. Though I suspect you wouldn't like that very much."

It was the dark man. He was standing next to me. Now I remembered where I'd seen this light before. It was the same that had come from the mirror when this fuckwad came and killed me.

He came closer, raising a hand to my face. "Tell me, Mr. Tyler, how did you come upon this place? You should be lost a long way away from here."

"Fuck you! That's all you're getting from me. You choked the life out of me, and now..."

His hand closed around my neck, lifting me from the ground. "And I'll do it again if you don't answer my question. It's very simple Mr. Tyler, I ask you a question and you provide an answer. Let's try again. Where did you come from?"

He loosened his grip from my throat. I pulled back and coughed, trying to catch my breath. "Some temple or whatever the fuck it was. I came in through this giant rock."

His eyes flamed with indigo light. "Where was this rock and temple?"

I pointed back in the direction I'd come from, or at least I thought I'd come from. "Back that way, a few hours of walking. I couldn't see anything else; it is after all pitch fucking dark in here."

His hand flew up again and I found myself cowering back. "Were there others there?"

"Yes, there were many there. It was like a fucking kumbaya jamboree or something. I thought I'd landed in a hippy commune of the dead, but with a twist of ancient Greece or something."

"Persephone!" he growled, more to himself than to me.

"Persephone? Who's that?"

"Never mind you. There's work to do. I'll deal with them later. I have something else to tend to at the moment. You'll be staying with me." He looked back through the windows.

"Who is she?" I pressed, nodding towards the figure behind the glass.

"Just a foolish girl about to learn a harsh lesson—one she won't forget in a hurry."

She was still making her way through the room of mirrors. I wondered if she could see him. See me.

"Before you entertain any thoughts of fleeing, Mr. Tyler, a brief introduction is in order." His voice sliced through the darkness, cold and precise. He stepped closer, the faint glow of the mysterious light casting deep shadows across his face. "I am Azrael Angue, but you will address me as Az. It's a name you'll find hard to forget." His tone was not inviting but commanding, his smile not warm but predatory.

He paused, his eyes narrowing as if he could see right through me. "Now, let's discuss your role in my grand design. How would you like a job?" His words dripped with malice, making it abundantly clear that this was not an offer but a summons. I realized in that chilling moment my fate was no longer my own to dictate.

The oppressive darkness around us seemed to thicken with his words, almost echoing his threat. My past choices had vanished, just like the light at the end of the tunnel, leaving me to navigate the looming shadows that Az now controlled.

CHAPTER 39: CLAY

WHAT HAD JUST HAPPENED? MY ARMS STILL DRAPED over the side of the pool, elbow deep in the water. Something had pulled Arianna down through the pool leaving no trace of her. How was it even possible for something to have come through the solid stone of the pool basin?

"Hey doc," I said, glaring at him to show my displeasure, "any particular reason you decided not to help there?"

"He still had a hold of her. I'm sorry, Clayton. I… I had to let him take her."

"Him? As in Az? Are you fucking serious?" My voice dropped to a dangerous whisper as I moved closer to Dr. Dawood, my anger barely contained. Grasping his robe, I hissed, "How the hell did he get past your defenses? You swore this was a safe haven!"

"Azrael is using reflections to his advantage. He's making gateways from them. It should've been safe here." Walking over to the pool, his head tilted down to the water. "I need to let the others know. We cannot stay here any longer, Clayton."

"What others are you talking about?"

"Clayton, as I've said before, there are others like me and others like you. Ava is waiting, but it's not just a simple journey—we have to prepare to face what's out there."

"Hold the fuck up! You knew where she was this whole fucking time and you, what, decided not to share that with me?"

"Your anger, Clayton. Please, try to remember you have to control it or he'll have you right where he wants you."

"I'm fucking close to not caring anymore, doc. You all are just full of shit—lies and deceit, one after another. You want calm? Fine! Then no more bullshit—just the straight truth. No more goddamn riddles, no more 'you're not ready' crap. Lay it all out, or I'm on my own. Got it, doc?"

"It seems we are at each other's mercy. Yes, we have a deal."

"Good. A few answers I need now. First, where did he take Arianna?"

"That I don't know. She's been taken somewhere the light doesn't touch."

"Okay, we'll keep working on that one. Second, where is Ava?"

"She is with the one called Persephone."

"How do we get to her?"

"We must leave the protection of this place and travel. The pool would've worked, however, knowing that he's traveled through it, we cannot risk that. We must head to the road, which will leave us exposed to Azrael if he wishes to locate us."

"Let him come then. I'll follow your lead doc. Let's get going. I've waited long enough to get back to Ava."

After our heated exchange, the cool air outside seemed to mirror the chill settling in my heart. We walked in silence, the weight of Arianna's absence a silent specter between us. As we approached the river, the usual straightforward path seemed altered by an ominous, unfamiliar presence lurking just below the surface. Dr. Dawood stepped into the river and walked until the water was up above his waist. I was about to follow him when he put a hand up to stop me.

Dr. Dawood halted, his hand raised in a cautionary gesture. "He'll not be pleased if you enter the waters right now. Wait here for a moment," he warned. Before I could question who "he" might be, the water ahead began to stir, and the front of a skiff emerged, heralding an arrival I'd only known from lore. Growing up, Charon the ferryman was nothing more than a spectral figure from stories and films, crafted to add drama to tales of the afterlife. Yet, here he was, manifesting from the river mists, as tangible and stern as any living being. His dark robe and the grim expression that promised no mercy matched the legends so perfectly that it was almost cinematic. The shock of encountering such a mythological figure in flesh and bones—or whatever eerie matter he was made of—was profound, reaffirming the surreal reality into which I had been thrust.

Dr. Dawood and Charon spoke for several moments while I remained on the shore. The doc stepped on to the skiff before summoning me over. When I approached and went to board, Charon's gaze fixed upon me as I approached the skiff. "You don't ride the ferry for free, boy!" he hissed, his bony, gray hand extending out to me.

Caught off-guard, I stammered, "I have no money to pay you."

His glare intensified, turning towards Dr. Dawood. "Then you don't ride! Anubis, what is the meaning of this nonsense? You think to call for me when your passenger has no means to pay the ferryman? We'll leave this boy to the river."

"Clayton," said Dr. Dawood, "you do in fact have payment for my dear friend. It seems you've only forgotten the token in your front pocket."

There it was, the cold sensation of the medallion I'd found back at the Appalachian House. I was amused that this had somehow come along with me from John Tyler's pants to mine. It was an object I held in the living world, but it had seemingly crossed over with me. I could feel its eternal coolness as I wrapped my fingers around it to pull it from my pocket.

Charon leaned closer, his eyes narrowing as he inspected the medallion, a serious weight to his scrutiny. "This shall suffice," he murmured, his voice carrying the echo of ancient rivers. "But let silence be your companion aboard this vessel, boy. And you, Anubis, spare me your tales today. The river is restless; as am I."

I complied, finding a small space at the front of the skiff, and as we set off, the shores of the familiar faded behind us, swallowed by mists that seemed to reshape the very fabric of the world I knew.

It was hard to believe that the fastest means of travel was going to be this little skiff, unless we were traveling not more than a few miles up the river. Our journey on the river stretched out, each stroke of Charon's pole a beat in the somber melody of our travel. I watched in my silence for a time as the dark night skies of Egypt faded and the swells of a turbulent sea came upon us.

Waves tossed the small boat from side to side. I clung to the figurehead with white knuckles as lights emerged from the depths below, catching my alarmed attention. I glanced back at Dr. Dawood and Charon, who stood at the stern, to see if they too were witnessing this spectacle. As we passed over the shadowy depths, the lights flickered like lost souls waving from underwater. Charon caught my gaze, his laughter booming over the water with resonant, age-old authority. "Behold the damned, boy. Trapped by their deeds, denied the light's return, their pleas echo across time. Here they remain, bound by the great sea, their penance a millennium in the deep. This, indeed, is their true Purgatory—such are the scales of justice weighed."

The more I learned, the easier it was to see all the false information that Az had been feeding to people. I nodded to Charon that I understood, but what did I really know? Anytime I thought I knew this existence, I was humbled again by its changing faces.

The great sea soon began to calm and in the distance I could see the sun beginning to shine. Soon, we closed in on land and the inlet to another river. By the time the sun had lifted overhead we had drifted up the river through several picturesque valleys. That's when I first saw the temple come to the horizon.

As the skiff approached the temple, the sight of its brilliant white columns piercing the horizon sparked a mixture of emotions within me. Each stroke of Charon's oar through the water seemed to beat in rhythm with my racing heart. As we disembarked, the cool, sacred ground of the temple felt like a boundary between worlds. Ahead, the gathered crowd blurred into indistinct faces, except for one.

There she was—Ava. I walked towards her, my steps hesitant yet urgent, each footfall a question of reality. Her presence soothed the chaotic churn of events and drew me in. When we finally embraced, the world around us dimmed, the murmur of the crowd faded into silence, and for a moment, it was just us—united amid the storms of our trials. As I was holding her, I saw another person further off in the distance that Dr. Dawood had engaged in conversation. Breaking from Ava I charged like an enraged bull at them.

"What kind of trickery is this!" I demanded.

"Calm yourself, Clayton," said Dr. Dawood.

Ava's arms came over my shoulder and turned me to her. "Clay, look at me. Clay... look at me!"

I looked down into her eyes; I was still seething that he would be here in that disguise. "What are you doing back here with him?" I asked Ava.

"Clay! That's not Az. It's the real Elizabeth."

"No, that's impossible. Grayson said she was ripped apart from the waist down and Az said she no longer existed. This is another dirty trick. He's fooling everyone!" I was getting worked up and could feel my anger spiraling out of control.

"I'm sorry for what he did to you. I'm really Elizabeth and though we've not met yet, I've heard many things about you. Grayson and Ava have told me your story." She reached out and touched my hand the way a mother does to comfort a distressed child. "Clayton, you don't have to trust me yet, but please, let's all go back to the temple and talk more."

Looking behind me, Ava gave me a reassuring nod. The group had begun walking to the temple. I stayed back for a moment; there was something else I needed to do. I suspected that Deanna hadn't been told about Arianna yet. I noticed when Dr. Dawood and I arrived she was looking around expecting to see her with us.

"Deanna, I'm sorry. He got her before we could leave. We're going to figure out how to get her back, I promise."

"Where did he take her?"

"I don't know. It all happened so fast. I had my arms out trying to pull her back. He was too strong and she slipped through my fingers. I hope she can hang on until we can get to her."

I wasn't sure I believed myself in that moment. If Az had her, there was no telling what might be happening to her. I hated to lie, but I needed to provide some comfort to Deanna, even if for a short time.

CHAPTER 40: ARIANNA

AS I CAUTIOUSLY STAYED IN THE CENTER OF THE HALL-way, my heart raced with dread and curiosity. Echoes of my steps filled the endless corridor lined with mirrors, deepening my sense of entrapment. Each mirror I passed introduced an unsettling familiarity—nothing changed, yet everything seemed ominously different.

Feeling compelled, I approached one of the mirrors on my left. At first it showed only my reflection and those across the hall. My breath caught in my throat as the reflections in the surrounding mirrors took on a life of their own, each moving in different directions. The sight was surreal, blurring the lines between reality and illusion. A cold shiver ran down my spine.

My focus snapped back to the mirror before me, and my heart sank. The reflection no longer mimicked my movements but offered a chilling, eerie smile instead. The laughter that followed, hollow and mocking, reverberated through the hall, sending waves of fear that I struggled to suppress.

She stood there, still as a statue, her eyes gleaming with a malevolent glint that sent a shiver down my spine. Her features were mine, yet twisted with a deviant smirk that seemed to mock my every breath. The smile on her lips was one of cruel amusement, as if she knew secrets I could never comprehend. Slowly, she raised a hand and beckoned me closer with a slow, deliberate motion, her fingers curling and uncurling with a predatory grace. I felt an involuntary pull, an inexplicable urge to step towards her, but I resisted, rooted in place by fear.

Suddenly, she turned and walked, stepping right through the mirror behind me and into an endless loop of mirrors. It looked like a picture of a picture, repeating endlessly, each image darker and more distorted than the last. The infinite expanse continued on, swallowing her up as she disappeared from sight. When the shock of that experience passed, I moved further down the hall of mirrors, my mind reeling from what I had just witnessed.

Azrael had placed me here for a reason. If I was but a pawn in his game it must mean he was trying to use me as bait to lure someone in. Clay would've been my first and only guess. Unless he was somehow leading Clay here, I'm not sure how he's going to find me. This place had no beginning and no end that I could see.

A bright light flickered further down the hall. I could see it was coming from one of the mirrors. I stepped up to it expecting to see my rogue reflection again. I wasn't looking for any more sudden surprises, but that was what I was expecting all the same. Turning to what I expected to be another mirror, my reflection was absent, replaced by a window-like view into dark, blue waters. The reality of the scene before me was jarring, as if the mirror had transformed into a portal to another, more ominous world. In the far distance there was a flashing light sinking deeper in the water.

"Arianna. Arianna… please, help me." I heard the voice plain as day. I knew the voice, but it couldn't have been. He swam up to the glass as I touched the mirror. He was struggling to swim, and the light I'd seen was grabbing at his legs, pulling him away.

"Eddie!" I yelled. He swam back, banging against the glass. I grabbed a mirror from across the hall and smashed it into the one Eddie was trapped in. The glass shattered with a deafening crash, unleashing a torrent of dark water that flooded the hall. Water surged around me, the mirrors blurring and then disappearing into the murky depths. While I was struggling to orient myself, the hall was replaced by an oppressive, watery grave.

I was in a panic at first. I didn't know which way was up or which way was down. Then I saw Eddie again. He was ten feet or so below me. I turned and swam with all I had to get to him.

The desperate struggle felt like a haunting cat and mouse game under the water's dark embrace. Each time I grasped his hand, a force pulled him further away, tearing at my resolve. My panic became overwhelming.

I wasn't sure how long I'd been under the water, but it occurred to me that I had no oxygen. No way of knowing where the surface is. If I didn't let go of Eddie soon, I would drown. We were moving faster and faster to what I'd assumed was the bottom of this body of water.

Below us, the darkness intensified, and a chilling realization dawned on me as I saw the water swirling in a slow, deliberate clockwise rotation. My heart sank as I understood: We were being drawn into an underwater whirlpool, its pull inevitable and strong. I was thinking I'd die if I didn't get air soon. Then, in spite of my panic, it hit me. *I'm already dead.* This thought, both liberating and terrifying, steeled my resolve. I tightened my grip on Eddie and pushed us into the center of the whirlpool.

I spun round and round in the darkness. At some point my hands lost their grip on Eddie. I watched as he spun further and further away from me. He wasn't moving any longer and as he drifted away, his eyes shone the light of cold death.

I did all I could to fight my way back to him, but I was sucked back to the darkness. The world was spinning and then I felt something solid at my feet. I kicked down as hard as I could bear to. There was a crack. I kicked it more until I felt whatever had been below me open up.

I forced my body down and could feel sharp cold edges of whatever I'd broken. It was cutting deep into my hands, but I didn't care. I needed to get out of this damn water.

As I pulled myself through the opening and opened my eyes, the world had flipped on its head. I was pulling down, yet I was coming up. It was a struggle to get on the unbroken ice. My hands were cut and my blood was freezing to the ice. After some struggle I finally gained my footing and pulled myself through.

I slid back from the hole slow and steady. The last thing I wanted to do was crack the already fragile ice. Once I was far enough back from the opening I lay on my back and looked into the sky. It was night, and I had no idea where I was.

I spotted a dim light on the shore, about a hundred yards to my left. Gritting my teeth, I started crawling on my hands and knees, each movement deliberate. The ice beneath me creaked with every shift of my weight. It was crystal clear, and under the moonlight, I could see the bottom of the lake. I kept my gaze fixed on the ice as I crawled, trying to tune out the unnerving sounds of cracking echoing around me.

As I neared the shore, about fifty yards away, a large, ominous shadow beneath the ice caught my eye. I approached, my heart pounding as I peered down through the clear, frozen surface. The sight that met my eyes made my blood run cold:

There, trapped beneath the ice, was Eddie, his eyes wide open in a silent, frozen scream. It was hell the first time I'd lost him, and now I was losing him again. If it hadn't been so cold I would've noticed the tears leaving frozen lines down my face.

But I knew this was another trick of Azrael. It wasn't really my Eddie. He had been dead for many years now. It didn't make the pain of seeing him any easier though. Hearing his call for me, feeling the touch of his hand against my own, these were causing small fissures in my psyche. For now I said goodbye to this Eddie and crawled the remainder of the way to the shore.

I was frozen and exhausted. There were several large pine trees that had no snow under them. I slid under them and allowed myself to have a few moments of rest. If I was already dead I figured I need not worry about hypothermia.

If this was the worst thing that Azrael could do to me I would show him that I could beat him at his game. Drawing in a deep, unsteady breath, I stood in the silent darkness of the night. Gathering my courage, I shouted into the void, "Is that all you've got, Azrael? Come on, you bastard! I refuse to be just a pawn in your twisted game."

I heard cracking about me. I guess Azrael had heard my declaration. The trees above me were engulfed in flames. I got up and ran from them, but everything in front of me was ablaze. I needed to get back to the lake.

CRACK. CRACK. CRACK. The tree came down hard and fast. I felt the flames kissing my skin as the tree's weight pressed my body deeper into the ground. Under the weight of this tree I fell into a deep unconsciousness.

CHAPTER 41: JOHN

"ARE YOU TRYING TO KILL HER?" I COULDN'T BELIEVE what I was watching through these windows.

"Mr. Tyler, you disappoint me. She's already dead. One cannot become more dead now, can they?"

"How in the hell am I supposed to know. The only thing I know about being dead is that you're the son-of-a-bitch who killed me."

"Do you really think you deserved to continue living? You do remember those things I whispered to you, Mr. Tyler. Do you think someone who's done such things should enjoy the benefits of life? I'll tell you I've taken many lives for my own good. Yours, well, let's say it was a little self-serving on my part, but your death by far was a blessing to the living world you knew."

Az's words bounced off me like water off glass. No shred of guilt shadowed my thoughts; instead, a smirk curled at the corner of my mouth. Why should I regret my actions? They had catapulted me to the pinnacle of success, reshaped the world on my terms. In my eyes, I wasn't a villain but a victor, some- one who seized opportunities where others hesitated. "Regret is for those who fail, Az," I retorted, my voice steady, infused with icy detachment. "I did what the greats do—I took charge, shaped the world around me. And I'd do it all again without a second thought. In this world, there are alphas who rule and others who serve. That's the order of things." I paused, watching his reaction to my defiance. "Now, about this job you mentioned—after seeing your little demonstration with the tree, I'm intrigued. What exactly do you need me to do?"

"I can see I've picked the right one for this. Still no guilt comes from you and your light is as dark as pitch." He draped one of his arms over my shoulder, guiding me away from the haunting scene visible through the windows. As we walked, the darkness around us seemed to pulse and shift, lit by an eerie indigo aura emanating from him.

"Mr. Tyler, you're going to be my messenger, my rider on the storm, if you will. Open your hand." He grabbed onto my wrist, his cold fingers turning my palm face up. Reaching into one of the pockets of his suit he pulled out a pocket watch and placed it into my hand. There was almost a sorrowful look in his eyes as his fingers let go of the watch. As Az placed the watch in my hand, its weight was unnerving, heavier than its size suggested.

The cold metal pressed against my palm felt like a physical manifestation of the dark pact being forged. The intricate engravings on its surface danced under the dim light, each line a sinister whisper of the power it held. I turned it over, feeling the engravings like braille under my fingertips, each symbol a cryptic message.

"What the fuck am I supposed to do with this?" I asked.

"You'll take it back to where you've come from. Then you'll go into the temple, open this watch, and place it in the center of the pool."

"You've got to be fucking kidding me. You're sending me back there after I just got away from those damn freaks."

"Fear not, Mr. Tyler. If all goes to plan, you'll not need to remain among them any longer than a few minutes after placing this."

"Why can't you go in and place it yourself?"

"Because, Mr. Tyler, I cannot enter the same way that you can. There are rules that I'm not going to spend time explaining to the likes of you."

"And what if I don't want to do it?"

He growled back at me with a dark and ominous laugh, "Do you remember our friend back through those windows?" I nodded to him. "Well, it will be something like that, but I promise you, much, much worse for you."

The thought of having to experience what that woman had made me gulp down hard. "Okay. I get your message. Now, how exactly do I find my way back? I had no way to see where I was going once I entered here?"

"Lift your eyes and step forward, Mr. Tyler," he instructed with a cryptic smile. As I raised my gaze, the surroundings seemed to fold in on themselves, distorting time and space. In a blink, what had previously felt like an endless march was reduced to a few steps. Standing before the stone entrance from where I'd made my escape. The rapid shift was disorienting, a stark reminder of the unnatural powers at play.

"How the hell did we get here so quickly?" I asked, my voice tinged with suspicion. The darkness had stretched endlessly before. Now, we stood in front of the stone entrance as if no distance had been covered at all. Az's smirk did nothing to quell the unease that knotted in my stomach.

"What exactly should I say if they ask where I've been?"

"You're a man very skilled in the art of lying. I'm sure your walk back will give you more than a suitable amount of time to come up with something believable."

There was a click as the door slid to the side. I was blinded by the light after being in the darkness for so long. Az moved to the side, keeping himself out of the direct light from the outside.

"Now go! You have a task to do."

I stepped out through the doorway. As it closed he said, "Oh, and Mr. Tyler, don't open that watch for any other reason than to place it in the pool. Off you go now."

The door closed tightly, once again appearing as nothing more than one of the rocks in the pile. In the light, I examined the watch, noticing its gold case with arrows pointing outward from the center in a circular pattern. Inscribed in the middle were the words, "MORTUM TUAM DUCAM. LUMEN TUUM AD ME PERTINENT." My Latin was rusty, but from what I could decipher, it roughly translated to "I am the bringer of death. Your light belongs to me."

All I had to do now was drop this thing in that fucking pool, and I could be on my way. Shouldn't be too hard. I would have to get past Elizabeth and maybe the ginger bitch, but I would do what was needed to take care of that. Afterall, Az was right—I'd done much worse things before.

CHAPTER 42: AVA

It was sweet to see the way that Clay tried to comfort Deanna, but I could also see the concern and something else in his eyes when he spoke about Arianna. I shrugged it off for the moment as I was so elated that he hadn't been washed from existence by Az.

After a fleeting embrace with Clay, the urgency of our circumstances pulled us apart, sweeping us back into the crowded temple where whispered strategies filled the air. The brief connection left me yearning for more—a moment of peace amidst the chaos.

Elizabeth had taken Clay down to the pool. This man that Clay had referred to as Dr. Dawood was talking with Deanna. That left Grayson and I standing on the sidelines without much to do. Our involvement seemed little needed right now.

"It seems there's yet a task for the two most important people here," I joked as I sat down next to him.

"Indeed. Though, I suspect in the end you and I will be much happier than the others." He took a long deep sigh. "Well at least for a little while." I couldn't help but notice the continued refinement in Grayson's speech. Most people didn't seem to notice this, but as part of my background in biology, I always observed the small things others ignored.

Feeling the weight of the stone walls closing in, I turned to Grayson, craving escape from the temple's oppressive atmosphere. "Let's get out of here for a while," I suggested, hoping to find solace under the open sky, far from the shadow of Az's indigo poison.

"That sounds like a wonderful idea, Miss Ava." He rose from his seat and extended his elbow to me.

I yelled back to the others that we were going for a walk. That was met with nothing more than a few palms waving goodbye. Glad to know we were going to be missed.

I really hadn't had the time to appreciate the beauty of this place since I'd come here. Everything was always this and that about Az or about learning what I truly am.

"Do you believe there is still beauty in the world?" I asked Grayson.

"I suppose it depends on what one defines as beauty. You know how the old saying goes, beauty is in the eye of the beholder. Who's to say what real beauty is? I'm not sure I could find beauty in the world Azrael has trapped us in and I saw no beauty in the darkness. Here… yes, maybe I can see beauty here."

As we walked, the natural beauty of the valley sparked a thought. Even in the darkest places Az created, I found beauty—not in the world, but in the resilience of the people I met. In the darkness, there was beauty in the simplicity of it all. And here, I see the beauty I remember from my life. Now, I just worry whatever is coming, all them back there, they've forgotten to look at the beauty. They're so focused on stopping whatever Az is doing or going to do that they're going to ruin all the beautiful things along the way."

"Yes, that they very well may. When people charge off to war they tend to become very much focused on the winning and not the damage that falls into their path. I think, Ava, that you'll find you do have a role to play in this after all. You'll need to become the collective consciousness for the group and make sure they don't burn everything on their path to Rome."

We walked further along the valley floor and away from the temple. I didn't want to go back anytime soon and listen to their plans. What Grayson had said made sense to me. Though, I was a little perplexed how I was going to get all of them to listen to me.

I knew how Clay could get once he got something in his head. I'd see it far too many times in life and then his relentless pursuit of the gateway. This could end badly for all of us if he wasn't using his better judgment. I needed him away from the rest of the group to have a conversation with him. I might be able to get him to listen to me, but I needed his full attention.

"Grayson, would you be willing to help me with something when we return?"

"And what might that be?"

"I need to have the others distracted long enough so that I can take Clay away for a few minutes. Not only do I need to know what happened to him and what he's planning, but I also need him of all people to hear me. I love him with all that I am, but if he goes on instinct alone, he'll get himself and the rest of us in more danger."

"I have no doubt about that. I tried to warn him about Azrael. He wanted nothing to do with the advice I had to offer. Yes. I'll help you, Ava. I think you might just be the guiding light that gets me back to who I am."

I smiled at him, knowing what I know now about the existence of all of us. "I think you'll find someday you'll be very pleased with what you find beyond the existences we've known."

Even as we savored the tranquility of our surroundings, a sense of unease began to build. Halfway through our walk, a brief glimpse of something—or someone—flitting between the rocks caught my attention, sending a shiver of unease through me. Who could it be, if not one of us? And if Az truly couldn't enter, what or who had just breached our sanctuary?

As we returned, the fleeting glimpse of that unknown figure near the rocks lingered ominously in my mind. Despite the assurances that Az couldn't come here, the shadow of doubt was hard to shake off. Were we truly safe here, or was this deceptive peace just the calm before an inevitable storm?

CHAPTER 43: ARIANNA

WHEN I REGAINED CONSCIOUSNESS, THE TREE THAT HAD pinned me down was charred to its core, a blackened skeleton among the ashes. The burn had made some room and I was able to slip myself out from under it. Reaching forward to pull myself free, I noticed the severe burns on my hands and arms. Each touch was agony, forcing me to grit my teeth against the sharp stabs of pain.

I fought for every inch I gained. The further out I got the more I realized how badly my body had been burnt. My clothes melted to the flesh, which was now black and blistering. My hair was non-existent aside from small smoldering clumps on my head. The jewelry I had been wearing also melted into my skin.

I got myself away from the remains of the tree and was in such pain that I tossed myself into the first snow pile that I could find. The snow's icy touch felt like thousands of knives thrust deep into my scorched skin, each movement a fresh hell of torment. I rolled to my back. "God! Somebody help me, please!" I screamed it as loud as my voice would carry. There was nothing but silence.

I tried to remind myself this was Azrael's trickery, yet the pain felt unbearably real. I tried to cry, but even my tear ducts seemed to have been burnt. I crawled back to the lake in the event any new surprise fires might spawn.

Looking down, my reflection stared back at me from the glassy ice of the lake. "Wow, you look like shit!" I rolled over, sliding back on my ass and hands. Azrael was standing above me.

"Stay back!" I gasped, my hands trembling and charred as I pushed myself away. I tried getting to my feet but I kept slipping back down.

"I thought you asked someone to help you. I am someone, and I can help you Miss Stone. You only need to help me." Azrael came over and grabbed me by the arm. I squirmed from the pain of my raw burns being touched.

He gripped my arm tightly, his unyielding strides dragging me toward and into the icy lake waters. I was about waist deep when I felt him take me by the head and shove me under.

The burning got much more intense. It was a feeling worse than when I had drunk the Waters of Lethe. I kicked and tried to claw back at Azrael's hands, but it was of no use, he was too strong for me. Exhaustion overcame my will to resist; despairing, I opened my mouth and inhaled the frigid lake water, surrendering the cold numbness.

I started choking as water flooded into my lungs. Then, something I wasn't expecting happened. His hands went loose—they were pulling me back up.

He hurled me onto the shore where I began puking water. "Don't think you're getting yourself out of it that easy. Now, will you help me or shall we continue on with this? Time is of no concern to me, but it may be for you."

"There's no way I'll ever help you, Azrael."

"Awe! Don't you want to at least know what it is that I'm asking of you? I promise you, it will be much better than the alternatives we've been exploring."

"Go to hell, Azrael!"

"Go there? Miss Stone, I've spent an eternity here. I guess we'll continue on with this then."

"Give it your worst. You can't kill what's already dead."

"Are you so sure of that? You shouldn't make bets on your existence if you are not one hundred percent certain of it."

He grabbed my arm. I was ready to wince again in pain, but I realized that all my burns had healed. I lifted my hands to my head, finding my hair miraculously restored.

"What… What did you do to me?"

"Taking life away is not the only power I possess. I can take you to the brink of death and back as much as I like. And maybe you're right. Maybe what's dead can't be killed again. But, oh my sweet lady, I can make you pray every moment for the rest of eternity that death will come. Now, what do you say? Will you help me?"

"GO… FUCK… YOURSELF!"

He chuckled darkly, his eyes gleaming with sinister amusement. "Suit yourself, Miss Stone." He took me by the hair and pulled me behind him into the woods. Not far from where I'd fallen from the fire there was a small cabin.

Azrael flung the door open and walked us to the far side of the building. I didn't have a chance to look around. All I could see was a tall floor mirror coming straight at my face. I closed my eyes expecting to feel glass breaking over it, but it never came.

I no longer felt the tight grip on my hair. I scurried back to my knees and looked around. Fuck! I was back in the mirror maze again. Looking around I didn't see Azrael anywhere. He must have thrown me through, but not come himself.

The air was cold and damp. Azrael had restored my skin to its unburnt state, a cruel mercy, yet he left me shivering, bereft of any clothing.

I knew standing still would get me nowhere. If I didn't at least try to move on, he would probably let me sit in this spot until I grew insane. The best bet I had was to get up and walk on.

He'd dropped me back in the maze not far from where I'd broken the glass to save Eddie. That mirror and the mirror I had used to break it still laid there shattered.

I did my best to avoid the shards of broken glass on the floor. A few stray pieces couldn't be avoided and my feet received several deep cuts. I didn't stop—I had to keep walking.

The hall seemed like it would go on forever, with mirrors stretching endlessly on both sides. On and on it went. Then I noticed something on the floor ahead. There was something different, something I hadn't seen yet… until I got close enough and realized I had.

The same broken mirrors lying on the floor and just beyond them, outlines of my bloody footprints. This place was a loop, but how? I never made a turn. Never changed direction. I didn't recall seeing any curvature to my path. If true, it meant there were no doors in this place. I had to try one more thing. I turned and ran back in the direction from which I'd come. Sure enough, I came back to the same spot with the broken mirrors again.

There had to be more to his plan than this. Yes, I would go insane sitting here, but that wasn't something I could see having me begging for death.

"Think, damn it, Arianna!" I said to myself. "You're smarter than this. What is it that you're not seeing?" Not see… ing. That was it, the mirrors! That was how he got me in here. If they were doors that meant that they work more than one way. Now the question was which one should I choose?

I ran back up the hall to get as far from the mirrors I'd broken, but close enough that I could still see them. I would start here and work my way back.

I put myself in front of the first mirror, but unlike last time, my own reflection wasn't there. I pushed on the glass, but nothing happened. I felt around the frame. Maybe there was a lock or button. Nothing again. *Fuck it*, I thought, *I'm going to run into the mirror as hard as I can.*

I backed up across the hall so I was in front of the other mirror. I counted to myself... one... two... thr... An arm reached out from behind me wrapping its hand over my face. It stunk of rotten flesh and didn't taste much better when I bit into its fingers.

It made no sound, even though I'd bitten it. It only pulled me back until I saw my feet being the last things dragged away from the outside of the mirror. Apparently, these mirrors operated on an invitation-only basis. My only question now was, where the hell was I just invited to?

CHAPTER 44: CLAY

"SERIOUSLY, AVA, I'M OKAY AND MY TEMPER IS UNDER control."

"Oh, so that's why you looked like you were about to stampede Elizabeth when you got here? Clay, all I'm asking you is to think a little more about whatever plans you were making before you go charging off to be the hero of the day. Yes, we want to stop whatever Az is doing, but shouldn't we make sure we protect what cannot protect itself?"

She'd come back from her walk with Grayson and had been on a rampage with me ever since. When she came over and said she wanted to talk to me I was hoping it would give us time to catch up. Time for us to talk about something other than Azrael.

I wanted to share with her what had happened when I drank the Waters of Lethe. I wanted to see if she'd already done that as well. I wanted to see what her experience had been. I didn't want to get lectured about what should or shouldn't be done next. It was bad enough the entire time she was gone that was all I heard from Elizabeth and Dr. Dawood.

"Ava, we have to do whatever is needed to stop Az. Yes, we want to protect as much as we can. I still don't even understand what the rest of them are expecting us to do. Have you gotten anything from them while you were here? I can't imagine that Elizabeth knows more than Dr. Dawood. He's another, like Az. Just, with him, it seems he's actually truthful with what he's told me."

"Elizabeth knows a bit, but she's not the one I spoke with the most."

"Then who was it?"

"Persephone. She's another one like Az and your Dr. Dawood."

"Is she gone? I must have missed her when we came in."

"No. She seems to not be like the other two in some ways. The only time I saw her was when I was at the temple pool. Come with me. Maybe we can get her to say hello."

The pool looked very much like the one I'd seen in Dr. Dawood's temple, the only difference being the emblem in the bottom. Dr. Dawood's had the Eye of Horus and this one had a flame.

"So how do you summon her or whatever it is that you do?"

"Umm… ha… ha… I don't really know. She summoned me last time. How do you call your doctor friend?"

"He's just there. Though, it never seems when I need him to be. Why do they all have to be so damn cryptic? Say what you mean and drop the fucking riddles."

"What fun would that be?" the voice replied playfully. As it echoed through the chamber, Ava and I spun around to locate the source. Positioned elegantly on the edge of the pool was a woman, draped in a flowing white robe.

Her dark hair cascaded down her back, reaching her waist. Adorned with countless pieces of jewelry, each piece crafted with the flame design that seemed to dance with a life of its own, she captured our full attention.

"I'm going to assume that you're Persephone?"

"And I'm going to assume that you're not going to be a pain in the ass while I try to explain a few things to you."

As Persephone was about to speak, the room's atmosphere shifted subtly. "He's already had plenty explained to him, Persephone," interjected a familiar voice. I turned to see Dr. Dawood stepping quietly into the room, his timing impeccable. Had he been listening all along?

"I thought I could smell wet dog. You could at least have the courtesy to bathe yourself before gracing us with your presence, Anubis."

"Dear sister, the blame lies with Azrael. His games forced us to summon Charon to transport us here.

"Glad you both are having a pleasant reunion and all," I said, "but maybe we can skip through that for now."

Persephone scowled at me, "Is he always this pleasant?"

"I would say that is rather mild for Clayton."

Dr. Dawood walked over to the pool and gave Persephone a hug. I turned back to look at Ava and from the back of the chamber I could see a shadow creeping along the walk.

The figure stayed close to the walkway as they moved, skillfully hiding behind one of the large statues of Persephone that adorned the room. I nodded to Ava to look in the direction of the shadow, but they had slipped too far back by the time she had looked up.

The figure lurking in the shadows caught my eye again. I wasn't sure if they belonged here, their presence sending a prickling sense of unease up my spine. People hiding in the dark usually have reasons, and seldom are they good.

"Dr. Dawood, how about we go back out with the others. I think it's only fair that we're all on the same page and have the same understanding."

"I'm sorry, Clayton. There are some things that they're not ready to hear. It's only for the ears of yourself, Ava, and if we find her, Arianna."

I interrupted the doc, "You mean WHEN we find her, doc, not if. IF is not an option." As I spoke, I caught Ava's glance; her expression heavy with unspoken words about Arianna. It was clear she would be our next serious discussion once we were alone. It was a topic that I needed to think about myself. My feelings for Ava had never waivered. I was confused, however, what my feelings for Arianna were.

Before it was the comfort of a friend helping when I was trying to escape; then, we drank the Waters of Lethe and I knew more about the three of us. There was still this mysterious fourth that I was unaware of. I only knew of our pasts as the light. When we take our worldly forms, you can only remember your own experiences. The others hadn't always been there with me, and we didn't always find one another.

Regardless of which existence I found myself in, my thoughts often wandered, pulling me into a labyrinth of memories and speculations that were hard to escape. Shaking my head I looked around the room noticing that the others were headed to the chamber door. Ava called back to me, "Clay, are you coming? We're about to head into one of Persephone's private chambers for a talk."

The shadow moved again; this time Ava had spotted them as well. She stepped back into the room nodding her head. There was now an understanding of what I'd been pointing out earlier.

The shadow crept closer to the pool, its movements deliberate and silent. Turning towards the creeping figure, I called out, "Who are you and what do you want? There's no use hiding any longer. I've seen you lurking around—now show yourself."

The tension in the room peaked as the shadowy figure finally stepped forward, emerging into the dim light of the chamber. The face that greeted us was unnervingly familiar. It was one that I'd worn for some time in my return to the living world.

"John Tyler, we meet at last."

CHAPTER 45: JOHN

DESPITE MY SILENT MOVEMENTS, SHADOW-LIKE WITHIN the chamber, I still don't know how he managed to spot me.

Upon entering the pool chamber, it initially seemed empty. Just a few steps from the pool, the ginger bitch and a man emerged, absorbed in deep conversation. Luckily, the focus on their conversation allowed me to swiftly slip into the shadows unnoticed.

A woman materialized out of thin air above the pool, unknown to me but clearly recognized by the ginger bitch. Not a moment later another man entered. I heard them addressing each other as Persephone and Anubis. There was something about them that told me to stay where I was until they were gone. The other two I knew wouldn't be much of a problem to deal with.

As they moved out of the room I crept back to the pool, and then, he called me out by my name—my full name.

As I stepped out into the light and got closer to the man there was a familiarity to his face. It was him, the one I'd seen when I was crossing through the darkness.

"John, what are you doing here?" the ginger bitch asked.

"Not important," I said. "How do you know my name?"

"I know plenty about you, John Tyler," the man sneered. "Your wife Emilia, your tech empire, even your dirty little secrets, like the affair and cutting your family out of your will. Oh, and let's not forget the other dark, disgusting things you've been up to."

"How? There's no way." I reached into my pocket and could still feel the watch there, its icy cold touch a reminder of what I needed to do.

"There is a way. When we last crossed paths, you ended up here and I, well, I ended up in your body. I'm sorry to have to inform you that you'll not be able to return to yourself. But, have no fear John, before I left, Emilia and I went and made a few adjustments to your will. She and the kids will be well taken care of after your most unfortunate death."

"You son-of-a-bitch, do you have any idea who you're fucking with? I will crush you. Everything you own will be mine!"

"Really, John? Will you? You no longer have your business. Your money. What power you thought you had didn't come with you. You have no power over any of us here."

"No power, huh," I thought to myself as I pulled the watch out of my pocket, letting it dangle by the chain. As they set their eyes on it I could see it was something they'd recognized. No doubt these two have met Az before.

"What are you going to do with that?" she asked. The man stepped protectively in front of her and advanced towards me, narrowing the distance. Meanwhile, I edged closer to the pool, calculating each step to ensure they couldn't stop me in time. Az had said as soon as I opened it to place it in the water, and I would be out of here.

"Oh this old thing?" I said. "It was a present from my new friend, Az. Do you like it?" I took a few steps closer, showing it to them. Only a few more steps and I was there.

"It's not exactly my style of watch, but something tells me that the value of this watch is about to far outweigh its cheap design." One more step.

I clicked the watch open and tossed it into the pool. The man, who I had come to realize was ginger bitch's man, Clay, charged at me. Then the ginger bitch dove towards the pool.

He tackled me to the ground; as we landed, an ear-piercing screech erupted. Glancing at the pool, I saw the water shift from clear to indigo, as if black ink was bleeding through. That had gotten Clay's attention.

He released me when he saw her reaching for the water. "Ava, no!" he shouted. As her hand touched the water, Az materialized just like the woman who had earlier. He had his pocket watch back, swinging from his fingers.

"Miss Sanderson, Mr. Mitchell. How splendid to see you both again." Az looked over to me. "Thank you very much for your assistance, Mr. Tyler. As promised you'll be leaving here in a few moments."

I got back to my feet and walked towards Az. I wasn't taking any chances at being left here. Clay grabbed the ginger bitch and pushed her behind him. "The ever valiant Mr. Mitchell," Az said as he stepped closer to them. "Here's what's going to happen: You're both going to come with me and we're going to be done with this once and for all."

"You'll have a snowball's chance in hell of making that happen, Az," Clay responded.

"Oh, the confidence, Mr. Mitchell! Think your friends will come to your rescue? Just like they did for Miss Stone, huh? Face it, there's nothing you or they can do."

"Mr. Tyler, please be so kind as to step inside the pool."

As I stepped into the pool, following Az's instructions, he reached out, seizing Clay by the arm with a swift, unexpected motion. Before there was a chance for anyone to comprehend what was happening, a blur of red hair pushed past Clay and the ginger bitch drove her shoulder into Az. His grip on Clay's arm was broken. Az and the ginger bitch both fell back into me, knocking me down into the water.

The moment Az touched the water again, it was as if a whirlpool had opened up and it swallowed us whole. Spinning. Spinning. Oh man, I needed this to stop.

The water violently tossed us out, and I skidded to a halt on a hard surface. As I blinked open my eyes, the overwhelming darkness enveloped me once more, returning me to a profound and chilling obscurity.

Struggling to my feet, I realized I was alone—neither Az nor the ginger bitch were anywhere in sight. It was dark but I could see my hands. I turned to the light coming from behind me. It was the windows again. Looking through them I could see Az and the ginger bitch inside. He was gripping her throat, his face inches from hers in what was clearly a hostile exchange.

I scanned the area for the other woman who had been present earlier, but she was nowhere to be found. Where could she have vanished to?

CHAPTER 46: ARIANNA

I LOOKED AROUND THE SHADOWY CORNERS OF THE room for several tense minutes, searching for any sign of what had dragged me through the mirror, but I was alone.

Where here was, I wasn't all that sure yet. I'd been pulled through a mirror that looked similar to the ones in the mirror maze, but this one was in a small bedroom.

The room was plain in regards to furniture and decoration. The linens on the bed were black with accented red threading. The bed posts were the most ornate things in this room. Each of them was a different shape with a letter carved into it.

At the head of the bed was a triangle with the letter N carved into it. Across from that was a circle with the letter E. The foot of the bed was an octagon with the letter S and its partner to the other side was a square with the letter W. I could only assume that the letters were compass directions, but I didn't understand the significance of the shapes.

I went over to the door and tried the knob, but it was locked. It was one of those old skeleton key type of locks. I was curious what was on the other side of the door. I got down on my knees and put my face up to the lock to look through.

A sharp, excruciating pain shot through my eye, piercing my calm with sudden, unbearable agony. My scream echoed off the cold walls, mixing with a rush of fear and confusion. Panic began to set in as I felt the blood trickle down my cheek. My hands rushed up to my eye. I could feel a pointed object now sticking into it. I tripped over my own feet as I backed away from the door, landing on the bed.

Bang! Bang! Bang! The relentless pounding on the door sent waves of terror through my body. Each thud felt like a hammer against my chest, intensifying the dread pooling in my stomach. I was trapped, with nowhere to hide. I slid back to the headboard, pulling my feet onto the bed. Reaching up I pulled the object from my eye. I was relieved that my eye hadn't come out with it. Looking through the good eye that I had left I could see a bloody knitting needle in my hand.

The banging on the door was getting harder. The door rattled with each hit it took. I could see it wasn't going to hold much longer. Whatever wanted in here was about to get its wish. I needed to find something to at least try and protect myself.

I reached for the bedpost with the letter N on the triangle. It looked like it would be a good option to swing at someone. The triangle looked like it may be sharp enough to do enough damage to give me a chance to get away. Grabbing just under the triangle I pulled up. The post wouldn't come free, but as my hand slid up under the triangle I felt that it was loose.

I was hoping that this was a bedknob and if I could get it free I could at least have something to throw at whatever is coming through that door. I turned it counter-clockwise and after a single rotation, I heard a series of several clicks, almost as if there were locks inside the bed post that were being released. I tried turning it more but it was stuck. I couldn't even turn it back to where it had been before.

Bang! Bang! Bang! I saw cracks coming down the center of the door. I jumped over to the other side of the bed and grabbed onto the circle with the letter E. It too was loose, but would only turn clockwise. This one made two full rotations—*click, click, click.* Then it seized up like the other.

Splinters were now flying off the back of the door where a small hole was forming. Through the splintering wood, a grotesque hand, its flesh decayed and peeling, clawed its way through, desperate to reach inside. In the place between its thumb and pointer finger I could see deep teeth marks. Whatever was trying to get me now was the same thing that had pulled me through the mirror.

I moved down to the end of the bed and the same thing happened with both the square and octagon bedposts. Several spins, a series of clicks, and then they seized up.

The arm had reached further into the room and was grabbing for the doorknob. Apparently this door was locked from both sides. It tried turning the knob, but the door wouldn't open. With that failing it returned to breaking off pieces of the door.

I looked for anything that might be able to be used as a weapon. It was useless. I went back to the mirror and noticed that it was no longer a reflection of this room. It was looking back into the mirror maze. I could see Azrael there with a woman. He had her by the neck and was yelling something at her.

The door burst open as this thing entered the room. It was a person I'd once known. It was Eddie, but it also wasn't. My heart sank as I faced the grotesque parody of a man I once knew. Grief mingled with horror, tearing at my nerves as the creature moved closer. The skin was sagging down to the bone and patches of skin were gone from where something had been gnawing on it. This is what Azrael's plan was? To keep showing me the one love in my life in as many painful ways as possible.

As I looked back in the mirror I knew what I had to do. I was either going to end up covered in glass, or I was going to be able to help out this poor woman that Azrael was harassing. I took a final look at Eddie, and with a deep, steadying breath, I turned and hurled myself into the glass.

CHAPTER 47: AVA

"DID YOU REALLY THINK I WOULDN'T FIND YOU? AFTER all I did for you. You could've been beside me for all this."

Az was enraged and had me by the throat. I tried kicking and shaking myself free, but it was no use; he was too strong. I grabbed onto his wrist trying to push it off of my neck. "No. You'll not get free, Ava. Not until I let you free." He spun us around, showing me the place he'd brought us to. "Do you see this? This is your fate now. You'll wander these halls for an eternity and each day you're going to pray that I'll come back and turn you into nothingness."

Out of nowhere we were flying forward and crashing down onto the floor. Az lost his grip on me and then there was another hand pulling me away from him. I couldn't see who it was, but I could feel that the person had soft and delicate skin. "Quick. Get to your feet," she said.

I reorientated myself and pushed up from the floor. The hand grabbed back on to my arm. Turning I saw that it was the woman that was on the floor back at the apartment. This was Arianna.

She was pulling me further down the hall. Az's boisterous laugh filled and echoed down after us. "Isn't this precious? Both of Mr. Mitchell's prized women protecting one another."

"Stay away from us, Azrael," yelled Arianna.

"Oh by all means, dearest ladies—you're welcome to run this maze. I shall not interfere. In fact, I'm most curious to see what might happen as you face it together."

What the hell did he mean by both of Clay's prized women? I was Clay's, not her. I pulled my arm back from her, but this only served to make Az laugh even harder. Arianna stood staring at me with a look of confusion on her face. I turned back to say something to Az, but he was already gone.

"You're Ava, right? I'm sorry if I've done something to offend you, I'm just trying to help."

"And you're Arianna. What's the deal with you and Clay? The pieces aren't fitting together for me."

"It's Az playing mind games, Ava. Clay and I are just friends. Let's keep moving and talk."

Looking in both directions, I could only see a hallway of mirrors stretching endlessly. "Is there anywhere to actually go other than this hallway? I don't see anything else."

"Yes, come. Each mirror leads somewhere—often to what you fear most. It can break you. The things it shows you will make you want to give up and die all over again."

"I doubt that. Az has already taken everything he could from me."

We walked down the hall a ways until we came upon two mirrors that were out of place and broken. The floor was damp and the air much cooler here.

"This is where I started when he put me in here," Arianna said. "He showed me something, and I broke the mirror and it took me in. If you don't mind, I don't want to talk about that experience right now. I've tried both directions and each time I come back around to this spot. It doesn't matter which way you go, you'll end up back here."

"So, we need to break all the mirrors to find a way out of here?" I asked.

"No. It doesn't work like that. Whichever mirror wants us, will take us, or that's what seems to be happening."

It didn't sound all that unbelievable, a little odd, but then again in the time I'd known Az this was the type of shit he did. "Okay. Do we keep walking and wait for something to happen?"

"I'm not sure, Ava. You know his ways better, since you were working with him."

I couldn't help but feel she was taking a cheap shot at me. "Yes. I was working with. Was, as in the past. Was, as in before I found out that he'd taken my life before it was my time, to serve at his pleasure. Was, as in before I found out that he killed Clay to make sure that I'd forget my own memories and serve him better."

Arianna had a shocked look on her face. "Oh, that's right. Clay didn't get to share that with you before he tried to be the hero of the day and recklessly dive through Az's gateway. I get that he wanted to keep from being erased by Az, but there were other ways. Ways that didn't involve getting back to the world of the living; leaving me here alone again."

"I'm sorry, Ava. Clay was desperate to escape and baffled by your alliance with Az. He couldn't understand why you'd shut him out."

"And he shared all that with you? Is that what your Book of Clay was all about?"

"It's not what you think. Clay feared Az's power to erase memories—he had seen it happen. The Book of Clay was something he asked me to write. It was the book of his life, his life with you and the love he has for you, Ava."

I didn't know what to say to that. I saw how beautiful Arianna was and felt insecure that someone else might take Clay away. She could sense I was confused and hurting and placed an arm over my shoulder. "We have more to talk about, but please, let's keep moving. And remember, whatever Azrael shows us, it isn't real."

"The damage to your eye looks very real to me."

"Yes, but I suspect it will go back to normal in time. I've already had most of my body covered in severe burns and I'm certain he's tried to drown me twice. Each and every time I've come back to normal."

"So he's only controlling what we see?"

"No, you're going to feel it as well. These things don't come without pain. In those moments you'll want to give up, or at least I have. But you can't give into him. We need to find a way out of here, and we need to stop him."

"You sound like Clay now. Yes, stop Az, but let's be careful not to destroy everything else in the process. He'll use us to bait Clay, who's already on edge. We need to reach him first, or shit's going to hit the fan for everyone."

"Let's find out where these mirrors lead, now."

Down the hall we went pressing against the glass of each mirror. Most were glass and nothing more. We each had one side of the hall. Thinking about what I knew of Az I stopped Arianna. "We need to work on the same mirrors. Separate mirrors might bring us to different places. We're going to be stronger together."

After testing several mirrors, one finally yielded. As our hands touched the glass, it rippled like water, allowing us to pass through. On the other side it had been water—a waterfall.

Beyond the waterfall was a small lake with sapphire colored water. We couldn't see the bottom, and I suggested we should see if there was a way to the shore without getting in the water. There was no telling what might be in there. I should've remembered never to underestimate Az. He knew I'd avoid the water, and so we walked right to the place he wanted us to be.

CHAPTER 48: GRAYSON

SINCE AZRAEL THREW ME THROUGH THE MIRROR, IT'S like something woke up inside me. I started knowing things I shouldn't—secrets that unfolded hour by hour. But there wasn't any time to make sense of it all, not with Ava and Clay's lives spinning out of control because of me. Amidst the chaos, I couldn't believe who I ran into: Elizabeth, right there in front of me. I never thought I'd see her again, but there she was, as real as the mess we were in.

Our reunion was cut short. Every attempt to catch up was interrupted by some new crisis. This time, while sitting outside the temple we'd stumbled upon, Clay's shouts echoed from inside, sounding dire. Knowing him as I did, his yelling was a sure sign trouble was brewing.

Elizabeth and I got up and ran inside. Clay's yelling was coming from the room with the fancy pool. When we got in there I could see that the water had turned black as midnight. Clay was leaning over the side of the pool yelling at the water. *Oh shit,* I thought, *this boy has finally lost his fucking mind.*

I walked over to Clay and put my hand on his shoulder. "What the hell happened?"

"That son-of-a-bitch took her! John Tyler helped him sneak in and snatch her right out from under me."

"Who took her?" This boy was back to muttering nonsense again.

"Az! He took Ava. He was trying to take me… Ava… She dove over and pushed him away. When they hit the pool they all disappeared."

"I see. Who the hell is John Tyler? Is that the new name Azrael is using?" It surprised me how much had happened to Clay since I'd last seen him. I wanted to get caught up on it all, but it would be hard with him in this worked up state.

"No, John Tyler's the bastard whose life I stepped into when I jumped back to the living world—total scumbag, fits right in with Az."

Elizabeth chimed in, a note of anger in her voice. "Clay, not everyone involved with Az is bad. Remember, Ava and I both worked with him once."

I couldn't help but look back at Elizabeth with an utterly shocked expression. Working for Azrael? That didn't sound right. She had despised him so much and never mentioned anything about that past to me. That would have to be a conversation for later. Clay was falling apart and he needed someone here for him.

I pulled Clay up by the arm. "Come on Clay. Let's go find that doctor friend of yours. I suspect we'll be needing to tell him what's happened. Elizabeth, are you able to close this pool thing? I don't suspect we want anyone going in or near that water with it looking the way it does."

"Absolutely. Get him settled down; I'll handle this mess. We don't need any more surprises."

Dragging Clay away from the chaotic scene at the pool, I led him to his friend, Dr. Dawood, hoping he could offer some stability. I was still a bit suspicious of him and this Persephone lady. I don't go putting too much stock in anyone I've met here. There was just something about it that told me whatever they were trying to do was more self-serving rather than to the benefit of everyone.

"Hey Dr. Dawood," I said. "There was a ruckus by the pool you all have down here. Clay says that some oaf named John Tyler was able to help Azrael get in here and now Ava has vanished."

"Clayton, is this true?" asked the doctor. Clay stood silently beside me with his fists clenched tight. I'd seen that look in his eyes before, and I suspected that he was about to have a meltdown of nuclear proportions.

"Why don't we let Clay have a few moments. You said that you all lost Arianna in a similar way and now Ava's gone. The boy needs a few moments to sort that stuff out."

I set Clay down in a chair and motioned the doctor to follow me outside. As we were walking out, the lady, Persephone, had come in and headed towards Clay. "Ma'am," I said, "I think Elizabeth could use some help in the pool room. She might need you for a few things." She seemed surprised that someone by the likes of me would be telling her what to do. After a reassuring look from the doctor she took off in that direction.

The doctor and I sat down outside where Elizabeth and I had been when this scene started. "What kind of doctor are you? I don't think I've had a chance to ask you that before with all the excitement and all."

"Doctor is only a role that I was playing as it was needed to get access to Clayton."

"I see. I see. So what's the big deal needing him so badly?"

"It's bigger than just Clayton. I was the one who could get close enough to earn his trust—not an easy feat."

"And I don't suspect you're about to go breaking that trust, now are you? That poor boy went through hell in Purgatory with betrayals coming in every direction. You and that lady friend of yours seem to have more than a little in common with Azrael."

"I'm offe..." the doctor started to say.

"Save your offended act, doc. I've seen enough to know when I'm being played. I may not be the smartest man, but don't think I don't notice you and Persephone off in the corner whispering every chance you get."

I slid in closer to the doctor and spoke in a hushed tone. "Let me share a little sunshine with you doc. We're blowing this popsicle stand soon, and before we do, you and your lady are spilling everything. No more games, no more secrets. We're tearing down the curtains, and you're gonna help us. If you think I'm going to let either of you two peckerheads harm any of this lot I've come here with… Well, you best remember, you're not the only ones who have secrets."

I slapped the doctor on the back. "Good, I see we have an understanding. I'll give you a few minutes to go back and speak with the lady friend. I'm gonna go back and check on Clay."

CHAPTER 49: ARIANNA

WINNING AVA'S TRUST PROVED TO BE HELLISHLY FRUS-trating. I couldn't pin down what had ticked her off so badly. If we were going to make it through what Azrael was putting us through we need to at least be able to work together.

Avoiding the water seemed like the right call at the time. I followed Ava as she skirted along the mound that led out from the waterfall to the shore. We moved cautiously, sliding our feet along the path. Other than a few loose rocks that had slid down into the water it looked as if we were going to make the shore without a problem.

A few feet from the shore I heard something and grabbed Ava's hand to get her to stop. I pointed up. There was something moving on the cliff above us. We took another slow step forward and were greeted by a fierce roar.

"Run!" I shoved Ava forward and we made a dash to the shore and into the surrounding woods. The roars grew louder, and I could hear the creature tearing through the brush and trees right behind us, closing in fast. There was only woods ahead, I knew what we had to do. "Ava," I said, gasping for breath. "We need to turn back to the water."

"Are you insane? That water's a fucking death trap, Arianna! We can't even see the bottom!"

"Please, Ava, just this once, trust me. We can't outrun that thing. The water—it might buy us some time."

Either her trust was growing, or she had seen what was chasing us—I hadn't dared look back yet. I needed to focus on running. Ava turned and was running at an angle, but it wasn't back to the water.

"What are you doing?" I asked.

"Blindly turning back is suicide. We'll loop around, keep our distance. I trusted you—now it's your turn."

She took us a quarter of a mile or more away before turning again and heading back towards the lake. My legs were getting tired and my skin kept getting cut from branches and pricker vines scattered along our path. Ava's pace outstripped mine; she was a natural runner, and I struggled to keep up. The lake had to be getting closer.

I felt we were at a safe enough distance as I could no longer hear anything following us that I could look back. That was a big mistake. It took a moment to register what it was I was looking at. It was the biggest goddamn bear I'd ever seen.

It had to have weighed well over a thousand pounds. Its brown fur was matted and soaked with blood from its last meal. I turned back to run harder, and slammed into Ava's back. She'd stopped short.

"What the hell, Ava! Move your ass, we're not safe yet!" She grabbed my head and turned it forward. The lake was not more than a few yards ahead of us, but before we could reach it there was a curtain of these thorny plants. The barbs looked deathly sharp, but still, sharp barbs or getting devoured by a bear. I knew which I was going to choose.

We gained a brief respite as the bear paused, eyeing us from a distance. I ran to my left to the closest tree grabbing a recently fallen branch. I took it back and started swinging away at the thorny plants. Every piece I hacked off sprouted two more in its place—like some sort of fucking hydra.

I threw my hand forward and pulled at one of the vines. I ripped at it and it came down. My hands were now bleeding and in pain, but the vine I'd torn down didn't regrow. I got it now. This thing had a toll to cross through it and the price was to be paid in blood.

Looking back, the bear wasn't charging but had resumed growling and making a slow stride towards us. "Ava, stick close to me and watch the vines. Grab a branch or something to fend them off. When we hit the lake, you gotta shove me under—hard. I'll struggle, but don't let up until I go limp."

"I can't just drown you, Arianna! That's insane!"

"We're already dead, Ava. Please, just do what I'm telling you." I didn't give her a chance to respond. I put my hands in front of me and began ripping at the vines. The more I pulled the more my hands bled. Soon the vines were ripping at my body as I got deeper into the patch. They weren't growing back and as far as I could see, Ava was unharmed by them.

By the time I broke through, my body was shredded, blood everywhere. I could feel blood running from every part of my body. As the last vine ripped free I charged forward into the water. You couldn't see the bottom, but it was there. My feet could feel the cool soft sands beneath me.

I looked back and Ava had made it through. The pain from the cuts was sinking in and I was becoming faint. "Please, Ava," I begged. She came forward, grabbed my head and neck, and shoved me under the water.

A moment later, I gasped back to life and coughed up lake water, no longer feeling the soft sand beneath us. All I could feel were Ava's arms wrapped around me.

"How long was I out?"

"Just a few minutes. I pulled you up as soon as you stopped struggling. I had to get us away from the shore. The bear is still standing over there, but so far it's refused to come into the water."

Looking back at the shore I saw the big brown beast of a bear pacing back and forth looking for a way to get to us. Ava had brought us out fifty or so feet from the shore.

"Thanks for that, I'm good to swim now." I pushed off and turned to look back at Ava. The few cuts she had were already healed over. Mine had done the same and the damaged eye had also been restored to me. I was right about the water, however, seeing that Ava had healed without having to have been drowned I thought the same could happen for me. Azrael had just wanted me to suffer before.

"What do we do now?" Ava asked.

The other side was about three hundred yards away from us; if we could make the swim over there would be no way for the beast to catch up with us. "Let's make a break for it over there." I pointed towards the rocks. "But shit, Ava, what's waiting for us there? Could be nothing, or something even nastier than our furry friend back there. Honestly, I'd rather feel sand under my feet than guess what's lurking below."

Ava nodded in agreement. "Alright, let's edge in closer first. The sand cuts off about twenty-five feet out. We'll skirt along the edge, see if that bastard follows. Maybe find a spot it can't get to us."

As we swam, the bear trotted along the shore following us. Azrael was going to make sure this wasn't easy. We'd gotten halfway around the lake and the bear hadn't stopped its pursuit.

"Look over there, Ava." Another cluster of rocks was jetting out from the shore. It looked too steep for the bear to be able to trek out to us. "Let's hold up there and get out of this damn water for a bit. See if that bear gives up the chase or decides to wait us out."

As it turned out, it would wait on us as long as we stayed there. I was right however. The bear couldn't make it out to the end of the rocks. That gave us time to rest ourselves and more importantly, provided a chance for Ava and I to talk.

It was small talk at first. I felt as though I had the upper hand in the conversation as I at least had the background on Ava that Clay provided when we preserved his memories. Ava was a wonderful listener as I shared the story of Eddie with her. In my line of work I'd often been the one listening, so it was a nice change having someone listen to me.

Later in our conversation, she apologized for her jealous outburst about Clay and I earlier. I told her it was nothing to worry about. I only hoped that moving forward we could trust each other more.

The sun was setting and the bear had fallen asleep on the shore facing us. I motioned to Ava to slide back into the water—I followed behind her. Back on the shore, the beast was still sleeping.

We made our way further and further from the rock pile; still no sign that the bear had followed us. We'd almost circled the lake with the waterfall coming back into view. Just before reaching it we came across a small cove. "Let's get out of here, but slow. There's no telling what else might be out here," I said.

Inching out of the water, one foot at a time, Ava and I made our way into the surrounding forest. Daylight had faded—the only light still visible was that of the full moon rising. It was a dull glow providing barely enough light to see a foot or two in front of us.

There were no paths in these deep woods. I was leading the way as my eyes had made a quicker adjustment to the dark. "Ava, look over there. Do you see it?" There was a slight downhill drop off and at the bottom, a temple. Though this wasn't like the one I'd seen in the desert. This one had old forest growth covering it and many of the columns were in a state of severe disrepair.

"Yes, but do you think it's safe?"

"There's only one way to find out. I was in one that looked like that when I was entering into death. It was where I'd met Dr. Dawood. It was the same place that Azrael had pulled me into this maze from."

"There was another one where I had been. Our situations are similar; he pulled me through as well. The temple I was at there was another like Az calling herself Persephone."

Walking closer to the temple we could see a light coming from inside, but could hear no other people around. As we were stepping up on to the first of the steps I heard something large breaking through the brush behind us. It was coming fast and with a purpose.

I took Ava by the arm and pulled her along with me into the temple. "It's that fucking bear again! We have to go inside. There has to be a door or something we can put between us and the bear." There wasn't; but we didn't need it.

The moment that bear tried to cross through the threshold of the temple it was turned into a pile of ash that fell to the ground.

Ava and I hugged each other. "That was a close one," she said.

The temple looked as though it was set up very similar inside to the one that Dr. Dawood had been in. I only hoped that meant there was a pool here as well. It might be that we could use it the same way that Azrael had.

The light I had seen was coming from a small torch on the wall. I pulled it down and began looking at which path to take. To the right, there was a door of gold with fine jewels decorating it. To the left, a door made of wood. It was rotting and mushrooms and mold grew from it.

Ava and I looked at one another for a moment before I stepped forward, grabbing a door handle. As the door swung open, behind it was a small chamber with a small floor mirror resting against the wall. I somehow had known that picking the less ornate of the two doors would bring us to what we were looking for.

"Do you think we should check the second one?" Ava asked.

"I don't think so. Something tells me that those foolish enough to think a golden door is better will find nothing but want and despair behind it."

Standing before the mirror, a hidden detail caught our eye. There was another room that had no door directly behind us.

Ava and I both turned to see that this wasn't the mirror playing tricks on us. There was a room and it had one of the pools that we'd both seen at other temples.

"I need to take a look at it before we try the mirror. Are you okay with that?"

Ava curled her lips. "I'm not much of a fan of those at the moment, but we need to stay together. If Az separates us I can't see things getting better for either of us. We can go take a look, but please, let's be quick about it."

"Deal!"

The chamber was almost an exact replication of the one I'd seen in Dr. Dawood's temple. "Does this look like the one you saw in Persephone's temple?" I asked Ava.

"A little dirtier and not as well kept, but yes, the layout is exactly the same. The other thing I see that's different is the symbol on the bottom of Persephone's pool is a flame."

I looked down into the pool and could see there were two different symbols below. "Yes, this is different from what I saw at the bottom of Dr. Dawood's pool as well. Do you think this might be Azrael's temple?"

"I don't think so," Ava said as she was wiping dirt and webs from the wall. You see this symbol, it's a..."

"It is a fish and a bodhi tree. That doesn't mean it may not be connected to Azrael."

"He's too vain to let something that belongs to him fall into this type of disrepair."

"Okay, let's go see if that mirror works. I don't want to be here much longer. It may or may not be his, but I don't want to find out who the owner is if they come back. If they let it look like this, I'm not sure they are going to be on the friendly side."

We went back across the hall and this time the mirror was not as complicated as the last. We both took a hand and pressed it against the glass as we stepped forward. It gave way, feeling like a gel washing over me.

When we came out on the other side we were back in the mirror maze, but something had changed. It was the same mirrors, or at least they looked the same, but the room was now a giant circle. The mirrors were all lined up against the wall. I wasn't sure if it was the same room until I saw that two of the mirrors were still broken.

I looked over to Ava. "He's going to make it harder now, isn't he?"

Ava took a big gulp of air, pointing at the mirrors. There was a man walking towards us from behind them, but it wasn't Azrael.

"Who's that?" I asked.

"John Tyler," Ava replied.

CHAPTER 50: GRAYSON

CLAY WAS STILL FUMING WHEN I GOT BACK TO HIM. THAT boy has such a hard time getting past his anger and focusing on what needs to be done. I figured I'd give him a little more time to cool down before I tried to talk to him. Elizabeth's and my conversation had been interrupted, and I intended to get back to that before anything else could disrupt us.

As Elizabeth slowly and deliberately cleaned the remnants of the previous chaos in the pool room, I watched her closely, the weight of past secrets hanging between us. "Elizabeth, can we finish that talk?" I asked, cutting to the chase. We dived straight back into the thick of it—my chaotic tumble through Azrael's dark mirror, my unexpected alliances with Clay and Ava. Every word was quick and sharp, reflecting the urgency of our messed-up world.

"All that bullshit I believed about the portal and Purgatory? It's all one big fucking joke. And poor Clay, I fed him those fairy tales, not knowing shit."

"Grayson," she said in that reassuring mom voice, "you shouldn't be so hard on yourself. You had no idea and I had no way to get back to tell you what happened."

"Maybe that's so. Tell me this, how well do you trust these other two?"

"Who might you mean, Grayson?"

"That doctor and the pretty lady that lives in the pool here."

"Her name is Persephone and I trust her enough. The doctor I'd never seen until he came with Clayton."

"I see. Well, to be honest with you I don't care much for either of them. Just something about them that's not sitting right with me, Elizabeth. While I'm being honest, there's something else that's not sitting well with me. How is it that you'd never come to tell me that you worked for Azrael?"

Elizabeth's shoulders dropped, and her head followed. "I was ashamed that I had. It was a long time before I'd met you. By then I was so focused on stopping what I knew he had been doing, and like Clay, I wanted back to the living world."

I shook my head, trying to piece together the fragments of what I'd learned. "When you first mentioned the gateway, you looked like you'd seen a ghost. But Ava—she seemed clued in from the get-go."

Elizabeth sighed, her gaze dropping briefly before meeting mine again. "When I worked with Azrael, he never let on about the gateway. All I knew was the indigo haze—it was his calling card. Looks like he didn't make the same mistake with Ava."

"And you got away without a scratch? That doesn't sound like something he'd let slide."

Elizabeth's face fell, shadows in her eyes. "Not all scars are visible, Grayson." Her voice was barely above a whisper, cracking with emotion. "Is that why you're doubting me?"

"I don't know just yet, Elizabeth."

She pursed her lips and sighed. "There are many things we shared Grayson and many things we didn't have the time to.

My omission about that period wasn't done to be deceitful. It was out of shame. Please, my friend, I ask for your forgiveness."

I grunted, unable to deny her the forgiveness she sought. Doubts gnawed at me, though, like rats in the walls of my conviction. As we stood there under the open sky, the air thick with unsaid words, I sensed bigger storms brewing. "There's more trouble ahead," I muttered, more to myself than to her. I also knew that there was something I was now keeping from Elizabeth and everyone else. I'd changed somehow. I'd been feeling it, but things were becoming clearer now. Clear about who I was or rather who I'd been. Pushing this to the side I got up and offered my hand to Elizabeth. "Let's go find these other two. I'm not much for standing around while Azrael is out causing harm."

We walked back toward the temple, the cool outside air clashing with my heated thoughts. As we approached, the distant echoes of a commotion grew louder, transforming into distinct shouts as we stepped inside. The familiar walls of the temple now echoed with the chaos of conflict. Clay was in the doctor's face, veins bulging, voice a ragged roar. "Move!" he bellowed, lunging for a door at the far end, only to be blocked by the doctor and that mysterious lady, Persephone. I knew by the look on that boy's face he was about to do something stupid again. I couldn't understand how someone so smart could be so damn dumb sometimes.

CHAPTER 51: CLAY

"GET THE FUCK OUT OF MY WAY! I'M SICK OF YOUR BULL-shit games and riddles. I drank your goddamn water, saw my past lives—SO THE FUCK WHAT? It's time to act, not play your twisted games! To hell with the both of you."

I shoved harder against them. Dr. Dawood's eyes began glowing bright. So be it, I thought. At least if someone took me out I wouldn't have to deal with this torment any longer. Either my light was going to burn out or I'd return to the great light.

I was dead set on making a final charge forward at them when I felt a hand touch my shoulder. "You really think that's a fucking smart move? Give me a minute to talk some sense into you, then you can go charging off like a goddamn mad-man if you still want to."

Grayson worked himself between Dr. Dawood and me. "Fine, let's go outside," I said.

"Clay, what the hell are you doing? You really think you can take on those… things by yourself?"

"I… I… yes I can. I know more than I did before. I know more about what happens to us and where we came from."

"It may be that you do. Does that knowledge give you any of the powers or strength that the doc or Azrael have? I suspect not my friend. You need to use that brain of yours."

Grayson leaned in closer to me. "You listen to me friend, I don't trust either of them. I think it might be wise if you started listening a little more to what they're saying. Seems to me they might be trying to send you, and by the looks of it, the rest of us out on some fool's errand. One that is likely going to benefit only them."

"What makes you think that?" I asked.

"It's just a gut feeling, Clay. Ever since I met those two, something's been off. They remind me too much of Azrael. Dress up a wolf in sheep's clothing all you want—it's still a wolf underneath."

"What am I supposed to do, Grayson? I've lost both Ava and Arianna in the last two days. I can't let Az have them. I just can't!"

"So what is it about that pool that had you ready to take on the doc?"

"Both of them were pulled through a pool by Az. There has to be a way to use that thing to get to him."

"So what are you gonna do, go jumping in the pool and end up with them? You think you're gonna take on Azrael by yourself? Clay, man… where the fuck did that get you the last time?"

"I need to do something, Grayson. What would you have me do, sit here and wait for those two to finally come up with a plan on what to do?"

"No, I wouldn't. I would have you think and be smarter about this. We don't know a damn thing about those pools other than what they've told us and what we've seen. Do you know for sure where it will take you? No. You don't. But we do know where something will take us and I suspect if you want to find Azrael, it will get you to him."

"What other place?"

"The darkness, Clay. It's the one place we've all been through at one point in time. It seems to be the one place that has connected each of us to the different places we've been to."

"Okay, but the last time I was there I had jumped through the gateway. I don't see one of those anywhere near here."

"Don't need to find that thing again. There's this place beyond the valley where the rocks open up and lead back out into it. It was where we came through."

"Great, tell me where it is and I'll be off."

"Not alone this time. I shouldn't have let you go alone last time. I'm not going to make that mistake again. First, though, we need to go back and find out as much as we can from those two fools. There's still more we need to know before we go chasing Azrael."

"I can't. I need to get..."

"You need to get your head out of your ass. You will get to Ava and Arianna. Listen to me for a minute boy. They are two very strong women and if by any chance they've ended up together, Az will be dealing with more than he's bargained for. Now get that sour look off your damn face and let's get this done."

CHAPTER 52: AVA

"KEEP THE FUCK AWAY FROM US, JOHN!" I SHOUTED, MY voice echoing sharply off the mirrors.

John smirked, unfazed. "Well, that's a rather cold welcome, Red!"

Having John Tyler walk through the mirrors was the last thing I was expecting. I knew from the temple that he'd fallen into working with Az. That still didn't answer why he would send John in here with us.

"Who's this friend of yours, Red?" John's tone was taunting.

"Call me Red one more fucking time, and you're gonna see your face smashed right into one of these goddamn mirrors," I snapped back, my fists clenched.

"My name's Arianna. Who the hell is this guy, Ava?"

I kept my eyes locked on John. "This piece of shit is John Tyler. It was his damn body Clay got stuck in when he returned to the world of the living. And yeah, he's also the reason we're all fucked right now."

"Oh, now I wouldn't go saying it was my fault. I do believe it was you who decided to come charging at me like a bitch in heat."

I moved in front of Arianna, at the same time stepping closer to John. Staring him down, my voice became low and fierce. "You do realize every damn thing Az promised you is a lie, right? He's just using you, John. And when you're no longer useful, you're out, just like that."

"How sweet of you to worry about me. I would be a very bad businessman if I hadn't seen that when I made the deal. Let's say for now that I have a few cards up my sleeve I can play when the time comes."

"So what are you doing here, John?"

"What, do you not appreciate a little male company? I know I would surely enjoy a little of either, or even better, both of your company. A man has needs, even in the afterlife."

My stomach started to turn. I didn't know much about John, but since our last conversation I knew that he was always giving off major creep vibes. We had to move and get away from him. I hadn't thought Az would go this low, but it appeared he was even darker than I thought.

For each step he would take forward Arianna and I would take one back. Looking over my shoulder I could see the glass from one of the broken mirrors. I took Arianna's hand in mine pulling her back with me to the shards of glass.

John must have realized what I was doing because in a moment he was on us. I had just enough time to reach down and grab a piece of glass. I felt it cut into my hand as I squeezed it tight.

Arianna let out a scream. John had her by the neck and was trying to choke her. I swung my arm as fast as it would go burying the glass deep into John's thigh. I reached back and grabbed another piece of the broken mirror to be ready for a counterattack.

"You fucking bitch. What the fuck did you do that for?"

John stumbled back, clutching his thigh as blood began to seep through his fingers, pooling on the floor. The sharp, metallic scent of blood filled the air, intensifying the already suffocating atmosphere.

"You keep your fucking hand off of us or I swear, John, I'll fucking castrate you."

I didn't think this would kill him. Arianna and I had already learned that while the pain here is a very real feeling, death never comes. All I needed was for John to think his life was in danger for a little while. I had no clue what would happen if he remained there bleeding and I had no intention of staying here to find out.

"Find another mirror," I said to Arianna.

"I don't know which one. It's all set up differently now."

"We need to get out of here before he can follow us. Whatever Az sent him here to do, I can promise our virtue was not of concern."

John began cursing and moaning as he pulled the glass free from his thigh. There was a slurping sound as it broke free of the flesh. "Fuck, that hurts. You damn ginger bitch, I'm going to pound every last bit of life out of you."

John grunted, tearing the sleeve off his shirt and roughly wrapping it around his bleeding thigh. After securing the makeshift bandage, he stooped to pick up the bloodied piece of glass, his eyes seething with rage as he started limping toward us, ready for retaliation.

"Arianna, now would be a good time to tell me which mirror." I repositioned my hand, ready to strike. I knew I'd be at a disadvantage with his longer arms. As I was readying to strike, a hand grabbed me from behind.

There was a sudden blur. I was underwater and I could see John banging on a piece of glass buried in the sand below me.

Arianna grabbed my hand and we pushed up and up. When we breached the surface I could see the familiar concrete shore of Lake Michigan. We were back in Chicago, but was it the same? For that matter, was I the same?

CHAPTER 53: CLAY

WHEN GRAYSON AND I HAD GOTTEN BACK TO THE TEMple, Dr. Dawood and Persephone were nowhere to be found. Elizabeth said they had gone to take a look at the pool. She went down a short time later to ask them a question, she found the water of the pool clear from the black sludge, but the two of them were gone.

"Don't worry, they'll be back soon," Elizabeth muttered, her eyes scanning the empty space. "Must be something big if they took off like that. We should grab some shut-eye; we're gonna need it when they lay it all out."

The others had settled in to sleep, but I couldn't. I was back to sitting and waiting again. I was dead serious when I told Grayson I was sick of this goddamn waiting game. I thought he understood me and that we were on the same page, yet even he had decided to wait and went to sleep.

The moon was bright, lighting the valley as much as the sunlight had when I stepped outside. My restlessness wouldn't allow me to sit and watch Grayson and Elizabeth sleep. As I looked around it was unclear to me where all the others here had gone as there wasn't a single soul stirring about. I began walking further and further away from the temple and in the direction Grayson had pointed when he mentioned where an entrance to the darkness was.

It was a half hour or so into my walk when I came upon a large mound of rocks. Most of them were good sized boulders, but there was one that stood out among the rest. This must be the gateway Grayson was going on about. It took me a few moments to figure out how it worked, but soon the rock rumbled as it slid open. A vast darkness expanded out in front of me.

I didn't want to let Grayson down—he was the closest thing I had to a friend here. But I couldn't leave Ava and Arianna stranded. I had to act, choice or not, and hoped Grayson would understand. Holding my breath I stepped forward into the darkness, the rock entranceway grinding to a close behind me.

The ground was flat beneath my feet, each step echoing into the void, sending ripples of sound through the vast darkness that enveloped me. My journey was slow as I didn't want to trip and faceplant should something get in my path—nothing ever came.

I walked for about two hours. If that was the amount of time I'd been gone I knew it wouldn't be long before Elizabeth woke and sent others after me. She was Grayson's only weakness. If she asked, I had no doubt he would tell her about our discussion earlier that day. That and the thought of finding Ava and Arianna were what kept me moving forward.

Several more hours passed. No one had found me and I had found no one. For all I knew I was walking in circles as there was no path that I could identify. No way for me to mark where I'd already been.

Stopping for a moment, I closed my eyes. I pictured again what I'd seen when I drank the Waters of Lethe. I was the light, we were all light. Then why couldn't I be my own light in the darkness? How did I become the light now? Once I'd become aware again, Dr. Dawood never spent time explaining anything else to Arianna or me.

I focused intensely, envisioning the light I'd glimpsed before. Opening my eyes, a faint glow emanated from me—not strong, but sufficient to illuminate my direct surroundings. It also must have turned me into a beacon for everything else in the darkness. More importantly it drew the thing that would take me to Ava and Arianna: Az.

His voice came before he did. "Mr. Mitchell, it seems you're learning more about yourself and your existence."

I spun in a full circle and didn't see him anywhere. "Show yourself, Az. Tell me what you've done with them."

"Or what, Mr. Mitchell? We've danced this dance, and you haven't got a fucking thing to threaten me with."

My eyes darted around looking for him as I replied back, "That may be the case, Mr. Angue. What I do know now is that your own capabilities are much less than you make them out to be." It was a total bluff on my part. I knew nothing more about him, but to challenge Az would be my best hope at drawing him out.

A white mist rose from the ground and it formed into a giant movie screen. "You see, Mr. Mitchell, I know why you've come here." Light started flickering on the screen. "They were far too easy to take and are much easier to manipulate."

It was Ava and Arianna; they were together. I could see Ava's hand was bleeding from a piece of glass that she was holding. "They're at my mercy. I think, maybe for you to understand how weak and vulnerable you are, they should pay a small price for that. Don't you think?"

"Back the fuck off them, Az, or so help me..."

"I see you're no longer making jokes. Let's give them a friend to play with."

The view on the screen changed and it was as though I was looking through Arianna's eyes. She was standing behind Ava. In front of them I could see John Tyler walking towards them. There was no sound but I could see a dark determination on his face.

"You're even sicker than I thought, Az. I have no doubt you know the type of person John is. Yet, you put him in there with them."

"Don't be so surprised. It was me after all who made it possible for him to come here and send you out there. Yet, somehow, here you are again. Was it not enough that I gave you what you'd been after? You were living again."

"It wasn't only about living again. It was about living again with Ava. It was about having the life that we were planning. You took that away from us."

"I did, your plans were nothing compared to my own."

I looked back at the screen and John was drawing closer to Ava. She took the glass in her hand and dove at him. I didn't get to see what happened next as the screen quickly faded to black. "I'd say that should be enough of that movie for now. Wouldn't you agree?"

"What the hell did you let happen to her? To them?"

"Have no fear, Mr. Mitchell. That was many hours ago. It seems that your dearest Ava is quite the fighter. She landed that piece of glass right into Mr. Tyler's thigh."

"Where are they now, what did you do with them?"

Az appeared in front of me; I may not have realized it was him had I not known about the light. His appearance was nothing more than a glowing orb of indigo light.

Seeing this form of him was starting to make many other things make sense: the world of Purgatory that we'd been in, the indigo light that appeared there, and the way it shone when he was around. The indigo light was his truest form; the others were just the way he wanted us to see him.

"I will tell you where they are… no… scratch that. I will take you to them, Mr. Mitchell. Before I do that, however, you're going to sit and talk with me. I'm anxious to learn more about which of my brothers and sisters have made it a mission to send you after me."

"I don't know what you mean, Az. Who are your brothers and sisters?"

"Don't play coy with me. You died as Mr. Tyler, yet, you didn't come back to me. I already had a claim to both of you. By all rights you should've been back here the moment you were separated from Mr. Tyler's body. That is unless one of my brothers or sisters interfered. Now my question is, which one was it?"

Was it wise to let him know? Grayson mentioned that there was something he didn't like about the doc and Persephone, but was it enough to reveal them to Az. Even worse, I knew Az may never actually take me to Ava and Arianna. I had to get something up front before giving him any information. I also needed a little more time to figure out if there was any risk to the others by giving them up. Ava had been right when she said we needed to be cautious about burning everything on the way to stopping Az. I needed to be smart enough to avoid doing that now.

"Listen, Az, you're gonna show me where they are first. No more fucking around. I'm not playing your twisted games anymore. I know you're cooking up something else and right now, you're not ready with whatever that is."

It was another gamble, but it paid off. "Very well," he said. He reappeared as the dapper man I'd seen in Purgatory. "Follow me, Mr. Mitchell, and be careful not to step outside of the path I show to you."

A series of small indigo stones flickered to life beneath our feet, casting an eerie glow as we ventured deeper into the darkness. For a surreal moment, I half-expected Az to start moonwalking and humming "Billie Jean," a fleeting attempt to lighten the gravity of my decision. But as the path stretched out ominously before us, the weight of potential peril pressed heavily upon me. I clung to the hope that this hidden route was distant enough to buy time for devising a better strategy—or that Grayson and the others were already on their way to intercept us. Every step forward was a gamble against the dark, my thoughts a swirling mix of dread and determination.

ASCENSION OF LIGHT

CHAPTER 54: JOHN

I COULDN'T FUCKING BELIEVE THAT BITCH STABBED ME. Another goddamn inch, and she would've castrated me—the very part I planned on using to teach her a lesson when I caught her. As the blood trickled down my leg, it wasn't just rage that festered inside me—it was a fucking inferno, screaming for payback.

I tried to follow them, but that ended, leaving me with a broken nose when I ran face first into the damn mirror. "Az, you prick, where the hell are you hiding? Those girls slipped through my fingers. What's the fucking trick to follow them, huh?"

He was the one who'd told me to come in here after them. Though, truth be told, I was more than happy to come in here after that little ginger bitch and her blonde friend. The only thing Az had told me was to come in and terrorize them. "Anything off limits?" I asked. And wouldn't you know, nothing was.

Az wasn't answering me so I needed to figure out these damn mirrors on my own. When he had me enter, it was simple enough. I walked through the windows we were observing from as if nothing was there. Now I couldn't even see those windows.

I suppose I could sit here and wait. They always seemed to end up back in this room. Still, that bitch had stabbed me and I wanted to give her some payback for that. I wondered if all the mirrors led to the same place. Only one way to find out.

I went to the mirror to the right of the one they exited from, no dice. Then to the left, when I touched this one the glass rippled and split like I'd just placed my hands into a pool of water. *Here we go John.* I closed my eyes and stepped into the mirror.

The other side was a mirror in a very tight bathroom. Was I on a plane? No, that couldn't be it. It wasn't loud enough. This was… a train?

I stumbled out of the bathroom, right into the dimly lit confines of a train's sleeper car. The cramped space felt like a coffin on wheels. Looking around a dark spot on the floor caught my attention. Dear God, it was dried blood. What the fuck kind of train had I ended up on?

Out the window I could see the train was moving at a good clip. The sky was a dark purplish color—looked like we were riding into a storm. I stepped over the blood and moved out into the narrow hallway of the train car. Glancing back at the door for the room number I noticed the door had a big piece of yellow police tape across it. The tape hadn't been there when I walked out. Or, had I walked through it?

I moved further down to the next car and then another before I finally saw another person in the dining car. A man stood behind the counter cleaning up. "Excuse me," I said. I got no response from him. "Hey, you deaf or just ignoring me? What shithole is this train headed to?"

I got closer still and waved my hand in front of his face. *Right, John, you fucking idiot, you're dead.* He couldn't see or hear me. I'd only been around other dead people since Az had taken me. This had to be a living person and to him I didn't exist. There had to be another way to find out where this train was headed. Right now, though, I still needed to find the ginger bitch and her friend.

It had been a fruitless search. By the time I reached the first car behind the engine I'd not seen anyone that looked even remotely close to the two women. I was able to determine that the train was heading west. Looking out one of the windows on my way back to the sleeper car I could see the sun setting behind a purple sky.

I moved through the sleeper car like a predator. Tension coiled in my gut with every door I flung open. The cars filled mostly with families or old-timers, nothing interesting. But the last door, now that was a whole different story.

The sounds hit me before I even reached it—those unmistakable noises of flesh on flesh. *THUD. THUD. THUD.* Mixed with breathy, sweet moans. Shit, it'd been ages since I'd heard anything like it—brought me right back to the night before that hospital fuck-up. I couldn't help myself; I had to see this.

What I saw was some raw, animalistic banging. The guy was old, maybe pushing sixty, sweating like a pig and panting like he was about to croak mid-climax.

The chick? Young, maybe barely twenty-three, putting on a moan show clearly more for his benefit than from any real pleasure. Watching just a bit, I could tell why. The old fucker was going at her like he was trying to strike oil—*THUD. THUD. THUD.* Lucky for her, the geezer might just break a hip and save her the trouble.

She was a looker, so I took a seat and enjoyed the show. Caught her checking her watch a few times amidst the geriatric drilling—clear sign she was a paid ride. This old timer had shelled out good money for her company, no doubt. After another grueling five minutes of his relentless jackhammering, he finally blew his load and rolled off her, just as the train's conductor announced over the P.A. that we were pulling into Chicago, Illinois.

I thought about heading back to try the mirror again, see if I could chase those bitches another way. But then, fuck it—why rush? I was free, in a fresh playground, and without Az or any of those Heaven's Gate assholes to cramp my style. Chicago awaited, and the ginger bitch could wait. It was high time I had a little fun on my own terms.

CHAPTER 55: ARIANNA

WHEN WE CLIMBED OUT OF THE LAKE IT DIDN'T TAKE US long to realize we weren't that far from Belmont Harbor. Everything looked the same as I had remembered it before I died, but now there was this dark indigo looming over everything, including Ava.

"We're back in Purgatory," Ava said. "Or… at least I think we are."

We weren't that far from my apartment so I suggested that we go there. Depending on how much time had passed it was possible that all my belongings were still there. After everything we'd been through I needed some comfort, some familiarity.

It was only a short walk from the lake, but I was getting my first experience of the strange world that Clay, Ava, and Hamilton had been living in. Truth be told, aside from the creepy light, it wasn't all that strange to me. Sure, people walked by and just about through us, but that didn't bother me much at all. Maybe hearing about it from them had taken some of the awkwardness out of it for me.

I could see from the street that the lights in my apartment were still on. I tried remembering if I had them on before Az came for me. Those memories were adrift from my mind and becoming harder to recall. I told Ava that we should be cautious going in until we knew the coast was clear. Turns out that the lights had been left on, but there was a bigger surprise waiting for me when we entered the apartment.

On the floor by the island counter lay my decomposing body. Seeing it face down—swollen and gray—sent a chill echoing through me. I was staring into my own mortality laid bare upon the floor; yet another reminder of my new reality. A part of me wanted to look away, but a darker curiosity compelled me to stare, to acknowledge this version of myself.

Ava grabbed on to my hand and pulled me away. "I'm sorry. I should've warned you. I just thought..."

"You thought someone might have come and discovered my body by now. I get it. It's okay, Ava. I mean, it's a little unsettling but I'm glad Deanna's cat, Arcane, hasn't started eating it yet. Speaking of which, where the hell is that cat?"

I found Arcane, hidden under my bed. As I reached out to comfort him, he recoiled and hissed—a response that stung more than I anticipated. "Arcane, it's me..." I murmured, my voice cracking. I tried for a few minutes to get him to recognize me, but it proved pointless.

He was okay; that would be good enough for me. I did, however, want to see about getting him food. I may be detached from my body, but I really didn't like the idea of it turning into meow-mix for Arcane. Ava was able to show me how to channel energy to temporarily get a hold of things in the living world. Which brought a memory back to the stunt that Clay had pulled on Jamie and thereby bringing me into this situation.

It took both Ava and me working together but we were finally able to get the bag of cat food knocked over and spilled onto the floor. Once we made sure my body wasn't going to be a kitty feast we sat down over in my pillowed meditation corner. "So where do we go from here?" I asked Ava.

"Your guess is as good as mine. I'm kind of surprised that we ended up here. I wonder if that means all the places we've been to through the mirrors are part of the living world as well?"

The thought of that shook me to the core. I hadn't told Ava about what happened in the first mirror. With what she was thinking that would mean that somehow I'd really come across Eddie and watched him die again in front of me. I couldn't bear that thought at this moment.

Ava jumped up and ran across the room. I slid back and looked around the room "What? What is it?"

"Sorry," she said. "We were talking about mirrors and I remembered something. Your floor mirror over there, that's where Az tossed Grayson through into the darkness. Maybe it's still a gateway back to the mirror room."

"Do we really want to risk going back? If that fucker John's still lurking, it's a hard no from me."

"Good point. Shit! What if he's figured out how to use these mirrors too? Is there anything we can smash or fuck up to block them?"

"Az came through my bathroom mirror when he came for me. I don't think breaking them is going to solve our problem. Also, think of how much work we had to put in to knock over a small box of cat food. Imagine how hard it would be to break a mirror in this world."

I put my hand on Ava's shoulder, "Let's take a few minutes and think all this through. For all we know breaking the mirrors could be exactly what he wants us to do."

The mirror looked no different to me than it had for the fifteen years I'd had it. It was a gift from my grandmother before she passed away from lung cancer. It was the last thing I had from her so I was going to be damned if I was going to let it be smashed to pieces without a good reason.

As I stood in front of it I saw nothing other than a reflection of the room. Raising my hands I approached it, the same way I had the other mirrors in Az's maze, until I would've been touching it. My hands didn't float into it the same way they did with the other mirrors. The ones that transported us to and from these places. However, my hands did go through it like they were smoke or some sort of visual illusion. "I don't think there's anything we can do with this one, Ava."

"I still don't trust staying here with it. Just because we can't use it doesn't mean Az or John won't be able to."

"Is there anyone else left in this world that we can trust? Anyone that you know?"

"No. Also, if we're back in Purgatory, Az is going to know what we're doing the moment he starts thinking about us, or at least that's what he made us believe before. This is all so confusing, Arianna," Ava sighed. "It feels like everything just leads to one contradiction after another."

Ava's words triggered a sudden recollection in me. My mind raced back to the first time I encountered the mirror maze—the entrance had been at Navy Pier. It was a different era I had glimpsed, but that didn't rule out the possibility of the building still being there.

"Ava, I need to tell you something about when I was dying. I think I might have figured out where Az has been keeping us, and more about his realm. Remember when you found me in the maze? That wasn't the first time I had been there."

CHAPTER 56: GRAYSON

I KNEW HE WAS GOING TO LEAVE. AS SOON AS THE REST of us decided to go to sleep that boy was itching to get up and out the door. I had hoped that he might have some better sense, but Clay always seemed to lead with his emotions and the rest of the world be damned on the outcome.

It was the old lady, Deanna, that was the first to notice that Clay was gone. She'd come over to me in the early morning hours shaking my shoulder. "Wake up," she said in a hushed whisper. "Clay's gone."

"He probably went for a walk—that boy's always had too much energy to sit still. But damn it, let me sleep."

"He's been gone since just after everyone went to sleep. In case you didn't notice it's early morning now and he hasn't come back."

I rolled over on the floor and wiped the sleep crust from my eyes. "So you mean to tell me you saw him leaving, but didn't think to come tell me before now?"

"I stayed out of it at first; he's always been quick to act when driven. But, to be honest, I'm relieved he hasn't returned yet—it means he's out there looking for Arianna and Ava. Like we all should be doing."

"Why wake me now, though? I saw it coming—Clay's always the first to jump into the fray, consequences be damned. Wish I could've convinced him to stay, but it's Clay. They," I pointed over to the entrance of the pool chamber, "have been waiting around with their fingers up their asses and it was driving him mad."

"I woke you because we have to go after him. I had a gift in life to be able to talk to those of you in this realm. It seems that in this existence it has transformed itself into premonitions while I sleep. Clay is in trouble. Azrael found him and for some unknown reason Clay has trusted him to take him to the girls. He has no intention of doing that, only using Clay against the rest of us."

"Against us? Miss Deanna, what you're saying is just crazy. Clay can get worked up, but he would never hurt the rest of us."

"It's his anger, Grayson. He thinks he's rid himself of it, but all he's done is suppress it deep in his shadow. Azrael seems to have recognized this as well. In Clay's new state it makes him a greater danger than Azrael if he can't keep the anger under control. I dare to bet that even Azrael doesn't understand what he's about to try and unleash."

"What new state? He looked the same to me when I saw him."

"Our friends," she pointed back to the pool chamber again, "have transformed them. We still see the forms of them that we know but they did something to them that..."

"What do you mean by them? I thought this was only Clay we were talking about."

"No. Whatever they did to Clay has also been done to Arianna and Ava. Whatever it was, they're no longer exactly the same as we remember them. My premonitions haven't shown me much more than that. I know only that we need to stop them and it's in you I must now put my trust."

I understood her immediately. It had to be us—no one else. Clay would only trust us, especially in whatever state he was in now. I only questioned when or if we would find him. "Okay, give me a minute here and we can get going." I thought things were getting strange the day I met Clay, but I'll be damned if they don't keep getting stranger every day.

I got myself up, and Deanna and I crept out of the temple. For a lady of her age she moved quite well. Death had done wonders on returning a spirit to her step.

We took off back to the entrance of the darkness as it was the only way either of us figured we could get out of here. I had suggested we call for that fellow with the boat that brought Clay. Deanna shook her head at me. "You don't call for the ferryman unless you can pay his price. We cannot."

I could see fresh footprints as we reached the rock entrance into the darkness. There was no doubt now that this was the way Clay had come. I had no excitement about walking into the darkness and what waited for us on the other side. But it was also in this place that I started to become aware again of who I am. I wondered if going in again might wake more up and when the time came might be able to help us with Clay.

CHAPTER 57: CLAY

"WHERE THE FUCK ARE THEY, AZ?"

We had walked for an hour only to come up to a series of windows that looked into a room filled with mirrors. As I examined it I could see this was the same room I had seen John coming after Ava and Arianna in. There was blood on the floor—I could only hope that Az had been truthful that it was Ava who had gotten John and not the other way around.

"They'll come back through soon enough, Mr. Mitchell."

"And what about John, where's he?"

Looking at me with indifference, he said, "He could be with them, he could not. Time will tell."

"Az, cut the shit. You promised they'd be here. Where the fuck are they?"

"I'll tell you when I damn well please and not a moment sooner."

I could feel my anger returning. I thought I had freed myself from this but there it was gurgling up from below the surface. I wanted nothing more in that moment than to take Az by the throat and strangle him.

"You're a damn fool if you ever took me at my word. I find though, that through the mistakes of your new friends, there's been a new gift you can give to me. You, Mr. Mitchell, weren't even near ready to drink the Waters of Lethe. There are reasons that no one is permitted to drink from those pools until they are ready to return."

"All it did was make me remember Az. It made me remember about the lives that I've lived before this one. It made me remember that I'm part of the great light, as we all are."

He couldn't contain his laughter. "Sure those memories are real, Clayton? Sure Anubis hasn't screwed you over like I have?" He stepped back and looked at my face, still laughing. "Oh… my. You really bought into all that you are the light bullshit. This is too delicious. Mr. Mitchell, you are far too naive for your own safety. If I had known it was that easy to manipulate you I would've tried that approach from the start. We could've avoided the mess we've come to and saved me a lot of time."

He continued laughing at me. Deep breaths, I told myself. I needed to control these feelings of anger. He was only trying to manipulate me with his lies.

"Why should I believe anything you say to me? It was you that has always been lying to me. It was you that took me from the world before I was done with it. It's you that keeps taking everything that matters to me."

"So dramatic. I may have taken Ava and Arianna; but I can assure you I was not the one to take your dear parents. For them, it was just their time."

"Don't you fucking dare talk about my parents." There was that anger again. The more I fought against it the more I could feel it escaping my control. It was like a dark sludge coursing through me, changing me. Why was he trying so hard to push me to anger?

"You know Clayton, if you like, I can take you into the room," he said, pointing through the windows.

"What good will that do me if I have no idea which one to find them in?"

"I didn't say I was going to make it easy. Which would you rather do, sit here with me or be proactive and go searching on your own? For all we know Mr. Tyler could be enjoying his revenge on them now. He did say he had a particular taste for ginger today."

I was breaking. Each time Az opened his mouth I could feel the anger boiling. I could feel the light in me growing darker. "Take me in then. You seem so much to want me in there. Take me in. Tell me how those damn mirrors work and I will."

The Cheshire grin came over his face, "If you say so slick..."

Az's physical appearance faded and I found myself engulfed by a dark indigo mist. I could feel myself moving but my feet were still. As the mist dissipated I found myself standing in the middle of the round chamber with mirrors all around me. No Az though. He'd only dropped me in the room.

"Az, you fucking coward! Get back in here!"

"Mr. Mitchell, you asked for me to bring you in and I did. I said nothing about me staying there with you. If you want to find your lady friends you'll need to go where they've been. I can tell you that you must start with the broken mirror."

"What the hell am I supposed to do with a broken mirror?"

I spun looking at all the broken shards of two mirrors. There came a crunching sound followed by a scraping one. The glass was moving.

"What you're supposed to do with it, Mr. Mitchell, is feel pain!"

The pieces of both mirrors came snapping at me. I didn't have a chance to dodge them before even the tiniest pieces of mirror were cutting through my skin.

Each sliver of glass made itself known with piercing pain. A particularly large piece slashed through my throat. Any chance I had to scream was turned into a gurgled whisper. Blood trickled down my neck, warm against my cold skin. I clutched at my throat, a failed attempt to stop the flow.

The room spun wildly around me. The pain was so intense I wasn't sure how much longer I had before I passed out. Death felt imminent, but then the absurd truth hit me—I was already dead. This body, this pain, was nothing more than an illusion crafted by Az to torment me. Desperate for escape, I realized to move beyond this physical torture I needed to return to the light I'd seen after drinking the Waters of Lethe.

As the mirrors somehow reassembled themselves, stained with my blood, I staggered towards the nearest one. The reflection that met my eyes wasn't my own bloodied body, rather I saw the deep blues and grays of the light I remembered—now darkened by a shadow.

I focused, determined to reconnect with the light that I truly was. The more I stared, the less I saw of my wounded self and the more the light took over. Pushing forward, the glass before me became like a thick gel, and I stepped through it, leaving the pain behind.

Emerging on the other side, I found myself submerged in deep waters. Nearby, a man was struggling against a violent whirlpool threatening to pull him deeper. Something about him seemed oddly familiar. Without hesitation, I swam towards him, gripping his hand to pull him free from the churning water. As we reached what I believed to be the surface, it turned out to be a solid sheet of ice.

I pounded on the thick ice. Below, I could see his face distorted by fear, bubbles escaping as he fought for air. Each strike of my fist caused the ice to crack ever so slightly, and with a final, desperate effort, it shattered, allowing us both to clamber onto the chilling surface.

Free from the ice it took a few moments for both of us to catch our breath. I rolled to my back and noticed that the cuts I had from the glass were no longer there. I felt up further to my neck and the gash across my throat was gone as well. I was still feeling pain, but this was the aching pain from the cold air hitting the water on my clothes and skin.

"We need to get to the shore," I said to the man. We crawled across the ice to the shore where we both were finally able to sit upright. This was where I got my first solid look at the man. His hair was pitch black and his eyes were a radiant blue that chillingly reminded me of Az's. Below his left eye was a scar that ran down to his lower jaw.

"How in the hell did you get stuck under that water?" I asked.

"I'm pretty sure I've been down there a long time. It's been a bit like the movie *Groundhog Day*. I keep waking up in the water and each time I keep drowning again. You're only the second person I've seen since I've been in it. The first one I saw here, I thought I must have been dreaming. She tried to save me but we didn't make it to the surface in time."

"What is the last thing you remember before you ended up in the water?"

"I went for a run by the lake and something got a hold of my feet. I tripped and fell in. The shock of the water, it was so damn cold. Then it was like something still had my feet and it kept pulling me down. I've been there ever since."

I could still see he was adjusting to no longer being in the water. "Which lake was it that you fell into?"

"Lake Michigan, in Chicago." He looked around and could see as well as I could that we were not in Chicago. This looked more like we were on the edge of a small pond somewhere in the north woods. "How did you get into the water?" he asked.

"It's a long story and I'm not sure you'd believe me if I told you. I think we need to get away from the water." I looked up and spotted a small cabin at the edge of the woods. It could be a trap set by Az, but it would be a chance we would have to take. "My name's Clay. You okay enough to walk to that cabin?"

"Yes, I think I need another moment and I can make it. I feel like I haven't used my legs to walk in a long time." I put my arm under his and helped him to his feet. "Thank you," he said. "My name's Eddie, by the way."

CHAPTER 58: JOHN

I'D BEEN WANDERING AROUND CHICAGO FOR OVER HALF a day. It was strange to walk among the living, feeling invisible and ignored. I visited a few of the offices my company maintained downtown. The news had hit of my death a few days before. The conversations I overheard consisted of stories of a gruesome murder on a train that was Chicago bound. Well, that explained the blood stains I saw. And then there were the whispers about my scheming bitch of a wife seizing control of my company. If I could only get back home to Richmond I would haunt her until the end of her days.

Hell, maybe I would talk to Az about that later. But first, the throb in my leg where that ginger bitch stabbed me was a constant reminder of what I needed to finish.

I could see others who were dead like me; at least I assumed they were because they looked right at me. As dusk approached, I'd grown tired of all this walking. I yelled out, "Alright, Az, you conniving bastard, if you want me to catch these girls, you gotta give me a goddamn clue! Is there another mirror, or do they all work the same?" There was no response, and I really wasn't expecting one. Az had left me to clean up his mess, not caring whether I succeeded since he could step in and finish the job without breaking a sweat.

Finding myself on the Magnificent Mile, I spotted the ginger bitch and the hippy bitch across the street. *Well I'll be damned.* Maybe Az was listening after all, or perhaps fate felt like tossing me a bone.

I tailed them, staying a half a block or so behind the two women. They were cautious; they kept stopping to look around—a sign they knew they weren't safe. The temptation to grab them was strong, but my curiosity about their destination kept me at bay. The ginger bitch knew something about this world; her friend still seemed lost, a damn hippy caught up in the breeze.

I kept up the cat and mouse routine with them until we reached Navy Pier. Still hanging back a ways from them I could see they were searching for something. They'd enter buildings—one would stay out as a lookout while the other checked inside. When they stopped at the end of the pier, staring out over the lake, I knew I had to hear their plan. There were enough people, living and dead, that I was able to blend myself in.

They were standing by a statue of a man sitting on a sofa. There was extra room on the sofa so I sat down turning my face away from them, but my ear towards them. The hippy bitch was insistent. "It has to be down here, Ava. The entrance was hidden under a tarp back then, maybe deeper inside one of these newer buildings. I told you when I was here it was another era like the 1900s or something. They must've built some of these buildings out more since then."

"I know Arianna, but let's be smart. Az loves his traps. Let's think this through before we dive into any more buildings. Maybe there's something we didn't see when we peeked in earlier. Maybe there will be something that triggers a memory for you."

Perfect, ginger bitch, keep searching those buildings. I'll be right behind you. They were looking for an entrance, but an entrance to what? I would need to let them find what they were looking for before I got them. My only hope was that the entrance they were looking for was one that led me away from here. I'd grown tired of Chicago.

CHAPTER 59: AVA

I DIDN'T WANT TO WORRY ARIANNA BUT I'D SEEN SOMEone following us since we'd gotten to Navy Pier. Or at least I thought someone was following us. I'd been around long enough to keep my senses aware. Az liked nothing better than a nice surprise.

I purposefully held us up at the end of the pier to see if anyone dared to approach us. I had no fear of jumping back into the lake if that's what we had to do. It didn't come to that. Whomever it was that had been following either stayed back or had given up.

Once I felt comfortable that no one was approaching us I started us back towards the buildings again. It wasn't that I didn't believe what Arianna had told me about the mirror maze—it sounded like something Az would do. My concern was that she had this experience before she was dead, or at least she believed it was before her death. There was no telling if this maze would be here and I didn't like making us be so vulnerable and out in the open. John Tyler could still be out there and right now I was more concerned with him than I was with Az.

"Let's make this search as quick as possible. Remember, keep your eyes open. Never put it past Az to have a surprise lurking around the corner."

Once assured we weren't being followed, we resumed our search through the buildings. The first three were disappointingly empty. As we approached the fourth, the chilling sense of being watched returned. This time, I was certain—we weren't alone.

"Arianna, hold up," I whispered, pulling her into a shadowed alcove. "There's someone following us. I don't know who, but there's someone back there. They've been on our ass since at least the beginning of the pier."

Her eyes widened. "Azrael?"

"Doubt it. He'd have shown himself by now," I murmured, peering around the corner. "Stay sharp. They are keeping their distance for now. Let's keep moving, but stay alert."

We started back through the buildings again. Buildings four and five had nothing to show. Building six was much older than the other ones around it. We'd almost completed our walk of the building when I felt Arianna grabbing on to my arm and pulling me to a stop.

She was staring at a door that was draped with what looked to be a painting tarp. "Is that it?" I asked. "It doesn't look very much like you described it."

"It doesn't look like what I saw Ava, but I'm just getting a feeling from it."

Before I could tell Arianna to wait she'd already started her march over to the door. I ran to catch up.

When I approached her she had moved behind the tarp. I should've been able to see her feet when she got behind it, but instead they'd vanished into a fine mist. Shit! She shouldn't have gone alone.

As I pushed the tarp aside, only the sight of a rusted old door greeted me. I was about to step further in when John's voice shattered the silence from outside. "Hey ginger bitch! You want to try stabbing me again?" Looking out I saw a red-faced John Tyler bull charging me from the other side of the building. My arm, still outside the tarp, snapped back as adrenaline surged through me.

I looked up from the floor. The door in front of me was now an open doorway. I ran through finding Arianna standing in front of an old ticket booth. "This is it, Ava. I told you it would be here. I didn't look around last time at anything out here. I just went in. Now we can take some time to see if I missed something."

"No we can't. We have to move!" I grabbed her arm and pulled her towards the entrance of the mirror maze. "John's out there. He's the one that's been following us. He saw me go behind the tarp. We have a moment or two before he is up our asses."

I ran right into the first mirror entering the maze and felt my nose shatter on impact. "Fuck! That hurts!" I put my hand up to my nose to slow the blood. We had to keep going, but my eyes were watering like crazy. "Arianna, I need you to lead the way until I can see again. Take my hand and move."

"Hey, you fucking bitches, I'm coming for you!"

He was close and getting closer. "Arianna, we need to move faster!"

"I'm moving as fast as I can. We need to find a way to lose him in here. I don't remember which way I went. I was following the floor and trying to keep myself from…"

"From being an ass like me and running into the glass? Trust yourself Arianna. You can do this. We have to get distance from him."

Arianna continued on with me holding on to the back of her shirt. My vision was starting to come back but I realized that the blood from my nose was leaving a trail behind us.

"Aww come on. I only wanted to talk to you. Wait up for a moment," John said as he shorted his distance to us.

"Shit! Shit! Shit!" Arianna had started shouting. Wiping my eyes I could see why. We were at a fucking dead end. Mirrors on three sides of us. Only one way to turn: back.

"Well lookie lookie what I've found." John came up behind us, blocking any chance of escape. Out of instinct I pushed Arianna behind me. I was the one who had stabbed him; better he took his anger out on me. It might give her a chance to escape.

He stepped closer. Arianna was now backed up to the mirror behind us. Of all the times we needed one of these damn mirrors to let us go somewhere it turns out to be a regular mirror. I could only hope to try and distract him now.

"John, what the hell is it that you want with us? Are you that whipped by Az that you're going to do all his bidding?"

"I do what I fucking want, ginger. Az doesn't pull my strings."

"Whatever you have to tell yourself, John." He took another step closer.

"Just wait until I wrap my hands around that little neck of yours. You won't feel the need to be so fresh then, will you"

He was going to do something whether I stood here or not. Why should I make it any easier for him? I wiped the remaining tears from my eyes and the blood from my broken nose. If he wanted to keep calling me a bitch, then it was time to show him how hard this bitch could bite. I charged forward with all the strength I could find.

I hit his midsection and could tell he hadn't expected it. He fell backwards, and I tumbled down on top of him. "Arianna, run!" I shouted.

John was more than double my size and was pushing up on me. It was only a matter of seconds before I was going to be rolled over on my back. Arianna should've passed over us by now. What the fuck was she doing?

I felt John's elbow bashing into my jaw. The impact moved me off of him. He rolled on top of me, kneeling on my legs and his hands, pinning my wrists to the floor.

He slid both of my hands above my head so he could pin them together. His other hand reached down and began ripping away at my shirt. If he'd been smarter he would have looked to see where Arianna was instead of trying to look at my breasts.

A foot came flying over my head and landed square in the center of John's mouth. I could hear the crunch of his teeth on contact. The splatter of blood from his mouth sprayed on me. He fell over to the side, holding his face as he yelled in pain. Arianna grabbed my hands and pulled me to my feet. We took off running back in the direction we had come from.

I knew we only had a few minutes before John would be back up and coming after us again. "See if we can make it back to the entrance," I said. "If we can escape out into the city I think we have a better chance of losing him."

"I… I don't think we can do that. When I was here before turning around to leave was what led to my death. There was no way out. It looks like the hall of mirrors we were in."

"Then head back towards the exit and start checking every damn mirror to see if it leads out."

I could still hear John's yelling but it was getting further from us. I was looking at the floor; if I could find the blood that had dripped from my nose earlier it might lead us back. The floor, however, was clean now. So either we were going in a new direction or the floors were self cleaning in here.

Bang! Bang! Bang! We hit each and every mirror that we passed. Nothing but glass and nothing other than our bodies to try and break the glass with.

We came into a straight path where the mirrors were only on our left and right side. You could see ahead a dim light glowing down at the far end of the passageway. "This is it," Arianna shouted. "This is the path I followed to the room I got boxed in. Please Ava, I don't want to go back there."

"I'm sorry, but we don't have a choice. If it's Az at the end, you have me with you this time. You're not alone." I grabbed her hand and gave it a squeeze. "Come on now, we have to move. It won't be long before..."

"Before I catch up to you two bitches!"

I didn't waste the time to look back. I kept Arianna's hand in mine and pulled her as I started running down the dimly lit pathway. It felt never ending. The only sound I could hear were the heaving, pounding, echoing from every one of John's footfalls towards us.

The dim light was getting closer. A few more strides and we would be there. From the depths of this maze came a thunderous boom; then every last ray of light was gone.

We came to a dead stop. Running full speed in a mirror maze is dangerous enough. Doing it in the dark was just plain stupid. John didn't get that memo. I could still hear him clomping up behind us. I can't say for sure what happened next.

I heard another loud thud that was followed by the sounds of shattering glass. Then the sound of John's feet came to a standstill.

"Put your hands up to the mirrors and keep walking," I said. "We have to keep moving." Off in the distance there were more footsteps coming. This time it was two different people.

CHAPTER 60: CLAY

EDDIE AND I HAD TAKEN TIME TO RECOVER IN THE CAB-
in. There wasn't much inside but it kept us out of the cold.
The one thing that was out of place in this cabin was a floor
mirror sitting in the corner. It bore an eerie resemblance to the
mirrors in Az's round room, its surface shimmering in the dim
cabin light.

I wanted to continue on, but Eddie was visibly disoriented, still grappling with the blurry passage of time and reality
after what he'd endured.

I did find it odd that he was also from Chicago. I was beginning to wonder what it was that Az had against people of
the Windy City.

"I have to get moving. You can tag along, but fair warning,
it might not get any better from here." He looked up at me
like a wounded animal.

"You're going back out there?"

"Not exactly. I'm going in there," I said, pointing to the
mirror. The look of confusion told me all I needed to know.
"There will come a time when I, or someone else, will be able

to explain all this to you. For now, can you tell me that you at the very least understand that you're dead?"

"Yes. Um… yes. I figured that out around the third time I got sucked down through the water and kept coming back to it. I just thought I had ended up in Hell or something. I mean I wasn't a horrible person in life or anything. It only seemed like that was what an eternity of torment would be like."

"As far as I know, this isn't Hell. Though I'm beginning to wonder. I can tell you what you've been experiencing is probably much nicer than what I'm walking into. My fiancé and a dear friend have been taken away by a… Well, I don't know how to explain what he is. But he has one hell of an ego complex and is more than happy to cause harm on anything or anyone that comes between him and what he wants. I happen to be his favorite punching bag at the moment."

Without a moment's hesitation he said, "I'm going with you. Anything's better than another second near that water. I'll admit this all sounds a little surreal, but you saved me from that water. I'm happy to help you if I'm able to."

"Okay, then let's get out of here." Approaching the mirror, I reached out. As my hands touched the glass, it morphed into the familiar gel-like substance. "Follow me as close as possible," I said. "I still don't have a clear understanding of how these mirrors work."

We were back in the room with all the mirrors again. Eddie came a stride or two behind me, looking bewildered that he'd just walked through a mirror.

I looked back over at the mirrors that had cut through me, and I could still see my blood infused into the glass. "We can stay away from those two," I said to Eddie. "Those are the ones that got me to you. I think the only way out of here is to try another one." Az's words repeated in my head that I would only find them if I followed their path.

Circling around the room I examined each of the mirrors. Next to the one with my blood I noticed a long blonde hair attached to the wooden frame. It was a perfect match for the color of Arianna's hair. This had to be the way they'd gone.

"This one over here!"

"Are you sure?" Eddie asked. "You might want to come take a look at this one first."

On the other side of the room I could see Eddie gazing deep into one of the mirrors. Stepping in front of him I could see why. What I saw started to bring the anger I had stuffed down back up again. Was this another one of Az's tricks? Another replay of something that had already happened?

It was John running after Ava and Arianna. They were in what looked like a long walkway and John was gaining on them.

Eddie's face registered a look of shock, his eyes wide and mouth slightly agape—a reaction I didn't quite understand. His hand trembled as he reached forward, fingertips inches from the mirror's surface. I quickly grabbed his wrist, feeling the tension in his muscles. "Hold up for a moment," I said, my voice steady but firm. "I told you, not everything is what you think it is here."

If we were going to be able to jump in this place I wanted to take John from behind and surprise him. I had been in his body and knew his strength. One-to-one there was no hope in me overpowering him.

As John appeared directly in front of our mirror from our vantage point, I seized the moment to surprise him. Pushing forward, the mirror slid open like a silent trapdoor. We were on a pane of glass plummeting downwards like a sled in the darkness, carrying us straight toward John.

The abrupt descent disoriented us, shards of glass nicking my skin as we tumbled. "Eddie, are you okay?" My voice echoed in the darkness, my hands feeling around, hoping I was pressing down on John and not Eddie.

"Yes, I think so. I have some cuts and they hurt like hell, but I'll be okay. How about you?"

"I'm cut up pretty good, but I don't think I'll die from it," I said with a chuckle. "I think our friend is down, but he's not going to stay that way for too long. We need to go, those are my two friends I was looking for."

"Is Arianna your fiancé?" Eddie said with a tremble in his voice.

How the hell did he know who Arianna was? Who exactly was this that I had found in the water?

"No. She's my friend. Ava is my fiancé." I stepped clear of him for a moment. "How is that you know Arianna?"

His voice softened, haunted by memories. "We were together—before I died. She wasn't just my lover; she was my entire world. She was also the other person I saw in the lake, but I didn't think it was real. Does this mean she's dead?"

"Yes, I'm sorry. You've stepped into the middle of a first class shitstorm and she's tied up in it as well."

I remembered the empty spot on Arianna's bed that had gone untouched. The spot I filled for two nights. Now here was her lost lover standing in front of me.

I put my arm over his shoulder. If Arianna had loved this man I knew he was a friend and not an enemy. "Come on, we need to catch up to them before they get too far ahead." Arianna was about to have the biggest surprise of her life… or the biggest surprise of her death, may be more appropriate.

CHAPTER 61: GRAYSON

"HEADING OUT INTO THE DARKNESS, HUH?" THE DOC, Persephone, and Elizabeth had snuck up behind Deanna and me as we stepped into the dark chasm ahead of us.

"Clay's taken off, and it looks like we're the only ones interested in finding him. You all seem content sitting around with your hands under your asses, so we're handling it ourselves." I could see the hurt in Elizabeth's face by my comment, but she was no longer the Elizabeth I remembered. She'd become a submissive drone to Persephone.

The doc was pacing about. "Do either of you understand what you're walking into? I thought Clayton was going to be my biggest challenge, but it seems that all of you are just as ignorant."

"If you spent less time in secret meetings and more on explaining things, maybe we wouldn't be so fucking clueless. Just get to the damn point or better yet, do something about it!"

"You know what I don't like, doc? The two of you ain't so different from Azrael. The longer I'm around you the more I'm seeing it. Whatever you've been up to stinks worse than a three-day-old fish."

"We're trying to help," Persephone said. "Anubis and I want what's best for everyone, but some things are beyond your understanding."

"So why aren't you or Anubis going after Azrael? Why does it always have to be us? What's the matter, scared of him? You all seem to have some voodoo powers and magic tricks. Seems a lot better matched to Azrael than what any of us have."

"If it were only so simple. We may have been created the same as Azrael, but what he has done has made him much more powerful than we are put together," the doc said.

"Come back to the temple with us. It won't be long now," Persephone said.

"Long until what?" Deanna asked. "Until Arianna, Ava, and Clay have been eviscerated from existence by Azrael? You play a game without sharing the rules. The only place I'm going is to find Arianna; the rest of you can do what you like."

Deanna took off into the darkness without hesitation, and I quickly followed, saying, "And the same goes for me. Those three kids need us."

"Wait!" I turned to see Elizabeth coming up behind me. "Please just hear them out, Grayson."

"If they've got something to say, they better keep up. We're not stopping for a chat." I took her by the hands. "Elizabeth, I can tell they're holding back a lot. There's more they're not saying, and it's weighing on me. Maybe they aren't keeping souls stored away like Azrael, but they're playing the same game. Please watch out for yourself around them. If we make it through this I will come to find you. I've had some revelations and changes I need to share with you."

I hugged Elizabeth goodbye and caught up with Deanna as the last of the light faded behind us. "You good to go?" I asked her.

"No, I'm not," she said. "But, when are we ever ready for anything life or death puts before us?"

"Very true, Miss Deanna."

The walk through the darkness dragged on. Every step felt like the ground might swallow us whole. Deanna, however, seemed to have a built-in navigation system in the dark. She moved with nothing but pure confidence, knowing exactly where our destination was.

Grabbing Deanna's hand, I pointed and said, "Look! What's that over there?" Off in the distance it looked like a half dozen fireflies suspended in the air. They had the indigo light of Purgatory. Whatever they were, I knew that they were somehow connected to Azrael.

"Yes, that's where we're going."

"Then why are you walking away from them?"

"Call it a sense of intuition. There are times when a straight line is not the best option. This place is a dark labyrinth. I don't know how I know the way to go—I just know that this is the way to get there."

I followed her steps and sure enough, walking in the opposite direction of the lights was bringing us closer to them. The closer we got we could see that they were not indigo fireflies but rather large floating windows with the light emitting from inside them.

"Welcome. Welcome. Welcome!" came a booming voice from all around us. "This is a most pleasant surprise. You two have saved me the trip of coming to find you. For that I thank you."

It was Azrael. I spun in circles looking for him but didn't see him anywhere. I stepped to the windows thinking he might be hiding inside there, but all I saw were mirrors lined up on the wall of a round room. "Well, you can see us Azrael, why not come out so we can see you?"

"This is much more fun, Mr. Devoe. Though, if you insist, I suppose I can make an appearance today."

I heard a squeak come from Deanna. Turning around I saw Azrael standing beside her with his hand resting on her shoulder.

"Get your filthy hand off me," she growled at him.

Azrael stepped back and came over to me. "I'm tired today, so before you ask—yes, they are, or were, in there. Yes, I'm going to send you in there. No, I will not tell you how to get them once you're in there."

"Azrael, if every conversation with you could have been that short, it might not have been that bad."

He grinned at me. "I would entertain you better, Mr. Devoe, but it seems that mutual friends entered the darkness not too long after you did. I'm surprised they would dare come in here."

I didn't bother asking any more. I knew that the doc and Persephone would come in after us. They only had Elizabeth left, and whatever they were planning required more than only her.

"Well, get on with it then. Send us along so we can go find them kids and you can go play with your friends."

"Find them you may, what condition Mr. Tyler has left them in will be another thing. I would say it won't be too long before he finds the both of you as well."

There was an indigo fog that seemed to seep up from the floor and surround us. It was thick and made both Deanna and I cough. Moments later when the fog dissipated we found ourselves in the round room that we'd seen beyond the windows. All around us, mirrors. Deanna pointed below our feet at the center of the room where there looked to be a pool of dried blood.

Looking around at the mirrors I could see that they all looked the same, with the exception of two. These two mirrors, opposite of each other, their glass looked to be streaked with red lines.

Deanna walked up to one of the mirrors. "How peculiar."

"What might that be?"

"These mirrors are all replicas of the floor mirror in Arianna's apartment. Don't you remember? That's where he threw you through."

"Can't say I paid much attention to that mirror when I was being tossed through it. You happen to see how he made it work?"

"He brought you up to it and tossed you through; nothing special was done."

"I suppose I can always toss myself into one of them and see what happens."

I was backing up when Denna grabbed my arm. "You don't have to jump through them like that." She walked up to each of the mirrors, showing me how she could place her hand through them. I watched and saw it was almost like her hand was breaking the surface of water.

"Grayson, come here and look at this."

The mirror she was standing at had no glass at all. Beyond the mirror frame was a dark hallway with a dull light glowing at the end of it. I stuck my head through and looked down. It was about a seven foot drop to the floor below. On the ground I could see broken glass and under that, a person. Deanna had seen it at the same time.

"We have to get down there. What if it's one of them? We can't leave them down there hurt. Quick, give me a hand and slide me down."

She already had one leg through the mirror when I pulled her back into the room. "Now hang on a minute. I know you haven't been there for long, but in case you hadn't figured it out yet, Azrael likes to mess with folks' minds. Jumping on into something you have no idea about is not the wisest of choices."

"So did you come all this way to stop now? I'm not going to let any of them be unattended to. So you can either help me down or I'll take my chances on my own."

I could see the family resemblance now. This stubbornness must have been a shared family trait with her and Elizabeth. Hadn't I known any better I would've assumed Clay was related to them as well.

"I'm not gonna let you go jumping in. Give me a minute and I'll lower myself down. Something tells me you'll be needed more than I will before this is over."

Brushing away the tiny fragments of glass still resting on the frame and then grabbing onto the frame, I spun myself over. I dangled there for a moment. Looking ahead where there should've been a floor there was nothing but open space. On this side, there was only an opening in the darkness where the mirror had been. I let go and dropped the foot or so to the floor. Under my feet all I could hear was the crunch of broken glass.

The person was face down and did look a bit like Clay. When I rolled him over I saw that it was Mr. Tyler, whom I'd seen a few days back at the temple. I wondered how he'd gotten here on the floor.

"It's John Tyler, Deanna. I don't know what he's gotten himself into, but he's cut up pretty good."

"Give me a hand, Grayson. I want to get down there."

I reached up and grabbed her by the waist and slid her down to the floor. She walked over to John and tapped him with her foot. "If the girls left him here, there was probably a very good reason. We're getting closer to them. Once we find them we can come back and check on this one."

"Well I don't suspect he can get any deader than he already is. Let's keep moving down the hall to that light."

I wasn't sure where the hell we were but I didn't like the fact that this hallway had mirrors on both walls for its entire length. Azrael had been using them too often, and I suspected he could use these if he so desired.

As we reached the end of the hall I could see two figures standing off to one side. "Clay?" I called out. One of the figures turned towards us. It had to be him. "Clay, that you? It's Grayson, and I've got Deanna with me."

"Grayson, hold up! This place is crawling with fucking traps. Stay put—I'll guide you through."

CHAPTER 62: CLAY

EVERY DAMN STEP WAS A TICKING BOMB. EDDIE FUCKED up first and stepped in the wrong spot right after we passed John.

Eddie took a single step forward, setting off a symphony of clicks and clanks, reminiscent of a jail cell slamming shut. In the dim light, I could make out the glass floor beneath Eddie's feet, layers shifting and sliding away into the chasm below. There was no telling how far one might fall into that void.

"Eddie, left—now!" As the floor slid out from under him, he leapt to a narrow ledge that was still intact, shuffling along the wall. I followed closely behind, keeping my steps tight to that same ledge.

Dodging similar traps, we navigated our way down the corridor. At the end, we came upon a golden door, distinguished by an indigo jewel at its center, seeming to mark another barrier. Where the hell had they gone? We saw them coming this way, but we hadn't heard nor seen the great door close.

There were no knobs, handles, or bars on this door. We were debating on how to open it when I by chance looked back and saw two other people entering from the same place we had. I tapped Eddie on the shoulder to look back. We could see that the two who entered were inspecting John.

"I'll head back and check who that is. If shit goes sideways, find a way to crack that door open." Just as I moved to investigate, Grayson's voice cut through the silence, calling out my name. *Shit.* He was clueless about the treacherous floor. One wrong move, and he'd plunge right into the void.

I hollered for him to stay put. I headed back down the path we had followed from the door.

"What the hell are you two doing down here?" As I neared I could see that it was Deanna that had come with him.

"You think I'd let you have all the fun? You should've woken me up, dumbass. I might've come with you."

"Where are the girls? Did you find them yet?" Deanna asked.

"We thought we had, but we've come across a door that we have no fucking clue how to open. They have to be on the other side of it. We weren't that far behind them."

"Take me up to it," Deanna demanded. "I'll see what I can make of it and see if we can get it open."

I took Deanna's arm. "Follow me, but step carefully and keep your footing stable. There are holes in that floor that you won't see until you are damn near falling through them. If you feel your balance getting shaky let me know and we can stop. Grayson, same for you. Don't stray away from the path I take."

Deanna wobbled a couple of times but quickly regained her footing, determined to push on. I didn't stop her; the old woman couldn't have weighed more than ninety pounds soaking wet. If she slipped I knew I could easily support her weight and keep a hold of her.

"Deanna, Grayson, this Eddie."

Deanna let out an audible gasp. "I don't believe it. Clay, do you know who this is?"

"Yes, Deanna. I just told you, this is Eddie. And yes, I'm aware that he is… was Arianna's fiancé before he died."

"We can go with 'is' for now. She can tell me if she feels otherwise when I find her, " Eddie said.

Deanna came up and hugged Eddie tightly. "I'm sorry," he said, "I don't remember who you are."

"You never would've known me. I didn't come into Arianna's life until after you had passed."

Grayson was feeling as impatient as I was. "I'm glad y'all are having this reunion, but I think we need to get a move on figuring out that door. Our friend back there is starting to stir and considering the state the two of you left him in, I am going to take a wild guess we don't want him getting to us any time soon."

"No, we don't." I led Deanna over to the door. "See, nothing there. Only a jewel in the center. But there's glass over it and no way to move…" Deanna's hand moved so fast I would've thought she was a boxer in another life.

The glass over the jewel fell into pieces on the floor. "If you want something, sometimes you have to take it," Deanna said. Her hand was covered in broken glass and dripping blood, yet somehow she still was able to give a delighted smile.

She handed me the round indigo jewel. It was ice cold, but nothing special aside from that. I looked closer at the space where the jewel had been resting. I could see a hole no bigger than two inches wide. Inside of that there was a black button.

"Be ready for anything," I warned them, pressing the button. It worked as expected; the door hissed open, sliding left to reveal… another fucking hallway.

There was no telling how far Ava and Arianna had gotten since we'd been dicking around out here to get this door open.

I shouted Ava's name several times and told her that if she could hear me they should stop until we caught up. Eddie was feeling the same desire to get back to Arianna. He started to dart forward. "Hold up man," I said. "Don't forget what we just walked through. There's no way for us to know if there's more of that ahead."

"We need to catch up to them," he said, his frustration spilling out."The slower we go the further away they are getting from us."

It was different for me having someone else acting off of pure instinct for once. "Yes, I get it. Let me take the lead. Something tells me that even if I fall into one of these traps I'm still more useful to Az existing than not."

I looked back at Grayson and Deanna. I'd forgotten about John, but he hadn't forgotten about us. He was running hard and fast. Somehow for him, the floor was not falling out beneath his feet. We didn't have time to do this right now. "Go! Run!" I commanded them.

"But what about..." Eddie started to say.

"It doesn't matter. John is coming and he looks pissed." I pushed them all through the door and we started running.

We had about a hundred yards on John, but he was making up the distance with each step. *Jesus,* I thought, *who the fuck is this guy, the fucking terminator?*

We hadn't cleared fifty feet before the door began to hiss shut behind us. John had dashed through just in time—well, part of him did.

Looking back I saw an arm sticking through the door. John had been reaching forward when the door had closed on it. The arm was crushed and we could hear John screaming in pain on the other side.

Everyone started to slow down. "Keep moving, don't stop." I wasn't taking any chances on John getting that door open. I was hoping that door would be the last we would see of that scumbag. Now I just want to get Ava and Arianna back and see us all out of this place.

CHAPTER 63: ARIANNA

"DID YOU HEAR THAT?" I ASKED AVA.

"Hear what?" she asked.

"I heard someone yelling your name. Do you think John is back up?"

"It could be; which is why we need to keep moving."

The maze continued on and on. Nothing but a long endless hallway filled with mirrors. This may not have seemed like Hell to anyone else, but I couldn't help feeling like this is what Hell would be like. One endless loop.

Ava," I heard the voice call again, clearer now. This time, she heard it too.

"That's not John… It's Clay! He's here!"

Ava spun on her heels, heading back the way we'd come. Before I could warn her, a massive glass panel slid across the corridor, blocking her path. I grabbed her arm and yanked her backward, pulling her to safety.

"Ouch! What the fuck did you do that for?" Ava snapped, rubbing her arm.

As the panel locked into place, I tapped on the glass. "This maze won't let us turn back. If you'd taken another step, it would have smashed you to pieces or broken your nose worse than it already is. Let's stay put until Clay catches up."

"You talk about this maze like it has a mind of its own," Ava said.

"I don't think the maze has a mind. It's got Azrael's will behind it, pushing us down this twisted path. If we veer from that path, he's correcting us. The question is, does he want Clay finding us?'

"Tell me more about what happened when you were here before."

I'd been dreading and trying to avoid this conversation; the mental trauma from those moments was still raw in my mind. I knew Ava wanting to hear this was inevitable. It had been such a harrowing experience that I was doing everything I could to not think about it. But if there was one person I could tell the story to, it was Ava, as she seemed to understand Azrael in a way that others didn't.

"In ways it was much like what we have been going through, though I was alone. I entered the maze and walked for hours. When I tried to turn around to get out the maze began changing. I found myself in a room where all the mirrors surrounded me. In each of the mirrors you were all in them.

"Deanna in one. Clay in one. You and Grayson each in your own. And Hamilton..." I paused, choking back tears as I recalled Hamilton's fate at the hands of Azrael. "Hamilton was in one. But then the mirrors all started closing in on me. I screamed, and they shattered, and everything went dark."

Ava reached out and touched my arm, giving it a sympathetic squeeze. "I'm so sorry. I know it must've been terrifying for you."

I nodded, fighting back the tears. "After that, I woke up by the lake with Clay and we were taken under the water by a giant wave. When I came up again we were in Anubis', err, the doc's temple." I left out the part about the kiss with Clay. I remembered it happened, but I still believed it was just his way of calming my panic under the water. I saw no reason to upset Ava with this right now.

"An obvious statement," Ava said, "but, it's something about the mirrors. Az will go through them and come out of them, but he is very cautious about his distance when being in front of them. I noticed when he was tossing Grayson through that he stayed off to the side of the mirror. And when we first got to your apartment from our side in Purgatory all the glass and reflective surfaces had been damaged."

"So what do you think, we have to get him in front of the mirrors?"

"It's worth a shot. But we might need more than one mirror to surround him. It should enclose him, just like you saw."

As we talked through our strategy, I turned to the glass panel, and my breath caught in my throat. Standing next to Clay was a face I thought I'd never see again—Eddie.

Every heartbeat skipped as I stepped closer to the glass. I could see him staring at me with longing eyes as we both walked up to the glass that separated us. He put his hand up, and mine followed. How could this be? I couldn't hold back the waves of tears now washing down my checks. Ava came over, asking, "Are you okay?"

A choked laugh escaped me. "Better than I've been in a long time. My Eddie… He's back."

CHAPTER 64: CLAY

SEEING THE REUNION BETWEEN EDDIE AND ARIANNA was heartwarming and all, but we had bigger problems to manage. First and most important was getting past the god-damn wall of glass blocking the hallway. "Want to try smashing this one, Deanna?" I joked. She only gave a tight-lipped smile. No one was in the mood for jokes.

I couldn't see any way around it; leaving us the option of trying to find a way to break it or head back the way we'd come from. Neither of those options excited me. If we were going to attempt to break it, the amount of broken glass that would be flying around had the potential to cause pain to all of us. Yes, we're all dead and it would seem we can't get any deader, but who the hell wants to feel the pain of glass slicing through them? I'd already done that once, and I was in no way looking to repeat that shit anytime soon.

Turning around would mean we'd have to face a one-armed John, and I suspected by now he'd be pissed off and looking to unleash his rage on someone. Maybe that was it. Maybe John could be useful for once and smash right through that glass. With what Emilia had shared about him, I wouldn't feel the least bit of remorse.

Whether it was, his power that turned him into a corrupt bastard or if he'd always been dark as fuck, John didn't deserve a peaceful afterlife. No fucking way he was getting a pass back to the light or another shot at life.

John's the type of person that stories of Hell had been created for. His soul deserved endless torment, not just for the evil he'd done but because he never showed an ounce of goddamn remorse for any of it. He didn't care who he hurt as long as he got his way. Until a soul has found remorse it deserves no rest.

John's hands were soaked in the blood of many people, but those were not the worst of his crimes. The worst were the children he had harmed. Emilia couldn't bring herself to share all the details as it was making her physically ill. John's tech companies were involved in exploitation and he did nothing to stop it. If that was not bad enough, this fuck had even gone so far as to exploit his own daughter. A beast like that deserves every wickedness that comes upon him and then some.

Az knew all about John's dirty secrets, and that's why it pissed me off to no end that he set that bastard on Ava and Arianna. Well, fuck it, two can play that game. I turned on my heels, determined to drag John back and give him the pain he deserved.

"Stay here," I barked at the others. "When you see me coming back, clear the fuck out and keep away from that glass. Make sure Ava and Arianna know to do the same."

"There's nothing back there, Clay," Grayson said.

"Oh yes there is. There's a piece of shit back there that will make a wonderful projectile for that glass."

I navigated my way back down the hall until I came to the door. John's arm still hung there but I no longer heard him screaming. With any luck the arm had been clipped clean off and he lay passed out on the other side.

I found the matching button at the back of the door and pressed it. The door hissed open. Unfortunately for John, his arm was still attached—just barely.

It looked as though it was more of a fusion of his clothing and flesh that kept the arm connected to his shoulder. John was being dragged with the door for a moment as it opened. His weight, however, became too much and he fell to the floor. If we hadn't already been dead, I would've thought he was.

His eyes were opened, and his mouth gaped as well. It was as if he were frozen. I tapped my foot against his leg and got no response. A few more taps at him and I got a low moan coming out of his mouth.

Good, he's waking up, now all I need to do is get him good and pissed off. Having lived as him and with the stories that Emilia had shared, I had more than sufficient ammo to do that.

I stepped on to his injured arm, putting all my weight on the small area where it remained attached. "Time to wake up and play, Johnny Boy!"

CHAPTER 65: JOHN

THE PAIN IN MY ARM WAS EXCRUCIATING. I FOUGHT MY-self back from the darkness to see this prick standing right on it. "What the fuck are you doing?" My voice came harsh and dry from my throat. "Get off my fucking arm!"

"What's the matter John, don't like the pain when you're the one receiving it?"

It was that fuckwit from the temple, the one hanging around the ginger bitch. How much did he actually know? Az knew far more than anyone should, but he was some sort of supernatural freak. This fuckwad, at least as far as I knew, was human. What he knew must have come from the people I used to know, or my dear darling Emilia.

I yanked my arm back—big mistake. The last tendrils of skin and muscle tore away. I screamed from the searing pain. *Get it together, John. You have to compose yourself. Don't let this asshole see you as weak.*

Blood poured down my shoulder, but I forced myself up the wall and to my feet. Missing one arm or not, I'd make him fucking pay for this.

He leaned down, grabbed my severed arm, and stuck it out, palm facing me. "Hi, John. Remember me? Remember helping Az snatch Ava away? What's wrong—your own hand too greasy for a handshake?"

He swung it and slapped me across the face with my own fucking hand. That was the last straw. I leaned forward and charged at him. He was quicker than I had thought. At the temple he'd been much slower; it had been the ginger bitch there that had the speed.

"You don't have a big door to save you this time!" I yelled after him, watching as he weaved across the corridor. He was being too deliberate, too cautious with every step. This prick was leading me into a trap.

From a distance it looked as though it was a solid floor but the further up the hallway I got I could see that in places there was no floor. Just wide open gaps that fell into a black nothingness. Was this his plan? To have me come running after him and fall into that blackness. I might have been in pain, but I hadn't lost my wits. Good, he's underestimated me. I would do the same with him that I'd done to others in the business world— let him lay his best trap and then devour him when it fails.

He was moving fast, but not fast enough. For each of his strides I was catching up by almost half. It was only a matter of another minute and I would have my hands… *hand* on him.

Up ahead, the others were huddled along the wall, watching. Why the hell were they standing there? What were they waiting for?

My eyes flicked back to the fuckwit as he darted aside. Too late. I couldn't stop my momentum. He snatched my remaining hand and flung me forward, straight through a glass wall.

For the second time today, I felt glass tearing into me, ripping my flesh apart. Pain pulsed through my nerves like fire, but it didn't kill me. I had been surprised the first time when it had fallen from above me, but I was even more surprised at the speed at which my skin healed from these cuts. The only thing I hadn't been able to shake off was the pain that came with it. There was the initial pain as the glass ripped through, then the secondary pain as it came back out the other side of me.

The glass was shattering all around me but the weight of my body was pulling me down and not all the glass had shattered. My body was spinning and as my eyes were looking down to the floor I saw a sharp triangular wedge of glass. It was coming right at my face. Fuck—that was all I could think as it pierced through my face and back out my skull. The pain sucked even worse this time, but the strangest fact was aside from the pain I was still thinking without issue. I was still aware. Still awake.

I could see the other people walking through where the glass had been and on the other side I could see the ginger bitch standing there. That's when the fuckwit came up and whispered into my ear, "If that's the worse you get, it will never be enough for those children. Your own daughter, you sick fuck."

CHAPTER 66: AVA

I COULDN'T BELIEVE WHAT I HAD JUST SEEN. ONE MOment Clay's running at the glass that had separated us and I was thinking he'd lost his mind. The next thing I see is a one-armed John Tyler flying into the glass.

It had been only a few seconds before when Arianna and I understood that they were trying to direct us away from the glass. On both sides we had to pull Arianna and Eddie away from it.

The glass came shattering down and the pieces were flying everywhere. I got my head back up and was brushing the glass off when I saw that John was now impaled and Clay was whispering something to him.

John began yelling, "I'll get you you damn fuckwit. You just wait. I'm not staying stuck here long. I'll get myself out, or Az will come for me. You know I'm right, and then I'm coming after you and your little ginger bitch." Clay lost it.

He turned back to John, placed a hand on both sides of his head and pushed it all the way down until John's head was split in two. "Fix that, you sick fucker."

Grayson went running back to Clay to calm him down. "No, leave me the fuck alone, Grayson! I'm so sick of this shit. People like that twisted bastard deserve way more than what he's getting. You know as well as I do that, before long, humpty-fucking-dumpty will be back on his wall."

"Clay, you can't be the judge of that."

"Oh, then who, Grayson? Az? Is he the one who decides who should be punished? Because it sure seems like he enjoys screwing with people who did nothing wrong, and then he lets that asshole come after us. How the hell is that fair to you?"

"No, it isn't. But it doesn't give you the right to make the decision either."

"Then who, Grayson? You're gonna tell me there's a God who we should leave this shit to?"

"I'm saying there's still things you don't understand."

Clay was… glowing. There was blue and white light bleeding through his skin. I went to reach him and as my hand touched him, I pulled back from the burning heat being emitted from the light. "Clay, what's happening to you?" I asked.

He hadn't seen it. I looked around to see if any of the others were seeing it. By the looks on their faces I knew I wasn't alone. "You're glowing blue and white light, Clay."

"It looks like when we drank the Waters of Lethe," Arianna said. "I watched you change to those colors of light. It looks like it's happening again."

"I didn't drink any more of the water and I'm not seeing any light coming off of me. Maybe it's the lighting in here."

"Mr. Mitchell," came Az's growling voice. "It appears you're closer to ridding yourself of that annoying skin of yours."

He was standing a few feet behind Clay, looking at John. "Well, it seems that Mr. Tyler has had a rough day. Why don't we give him a little break from this glass." Az reached down, grabbed John's head and picked it up as if it were a child's toy.

An indigo mist swirled around John and as it faded we could see that John was whole again. He looked to be still unconscious but his arm was back and his head no longer split in half. Az nodded in approval at his work, then turned back to Clay.

I did my best to move closer to Clay but the heat from the light coming from him was too hot to tolerate. The larger the light was getting the more the heat was driving me back. It didn't seem to bother Az, however; he walked right up and placed his hand on Clay's shoulder.

"Get your fucking hands off of me." Clay pulled back. "Why the hell did you fix that sack of shit up? He deserved every moment of pain he was getting." The blue light coming off of Clay was turning into a darker grayer color as his anger increased.

"I think you've provided Mr. Tyler with more than adequate pain for today, Mr. Mitchell. Though I do appreciate your certain spunk for justice. If only it had been under different circumstances you would have served me much better."

"I would never serve you, you sick demented fuck. I'll spend the rest of eternity trying to figure out how to rid this world and every world of you."

The gray light had turned into a black light with the hot white light expanding as an aura outside of it. Grayson said to Clay, "You need to control your anger, Clay. Something's happening."

"NO... I... DON'T!" Clay replied.

His skin was fading away, the light ripping him apart. I looked at Az who was smirking. He was intentionally trying to piss Clay off. He knew what was going to happen. He wanted this to happen. When Az could see the dark light he went for the jugular. He came over, third-arm out, at me. Everything happened very quickly after that.

Clay charged at Az. Grayson dove at Clay. I tried to take a step back but the wall was right there and I had nowhere to go. Clay as I had known him was gone. There was no Clay, there was only a hot ball of dark light. As Az's hand touched me the ball of light that was Clay went supernova. Everything in the maze hallway shook. The mirrors shattered and parts of the floor were cracking as well.

Grayson had been too close to Clay when this happened. I caught a glimpse of a radiant golden light flash and then there was only ash falling where Grayson had been.

I pulled away from Az who was laughing at everything that had just happened. Clay's dark light blew out in so many directions and then it was gone. What the hell had happened? Was he gone for good now?

I felt Arianna's hand on my shoulder pulling me back to those of us remaining. Az turned his attention back to us. "If you thought there was pain before, you've no idea of what you're about to experience."

The hall started to spin faster, the walls blurring as the ground cracked open. It felt like we were in a whirlwind of pure chaos. I couldn't tell up from down, my grip on Arianna the only anchor I had as the dark indigo mist engulfed us. My head felt like it would explode from the pressure.

Then, a jolt snapped us like a whip, slamming us back into something wet and cold. My eyes squeezed shut from the impact, and when I finally dared to look, we were submerged in water.

As the mist lifted, we found ourselves drenched in Persephone's pool, the calmness of the water a stark contrast to the nightmare we had escaped. The surrounding columns cast long shadows on the shimmering surface, and for a moment, I was too stunned to speak.

Arianna's hand gripped mine tightly, her breath quick and shallow. Eddie looked like he'd gone green with sickness, while Deanna muttered incoherently under her breath. We sat there, stunned, as Elizabeth stood in the doorway, staring at us, her mouth agape.

CHAPTER 67: JOHN

"WHAT IN THE FUCK JUST HAPPENED BACK THERE? " I asked Az.

"Everything that needed to. Mr. Mitchell is now out of the way and I can proceed with collecting the remainder of those that I need."

"The remainder you need for what?"

"You'll be the first to see when the time is right Mr. Tyler. I can assure you of that. Now, if you'll excuse me, I have a task I must tend to."

"So I get to be stuck back in this dark void again?"

"If you like I can put you back in the maze. I'm sure if you hurry you can catch up to them and get yourself impaled again."

"I'd prefer not to, but fuck, it might be better than standing around here scratching my ass."

"Very well." The indigo mist rose up from Az again. When it cleared I was standing in my office back in Richmond. "You can't be seen or heard by any of them, but this should be sufficient for you until I get things finished."

"Yes, this will do quite well." I turned to thank him but Az was already gone.

Looking around I could see that Emilia had already been hard at work making over my office. The warm smell of scotch and cigars had been replaced by something flowery and nauseating. The dark leather furniture had been replaced with lighter color cloth furniture. Then the biggest change: the name on the door. Not only had that bitch removed my name, she'd already changed hers back to her maiden name, Emilia Stewart.

I saw a number of people walking to the conference room that was next to my office. Figuring that Emilia must be in there I went over to see what else she was up to.

The conference room was packed wall-to-wall with people. At the head of the table I could see Emilia and an older gentleman standing next to her. "Thank you everyone," she said, calling the room to order. "I promise we'll keep this short and to the point. As you know we've continued to make changes since John's untimely death. As sad as many are about John's passing it has presented us with an opportunity to rebirth this company and rid some of the poison that has been running through it."

What the fuck was she doing?

"I would like to introduce all of you to Special Agent McMillian. He and his team have been investigating my late husband and this company for the past four and a half years. I will not get into the details of the investigation, but I'm sure many in this room already know what it's about. Following John's death and taking over I've come to learn the truth about the darker elements of this company. I must say with all I've seen… each and every one of you in this room is a vile, despicable piece of human garbage. Human Resources had advised me to leave that out, but a woman can't help how she feels. I promised it would be short and sweet, so here it is: as of this moment you are all officially terminated."

There was no way she found anything out. There was no way any of these people had been dumb enough to leave the files I had ordered destroyed once they were no longer of use to remain in existence. This was nothing more than the feds digging around for something.

"Special Agent McMillian, I'm going to leave all this scum in your capable hands. You and your team have access to all of our conference rooms for the remainder of the day. I will see that you're not disturbed."

Emilia walked by me exiting the room. As if on cue when she stepped out fifteen more federal agents filled the office, blocking those trying to leave.

Emilia went back to my office and took a seat behind the desk. I stormed in behind her. "You're going to destroy this company, Emilia. As soon as word gets out about a federal investigation our stock price is going to fall. Our investors will back out. We will lose customer confidence. Your single handedly just fucked this company into the fucking ground."

Emilia's cell phone began ringing. "Hello? Yes, it's done. So do we still have a deal? Will you buy the company once the news hits? I'm only asking for a quarter of the price that it's worth. However, that contract must stipulate that two percent of company profits go into a trust for the kids every year. Yes. I'll back out of the company completely. I'm looking forward to a nice long vacation in Puerto Rico. Okay. I'll call you with the final details tomorrow."

"Fuck you, Emilia!" She looked over as if she'd heard me.

"No, John… *Fuck you.*" She reached into my desk drawer, pulled out a cigar and lit it. All the lights and electronics in the room were having a sudden power surge. The lights got brighter and the surge protectors clicked over. Looking to the back corner of the room I saw an antique grandfather clock that was not something I'd purchased or ever seen before.

There was a light coming from the mirror at the back of it. As I got closer to it I could see that strange black light Clay had turned into back in the glass hallway.

The light swirled in the mirror as I watched it. I noticed that the glass was starting to crack from the center. I turned back away from the clock but I was not fast enough. The mirror in the clock shattered and the dark light came pouring out of it.

It must have been only me that could see it. When I looked over to Emilia, she was still sitting casually at the desk smoking a cigar as though nothing had happened. I was sucked into the light and as the view of my office faded away, Emilia said with a long exhale, "Thank you, Clay."

CHAPTER 68: ARIANNA

I HADN'T LET GO OF EDDIE'S HAND SINCE HE CROSSED through the broken glass. There was no time for us to even have a conversation. Everything was moving fast and seemed to only be getting faster now.

When we landed in the pool it was only a matter of minutes before both Dr. Dawood and Persephone had come into the room. They claimed that they had gone into the darkness to look for us. However, coming to their better judgment, they turned around and came back here to wait. I'm not sure anyone was buying into that, especially Ava.

I could see more and more what it was that Clay saw in Ava and why he had gone through all he had to get back to her. Even under the craziness of all that was going on, she explained what happened to them with so much poise and grace it was barely believable. Had I tried I would've been stumbling over each word.

The look of concern on their faces grew when she described what happened to Clay. It told me all I needed to know about the seriousness of it. It was something very bad, and it was only the beginning of the terrible things that were about to start happening. The first of which we noticed when we stepped outside of the temple. The blue skies that had once been home to this place were being replaced by dark indigo and black storm clouds.

Dr. Dawood was the first to comment on them. "It seems Azrael has gotten what he wanted. I had hope that Clayton would be able to keep his anger under control. It's the rage inside of him that is fueling this change," he said, pointing to the sky.

"Care to elaborate a little more?" Ava asked.

Dr. Dawood looked back at Persephone who gave a shrug of indifference. "I suppose we must share now as it makes no difference. I don't know a way to reverse what's happened and to prevent what will happen. Ava, Arianna, you're already aware that all of us come from the same great light. Even those in the human world who are referred to as gods stem from this same great light. Those of you who were fortunate enough to a life or some even multiple lives as a human are transformed for a time. When the mortal flesh expires, your light is returned to the Great Light. When you return you keep your knowledge and experiences from each lifetime. It is the great cycle; everything must eventually return to the great light. Azrael has made a mockery of this rule and has been collecting light for at least the last two millennia. At first other guardians didn't notice this. Over the last two hundred years it was becoming more apparent that light was going missing. It was by pure accident that we stumbled across the fact that they were all coming from lights claimed by Azrael."

"Okay, but what does this have to do with what happened to Clay or any of us for that matter?" I asked.

"All but you, Arianna, were at a time claimed by Azrael. Even this place we are in has been tainted by Azrael's poison. Clayton's anger got the best of him and didn't allow him to hold the human form. When that broke apart on him he returned to his light, but doing so in the darkness of Azrael's realm of control has transformed him into Azrael's new poison."

"How do we save him?" Ava asked.

"We don't. We can't. Everything that Clayton's light touches now will be absorbed back into Azrael's collection," Dr. Dawood said.

"Wait. You still haven't said why Azrael is collecting this light. What is it that he can do with the lights that he's captured?" I asked.

"The reason we all return to the great light is because it is the great light. Think of it the same way that the moons orbit a planet or a planet orbits the sun. Whatever has the greater mass will pull the lesser to it. Azrael is trying to make himself the Great Light by keeping all the lights he's captured," Persephone said.

"So what you're saying is he's trying to make himself The God among gods," Deanna said.

"Yes, but gods isn't really the right way to describe it. It's not the same as you think of it. There's not this omnipotent being at the center of it. The Great Light is a source from us all. We've all been born of it and at some point we shall all return to it."

Ava had enough at this point and walked over to Dr. Dawood and grabbed him by the collar of his robe. "I'm not giving up on Clay! I don't believe that it's hopeless to fight for him. There's no cost too great to get him back."

Persephone stepped in and slid Ava back from Dr. Dawood. "I'm sorry dear woman. You'll never see him again in the human form you remember him as. That version of him is gone to the ether. He will keep the memories of you and the lives you lived together. But, he's a dark light now; everything that he touches will be absorbed wherever Azrael is storing it. For many years we thought it was in the dark space that you were pulled from. It was where he was throwing everyone that we helped to rescue. Even the numbers you see here aren't close to half of what he's taken over the years."

"So that's it? You're both going to lay down and let Az win?" Ava was pacing back and forth shaking her head. "You're right—you're not gods. I can clearly see that now. How you ever were considered greater lights than the rest of us I will never understand. You two are the biggest cowards I've come to know. Grayson was twice the light either of you could ever hope to be. Clay was changing, Grayson dove in to try and help him. Can't see either of you doing anything that selfless. Clay was right about you two. You're no different than Az; you're both just worried about your own best interest."

As Ava was giving them the third degree something she said stuck out in my brain. They were saying that whatever Clay touched was absorbed into him, but I remembered that didn't happen with Grayson. The light from Grayson was not pulled in, but rather it blasted off into the space around the mirror maze. So either they weren't telling us the truth or...

"It's the maze!" I yelled out. Everyone turned to look at me. "It's the maze. That's where he's keeping the light. You all had to have seen it as well. When Grayson went to grab Clay his light wasn't absorbed. If Clay was where Azrael was wanting the light to go, why would it go away from him? We have to go back and figure out where the light is hidden."

"No," Ava interrupted. "We have to go back and save Clay first. If we can't save him I need to find a way to stop him."

"Ava... do you remember the pool that we saw? I wonder if we can get in through that. It was right across the way from the mirror."

It took Ava and I some time to explain everything we'd been through to the others but I knew I was on to something.

Persephone recalled that there had been one other like them that had gone missing a few thousand years ago, but it was always assumed he'd gone back to the Great Light for good. This one was known to have been friendly with Azrael but then later was betrayed by him. Dr. Dawood remembered what the temple had been like and said what we described did sound close.

"So we can use Persephone's pool and get back to it?" Ava asked.

"If there was still water in it, then yes, it may be possible to get there. The pools are all connected. However, Azrael will know that you've gone through. He's tainted that pool and I suspect he's done the same to the one you saw as well. You'll need to move quickly. Who among you will go?"

"Are you fucking kidding me," Ava yelled at Dr. Dawood. "Even after all that you're still going to stay here with your tail tucked between your legs? Un-fucking-believable." Ava looked around to the rest of us. "Anyone else brave enough to come along?"

One by one we all stepped forward. Eddie and I first, then Deanna, and at last Elizabeth stepped forward.

"Elizabeth, you can't go," Persephone demanded. "This is where you belong. Not out there."

"Seems to me like this is where the cowards are staying. I never backed off when it came to Azrael, and I don't intend to start doing so now. These nice folks with my niece need me and I owe it to Grayson to see if I can find him as well. None of these kids would have been in this mess had it not been from me first breaking through that gateway years ago."

There wasn't much more to be said after that. Dr. Dawood led us down to the pool and I watched him fiddle with a device that looked like a compass at the side of the pool. "When you're ready, step in. It will take a moment, but the waters will wash over you like a wave. When they clear you will be in the temple of the Golden Light."

We each stepped in holding the hand of someone else. We didn't want to get separated. Ava and I each took an end. We were the only ones who had navigated Azrael's maze before. If for some reason we got split up we would be able to keep any that remained with us as safe as possible.

The wave came up and washed over us. I felt Eddie squeeze extra hard. I think he was still having a hard time with water after having been trapped beneath for so long.

One… two… three… four… I was counting in my head. I got to twenty-five before I felt the waters fall back off of us.

We had all made it and were standing back in the pool of the abandoned temple. Though it looked different now. Where there had been rotted plants and overgrowth there were now beautifully manicured plants and flowers blooming. I could smell sage and sandalwood burning from somewhere close by.

I looked at Ava and could see she was just as confused as I was. This was not at all what we'd seen before. I hoped we ended up in the right temple.

"You have." A voice came from the outer chamber.

"You have what?" Deanna asked.

"You've come to the right temple. Arianna was thinking you'd come to the wrong one, but you've come to the correct one."

We all let out a sudden gasp. There in a glowing white tunic with a radiant golden aura stood… Grayson.

CHAPTER 69: AVA

WHEN I SAW GRAYSON WALK INTO THE ROOM I COULD tell right away something was different about him. There was the obvious that he was somehow reading Arianna's thoughts. That and the fact he had a glowing light coming from him, the same that I'd seen fly off when he touched Clay.

"Grayson, I'm so glad to see you're okay. We need to find..."

"You need to find Clay, yes, I know. That's why I've waited here for you."

It hit me then; he wasn't speaking the same. I had thought I had heard the changes before but now it was much more pronounced. His speech had a much more defined rhythm to it. It was a more educated way of speaking. Shit, I was just thinking that.

"Yes, you were. It's okay Ava. I am different than when you last saw me. It's thanks to Clay that I was freed from an identity I had found myself trapped in for many years. It started when I was tossed into the darkness. These memories I started having, knowing more than I should. There was another voice that was calling out from inside of me. Turns out, it was my own voice."

"So wait," Arianna asked, "are you the Golden Light, or whatever it was that Dr. Dawood said?"

"That's one of my names, but it doesn't matter now. Our priority is finding Clay. Did Dr. Dawood and Persephone explain what's happening?"

I shared with Grayson what they had told us and my feelings about the two of them.

"You're right to call them self-serving. They've always been that way. Though, they are not at the same level as Azrael. His is a lower level of depravity. They are just trying to save their own existence. They are the gray area, neither good nor bad. Come with me and we will talk more as we get you back to the maze."

We walked out of the pool chamber and across the hall to the mirror room. Elizabeth was the last in the group. I hung back and caught a moment between the two of them. Grayson reached out and hugged her. "My dear friend Elizabeth," he said, "so many secrets we had. Yet, there really were none at all. Did you always know who I was when you started helping me?"

"I wasn't sure, but I had a good idea." He took her hand and followed the rest of us to the mirror.

"Ava, Arianna, I trust that you know the way to where you are going?" Grayson asked.

"Yes," I said. "Are you not coming with us, Grayson?"

"I am, however, even I do not know the way through these trials that you've already seen. I only know that which I saw when I was with you."

"We really only know what we've seen as well," Arianna said.

"What exactly are we looking for? The other two were vague, like usual, just saying Az has stolen lights. And how do we get Clay back from whatever he's been turned into? Dr. Dawood and Persephone said it's impossible, but I don't buy it."

"Ava, I'm sorry. They weren't lying. We can't bring Clay back to the way you knew him, but we can return him to his pure light. When the time comes, you'll know what to do. As for the lights, they aren't in the maze—they're inside Azrael. He leaves them in the darkness until their will breaks and he can consume them. They need to have nothing left to hold on to—no hope, no..."

"No memories of the living world or their lives," I said. Grayson nodded. "So that's why he was always so hellbent on getting everyone to forget. The maze, that was to break those that the darkness could not bend. But we..."

"Yes, Ava. All of you made it through. The bond between you extends beyond a single lifetime and it was too strong for Azrael to break. He had captured me, but knew because of who I am he would never break me. So while I was in his realm the memories of who I am had been taken away from me. It was only after passing through the darkness that I became free and the rest began to be restored to me. I still needed to shed the mask and hold that Azrael had placed on me. When I saw Clay changing I knew his dark light would rip apart the façade and free me."

"So how do we free the lights from Azrael if they are in him?" Deanna asked.

"He must see himself from all angles. He must be the only thing that he sees. If you think back you will see he always avoids being in front of the mirrors."

"Arianna suspected as much," I said. "We need to lure Azrael into the maze."

"I know where we need to go," Arianna said.

"Lead the way—we're here with you," I said.

CHAPTER 70: ARIANNA

ONE BY ONE WE CROSSED THROUGH THE MIRROR BACK into the round chamber with mirrors around its circumference. Grayson was the last one to step through. As he cleared from the mirror it shattered into an unknowable amount of pieces and then fell to the floor.

"There's no turning back now," Grayson said. "Azrael knows we are here and I suspect he knows what we are after. Arianna, which of these mirrors should we go through to get back into the maze?"

I walked around the room inspecting each of the mirrors. The ones I had broken before were now pieced back together and there were deep red lines fused into them. I kept examining until I came across one that I noticed had a small bloody fingerprint at the edge of its frame. This was it, this was the one we had gone through after Ava had stabbed John in the leg.

"This one here, but it doesn't take us into the maze, it only takes us into Lake Michigan. We had to go to a building on Navy Pier to get into the maze."

"There's another way in," Eddie said. He'd been so quiet since we'd found each other. I could only imagine what he was going through, having just been pulled up from ten years of death's ugly grip, stuck in an endless loop of drowning, and now having all these people with one clusterfuck of a situation. "Clay and I used this one to enter. Grayson, I think yourself and Deanna may have come the same way. The only difference is the glass is back now."

"Are you sure that's the right one?" Elizabeth asked.

"Yes, it's the one that Clay's blood is infused into. He told me that the two mirrors had ripped through him and pieced back together. Anyways, yes, I'm sure this is it."

I trusted Eddie; to hell with them if they had questions. I took his hand and we pressed against the mirror. There was a crunching sound as we pushed the glass further forward and then it slid in and down. Instead of shattering on the floor this time it turned into a set of glass stairs.

"It looks like he's welcoming us in," Grayson said.

"That's the dumbest thing he will ever do," Ava said.

I was becoming more concerned about her. I knew she was hurting because of the fate that had befallen Clay. Someone had to keep an eye on her. We couldn't risk having her do something stupid that would put her in the same state as Clay. Had she forgotten, I wondered, that we both drank the Waters of Lethe as well? That had to mean we were both as vulnerable as Clay to becoming dark lights.

Back in the maze again—the mess that had been made from Clay going supernova was no more. The path we had followed looked the same, everything in its place. This time we traveled even further on it. I had to stop here and there to get a fix on what had happened the first time I was here.

The group was not very talkative. A growing tension of what was to come was weighing down on all of us. Ava had walked up beside me and Eddie had fallen back behind us. "This is too quiet for me," I whispered to Ava.

"I know what you mean." She replied with a deep sigh. And then, then she did something that I don't think any of us were expecting. She started singing. It was something absolutely beautiful.

Clay had told me that she could sing and how great it was, but to hear for myself how rich and soulful her voice was, was an experience all on its own. It took the dark feelings this place was giving me and sucked them away. She first sang "Amazing Grace" and sang it with such an emboldened passion with a voice full of a raspy pain, not a single one of us had a dry eye when she was done.

I squeezed her hand when she finished singing. "I have one more for you," she said, her voice wavering as the tears welled up in her eyes. Her breath shuddered as she started again, "You are my sunshine, my only sunshine," each word charged with emotion. I stepped back and took Eddie's hand, both of us feeling the weight of her sorrow. "You make me happy when skies are gray." Grayson clasped Deanna and Elizabeth's hands in his, and the tension rippled through us. "You'll never know, dear, how much I love you," she sang, her voice cracking as she brushed a curl of hair out of her dampened eyes. "Please don't take my sunshine away." Her melody wrapped around us, carrying the depth of her longing like an invisible thread binding us together. Ava was calling out to Clay, hoping he could hear her from wherever he was. In that moment, I prayed we'd have the strength to bring him back to his pure light.

Ava's singing had helped to calm my nerves and as they did the way I needed to go became clearer. The long dark hallway that seemed never ending had transformed back into a more familiar house of mirrors. We weren't far from the room that had transitioned on me. I could only hope that when the time came someone among us would know what to do.

Ava continued humming softly to herself. She'd fallen to the back of our band of travelers and Eddie had stayed up by my side. "I never believed it had been you in the water. I thought after all the years of living in the loop my mind was finally breaking. But it was the best vision to see you."

"What happened to you? You went out for a run by the lake and you never came back to me. I mean I know you'd fallen in the lake but that was only because you washed up on the beach a few days later."

"I went for my run at Belmont Harbor, but my sneakers came untied as I made the turn. Not wanting to faceplant again like last summer, I stopped to tie them. I had moved back from the shore because of the big waves, but somehow I was just a foot away from the lake when I looked up. Before I could react, a massive wave slammed into me, dragging me down into the freezing water. I tried to fight, but the cold kept pulling me under. My lungs screamed for air, and I finally had to inhale. The icy water flooded my lungs, and I coughed, only swallowing more water. I realized I was going to die there, so I spent my last moments thinking of you—how much I loved you and how I wanted you to see all the things we'd dreamed of together. You were my last thought before everything went dark."

I was crying now. I wasn't sure I could tell him how I had tried to join him well before I got here. Tell him how I had been given a special gift of talking to the dead. How I had spent many years asking all the dead people I would meet if they had seen him. I would need to share it with him at some point but now wasn't the time for that. I leaned over and kissed his cheek. Even though we were dead he still had that same musky scent I had always loved about him. I was content now, knowing we could come through this okay.

It wasn't long after that we came to a dead end, but it was "THE" dead end. "This is it," I said. "This is where the mirrors turned in on me. I saw five people reflected in them, but not all five are here now. I don't know if that means anything. Grayson, do you know anything more about these mirrors? I'm sorry to say I don't know how he turned them on me, only that he did."

"I don't. It seems to me that Ava is already working on that." I looked over to see she was examining the mirrors. She was pressing all around the frames, looking for something. It didn't take her long to figure it out. In the upper right corner of the frame was a small indentation about the size of a thumb. She pressed her finger into it and the mirror spun out to her.

Each mirror had a central rod and tracks in the floor that let them slide and be repositioned. "Grayson, why would he make it this simple?" I asked. "He must know what we're trying to do."

"It's easy for his own use, and he probably doesn't think anyone would dare put themselves in this position." Grayson grabbed Ava's hand just as she reached for the last mirror. "No! Don't turn that yet. This reflection can trap any of us like it will trap Azrael. Stay outside and leave that mirror alone."

"So now what?" I asked. "Do we hang here patiently waiting for Azrael to stumble into a trap we've set for him?"

"I don't think we'll need to wait very long," Elizabeth said, pointing down the hallway to a mass of dark light coming right at us.

"That's not Azrael," Ava said. "It's Clay."

CHAPTER 71: AVA

I DIDN'T NEED TO SEE CLAY TO KNOW THE DARK LIGHT was him. When you are connected to one another the way we are… were, you come to recognize them in all their forms.

It hurt me to see him like this and feel as though there was nothing I could do. Grayson had told me that when the time came I would know what to do. But, I was having no sudden epiphanies.

Clay had honed in on us and his dark light was moving toward us. "Grayson, what am I supposed to do?"

"Trust yourself, Ava," Grayson said, "You're the only one who can stop him."

Great, a lot of help that was.

I looked back at everyone. "Make sure when Az comes you get behind those fucking mirrors." I took off walking in Clay's direction.

So what was it that had turned Clay into this? It had been his anger. The angrier he got the more the dark consumed him. Whatever I did, I had to keep my anger in check. Clay was always quick to anger and at times I wasn't much better.

"Clay," I called out, my breath catching as I approached. "It's me, Ava. I know you're still in there somewhere. You need to hear me right now. This isn't you. Az is using you, and everything you touch is feeding into his darkness. Please, come back."

There was a loud piercing squelch in my head, and I fell to my knees. "You're wrong! You're wrong! You're wrong!" It was Clay's voice, but it was only in my head.

I fought back up to my feet. "What is it that I'm wrong about Clay?"

"He will not be the most powerful thing, I will. He's not getting the light, I am."

"Clay, he's making you think that so that you keep doing his dirty work for him. You have to..."

"I don't have to do anything Ava! I have already taken many lights and they are with me, not with Az."

"Clay, you need to stop. It's not you; you're acting no better than Az. Stop it!"

The dark light came just inches away from me. I could feel the intense heat coming from it. I was worried that nothing was left of the Clay I had known. Dr. Dawood and Persephone were right, there was nothing I could do.

Clay was getting closer and the heat from the light was becoming unbearable. I couldn't stand it and had to move back. "Is this what's going to happen now, Clay? You're going to absorb my light as well? Are you going to take me away from existing so you can feel stronger?"

I scanned the area and noticed one of the mirrors had a dull indigo glow around the frame. Great, I'm trying to deal with this and now Az is going to show up. Fuck my life today.

"Well, well, Miss Sanderson. What a surprise to see you here, still fighting for poor Mr. Mitchell, I see. It must be painful watching him unravel, yet you stand here clinging to a fool's hope, thinking your love can save him."

"Whatever you thought you did with him—it's backfiring, Az."

"Not at all, my dear," Azrael chuckled. "He did just what I wanted, and now those lights are mine. Clayton thinks he's strong, but he's just a puppet. I only need to lead him to the rest I have… saved up."

"How's that going to help you if he has all the lights?"

"I think your friends forget to tell you, or maybe they have forgotten themselves; the lights must be given willingly. Clayton hasn't taken them willingly, but he will give them away to me when the time is right. Light that is given away unwillingly will only destroy the one who has taken them. As powerful as Mr. Mitchell is feeling at the moment, it will not be long before he begins to feel himself being torn apart into a million pieces as each of the lights tries to escape his binds."

I was trapped with Clay on one side of me and Az on the other. There were two things I had to do and I wasn't sure how. I knew one thing: I needed them both to follow me to the mirror we had set up. It was a long shot, but I think I had gotten an idea of how this would work out.

"Okay, Az," I said. "Let's get him where you need him." I needed to put on the act of my life to get Az to believe what I was saying. As I suspected he was already suspicious.

"That's a rather abrupt shift in stance, Miss Sanderson. Why is that so?"

"Because Az, I think the only way I'm going to get Clay back is to let you finish getting what you want. Be it here or whatever you have planned for us, at least we will be together."

"Whatever do you mean? You're together right now. Are you not?"

"Az, you know that's not Clay. You've twisted him into a hollow shell, a monster driven only by the anger that you pulled out of him. But I know my Clay is still in there, and I won't let you destroy him. I can only hope that once you have what it is you are looking for you will release him from that and return him to his pure light."

"You're putting too much faith in me, Miss Sanderson. I have no intentions of returning him to anything. I very much like this Clay 2.0. It is a much better model than the original."

Az's guard had come down and he hadn't seemed to realize that we had been walking and talking at the same time. Clay continued following at a distance. I only need to get them a few hundred feet more into the mirrors. The rest of the group must have seen us coming and each of them moved behind the enclosure. Grayson was behind the free mirror. I looked up at him as I passed, and he gave me a nod. I sure as hell hoped that meant I was doing the right thing.

"Then whatever is it you're going to do with me, so be it. I'm too tired to go on like this any longer. Congratulations Az, you've worn me out. You win."

I had walked Az into the dead end of mirrors but now I need to get Clay in while also keeping Az there. "Do you mind if I say goodbye to him?"

"If you must," Az said, laughing at me.

I stepped back out to Clay but went just beyond him in the hall. I stood there looking at the light for a moment. "Clay, I know you can hear me, even if it's not all you in there. I'm going to let Az take me now. I'm done with this game the two of you keep playing. It brings nothing but pain to everyone else. But I need you to know—I love you, and I'll never stop."

The tears coming down my cheek were real. I knew this could be the end of the road for not only Clay and me, but also everyone else if this didn't work out.

I turned away from Clay and walked slowly back to Az. As I approached him I saw his third arm slipping out from his waistcoat. My hands were trembling as I stepped forward, my pulse racing. Could I do this? I walked forward to Az's left arm. I felt the sudden heat of Clay from behind me. It moved right through me and went crashing into Az.

"Now, Grayson!" I yelled.

The final mirror came sliding back. "Ava, you need to get out so I can close it," Grayson urged.

I grabbed the mirror from the inside. "No Grayson, I'm sorry it has to be this way." I pulled the mirror towards me and sealed off the reflective chamber and my fate.

CHAPTER 72: ARIANNA

AS THE EXPLOSION OF LIGHT ERUPTED, IT WAS LIKE BE-
ing thrust into a symphony of colors in the void. A brilliant
burst of hues crashed over us, the force slamming us to the
floor. The light radiated in wild, swirling patterns, each col-
or spinning and weaving into the next like a frenzied dance
across the dark canvas. The air vibrated with a loud, harmonic
tone that shook our bones, echoing through the void. I was
breathless and stunned as the eruption of colors faded back
into the darkness. I couldn't believe it; Ava had pulled it off.
She had led Azrael in and we got him!

I helped Eddie up from the ground, and we stumbled
forward to where Grayson stood, his face solemn and etched
with grief. "Ava," I began, "I can't believe you did…" But as
I scanned the room, I felt my breath catch. Ava wasn't there.

"Where did Ava go?" I asked Grayson, my voice cracking
under the strain. He didn't respond, simply raising a trembling hand to point at the final mirror that had been slid and
locked into place. My stomach twisted with a deep, hollow
ache. Deanna and Elizabeth joined us, confusion and disbelief

mingling with their sorrow as the realization sank in—Ava was gone.

But before the weight of our loss could truly settle, the light within the mirror chamber grew increasingly volatile. Mirrors along the hallway splintered with sharp cracks, and the glass floors spiderwebbed beneath our feet. There was no time to mourn; we had to move.

"We need to get out of here," Grayson said. "Follow me."

Everything was shattering as we navigated our way back to the glass stairs we'd entered through. I was the last up. As I turned to take a final look back there was a cataclysmic explosion of light. The mirrored maze and then the chamber around us burst into a crystalized dust.

We were back in the darkness with nothing but a white dust that looked like tiny stars falling in a golden aura that shone from Grayson. "I know the way from here," Elizabeth said.

In the end we were back at Persephone's temple. The sky had returned to its beautiful cloudy blue and there was now a sense of ease among everyone.

Dr. Dawood and Persephone stood stunned, their disbelief hanging in the air as they exchanged bewildered glances. Persephone opened her mouth to speak but faltered, her voice cracking under her realization. Dr. Dawood blinked rapidly, his fingers nervously tracing the folds of his robe as he struggled to accept the truth before him. When Grayson finally touched their shoulders, a soft, radiant glow radiated from his hands, and they both fell to one knee, their expressions a mix of reverence and remorse. Joy and fear flickered across their faces as the enormity of Grayson's true nature dawned upon them. I still didn't get what was so special about him aside from he was one of them. It was also sickening me to see everyone else feeling so delighted and carefree when all I could feel was the loss of Ava and Clay.

"I don't want to stay in here right now," I said to Eddie. "Come on, let's go for a walk or something."

We were heading out the door when Deanna came up to us. "Do you two mind if an old lady joins you? It's a bit uncomfortable in there for me."

"Of course. I was feeling the same way myself. You think once you're dead you no longer have to worry about losing the ones you love and care for. I've been fortunate to gain one that I love back, yet, in the same stroke, I've lost two others that I loved as well."

"Yes," she said. "I can see how it feels that way. But I don't believe they're truly gone, my dear. There's been talk of being wiped out from existence, this or that. But if what they say is true, if we are all light, then we can never be gone." She gently placed her hand over my heart, her gaze steady and comforting. "In even the darkest of places, there is always a light within us."

I wasn't sure about that at that moment. I knew she was trying to comfort me, but I just couldn't shake the feeling of a giant hole torn into me again. It was the same feeling I had when I lost Eddie. Then again, he wasn't all that gone, just misplaced, as Clay would've put it.

I wasn't sure what was next for us. Did Eddie go and drink the Waters of Lethe and we go back to our pure light? Would that be where we find Ava and Clay again? I just didn't know.

CHAPTER 73: AVA

I'LL NEVER FORGET THE LOOK THAT AZ GAVE ME AS THE last mirror closed behind us. "What have you done you foolish woman?"

"I did what needed to be done Az." As the final mirror clicked into place there was nothing for any of us to look at except our own reflections. No matter which way you looked it was all that you could see. Az kept his head down and began pushing at different mirrors but they wouldn't move.

Realizing he wasn't going to move them like that he changed into the indigo mist. Up until now the heat from Clay's light was making it feel as though my skin was burning off. I held on until I could take it no longer. "Clay, release them. Don't let the darkness consume you."

I stepped closer to Clay's light, driving myself against the overwhelming heat. The searing pain was almost unbearable, but I had to reach him. It wasn't much different from the feelings after drinking the Waters of Lethe—painful, yes, but not the worst thing I'd felt. I knew the bodied version of myself was gone now, but I found myself still able to maintain independent thoughts. It was the thought of the bond we'd forged across lifetimes, our shared dreams and promises, that held me steadfast. I wouldn't leave without him.

The experience was something of what I would imagine it to feel like being stuck in a plastic bubble with a very bright light shining down on you. I tried to push out beyond the light but was continually thrown back. I could see there were other dimmer lights inside here with me. There in the center of it all I could see the dark light that Clay had become.

I drifted towards him, but I could only get so close before I was brought to a halt. It felt as though we were two magnets of opposite charge repelling one another. "Clay, I'm here now. Please hear me. This is our chance to stop Az from harming others. Our chance to be free from him once and for all. He's right out there; all that needs to be done is for him to look into his own reflection. Clay, remember us—the life we imagined together. If you release your anger, we can finally be free. Let the lights go, for both of us."

"Ava?" I heard a confused Clay ask. "Ava, what's happening? I was so angry and then I don't remember. I blacked out."

"Clay, you need to pull away from your anger. It's transformed you into something else. Something that Az has been using to collect others. Look around you, Clay. If you don't let them go they are going to consume you. That's what Az is counting on. He is waiting for you to break down and hand them over. Free them now and he has no more power over you. Please, Clay."

I saw threads of blue light weaving around the black, slowly overtaking the darkness that shrouded Clay. The dark light waned until it was replaced entirely by a vibrant rainbow of colored lights, each one escaping in a brilliant cascade. Clay's transformation was complete; he stood before me in his purest form, free from the darkness. It was just us now. "I'm not leaving you," I said. "Whatever happens to us now, happens to us together this time."

Meanwhile, Azrael reverted to his physical form, desperately trying to escape above us in an indigo mist. But the freed lights of those he tormented flooded around and above, forming a radiant barrier that trapped him. He knew his fate was sealed.

As Az reverted to his bodied self he took one look in the mirrors and that was the end of him. I watched as he was shredded from flesh to mist and then pulled into each of the surrounding mirrors. I could feel the pull on Clay and I as well, but that was okay, we were going together.

After all visible signs of Az were gone the mirrors cracked and shattered, releasing an echoing burst of sound and light. From that came Azrael's primal yell which reverberated through the air before dissolving into silence. I could feel Clay and I being hurled away at speeds faster than I could explain. At last, we were free. Free from Az's grasp, free from torment. With Clay by my side, we were finally unchained, and I could sense the weight of that liberation in every fiber of my being.

CHAPTER 74: GRAYSON

"DID WE CAPTURE HIM?" ANUBIS ASKED.

"It seems so," Grayson replied. "But everything turned to dust as we left. I can't say if he was fully contained."

"And what of the other two?" Persephone asked.

"They have names and it's okay to say them. Ava and Clay. They were inside when the explosion happened. It may be they were trapped along with Azrael, but I still have hopes they were returned to the Great Light. There's only one way we'll know for sure and that's to call the council together."

I saw a twinge of panic in both of their eyes. The council consisted of all the greater lights, like us, that kept order of the lesser lights. The suspicions I had of these two still felt very valid. Neither of them seemed to be forthcoming with Ava, Arianna, or Clay. Our roles had always been clear, be honest with all questions asked of us. They instead chose to play games of deceit and leading my friends in circles. If the council became aware of this there would be a price to pay.

I let my brother and sister rest in their concerns and I went back to find the others. I knew they had questions and it was far past time for someone to answer them with a sense of truth.

Elizabeth was the first that I found and she was by far the easiest to have the conversation with. She'd been around both this world and Purgatory long enough to understand. I found her at the outer doors of the temple.

"Hello my dear friend." My greeting was met with her warm smile. "It feels like it's been such a long time. You must know how glad I am to have found you still well. Even more so to have found that you were not consumed by his darkness. I do have to ask, what was it that gave it away to you as to who I am? You hadn't known me in any lifetime before that I recall. You only know me as a simple homeless man who was confused and lost."

"It was the look on Azrael's face the first day that we met. You may not have noticed because you were in shock learning about your death, but oh did I ever see it. There was a sense of fear in him when he saw you. I will admit I didn't know at the time exactly who you were. I only knew that you were someone important. Anyone who could put fear into him had to be important. It was also what had made me braver than I should've been. I thought if he feared you that would let me cross without question."

"Fear is a powerful thing but fear alone would never bring Azrael to submit to another."

"Yes, we did learn that, didn't we? It wasn't until I came here that I learned about being made of light. I didn't question it too much, just tried to learn what I could from Persephone. Though I say she was never very forthcoming herself. She never spoke to me until Ava arrived. Prior to that, she would kind of zap images into my head. I would be left trying to figure out what it all meant. But when we found you in the darkness, I saw something different about you. The golden light that shone off of you I had seen it in the back of almost every vision that Persephone had given me. Even now, Grayson, I cannot say I fully understand or appreciate who you are or how Azrael brought you through life and into Purgatory. To me you will always be my friend and confidante."

"And I see no reason for us to complicate that. I would recommend that you go visit Persephone by the pool. The time has come to free you of this place. Drink the Waters of Lethe and return to the light, my friend. I will see you again."

I reached out and pulled her in for a hug before sending her on her way. It was good to know that she would soon be freed from this chaos. I moved on to Deanna who I found in the first chamber of the temple. She had become fixated watching the water droplets falling from a slight skewed stone.

I spent only a few moments and told her what I must. She had no change in her stoic expression. When I was done she got up and walked into the pool room behind her aunt. The last two I needed to talk to would be Arianna and Eddie. I feared this would be the hardest of my conversations.

Arianna had already been freed by the Waters of Lethe; however, because of her attachments she had chosen to remain in the form she now projected. She could not drink the waters until she had come through the cycle again. It would take several hundred years for her to fade from this form and return. Her lover, Eddie, would be able to drink the waters and be freed. He could choose to stay with her for a while but in time all things must return or perish. I knew that she wouldn't want him to be gone again, but even more so, she wouldn't want him to waste away.

I found them in the innermost chamber of the temple. They held hands as Eddie lay with his head in her lap looking up into her eyes. I sat down beside them in silence for a moment. Arianna knew something uncomfortable was coming.

"Grayson, just get to it. We're all tired and worn down from every dark nightmare. I still don't understand who you are, but I can see by the look in your eyes that I'm not going to like a single thing that is about to come out of your mouth.

Rip off the Band-Aid, and rip it off quickly. Please don't make us suffer in silence any longer."

It surprised me to see that it was Eddie who was brought to tears by the news. I had figured it was the other way around. He panicked and started trying to bargain with me. "There has to be something we can do. Isn't there anyone else like Clay that we can take her to? Can't we have me do the same as she did, you know, drink the water of whatever it is and decide this is the form I'm gonna stay in?"

"I don't know that you'll be able to Eddie. The truth is that Arianna, Ava, and Clay were a very special case. It may be that your attachment to Arianna is strong enough to bring you back and hold you in that form, or, it may be that you end up returning to the Great Light."

"Is there any risk in trying?" Arianna asked.

"So long as he doesn't hold anger the way that Clay did, then maybe not. Arianna, I will leave that for you to be the judge of. I know many things, but what's in his heart you know better than I do."

"Who are you?" she asked. "You were just a homeless man helping Clay search for Ava. Now you have a temple. I know Anubis and Persephone, but I've never heard of the Golden Light."

"Yes, that's not a common name among those you call gods or goddesses. In the world you have known I stand for more than one. To some I am the one who sat beneath the bodhi tree. To others I am the one who spent forty days in the desert. And for others I am something very different. I'm the most direct connection to the Great Light." That was enough for Arianna to understand what I was getting at. Poor Eddie was still looking a little confused, but I knew Arianna would help him get there.

"I would have never believed it with how you were when we met," Arianna said.

"That's because Az found a way to trap me with the rest of Purgatory. Just because I am who I am doesn't make me all powerful. Outside of the Great Light, we are all the same in form. Some just don't realize the strength they have."

"What happens now?" Arianna asked.

"We begin again. Less has been lost than it feels like. The lights that were captured will all be returning to the Great Light. From there, they will refresh and share what they've learned in their last existence. Then the Great Light will send them back out again for new experiences."

"What happens to Azrael? Was that the end of him in the explosion? Did it like, vanquish him or something?"

"Nothing of the sort. We are all light. You cannot get rid of light, only change how and where it is seen. If things went as expected, Azrael is trapped in a darkness similar to what you experienced. He can't escape."

"So that's it, he just stays there? Seems like he's getting off pretty easy if you ask me," Eddie said.

"Not as easy as you would think. There will be a meeting of others that are like Anubis, Persephone, and myself. We will weigh Azrael's deeds and it will be determined what will become of his light. While you cannot destroy the light, those that are dark within can be placed where they can do no harm to others. It is very similar to what you experienced, Eddie, under the water. Or what you experienced, Arianna, in each of those mirrors. Now, I think it's time that you take Eddie back to the pool and see what happens with that water."

"One last question before we go, Grayson. What's become of Clay and Ava?"

"I suspect that they've returned to the Great Light. In time I promise we all will be joined together again. The wheel of light and life is and shall always be infinite."

CHAPTER 75: CLAY

WHEN WE FIRST ENTER INTO OUR WAKING LIVES WE ARE thrust into a mysterious and complex universe. We have little understanding of how it all works. It is up to us to learn how to navigate the complexities and contradictions of it all. Along the way we must be ever diligent of where we step as the number of pitfalls seemingly grow the longer our journey extends.

After everything that Ava and I had been through, the final journey had become the most beautiful of them all. Her final act of love helped free me from the anger that had dragged me into the darkness. When the moment came it was her sacrifice of love to stay with me that was my saving grace.

I'd always been so angry about everything that I didn't have or that I felt had been taken away from me. I never took time to stop and see the many things I had, Ava most especially.

I had my love and attraction to her, that was the truth. Until that final act she made for me, I didn't understand what it meant to have a true and unconditional love.

In the moments after the explosion everything was born anew. It wasn't only that we'd been freed from Az, we'd been freed from the final ropes binding us to the lives we had lived.

To be honest, I couldn't recall ever seeing something as beautiful as those last moments. All those lights freed from myself—freed from Az's captivity.

Every color imaginable zooming around us as Ava and I lifted higher and higher. There was but a brief moment of darkness before we found ourselves before the brightest and most beautiful light I'd ever seen. In that moment I saw all my lifetimes playing out before me in an instant. Not just the good, but the bad and painful as well. For the first time, I recognized the beauty in every part of my journey.

As the Great Light began to dim I couldn't help but to have a moment of aching sadness again. That was short lived when I saw what came next.

I found myself gliding high in a cerulean sky dotted with clouds round and white. As I descended I first came upon snow-covered mountains rising high up in the air. Then lower I drifted into a warm and sun-kissed valley. There I found a river winding for miles on end. And there, at the furthest reaches of the valley stood a blue house with red shutters. Waiting for me at the door of that house was the most beautiful sight of all my days–my dearest love–Ava.

EPILOGUE: AZRAEL

Left in the darkness of my own design, I was a touch surprised to find the Golden Light had returned. Without him they would've never known to trap me in the mirrors. I do suppose that was his payback after me trapping him in that body for several millennia.

What they hadn't counted on is that there was nothing that I feared, nothing that could hurt me. You cannot torment darkness with darkness. I knew in time that they would call a meeting of the council. I knew that in time I would be removed from the darkness and my work could begin again.

I wandered for a time and thought back on how Miss Sanderson had complained about being bored when she first came to me. I think I'm starting to understand that now. I had always been doing something, yet, now all I can do is think and walk. It was great for planning what I would do when I was back beyond the darkness, but even then the thoughts became dull and mundane.

This was their plan for me, wasn't it? They were going to torment me with boredom. Ha-ha. I laugh at their plan. Yes, it might be trying but it was nothing. As I walked I came upon a dull light ahead. I wondered if those fools had indeed trapped me in my own darkness. That would tell me that my hall of mirrors had survived and that was the light I was seeing ahead.

I quickened my pace and sure enough, as I got closer I could see the windows that led to the hall. Those damn fools, they had just given me the keys to my freedom! I reached the windows, but there was a difference.

If this was mine, it glowed the wrong color. Why had I not noticed that before I came rushing forward? These had a golden glow to them.

I didn't dare touch the windows, but I looked through them and on the other side I saw hundreds of… little people? No, that couldn't be right. These were children and at the center of them there was a man tied down. It was John Tyler.

I watched as one by one a child would walk up to John and cut him with a sharp blade. Each slice I could see John trying to fight the pain. There was no use for him to even try and fight it. The pain would keep coming and he would not die from it.

I turned to walk away; this room would do me no good. As I stepped away I heard John scream, "Damn you, Azrael! Damn you! This is all your fault that I'm here."

"No John, it is your fault that you are in there. You don't want to be tormented by children, you should have thought better about doing that to them when you were in the flesh."

I left him there. There was nothing that I owed him. I continued to walk. I knew in time I would find something else that the Golden Light had left in here for me.

Time passed as it does and as I thought, they delivered me to the council. My brothers and sisters thought it would be wise to keep me in my prison of darkness and they cleverly used a mirror in which they could all see and speak with me.

The questions started coming almost immediately. As I looked around those that I could see, the looks of disgust for me were more than apparent on their faces. Who did they think they were to judge me? If one were to dig deep enough into each of their doings you would find no true angels among us.

Their bombastic questions were nothing more than a chance for each one to sound more pious than the next. When the time came and I had had enough of this I spoke, trying to bring this flock of hens to reason.

"You must understand all that I did was for them. None of them would have ever been freed had it not been for me. You all stand and look at me as though what I did was something borne of evil. I would wager that each and every one of you has considered doing it. I was just bold enough to be the one to try it."

The Golden Light might think he has me cornered but he doesn't know the fight he is in for. For them to bring me to a full council was the dumbest move he could have ever made.

Whilst he might have been the jolly do-gooder, many of my brothers and sisters had also grown rather tired of having to tend to these lesser lights. While they get to experience this divine world created for them we are left to watch and want for what they have. What do they do when they have it? They complain about every little discomfort. Let me tell you, try working the same job for ten thousand years and then tell me about your poor aching back.

"Azrael," Odin came with a scolding voice. "You withheld souls from the Great Light to further your ambitions. What justification can you offer for such transgressions?"

"Isn't that what the Great Light has done since the beginning—hoard their light and experiences to themself. Why should we not have a taste of that? Is it only for us to be servants of the Great Light? I tell you my brothers and sisters, I have no use for that."

"So then you admit you are guilty of these violations and perversions," Anubis said.

"Guilt, hmmm. Yes. That is such a wonderful thing. While you all had the joy of tending to happier places it was I who had been placed in Purgatory. The place where each and every one one of them is soaked in guilt. I tell you now, Anubis, I feel no guilt for any of it. So I could not admit to being guilty."

What did these simpletons know about guilt? I looked at Ares who I knew would be on my side. I just wondered how long these dullards would ramble on before getting to the point.

"Azrael," the Golden Light said, "you can and will be punished for the disturbances that you've caused. You'll remain in the darkness that you have created for the next thousand years. At that time the council will review your state and decide if you are fit to return to your duties. Do you have anything else to say for yourself?"

Ha-ha-ha. They really thought a thousand years in here was going to change me, not at all. It was going to give me more time to plan and correct the mistakes I had made this time. "Oh, Golden Light," I said, "I think that's a fitting punishment and I shall be looking forward to our reconvening in the coming millennium." Such a ponderous fool.

"Brothers and Sisters," said the Golden Light, "it appears that Azrael mocks our decision. It might be that we ought to consider something more severe to see he understands where he has erred."

More severe? If he really wanted to punish me he just needed to keep talking for the next millennium. That would be enough to make anyone want to repent. "And what is it that you imagine to be worse for me, dear brother?"

A strong blast of air pushed me back from the window I had been looking through. I got back to my feet and the Golden Light was standing before me. "Brother," I said, "are you so naive to think you would be safe coming in here with me? Did you not recall what happened the last time you chose to face me? I seem to think there was a full two millennia where you were a pet in my precious purgatory."

"Have no fear my brother. I haven't come alone this time."

"I see you are losing more than your senses. I see no one here but us." That was when I saw her move out from behind him. "Ha-ha, you cannot be serious about this. Why, what is it that this lesser light can do to me? Do you forget it was me that brought her here in the first place?"

She took a step further out away from the Golden Light. "Yes, my little pet, please just take a few more steps forward and I will claim that precious light of yours for my own. There is nothing that you or this old buffoon are going to be able to do to stop me."

He put his hand out to stop her advance. "Oh that's right, I forgot to tell you, Azrael. Since we're not going to have you around for a thousand years, your position overseeing Purgatory—we gave it to her."

"But that's impossible! She's a lesser light; she's not fit to do our work."

"She *was* a lesser light, you mean. The Great Light saw it fit that she had earned a chance to prove herself beyond that. Not only will she hold the keys to Purgatory, but she will also be the one who oversees this prison that you so kindly created."

THE END...

ACKNOWLEDGEMENTS

Throughout the journey of crafting Broken Reflections, I have been fortunate to be surrounded by an incredible group of individuals whose unwavering support has meant the world to me. Their insights, encouragement, and dedication to this project have made all the difference.

To my cherished readers and confidants—Samantha Loza, Reneelyn Proctor, Donny Wise, Tina Underwood, Veronica Millen, Elizabeth Lareau, and Lois Quinn—thank you for your invaluable feedback, encouragement, and belief in my vision. Your thoughtful critiques and support shaped the heart of this story, and I am forever grateful for your involvement.

A special thanks to Melissa Black and Lisa Miller, whose sharp eyes and careful attention to detail caught the typos and errors my own might have missed. Your commitment to perfecting this book has been indispensable.

Krystal Fortin and Adam Gramatikas, thank you for your unwavering support and for making Echoes of Reckoning the first novel to grace the shelves of Level Up Gaming. Your belief in my work has been an incredible source of inspiration.

I also want to extend my deep gratitude to my Ziflow teammates for their continued support and encouragement along the way.

Leilani Dewindt, your brilliance as an editor has transformed Broken Reflections into its best possible version. Your dedication, skill, and care in every revision are a true gift.

And to Danna Mathais Steele, your vision for the cover and layout is nothing short of remarkable. Thank you for giving my words a beautiful and captivating home.

Lastly, to every reader who opens the pages of Broken Reflections, I offer my deepest gratitude. In every crack and shard of this story, you'll find pieces of yourself, and for joining me on this journey of self-exploration and reflection, I am endlessly thankful. You are, and always will be, part of the mirror.

ABOUT THE AUTHOR

RON SHAW lives in New Hampshire, where he writes under the watchful eye—and occasional ambush—of his cat, Ophelia. With a master's degree in Public Administration from Norwich University, he balances a full-time tech career with his passion for storytelling. When not lost in the dark and twisted worlds of his novels, you can find him expanding his vintage NES collection or pondering life's mysteries with a healthy dose of sarcasm.

9 7 9 8 9 8 9 1 2 4 0 4 6